POPULAR TALES FROM NORSE MYTHOLOGY

George Webbe Dasent

DOVER PUBLICATIONS, INC.
Mineola, New York

Published in Canada by General Publishing Company, Ltd., 895 Don
Mills Road, 400-2 Park Centre, Toronto, Ontario M3C 1W3.
Published in the United Kingdom by David & Charles, Brunel House,
Forde Close, Newton Abbot, Devon TQ12 4PU.

Bibliographical Note

This Dover edition, first published in 2001, is an unabridged republication of the work published in 1907, in an Imperial limited edition, in
the series Norroena Anglo-Saxon Classics, for the Norroena Society, by
George Routledge & Sons, Ltd., London.

Library of Congress Cataloging-in-Publication Data

Dasent, George Webbe, Sir, 1817–1896.
  [Collection of popular tales from the Norse and north German]
  Popular tales from Norse mythology / George Webbe Dasent.–
Dover ed.
    p. cm.
  Originally published: A collection of popular tales from the Norse
and north German. London : George Routledge & Sons, Ltd., 1907, in
series: Norroena Anglo-Saxon classics.
  ISBN 0-486-41812-X (pbk.)
    1. Folklore–Scandinavia. 2. Mythology, Norse. I. Title.

GR205 .D3 2001
398.2'0948–dc21

                                                    2001028588

Manufactured in the United States of America
Dover Publications, Inc., 31 East 2nd Street, Mineola, N.Y. 11501

CONTENTS.

(Norse Popular Tales and Legends)

CONTENTS

INTRODUCTION.

NORSE POPULAR TALES.

THE NORSEMEN came from the East, and brought a common stock of tradition with them. Settled in the Scandinavian peninsula, they developed themselves through Heathenism, Romanism, and Lutheranism, in a locality little exposed to foreign influence, so that even now the Daleman in Norway or Sweden may be reckoned among the most primitive examples left of peasant life. We should expect, then, that these Popular Tales, which, for the sake of those ignorant in such matters, it may be remarked, had never been collected or reduced to writing till within the last few years, would present a faithful picture of the national consciousness, or, perhaps, to speak more correctly, of that half consciousness out of which the heart of any people speaks in its abundance. Besides those world-old affinities and primæval parallelisms, besides those dreamy recollections of its old home in the East, we should expect to find its later history, after the great migration, still more distinctly reflected; to discover heathen gods masked in the garb of Christian saints; and thus to see the proof that a nation more easily changes the form than the essence of its faith, and clings with a toughness which endures for centuries to what it has once learned to believe.

In the Norse mythology, Frigga, Odin's wife, who knew beforehand all that was to happen, and Freyja, the goddess of love and plenty, were prominent figures, and often trod the earth; the three Norns or Fates, who sway the minds of men, and spin their destinies at Mimirs' well of knowledge, were awful venerable powers, to whom the heathen world looked up with love and adoration and awe. To that love and adoration and awe, throughout the middle age, one woman, transfigured into a divine shape, succeeded by a sort of natural right, and round the Virgin Mary's blessed head a halo of lovely tales of divine help beams with soft radiance as a crown bequeathed to her by the ancient goddesses. She appears as divine mother, spinner and helpful virgin. Flowers and plants bear her name. In England one of our commonest and prettiest insects is still called after her, but which belonged to Freyja, the heathen "Lady," long before the western nations had learned to adore the name of the mother of Jesus.

The Norseman's god was a god of battles, and victory his greatest gift to men! but this was not the only aspect under which the Great Father was revered. Not victory in the fight alone, but every other good gift came down from him and the Æsir. Odin's supreme will was that treasure-house of bounty towards which, in one shape or the other, all mortal desires turned, and out of its abundance showers of mercy and streams of divine favour constantly poured down to refresh the weary race of men. All these blessings and mercies, nay, their very source itself, the ancient language bound up in a single word, which, however expressive it may still be, has lost much of the fullness of its meaning in its descent to these later times. This word was "Wish," which originally meant the perfect ideal, the actual fruition of all joy and desire, and not, as now, the empty longing for the object of our desires. From this original abstract meaning, it was but a step to pass to the concrete, to personify the idea, to make it an immortal essence, an attribute of the divinity, another name for the greatest of all Gods himself. And so we find a host of passages in early writers, in every one of which "God" or "Odin" might be substituted for "Wish" with perfect propriety. Here we read how "The Wish" has hands, feet, power, sight, toil, and art. How he works and labours, shapes and masters, inclines his ear, thinks, swears, curses, and rejoices, adopts children, and takes men into his house; behaves, in short, as a being of boundless power and infinite free-will. Still more, he rejoices in his own works as in a child, and thus appears in a thoroughly patriarchal point of view as the Lord of creation, glorying in his handiwork, as the father of a family in early times was glad at heart when he reckoned his children as arrows in his quiver, and beheld his house full of a long line of retainers and dependents. For this attribute of the Great Father, for Odin as the god of Wish, the Edda uses the word "Oski," which literally expresses the masculine personification of "Wish," and it passed on and added the word, *osk,* wish, as a prefix to a number of others, to signify that they stood in a peculiar relation to the great giver of all good. Thus, we have *oska-steinn,* wishing-stone, *i. e.* a stone which plays the part of a divining rod, and reveals secrets and hidden treasure; *oska-byrr,* a fair wind, a wind as fair as man's heart could wish it; *osk-barn* and *oska-barn,* a child after one's own heart, an adopted child, as when the younger Edda tells us that all those who die in battle are Odin's *choice-bairns,* his adopted children, those on whom he has set his heart,—an expression which, in their turn, was taken by the Icelandic Christian writers to express the relation existing between God and the baptized; and, though last, not least, *oska-maer,* wish-maidens, another name for the Valkyries—Odin's corse-choosers,—who picked out the dead for him on the field of battle, and waited on the heroes in Valhalla.

Now, let us see what traces of this great god "Wish" and his choice-bairns and wishing-things we can find in these Tales, faint echoes of a mighty heathen voice, which once proclaimed the goodness of the great Father in the blessings which he bestowed on his chosen sons. We have the "one-eyed Odin," degenerated into an old hag, or rather —by no uncommon process—we have an old witch fused by popular tradition into a mixture of Odin and the three Nornir. Again, when he gets that wondrous ship "which can sail over fresh water and salt water, and over high hills and deep dales," and which is so small that he can put it into his pocket, and yet, when he came to use it, could hold five hundred men, we have plainly the Skithblathnir of the Edda to the very life. So also in the Best Wish, the whole groundwork of this story rests on this old belief; and when we meet that pair of old scissors which cuts all manner of fine clothes out of the air, that tablecloth which covers itself with the best dishes you could think of, as soon as it was spread out, and that tap which, as soon as it was turned, poured out the best of mead and wine, we have plainly another form of Frodi's wishing-quern,—another recollection of those things of choice about which the old mythology has so much to tell.

The notion of the arch-enemy of God and man, of a fallen angel, to whom power was permitted at certain times for an all-wise purpose by the Great Ruler of the universe, was as foreign to the heathendom of our ancestors as his name was outlandish and strange to their tongue. This notion Christianity brought with it from the East; and though it is a plant which has struck deep roots, grown distorted and awry, and borne a bitter crop of superstition, it required all the authority of the Church to prepare the soil at first for its reception. To the notion of good necessarily follows that of evil. The Eastern mind, with its Ormuzd and Ahriman, is full of such dualism, and from that hour, when a more than mortal eye saw Satan falling like lightning from heaven, the kingdom of darkness, the abode of Satan and his bad spirits, was established in direct opposition to the kingdom of the Saviour and his angels. The North had its own notion on this point. Its mythology was not without its own dark powers; but though they too were ejected and dispossessed, they, according to that mythology, had rights of their own. To them belonged all the universe that had not been seized and reclaimed by the younger race of Odin and Æsir; and though this upstart dynasty, as the Frost Giants in Promethean phrase would have called it, well knew that Hel, one of this giant progeny, was fated to do them all mischief, and to outlive them, they took her and made her queen of Niflheim, and mistress over nine worlds. There, in a bitterly cold place, she received the souls of all who died of sickness or old age; care was her bed, hunger her dish, starvation her knife. Her walls were high and strong, and her bolts and bars huge; "Half blue was her skin, and half the colour of human flesh. A goddess easy to know, and in all things very stern and grim." But though severe, she was not an evil spirit. She only received those who died as no Norseman wished to die. For those who fell on the gory battlefield, or sank beneath the waves, Valhalla was prepared, and endless mirth and bliss with Odin. Those went to Hel who were rather unfortunate than wicked, who died before they could be killed. But when Christianity came in and ejected Odin and his crew of false divinities, declaring them to be lying gods and demons, then Hel fell with the rest; but fulfilling her fate, outlived them. From a person she became a place, and all the Northern nations, from the Goth to the Norseman, agreed in believing Hell to be the abode of the devil and his wicked spirits, the place prepared from the beginning for the everlasting torments of the damned. One curious fact connected with this explanation of Hell's origin will not escape the reader's attention. The Christian notion of Hell is that of a place of heat, for in the East, whence Christianity came, heat is often an intolerable torment, and cold, on the other hand, everything that is pleasant and delightful. But to the dweller in the North, heat brings with it sensations of joy and comfort, and life without fire has a dreary outlook; so their Hel ruled in a cold region over those who were cowards by implication, while the mead-cup went round, and huge logs blazed and crackled in Valhalla, for the brave and beautiful who had dared to die on the field of battle. But under Christianity the extremes of heat and cold have met, and Hel, the cold uncomfortable goddess, is now our Hell, where flames and fire abound, and where the devils abide in everlasting flame.

Still, popular tradition is tough, and even after centuries of Christian teaching, the Norse peasant, in his popular tales, can still tell of Hell as a place where fire-wood is wanted at Christmas, and over which a certain air of comfort breathes, though, as in the goddess Hel's halls, meat is scarce.

We have got then the ancient goddesses identified as evil influences, and as the leader of a midnight band of women, who practised secret and unholy rites. This leads us at once to witchcraft. In all ages and in all races this belief in sorcery has existed. Men and women practised it alike, but in all times female sorcerers have predominated. This was natural enough. In those days women were priestesses;

they collected drugs and simples; women alone knew the virtues of plants. Those soft hands spun linen, made lint, and bound wounds. Women in the earliest times with which we are acquainted with our forefathers, alone knew how to read and write, they only could carve the mystic runes, they only could chant the charms so potent to allay the wounded warrior's smart and pain. The men were busy out of doors with ploughing, hunting, barter, and war. In such an age the sex which possessed by natural right booklearning, physic, soothsaying, and incantation, even when they used these mysteries for good purposes, were but a step from sin.

It is curious indeed to trace the belief in witches through the middle Age, and to mark how it increases in intensity and absurdity. At first, the superstition seemed comparatively harmless, and though the witches themselves may have believed in their unholy power, there were not wanting divines who took a common-sense view of the matter, and put the absurdity of their pretensions to a practical proof. Such was that good parish priest who asked, when an old woman of his flock insisted that she had been in his house with the company of "the Good Lady," and had seen him naked and covered him up, "How, then did you get in when all the doors were locked?" "We can get in," she said, "even if the doors are locked." Then the priest took her into the chancel of the church, locked the door, and gave her a sound thrashing with the pastoral staff, calling out, "Out with you, lady witch." But as she could not, he sent her home saying, "See now how foolish you are to believe in such empty dreams." But as the Church increased in strength, as heresies arose, and consequent persecution, then the secret meetings of these sectarians, as we should now call them, were identified by the hierarchy with the rites of sorcery and magic, and with the relics of the worship of the old gods. By the time, too, that the hierarchy was established, that belief in the fallen angel, the Arch-Fiend, the Devil, originally so foreign to the nations of the West, had become thoroughly ingrafted on the popular mind, and a new element of wickedness and superstition was introduced at those unholy festivals. About the middle of the thirteenth century, we find the mania for persecuting heretics invading tribes of the Teutonic race from France and Italy, backed by all the power of the Pope. Like jealousy, persecution too often makes the meat it feeds on, and many silly, if not harmless, superstitions were rapidly put under the ban of the Church. Now the "Good Lady" and her train begin to recede, they only fill up the background while the Prince of Darkness steps, dark and terrible, in front, and soon draws after him the following of the ancient goddess. Now we hear stories of demoniac possession; now the witches adore a demon of the other sex. With the male element, and its harsher, sterner nature, the sinfulness of these unholy assemblies is infinitely increased; folly becomes guilt, and guilt crime.

The frequent transformation of men into beasts, in these tales, is another striking feature. This power the gods of the Norseman possessed in common with those of all other mythologies. Europa and her Bull, Leda and her Swan, will occur at once to the reader's mind; and to come to closer resemblances, just as Athene appears in the Odyssey as an eagle or a swallow perched on the roof of the hall, so Odin flies off as a falcon, and Loki takes the form of a horse or bird. This was only part of that omnipotence which all gods enjoy. But the belief that men, under certain conditions, could also take the shape of animals, is primæval, and the traditions of every race can tell of such transformations. Herodotus had heard how the Neurians, a Slavonic race,

passed for wizards amongst the Scythians and the Greeks
settled round the Black Sea, because each of them, once in
the year, became a wolf for a few days, and then returned
to his natural shape. The Latins called such a man, a *turnskin,—Versipellis,* an expression which exactly agrees with
the Icelandic expression for the same thing, and which is
probably the true original of our *turncoat.* In Petronius the
superstition appears in its full shape, and is worth repeating.
At the banquet of Trimalchion, Niceros gives the following
account of the turnskins of Nero's time :—

"It happened that my master was gone to Capua to dispose
of some second-hand goods. I took the opportunity, and per-
suaded our guest to walk with me to the fifth milestone. He
was a valiant soldier, and a sort of grim water-drinking Pluto.
About cock-crow, when the moon was shining as bright as mid-
day, we came among the monuments. My friend began address-
ing himself to the stars, but I was rather in a mood to sing or
to count them; and when I turned to look at him, lo! he had
already stripped himself and laid down his clothes near him.
My heart was in my nostrils, and I stood like a dead man; but
he 'circumminxit vestimenta,' and on a sudden became a wolf.
Do not think I jest; I would not lie for any man's estate. But
to return to what I was saying. When he became a wolf, he
began howling, and fled into the woods. At first I hardly knew
where I was, and afterwards, when I went to take up his clothes,
they were turned into stone. Who then died with fear but I?
Yet I drew my sword, and went cutting the air right and left,
till I reached the villa of my sweetheart. I entered the court-
yard. I almost breathed my last, the sweat ran down my neck,
my eyes were dim, and I thought I should never recover myself.
My Melissa wondered why I was out so late, and said to me,—
'Had you come sooner you might at least have helped us, for
a wolf has entered the farm, and worried all our cattle; but he
had not the best of the joke, for all he escaped, for our slave
ran a lance through his neck.' When I heard this, I could not
doubt how it was, and, as it was clear daylight, ran home as fast

as a robbed innkeeper. When I came to the spot where the clothes had been turned into stone, I could find nothing but blood. But when I got home, I found my friend the soldier in bed, bleeding at the neck like an ox, and a doctor dressing his wound. I then knew he was a turnskin; nor would I ever have broken bread with him again; no, not if you had killed me."

A man who had such a gift of greed was also called lycanthropus, a man-wolf or wolf-man, which term the Anglo-Saxons translated literally in Canute's Laws *vere-vulf*, and the early English *werewolf*. In old French he was *loupgarou*, which means the same thing; except that *garou* means man-wolf in itself without the antecedent *loup*, so that, as Madden observes, the whole word is one of those reduplications of which we have an example in *lukewarm*.

It was not likely that a belief so widely spread should not have extended itself to the North; and the grave assertions of Olaus Magnus in the sixteenth century, and his Treatise de Gentibus Septentrionalibus, show how common the belief in were-wolves was in Sweden so late as the time of Gustavus Vasa. In mythical times the Volsunga Saga expressly states of Sigmund and Sinfjötli that they became were-wolves,—which, we may remark, were Odin's sacred beasts,—just in the same way as Brynhildr and the Valkyries, or corse-choosers, who followed the god of battles to the field, and chose the dead for Valhalla when the fight was done, became swan-maidens, and took the shape of swans. In either case, the wolf's skin or the swan's feathery covering was assumed and laid aside at pleasure, though the *Völundr Quidr*, in the Edda, and the stories of "the Fair Melusina," and other medieval swan-maidens, show that any one who siezed that shape while thus laid aside, had power over its wearer. In latter times, when this old heroic belief degenerated into the notion of sorcery, it was supposed that a girdle of wolfskin thrown over the body, or even a slap on the face with a wolfskin glove, would transform the person upon whom the sorcerer practised into the shape of a ravening wolf, which fled at once to the woods, where he remained in that shape for a period which varied in popular belief for nine days, three, seven, or nine years. While in this state he was especially ravenous after young children, whom he carried off as the were-wolf carried off William in the old romance, though all were-wolves did not treat their prey with the same tenderness as that were-wolf treated William.

But the favourite beast for Norse transformations in historic times, if we may judge from the evidence afforded by the Sagas, was the bear, the king of all their beasts, whose strength and sagacity made him an object of great respect. This old belief, then, might be expected to be found in these Norse Tales, and accordingly we find men transformed into various beasts. Of old these transformations, as we have already stated, were active, if we may use the expression, as well as passive. A man who possessed the gift, frequently assumed the shape of a beast at his own will and pleasure, like the soldier in Petronius. Even now in Norway, it is matter of popular belief that Finns and Lapps, who from time immemorial have passed for the most skillful witches and wizards in the world, can at will assume the shape of bears; and it is a common thing to say of one of those beasts, when he gets unusually savage and daring, "that can be no Christian bear." On such a bear, in the parish of Oföden, after he had worried to death more than sixty horses and six men, it is said that a girdle of bearskin, the infallible mark of a man thus transformed, was found when he was at last tracked and slain. The tale called "Farmer Weathersky," in this collection, shows that the belief of these spontaneous transformations still exists in popular tradition, where it is easy to see that Farmer Weathersky is only one of the ancient gods degraded into a demon's shape. His sudden departure through the air, horse, sledge, and lad, and all, and his answer, "I'm at home, alike north, and south, and east, and west;" his name itself, and his distant abode, surrounded with the corpses of the slain, sufficiently betray the divinity in disguise. His transformation, too, into a hawk answers exactly to that of Odin when he flew away from the Frost Giant in the shape of that bird. But in these tales such transformations are for the most part passive; they occur not at the will of the person transformed, but through sorcery practised on them by some one else.

But we should ill understand the spirit of the Norsemen, if we supposed that these transformations into beasts were all that the national heart has to tell of beasts and their doings, or that, when they appear, they do so merely as men-beasts, without any power or virtue of their own. From the earliest times, side by side with those productions of the human mind which speak of the dealings of men with men, there has grown up a stock of traditions about animals and their relations with one another, which form a true Beast Epic, and is full of the liveliest traits of nature. Here too, it was reserved for Grimm to restore these traditions to their true place in the history of the human mind, and to show that the poetry which treats of them is neither satirical nor didactic, though it may contain touches of both these artificial kinds of composition, but, on the contrary, purely and intensely natural. It is Epic, in short, springing out of that deep love of nature and close observation of the habits of animals which is only possible in an early and simple stage of society. It used to be the fashion, when these Beast traditions were noticed, to point to Æsop as their original, but Grimm has sufficiently proved that what we see in Æsop is only the remains of a great world-old cycle of such traditions which had already, in Æsop's day, been subjected by the Greek mind to that critical process which a late state of society brings to bear on popular traditions; that they were then already worn and washed out and moralized.

The horse was a sacred animal among the Teutonic tribes from the first moment of their appearance in history, and Tacitus has related, how in the shade of those woods and groves which served them for temples, white horses were fed at the public cost, whose backs no mortal man crossed, whose neighings and snortings were carefully watched as auguries and omens, and who were thought to be conscious of divine mysteries. In Persia, too, the classical reader will remember how the neighing of a horse decided the choice for the crown. In England, at any rate, we have only to think of Hengist and Horsa, the twin heroes of the Anglo-Saxon migration, as the legend ran,—heroes whose name meant "horse,"—and of the vale of the White Horse in Berks, where the sacred form still gleams along the down, to be reminded of the sacredness of the horse to our forefathers. The Eddas are filled with the names of famous horses, and the Sagas contain many stories of good steeds, in whom their owners trusted and believed as sacred to this or that particular god. Such a horse is Dapplegrim, who saves his master out of all his perils, and brings him to all fortune, and is another example of that mysterious connection with the higher powers which animals in all ages have been supposed to possess.

Such a friend, too, to the helpless lassie is the Dun Bull in Katie Woodencloak, out of whose ear comes the "Wish-

ing Cloth," which serves up the choicest dishes. The story
is probably imperfect, as we should expect to see him again
in human shape after his head was cut off, and his skin
flayed; but, after being the chief character up to that point,
he remains from that time forth in the background, and
we only see him darkly in the man who comes out of the
face of the rock, and supplies the lassie's wants when she
knocks on it. Dun, or blue, or mouse-colour, is the favourite
colour for fairy kine. Thus the cow which Guy of War-
wick killed was *dun.* The *Huldror* in Norway have large
flocks of blue kine. In Scotland runs the story of the
Mouse-coloured Elfin Bull. In Iceland the colour of such
kine is *apalgrar,* dapple grey. This animal has been an
object of adoration and respect from the earliest times, and
we need only remind our readers of the sanctity of cows and
bulls among the Indians and Egyptians, of "the Golden
Calf" in the Bible; of Io and her wanderings from land to
land; and, though last, not least, of Audhumla, the Mythic
Cow in the Edda, who had so large a part in the creation
of the first Giant in human form.

We now come to a class of beings which plays a large
part, and always for ill, in these Tales. These are the
Giants or Trolls. In modern Norse tradition there is little
difference between the names, but originally Troll was a
more general expression for a supernatural being than
Giant, which was rather confined to a race more dull than
wicked. In the Giants we have the wantonness of boundless
bodily strength and size, which, trusting entirely to these
qualities, falls at last by its own weight. At first, it is true,
that proverbial wisdom, all the stores of traditional lore, all
that could be learnt by what may be called rule of thumb,
was ascribed to them.

This race, and that of the upstart Æsir, though almost

always at feud, still had their intervals of common intercourse, and even social enjoyment. Marriages take place between them, visits are paid, feasts are given, ale is brewed, and mirth is fast and furious. Thor was the worst foe the giants ever had, and yet he met them sometimes on good terms. They were destined to meet once for all on that awful day, "the twilight of the gods," but till then, they entertained for each other some sense of mutual respect.

The Trolls, on the other hand, with whom mankind had more to do, were supposed to be less easy tempered, and more systematically malignant, than the Giants, and with the term were bound up notions of sorcery and unholy power. But mythology is a proof of many colours, in which the hues are shot and blended, so that the various races of supernatural beings are shaded off, and fade away almost imperceptibly into each other; and thus, even in heathen times, it must have been hard to say exactly where the Giant ended and the Troll began. But when Christianity came in, and heathendom fell; when the godlike race of the Æsir became evil demons instead of good genial powers, then all the objects of the old popular belief, whether Æsir, Giants, or Trolls, were mingled together in one superstition, as "no canny." They were all Trolls, all malignant; and thus it is that, in these tales, the traditions about Odin and his underlings, about the Frost Giants, and about sorcerers and wizards, are confused and garbled; and all supernatural agency that plots man's ill is the work of *Trolls,* whether the agent be the arch enemy himself, or giant, or witch, or wizard.

In tales such as "The Old Dame and Her Hen," "The Giant who had no Heart in his Body," "Shortshanks," "Boots and the Troll," "Boots who ate a match with the Troll," the easy temper of the old Frost Giants predominates, and we almost pity them as we read. In another, "The Big Bird Dan," we have a Troll Prince, who appears as a generous benefactor to the young Prince, and lends him a sword by help of which he slays the King of the Trolls, just as we sometimes find in the Edda friendly meetings between the Æsir and this or that Frost Giant. In "Tatterhood," the Trolls are very near akin to the witches of the Middle Age. In other tales, as "The Blue Belt," "Farmer Weathersky," a sort of settled malignity against man appears as the direct working and result of a bad and evil spirit,—the supernatural dwellers of the woods and hills, who go to church, and eat men, and porridge, and sausages indifferently, not from malignity, but because they know no better, because it is their nature, and because they have always done so. In one point they all agree,—in their place of abode. The wild pine forest that clothes the spurs of the fells, but more than all, the interior recesses of the rocky fell itself, is where the Trolls live. Thither they carry off the children of men, and to them belong all the untold riches of the mineral world. There, in caves and clefts in the steep face of the rock, sits the Troll, as the representative of the old giants, among heaps of gold and silver and precious things. They stride off into the dark forest by day, whither no rays of the sun can pierce; they return home at nightfall, feast themselves full, and snore out the night. One thing was fatal to them,—the sight of the sun. If they looked him full in the face, his glory was too great for them, and they burst, as in "Lord Peter." This, too, is a deeply mythic trait. The old religion of the North was a bright and lively faith; it lived in the light of joy and gladness; its gods were the "blithe powers;" opposed to them were the dark powers of mist and gloom, who could not bear the glorious face of the Sun, of Baldr's beaming visage, or the bright flash of Thor's levin bolt.

In one aspect, the whole race of Giants and Trolls stands out in strong historical light. There can be little doubt that, in their continued existence amongst the woods, and rocks, and hills, we have a memory of the gradual suppression and extinction of some hostile race, who gradually retired into the natural fastnesses of the land, and speedily became mythic. Nor, if we bear in mind their natural position, and remember 'how constantly the infamy of sorcery has clung to the Finns and Lapps, shall we have far to go to seek this ancient race, even at the present day. Between this outcast nomad race, which wandered from forest to forest, and from fell to fell, without a fixed place of abode, and the old natural powers and Frost Giants, the minds of the race which adored Odin and the Æsir soon engendered a monstrous man-eating cross-breed of supernatural beings, who fled from contact with the intruders as soon as the first great struggle was over, abhorred the light of day, and looked upon agriculture and tillage as a dangerous innovation which destroyed their hunting fields, and was destined finally to root them out from off the face of the earth. This fact appears in countless stories all over the globe, for man is true to himself in all climes, and the savage in Africa or across the Rocky Mountains, dreads tillage and detests the plough as much as any Lapp or Samoyed. "See what pretty playthings, mother!" cries the Giant's daughter, as she unties 'her apron, and shows her a plough, and horses, and peasant. "Back with them this instant," cries the mother in wrath, "and put them down as carefully as you can, for these playthings can do our race great harm, and when these come we must budge." "What sort of an earthworm is this?" said one Giant to another, when they met a man as they walked. "These are the earthworms that will one day eat us up, brother," answered the other; and soon both Giants left that part of Germany. Nor does this trait appear less strongly in these Norse Tales.

Enough surely has now been said to show that the old religion and mythology of the Norseman still lives disguised in these popular tales. Besides this internal evidence, we find here and there, in the written literature of earlier days, hints that the same stories were even then current and continue to be so, among the lower classes. Thus, in King Sverri's Saga we read, "And so it was just like what is said to have happened in old stories of what the king's children suffered from their stepmother's ill-will." And again, in Olof Tryggvason's Saga by the monk Odd, "And better is it to hear such things with mirth than stepmother's stories which shepherds tell, where no one can tell whether anything is true, and where the king is always made the least in their narrative." But, in truth, no such positive evidence is needed. These mythical deep-rooted germs, throwing out fresh shoots from age to age in the popular literature of the race, are far more convincing proofs of the early existence of these traditions than any mere external evidence.

KING GRAM.

SKIÖLD, King of Yutland (Denmark), and the border-
ing districts of Sweden and Norway, ruled his people with
love and kindness. He abolished all cruel laws, introduc-
ing in their stead just and humane regulations. It was
said that he had come over the sea on a shield from unknown regions, having been sent by his father for the
welfare of his people. By means of a bloody duel with a
rival, he had won his beautiful and clever wife, Anhild.
She gave birth to a son, who received the name of Gram.
He resembled his father in mind and body, but was of a
very passionate nature, and therefore constantly engaged
in war and strife. He was accompanied on all his expeditions by his faithful comrade, Bessi, who protected him
in battle with shield and sword. For this reason, Gram
gave him Hroar's fair daughter in marriage; whilst he
himself sued for the hand of Gro, a daughter of Siglrygg,
King of Sweden, celebrated for her beauty and courage.
But he received a scornful refusal, and was informed that
she was already promised to a more desirable suitor.
Gram immediately started with an army and a fleet in
order to avenge the insult; and having heard that his en-

emy could only be wounded with gold, he took with him a club encased in that metal, instead of a sword. Landing on the Swedish coast, he clothed himself in goat's skins, and in this disguise wandered for many weeks, a terror to all whom he encountered. It chanced that the beautiful Gro was walking one day in the same direction. She did not fly at such an unusual sight, for she soon perceived that the seeming monster was filled with admiration at the sight of her, and stood like one enchanted. Besides, he spoke so kindly and pleasantly that she willingly answered him; and then, throwing off his disguise, he revealed to her astonished gaze a hero and a king. Each felt and inspired a mutual passion, and then and there they exchanged vows of eternal love. Gram now requested the consent of the king, who, being averse to his proposal, marched against him with a large army. But Gram's invincible valour spread confusion among the enemy, who fled in all directions, whilst both Gro's suitor and the king were numbered among the slain. Hereupon, Gram conquered the whole of Sweden, and on the day of his marriage he placed the royal crown on the head of his fair young bride.

Gram's next care was to have his fleet splendidly decorated, and all the vessels painted, so that the dragon's heads in the bowsprit could be seen from a very great distance. A specially large and curiously shapen vessel was built for himself and his queen. It resembled the form of a dragon; in front, the head was ornamented with a golden crown, silver teeth, and a blood-red tongue; the helm at the back represented the tail of the dragon, the sails the wings of the monster, and the rudders his feet. When all was completed Gram set sail, and steered under a favourable wind towards Hledra. The crew were stationed on the deck in gay apparel and glistening armour. The shield of peace, composed of pure silver, sparkled from the mast of the *Orlog* ship, and the king himself, with the queen at his side, sat on the throne overlooking the whole procession. It was thus that Gram entered the harbour of the capital. Old Skiöld stood on the shore with his comrades and a large assembly of people. They welcomed the victorious hero, whose celebrated deeds were sung in all northern lands; and when they reached the court, Skiöld proclaimed loudly that from that time forth Gram should rule in unity with him over Denmark. All the nobles present joyfully assented to this, except Earl Ingo, who envied the young king his fame and power. Furtively he stole from the assembly, and spread the report among his vassals, and, indeed, throughout all Denmark, that "Skiöld was too old, and Gram too young; the government should belong to a better and more experienced man." As a raging fire often arises from a tiny spark, so this secret discontent ripened into a general rebellion. Then Gram arose in arms at the head of his faithful followers. Victory attended him everywhere; and Ingo, after having been defeated in a great battle, fled to Swipdager, King of Norway.

Gram now returned to Hledra, generously rewarded his warriors, and freed the people from their taxes for several years. At the same time he was heavily afflicted by the loss of those who were nearest and dearest to him on earth. First, his father died; then Gro also breathed her last, after having presented him with a son, and when his faithful comrade, Bessi, was also gathered to his forefathers, Gram was left alone in the midst of his worldly prosperity.

The news that Swipdager, at the instigation of Ingo, was preparing to invade Denmark, first aroused him from the melancholy into which he had fallen. He gathered all his brave warriors together, and was preparing to march against the enemy, when a Finlander came to him with the news that Humbel, the ruler of Finland, had a wonderfully beautiful daughter, whom he kept in confinement, because it had been prophesied that her marriage would cause some great misfortune to fall upon him. The old man showed him the picture of the maiden in a magic mirror, and the king was so enraptured with her loveliness, that he forgot his former queen, and the war by which he was threatened, and straightway sailed with his fleet to Finland. The king of that country not being prepared to oppose him, received the royal hero at his court, and told his daughter Signe to fill him a goblet of mead. Gram on seeing the maiden, thought that in reality she was far more lovely than in the magic mirror, and when she sang a song to the sweet tones of the harp, praising the hero who had slain many a giant with his club, and had successfully fought for the crown of Swithiod, he fell so deeply in love with her that he then and there sought her hand in marriage. Humbel, not daring to refuse him, granted his request, whereupon Gram set sail, in order to terminate his quarrel with the Northmen. But, just as he was on the point of opening the battle, the old Fin-lander again appeared before him, holding the magic mirror in his hand. When Gram looked into it, he saw a sight that filled him with rage. The court of Finland rose before his view, and there he saw a princely hero in glis-tening armour, and in his hand Humbel was placing that of his daughter, although evidently much against her will.

"It is Henry, the celebrated Duke of Saxony, whom thou now seest," said the magician; "the faithless king has promised him the hand of the noble Signe, and the wedding will soon take place." Gram lifted his sword in his fury, in order to destroy the mirror and its hateful representation, but both man and mirror had vanished like a passing shadow from before his eyes. He rushed like one distraught to the shore, embarked on one of his vessels, and sailed for Finland. Wind and weather were favourable, the ship bounded swiftly over the crested waves, and they soon reached their place of destination. The king wrapt himself in a large cloak to hide his costly apparel, drew his hat low over his forehead, and thus approached the palace, whence sounds of feasting and of revelry proceeded. He passed himself off as a man skilled in medicine, who was capable of healing all wounds, and of curing pains of every kind. On hearing this the king was pleased, and offered him a seat among the men in waiting.

Beer and mead were drunk to such an excess that the minds of the guests succumbed to their potent influence. Then Gram took a stringed instrument from one of the singers, and as he sang the praises of manly courage and womanly faith, Signe, who sat next to her bridegroom, raised her soft eyes to his face. She recognised him,—she rose. Then the king threw off his disguise, rushed among the intoxicated guests, drew his sword and killed the duke and all who opposed him, and finally carried the maiden away to his vessel in safety. Lightly their ship bounded over the waves, as if drawn by invisible hands, and the sea-nymphs laughed, and the nixies sang marriage-songs, and the wedding was soon after celebrated in the castle at Hledra. The king was beside himself with joy in the possession of his fair bride, who won all hearts by her beauty and wisdom. Moreover, they were now no longer threatened by war, for the Northmen had retreated, without venturing to engage in battle.

Years went by, rich in love and happiness, till suddenly the report spread that Swipdager had once more risen in arms, and was expecting the forces of the Saxons, who were coming to his aid. The energies of the king were thus again awakened by this approaching danger; he summoned his soldiers to battle, and the warriors of Denmark and Swithiod, eager for fame and plunder, readily enlisted under the banner of their great ruler.

The hostile factions soon found themselves face to face. When the first rays of the sun shone through the morning mist, horns were sounded for the attack. Then the war-cry arose; arrows and javelins whistled through the air, swords and lances clashed against helmets and shields. Gram and his warriors broke wildly through the ranks of their adversaries, filling all hearts with dismay. The hostile forces retreated before the superior strength of the foe, until at last all had fled except the rear-guard, commanded by Swipdager. Just at this moment, white sails appeared in the distance, coming nearer and nearer, till the vessels reached the shore. Many armed warriors disembarked, arranged themselves in ranks, and marched against the enemy, who, confident that the victory was won, were scattered hither and thither, pursuing the flying Northmen. When Gram saw the Saxons, he knew well the extent of the danger which threatened him; and determined either to make himself master of the occasion by killing Swipdager, or else, if the fates so willed it, to lose his life upon the field of battle. When the combat was at its fiercest, a bold Saxon suddenly forced his way through the ranks. He clove in two the shield of the Danish king, who thereupon grasped his sword to aim a desperate blow at his adversary, but it unfortunately caught in the boughs of a neighbouring oak, and before he had time to disentangle it, he was felled to the ground by Swipdager's sword.

Swipdager was victorious; many of his enemies lay dead on the battle-field, and the rest he had put to flight. Denmark was tributary to him, and he now made preparations for fresh conquests. He marched into Hledra, and gave orders that the two sons of the slain king should be brought to him, so as to prevent them, when older, from avenging the death of their father. But nowhere could they be found; they seemed to have disappeared from off the face of the earth, for since Gram's death no one had seen them. Swipdager now marched against Swithiod, in order that that land also should be subject to him. As the Swedish warriors were headed by no very able man, it took him but a very short time to subdue them. In consequence of his many conquests, Swipdager was now looked upon as the greatest monarch of his time, and ambassadors were sent from distant lands to do homage to the great ruler of the North. He had been successful in everything, except in his search for Gram's sons, to whom he was desirous of offering compensation for the loss they had sustained at his hands. For Swipdager was in reality a good and kind man, and it was only through the cunning of Ingo that he had been induced to take part in any violent proceedings; after the death of the latter his better feelings prevailed, and he longed for reconciliation.

Meanwhile, the princes, Guthorm and Hadding, had been in safe keeping. A mighty warrior named Wagnoft had taken the children during the battle from the arms of their dying mother Signe, and had fled with them into an almost inaccessible wilderness in Sweden. He thought it better that they should be brought up among bears and wolves than that they should fall victims to the fury of the enemy. They grew into fine strong youths, who learnt under his tuition to bend the bow, to wield the sword, and to slay the wild beasts of the forest. As they grew older, their expeditions took them into more inhabited parts, and people began to suspect who the brothers were. When the rumour reached Swipdager's ears, he immediately sought out the strangers in their retreat, and spoke to them kind words of reconciliation. He pointed out to them the poverty of their present mode of life, and promised them not only abundance of wealth, but also that he would give them to hold, as his vassals, their father's kingdom of Denmark. Guthorm, who was of a kind and friendly disposition, laid his hand in that of the king, and gladly acceded to his proposals; but Hadding answered never a word. The image of his dead father seemed to rise before his view, while at his side stood Wagnoft, like a spirit of vengeance, knowing of no atonement.

Swipdager, despising the anger of his obstinate opponents, left them to their fate, and returned to the castle, accompanied by Guthorm.

Hadding and Wagnoft now felt that their hiding-place was no longer secure, and they therefore wandered over hill and vale, till they reached the sea-shore. Some pirates, who happened to be sailing by, took them on board, and on hearing that Hadding was of royal descent, chose him as their king, and under his guidance gained much fame and plunder. One of their most important battles was fought in Kurland, against Lokir, the king of that country. Hadding pressed through the thick of the battle, in order to fight face to face with the king, but he soon found himself in a most perilous situation, surrounded on all sides by the enemy, separated from his friends and deprived of all weapons of defence. Death seemed inevitable, when suddenly an old man, blind of one eye, and whom no sword or spear could harm, approached. He strode over the battle-field, towering above all other men, as if he were a god come to rule the

9

earth. Hadding felt himself enveloped in the old man's mantle, raised in the air, and carried away with lightning speed. When at last he was set down on firm ground, he found himself on a lonely coast, but the old man had disappeared as soon as the cloak had been withdrawn from him. Nevertheless, when Hadding once more ventured into the interior of the land, he again fell into Lokir's power, who gave orders that he should be thrown before a wild bear. But, fortunately, he had learnt in his youth the nature of wild animals, and lay on the ground stiff and motionless as a corpse. The bear turned him from side to side with his paws, when suddenly Hadding sprang to his feet, threw himself on the monster, and strangled him. The young hero, whose great strength had awakened much admiration, was once more conducted to his prison; but he sang the guards to sleep, and escaped from the dungeon where he was confined into a fresh green wood. There the little birds welcomed him with sweet songs, and inspired him with hope and happiness.

After many years Hadding again met with his former companions. At their head he devastated the country far and wide, revenged himself on Lokir, conquered the stronghold Düna, and demanded, as ransom, an amount of gold equal to the weight of the governor of the town. As the latter was a very fat man, and weighed no less than three hundredweight, he had to give up all the gold in his kingdom.

Hadding now crossed over to Sweden with a formidable army, in order to avenge himself on Swipdager, and thereby fulfil the oath which he had sworn as a boy. For by day and night the spirit of his father was ever before him, reminding him of the filial duty he was called upon to perform.

The great king of the north thought it would be no difficult matter to overcome this adventurer, but he was somewhat alarmed when he saw that Hadding was accompanied by a very large army. He would gladly have deferred the battle till he had obtained some reinforcements, but Hadding discovered his enemies among the mountains, where they had pitched their camps and straightway commenced the attack.

Amidst the roar of the battle and the flashing of the swords, Hadding's one care was to find out the conqueror of his vanquished father. Revenge was the one desire of his heart; revenge was his battle cry!

At last he saw his enemy encouraging his disheartened soldiers, and leading them on to battle. Hadding pressed forward—at last he stood before the great king, and with the cry, "Gram's son sends thee to hell!" he felled him lifeless to the ground. Thus the battle was terminated, and the Northmen were either dispersed, or shared the fate of their king, and found their death on the battlefield. Denmark and Swithiod fell into the hands of the conqueror; it was only in Norway that Asmund, Swipdager's son, asserted himself.

Hadding was guilty of bloodshed, and Asmund, swearing that he should be made to repent it, sold all his possessions in order to collect a formidable army with which to march against him. His sentiments were shared by his lovely wife Gunhild, to whom Swipdager had been as a second father. She accompanied her husband as far as Upsala, where he was met by Hadding. The latter was threatened by great dangers during the combat, for the bravest of his warriors lay lifeless around him, and he was hard pressed by the enemy on every side. Breathless and exhausted, he rallied himself for one last desperate effort to ward off his impending fate.

Then Asmund, thirsting for revenge, and elated at his success, made a bold attack upon his enemy, when suddenly a mighty warrior rose, as if from the ground, between him and Gram's son. It was Wagnoft, who had saved Hadding from destruction when a boy. He killed Asmund with one blow from his club, and then led on Hadding's warriors to victory.

Hadding gave orders that the corpses of the slain should be solemnly burnt on two large funeral piles, and the ashes of friends and foes honourably interred; he also commanded that Asmund's body should be buried in the ground with all the observances of royalty. Before the grave was filled in, a fair woman approached, clad in deep mourning. She did not lament, nor did she utter a word; but her tears fell on the coffin. It was Gundhild, the young widow of the slain king, who, beautiful and noble as a goddess, mourned for him whom she loved. First she looked down into the depths of the grave, then, raising her beautiful eyes to the bright blue sky above, as if she would say: "From earth to heaven; from the night to light," she hastily drew forth a dagger, and pierced her heart, so as to be for ever united with him she loved so dearly. A lofty mound was afterwards raised over the grave of Asmund and Gundhild, as a memorial of their love and fidelity.

Uffo, a brother of Asmund, now ruled in Norway, and determined to carry on the war, as he was eager to avenge the death both of his father and his brother.

During the first year no events of importance took place. Then the Swedes sent an invitation to the king of the Northmen, inviting him to be their ruler. Bitterly resenting their desertion, Hadding marched into Swithiod with a great army, and laid waste the fertile country of his enemies far and wide. But when, after five years, he sent his fleet on an expedition, misfortune also fell to his share. His warriors suffered from the most pressing want, the horses and even the dogs were slaughtered and consumed, until at last roots and herbs were the only means of subsistence left to them. Under these trying circumstances, when many of his soldiers were ill and others had deserted him, Hadding was forced to join with the enemy in battle. He fought nobly and bravely to the last, but his efforts were in vain, and he was forced to fly with a handful of followers into his own kingdom. Here he found that his treasury had been robbed by the faithless officials to whom it had been entrusted, but the men of Denmark still remained true to their king, so that the enemy did not attempt an invasion.

For some little time Hadding occupied himself with home affairs, but his restless spirit soon drove him on to fresh enterprises. One of these brought him to Noreg, where an earl named Hakin was about to marry his lovely daughter Regenhild to a man whom she both hated and feared. The maiden's complaints were all in vain; the wedding-guests were already assembled, and the goblet was circulating freely, when an uninvited guest appeared, in the person of Hadding, who with his followers walked straight up to the bridegroom, and killed him with a mighty blow from his club. He then requested the earl to bestow upon him the hand of the fair Regenhild, and Hakin, not daring to refuse him, complied with his request. After the wedding Hadding returned to Hledra, where he would gladly have remained quietly in the company of his noble and lovable wife, had not the enemy forced him to take up arms once more.

Uffo, the brother of Asmund, was still thirsting to revenge himself on Hadding, yet did not dare attack him in his own country. At length he invited him to a reconciliation at Upsala, to which Hadding readily consented, appearing on the appointed day with a suite of armed followers. According to agreement, Swithiod was to be divided between the two rulers, and the past was to be forgiven and forgotten. After a grand banquet, Hadding's followers passed out one by one through a narrow doorway, outside which Uffo had had a cunning contrivance erected, by means of which each one that passed through it had his head dissevered from his body. Meanwhile Uffo detained Hadding with flattering speeches, so that he would not have noticed the strategem had not the last of his warriors uttered a piercing cry. Then he understood it all, and turned upon Uffo with drawn sword, but he found that the traitor had vanished.

On looking around him, he perceived a small iron door, which with some difficulty he broke open, and passed into the open air. A protecting god spread a thick fog around him, so that his enemies could not pursue him, and he escaped in safety.

Uffo, disappointed in his expectations, now promised the hand of his daughter and his whole kingdom to the man who would bring him Hadding's head. There was only one who was willing to undertake such a dangerous enterprise, and that was Thuning, who had loved the beautiful princess for many years. He collected a large number of the people who lived on the icy shores of the White Sea, and who honoured neither God nor man, and with these and the Northmen he marched against Denmark.

Hadding, wishing to save his own land from devastation, sailed with an army and fleet along the Norwegian coast. In passing an island, they were surprised at the sight of an old man, wearing a broad-brimmed hat low down on his forehead, and a long, flowing mantle of pale blue, who beckoned to them as they passed. In spite of the remonstrances of his companions, Hadding took him on board. Then they noticed that the old man had only one eye, which shone like the sun, and, moreover, his whole appearance seemed to change, and he looked so tall and imposing that the sailors whispered to each other that Odin had come among them, and they willingly obeyed his commands. After the army had landed in safety, the old man placed the warriors in ranks, while he himself remained stationed with the rear-guard.

The battle commenced as usual with the sound of the horn and the battle-cry. The mysterious old man shot seven arrows simultaneously from a huge bow, and they never missed their mark. When the enemy saw that fortune was against them, they had recourse to magic, and drew down a thick fog over the Danish army, so that they could no longer distinguish their opponents. On the other hand, the voice of the one-eyed stranger was heard like the rolling of thunder, and at the same time a cloud passed over them with lightning-speed, which dispelled the fog, and drove hail and sleet into the faces of the enemy. In the confusion which ensued Hadding killed the traitor Uffo, and also his enemy Thuning.

But there was still one man left who could carry on Uffo's work of revenge, and that was Hunding, Swipdager's youngest son. As, however, he was of a peaceful disposition, Hadding invited him to a reconciliation in the holy temple at Upsala. Here these two men stood face to face, whose forefathers had hated each other so long, with such a deadly hatred, and here they were finally reconciled to each other. Soon after Hadding received the sad news that his beloved wife Regenhild was on her death-bed. He travelled with all speed to Hledra, where he found his queen at the point of death. Softly she whispered these words in his ear: "I will hover about thee, and guard thee from all harm and danger," and then her gentle spirit took its flight.

Hadding felt very lonely and forsaken after the death of his fair queen, for all his old comrades had been called to their last resting-place, his son Frodi was absent on various expeditions, and his daughter Ulfhild, who had married a rich man named Guthorm, cared little for her old father. While resting one day upon his couch, he heard the tones of a harp, and a soft, sweet voice singing. It was the voice of his departed queen, and as he raised himself to listen, he saw her standing before him, with the silvery rays of the moon lighting up her transfigured form. He would fain have taken her in his arms, but she motioned him away, and told him she had come to warn him against the wickedness of his own daughter. Then she gradually disappeared from before his gaze, and only the soft tones of the harp convinced him that it was not all a dream. Soon after a messenger came from his daughter Ulfhild, asking him to attend at a grand feast given in his honour. He accepted the invitation, but remembering the prophetic warning he had received, he wore armour under his outer garments, and commanded his followers to do likewise. They soon found themselves seated round the banquet-table at Guthorm's court. Then Ulfhild rose, and crying, "Happiness to the great king!" she poured a goblet of wine over the table. This was the appointed signal, and the serving-men, drawing forth daggers, attacked the unsuspecting guests. But Hadding and his companions, who were protected by their armour, drew their swords, and punished the men as they deserved. When, however, fresh numbers came to the aid of their assailants, Hadding found himself in a most perilous situation; a few of his followers stood by him faithfully, others escaped on horseback to tell the sad news wherever they went that the great king had fallen a victim to the cunning of his unnatural and wicked daughter.

Meanwhile Hunding had passed his days in peace and happiness. When he heard of the violent death of his friend Hadding, he was deeply grieved, and ordered a great banquet to be prepared in his memory, to which he invited all the chief men of his kingdom. The feast was still progressing when the door suddenly opened, and Hadding entered. Hunding fell upon his neck and wept like a child, while he heard with delight how his friend had escaped from the hands of his would-be-assassins.

But that same night, Hunding, in groping his way through the banqueting-room, after dark, fell into a huge cask of sweet mead, and was drowned.

Sadly Hadding returned to Hledra, for now that his friend was dead it seemed as if the last tie that bound him to earth was rent asunder. The image of his beloved wife often appeared to him in his dreams, beckoning him to follow her; he felt the touch of her hand and of her kiss upon his lips, and he knew that his earthly joys and sorrows would soon be over for ever. He bequeathed his crown and kingdom to his son Frodi, and then he gladly went whither his beloved called him.

HELGI, SON OF HIORWARD.

"EARL Atli, my trusty friend wilt thou journey to King Swavnir, and woo his fair daughter Sigurlin for me? Last Yule I beheld her in her father's court, where I tarried as a winter guest, and I have not forgotten her since." So spoke King Hiörward to his foster-brother Atli. "So late in the season it will be hard to cross the icy mountain-crests and the swampy fens of the valleys," answered the Earl; "nevertheless for my liege lord I will adventure the fight with the fierce frost-giants (hrîm-thurses)."

Well found in arms and royal gifts, Atli journeyed to Swavnir. He was hospitably received; but when he named the suit he was come upon, Earl Framnar, Sigurlin's governor, bethought him that King Hiörward had three wives already, and his foster-child was too good to be an understrapper. So the wooer was sent away with a flea in his ear. Not discouraged by the evil tidings the Earl brought him, the King determined to make another attempt himself, and take an army with him. When with much toil they had gained the mountain crest, he looked down on Swavaland, and saw towns and villages on fire, and parties of horse riding about, laying waste the land. He learnt from fugitives that Hrodmar, a neighbouring king, who had also sued for Sigurlin's hand and been rejected, had in a pitched battle beaten and slain Swavnir, and now with cruel ravages was hunting about for his daughter, whom Earl Framnar had hidden away by magic. On hearing this, the King and his men moved down the mountain, till they came to a river, and there pitched their camp. Atli, who had the night-watch, quietly crossed the water, and soon arrived at a great building, whose entrance was guarded by a giant eagle. He pierced him through with his javelin, and in the house he found the fair Sigurlin, and Framnar's daughter Alof. The maidens were in great alarm, but the brave Earl pacified them, and brought them to his lord. Having thus found what they sought, the King ordered a retreat. The two maidens soon began to trust and love their deliverers, and consented to a wedding, which was held with great splendour in the royal castle.

The fruit of the royal marriage was a son, who grew up strong and handsome; but to the great sorrow of his parents, he was dumb. He heard and understood all that was said, but he never learnt even to say father and mother. All the pains taken to get him to speak were thrown away; and so it came to pass that he was thought little of, and had not so much as a name given him. It was only his older half-brother Hedin that paid much attention to him, taking him out for forays in the woods and fields, and when they grew older, on more serious expeditions. One day, as they were resting on the edge of the forest after a hard fight, they saw nine valkyries on their white steeds high up in the air. One of them let herself down, and halted in front of them, beautiful as Freya's companion. Coming up to the dumb youth she said: "Helgi, for so thou shalt be named henceforth, the hour is come for thee to shew the hero-spirit that sleeps in thy soul. I am Swava, King Eilimi's daughter, and am appointed to shield thee in the shower of spears." The youth in amazement gazed at the wondrous apparition: "You have given me a name," he cried, "but I will not have it without you."

"It is too soon to speak so bold a word; first prove by deeds that thou deservest a shield-maiden's love." So saying, she hastened after her companions.

"Happy Helgi!" cried his brother Hedin, "thou wilt win the glorious maid, and skalds shall one day sing thy fame."

Great was the joy in Hiörward's hall when the dumb son came before his sire, and in a clear voice asked for a band of warriors, that he might avenge his mother's father on King Hrodmar, who had slain him. Many warriors mustered round him, and he marched away as if to certain victory. The war soon blazed in the enemy's land, and the young hero was ever foremost in the fray. And if the storm of battle pressed him sore, and the strength of his arm grew slack, he saw the valkyrie hovering above him, catching the shot on her shining shield, and he felt new strength to tread the path of victory. In vain did Hrodmar hope to avoid him by skulking in the rear; he sought him out and felled him with a fatal stroke of the sword. In vain did the giant Hati seek to avenge his lord; he too was stricken to death, and sank on the bloody ground. Terror went before Helgi, and the hosts of the enemy turned their faces to flight. Victory followed him by land and by sea. Hati's daughter Hrîmgerd, a grim sea-maiden (meerminne), tried to sink the hero's fleet, but Swava came sailing in the storm-cloud, and guided the black-bosomed sea-drakes safely into harbour. Crowned with glory, the hero came home to the castle of his fathers, and the harps of skalds rang with his praises. He had now fulfilled the conditions prescribed by the shield-maid; and the next spring he set out for King Eilimi's court. When he made known his suit, the king gave a willing consent, and the loving Swava was not loth to obey her father. The feast of betrothal was held at once: Helgi fastened the golden circlet round the slender arm of his affianced, and when her lips rested on his in a long kiss of troth, he felt such rapture as the wounded hero feels on the battle-field, when with a kiss the valkyrie lifts him out of earthly trouble to immortal bliss. But the bridal was put off till Helgi should return from an expedition against Alfur, the son of Hrodmar, who threatened him with war because he had refused to pay the fine for killing his father. At parting, Swava held him long in her arms: she was loth to let him go, feeling that she had no longer the power to protect him, for by affiance to a mortal man she had stept out of the ranks of shield-maidens.

Alfur was well provided for war, and a skillful general. The fortune of battle shifted from side to side all the summer; at length Helgi won a victory, and drove his antagonist into the bleak highland. He took towns and castles, but could not wholly overcome the resistance of a people fighting for their freedom and their ancient line of sovereigns. Petty warfare went on even in the winter. Still Helgi was everywhere victorious; he meant to keep Yule at his father's court, and in the spring to fetch home his beloved Swava. Snowstorms delayed him on the journey, and before he could reach home, tidings came that Alfur with many warriors had forced his way back into his kingdom, had raised the whole population, and defied him to the "holm-gang." This was joyful news to Helgi, for now he hoped to finish the never-ending strife at a blow. But first he continued his journey. On his way he saw his brother Hedin come riding in wild haste and with distracted looks, aside from the main road. The moment he spied Helgi, he galloped toward him, and fell weeping on his neck. "Save me, brother!" he cried, "save me from myself. I have done wickedly, and brought heavy woe upon us." Then, in broken sentences, he went on: "On Yule-day there met me a strange woman, riding on a wolf. She was neither old nor young, neither foul nor fair; she offered me her attendance. I took her for a wanton, and spurned her away. She answered, threatening, that I should rue it at the Bragi-drinking. That evening we drank deep, and were at the height of our mirth, when the boar of Freyr was brought in, and the Bragi-cup was handed round. Every one bragged of some bold action he would do, and I—the dark Norn whispered the words in my ear—I vowed that I would win my brother's bride from him, the shield-maid Swava. But never will I fight the man that I love best on earth. I will wash out the wicked vow in my own blood. Fare well and happily!" He was rushing away, but Helgi held him back, and said: "Hear me, brother, while like a vala I foretell the future. My fylgia has parted from my side, and has turned herself to thee; therefore in the fight with Alfur I shall fall, and Swava, if she hearken to my prayer, will give her hand to thee. Look, Hedin, the coward begs hard for a bit more of earthly bliss; the hero looks the dark Norn boldly in the face, and says, Ay, spin thy black thread, and northward cast it for me! it reaches no farther than to dying; the entrance to Odin's Hall it cannot bar against me."

It was in vain that Hedin tried to keep him away from the battle, that he offered to lead the army for him, and to die in his stead: he kept to his purpose. In the spring the two brothers marched against Alfur, who fell back before them to the borders of King Eilimi's dominions. There he made a stand, and a stubborn fight began. It lasted all day, and still was undecided; but Helgi had received his death-wound from the sword of his desperate foe. In the evening Hedin and his comrades in arms stood round the dying hero. Swava, too, having heard of the fight, had come in haste from her father's castle, which stood near. Helgi knew her, and a glad smile hovered round his pale lips. "Give me the bridal kiss, my beloved, the valkyrie's kiss that summons me to Odin; then rest in Hedin's arms, he is worthy of thee." She made no wailing, she shed no tears; she said: "A true woman loves but once, and not again. Take, Hedin, the sister's kiss, but thou, Helgi, whom alone I can love, the kiss of the valkyrie. We shall soon meet again at the blissful gathering in Freya's Folkwang."

Her lips rested on his, as though she would catch his last breath. She stayed in the camp till the mound was raised over the departed hero, and then returned to Eilimi's castle. Her words came true; she died soon, and found, as she had wished, a resting-place beside the man whom alone she had loved.

LEGEND OF TANNHAUSER.

ONE evening when the noble knight Tannhäuser was sitting in a miserable wayside inn, grumbling over the fate that had made him a poor man instead of a prince, he was startled by a loud knocking at the door. He felt a moment's terror lest it should be the bailiffs come to arrest him for debt; but instead of that, it was his good lord, Duke Friedrich of Badenberg, who ruled the rich Danubian land of Austria.

The duke chid the young man for his debts and follies, and then, giving him a purse full of gold, desired him to return to court, where his music and society were much missed.

So Tannhäuser once more returned to court, and took part in the gay doings there. He also aided his liege lord in many a famous battle waged against the enemies of the realm. He was a great favourite of his master, both because of his gift of song, and because of his bravery. So Friedrich gave him the fair estate of Leopoldsdorf, near Vienna, as well as a large sum of money.

The Hohenstaufens, too, looked upon him favourably, both the Emperor Frederick II., and his son Konrad, who ruled in Germany after him. The minstrel received many gifts at their hands, and was devoted to their service.

But although large sums were thus continually passing into his coffers, he was always in debt. In course of time his patron the Duke was killed in the battle of the Leitha. He mourned him deeply, and wrote a number of beautiful songs in memory of the man who had been so kind to him. But at length his poetic soul began to turn with more pleasure to cheerful themes, so he collected what little remained of his wealth, and, setting out in the bright summer days, he wandered from castle to castle, and from town to town, sometimes hungry, sometimes happy, as he was ill or well received. He travelled through Bavaria, and remained some time at Nürnberg, where song was loved and studied; and after that he crossed the Alps into Italy. At Pavia, he made the acquaintance of a German knight, who was much drawn to the fascinating minne-singer, and he, in his turn, to the knight's fair daughter, Kunigunde. The old knight, on being asked for his daughter's hand, replied that he liked Tannhäuser very much, and would give him his daughter willingly if he had the wherewithal to support her. Minstrelsy was all very well, he added, but it would not keep a family in bread and butter. "You have both your sword and your harp to trust to," he concluded with a smile; "go, and make enough money to set up house, and then I will give you Kunigunde."

Tannhäuser took leave of his lady-love, promising to return in a year with the needful provision; and he hopefully intended to keep his promise.

He rode away sad at heart; but the weather was so beautiful, and the birds were singing so gaily, that he could not remain sad long. He sang wherever he could get an audience, but sweet and joyous as was the music he made, it brought him no gold. He therefore tried what his sword could do for him, and fought under the banner of King Konrad, against his rival Heinrich Raspe, the "pope's king," thereby helping to win the battle of Ulm. He was handsomely rewarded for his assistance. Then he went back to Italy, and fought there also for the Hohenstaufens, for which service he was richly paid. Once, soon after this, he sought and found shelter for the night in a castle where many knights were assembled. After supper he delighted every one with his minstrelsy. But immediately after he had ceased to sing, a stranger came in, dressed in black garments embroidered with gold, and wearing black feathers in his cap. He had a harp in his hand, and, seating himself, began to play and sing in a deep, powerful, and yet melodious, voice. His song was strange and eerie in its effect. The guests all glanced at each other in silence when it was done. They felt ill at ease, they knew not why.

Tannhäuser, throwing off the unaccountable feeling that possessed him, caught up his harp, and sang a merry ditty about woods and birds and flowers, and soon both he and the other guests were restored to their former cheerfulness. After that, they all began to play at dice. Tannhäuser won large sums, and lost them again immediately to the black stranger, and not only these, but some of the money he had put aside for his marriage.

The next day, when he left the castle, the stranger went with him, remained with him all day, and before night fell, had won all his money from him. Seeing how sad Tannhäuser looked, the stranger laughed, and said:

"Do not pull such a long face over so small a matter as the loss of a few gold pieces, but come with me to Wartburg; Landgrave Hermann has summoned a minstrel tournament to meet, in which the prizes are lands and wealth, but he who fails will lose his head. My name is Klingsohr, and I come from Hungary. I am willing to enter into an alliance with you. Your songs are like the bliss of heaven; mine, like the horrors of hell. If we are successful, you may have the wealth—I shall take the heads; if, on the other hand, we lose, we shall go together to heaven or hell; what does it matter which? You shudder like a weakling to hear me talk thus, for you believe the tales the priests tell you about fire and brimstone; but instead of that, it is the realm of Dame Venus, who gives her friends the most exquisite pleasures earth can afford, and both silver and gold in abundance. If you do not care for the minstrel tournament, you can visit the fair queen on the road to Wartburg, for she lives in the Hörselberg, which we shall have to pass."

Tannhäuser listened to his companion with a shudder; but when he went on to describe the unspeakable glories of the Hörselberg, and to tell of the marvellous charms of the queen, he felt a growing desire to see Dame Venus with his own eyes. So he set out with his strange companion, forgetting, or nearly forgetting, Kunigunde, and his love for her.

When the travellers approached the mountains of Thuringia they were joined by a tall and stately man in full armour, with his sword at his side, and a white staff in his hand. As they walked on together, they exchanged confidences as to who they were, and from whence they came. The new-comer said:

"People call me the faithful Eckhard, the Harlung's comfort, for I took care of the noble youths for many years; but, alas! wicked Ermenrich, and his evil counsellor Sibich, slew them in my absence, and all I could do was to avenge their death."

"The Harlungs, Ermenrich, Sibich," repeated Tannhäuser thoughtfully, "it must have been long ago."

"Three or four hundred years or even more may have passed since then," answered Eckhard. "I find it difficult to reckon time after the manner of men; but ever since those old days I have been busily employed in warning people away from the Venus Mount."

Klingsohr burst out laughing, and cried, "Spare your words, old fool; so you are one of the idiots who blaspheme Dame Venus."

"Get thee behind me, tempter," said Eckhard; "I am going to take the good knight to the Wartburg, where he may win glory and wealth."

"And I am going on to prepare his lodging in our queen's palace," answered the other, as he set off at a brisk pace towards the mountains.

The minstrel and Eckhard continued their way quietly, talking the while. At last they came to the beautiful Hörselthal, with its meadows, trees, and rushing stream, and, a little farther on, to a bleak mountain, out of which came a confused sound as of waves beating a rock-bound coast, the roar and clatter of a water-mill, human cries of rage, and the howling of wild beasts. "That is the Hörselberg," said Eckhard, "the place where Dame Venus holds her court, with the wicked who are under her dominion. Keep thine eyes and ears both shut, lest the temptress entangle thee in her net."

The nearer the travellers came to the mountain, the more the confused and discordant sounds they had at first heard resolved themselves into harmony. Through a door in the rock they could see knights, beautiful women, and dwarfs. All seemed to be enjoying themselves to the utmost. At the entrance sat a fair woman in royal robes. The moment she saw Tannhäuser she smiled, and signed to him to approach. Eckhard in the same moment entreated him by all he held sacred to beware of the temptress, who was outwardly like an angel of light, but inwardly a fiend incarnate. He would have said more, but Venus interrupted him by beginning to sing a wondrous song about all the joys that awaited those who entered her kingdom; and Tannhäuser, as thoroughly enchanted as though a magic spell had been cast over him, thrust Eckhard aside, and hastened to the queen of beauty, who stretched out her arms towards him. She half drew him over the threshold, and he half staggered across. Then the door shut, and the faithful Eckhard saw him no more.

It would be impossible to describe all the wonders and delights that greeted the eyes and ears of the lost knight. Every day brought new pleasures, which he enjoyed to the utmost. But at length he began to tire of it, and confessed to himself that satiety was not happiness. He had a horror of himself, and of the self-indulgent life he was leading; and his conscience, once awake, left him no peace. After an inward struggle, he made up his mind to go and seek out a pious priest, tell him all, and entreat him to show him how he might gain absolution.

Tannhäuser felt much happier when he had formed this resolution. He went to Queen Venus, and asked her to let him go. At first she refused, and then consented, saying that he might come back to her if he did not find what he was going away to seek. So he went out into the sweet fresh air, which was so pure that it gave him new life, but in a little while his resolution faltered. Could he be able to find a priest to shrive him!

He told his tale to priests, abbots, and bishops, but they one and all declared that they could not help him, that the Holy Father at Rome was the only person on earth who had power to absolve a sinner who had had dealings with the powers of the under-world.

He went to Rome, and confessed all his sin and sorrow to the Pope, whom he found walking in the garden, and awaited the answer of his Holiness with a broken and contrite heart. But the Pope replied with harsh voice and unbending brow:

"You are an adherent of the cursed race of Hohenstaufen; you have dwelt among the lost spirits in hell, and have been one with them: I tell you plainly that God can no more pardon you than this dry stick can put forth leaves and flowers"; so saying, he thrust his gold-headed walking stick into the ground, and walked away leaving it there.

Tannhäuser then exclaimed in his misery, "What shall I do? The high-priest of the Lord has cast me off, heaven is closed against me, and men will have nought to do with me."

At this moment an unknown voice broke in, "There is a higher than this priest, even He whose dwelling is in heaven, and He that came to redeem men from their sins, and who said, 'Come unto Me, all ye that are weary and heavy laden, and I will give you rest.' "

Tannhäuser started when he heard himself addressed, and, turning around, beheld the faithful Eckhard.

"Alas," he answered, "it is too late; I cannot, dare not, pray any more. I will now return to Dame Venus, and the pleasures she offers me."

So he went back to the Hörselberg in spite of Eckhard's entreaties; for he was utterly hopeless.

Now it came to pass, three days after, that the Pope again walked in his garden, and behold, the walking-stick which he thrust into the ground had taken root, and put forth leaves and blossoms. The sight filled him with amazement, and he remembered the words of the Saviour: "Be ye also merciful, even as your Father in heaven is merciful." And he sent out messengers in search of Tannhäuser; but he could not be found, for he had returned to Dame Venus.

THE WEREWOLF.

SWEDISH.

THERE was once a king, who ruled over a large kingdom. He was married to a beautiful queen, by whom he had only one child, a daughter. Hence it naturally followed that the little one was to her parents as the apple of their eye, and was dear to them beyond all other things, so that they thought of nothing with such delight as of the pleasure they should have in her when she grew up. But much falls out contrary to expectation; for before the princess was out of her childhood, the queen, her mother, fell sick and died. Now, it is easy to imagine that there was sadness not only in the royal court, but over the whole kingdom, for the queen was greatly beloved by all. The king himself was so deeply afflicted that he resolved never to marry again, but placed all his comfort and joy in the little princess.

In this manner a considerable time passed on; the young princess grew from day to day taller and fairer, and everything she at any time desired was by her father immediately granted her; many attendants being placed about her, for the sole purpose of being at hand to execute all her commands. Among these there was a woman who had been previously married, and had two daughters. She was of an agreeable person, and had a persuasive tongue, so that she well knew how to put her words together; added to all which she was as soft and pliant

33

as silk; but her heart was full of artifices and all kinds of falsehood. No sooner was the queen dead than she began to devise plans how she might become consort to the king, and her daughters be honoured as kings' daughters. With this object she began by winning the affection of the young princess, praised beyond measure all that she said or did, and all her talk ended in declaring how happy they would be if the king would take to himself a new wife. On this subject the conversation oftenest turned both early and late, till at length the princess could not believe otherwise than that all the woman said was true. She therefore asked her what description of wife it were most desirable that the king should select. The woman, in many words, all sweet as honey, answered, "Ill would it become me to give an opinion in such a case, hoping only he may choose for his queen one who will be kind to my little princess. But this I know, that were I so fortunate as to be the object of his choice, I should think only of what might please the princess; and if she wished to wash her hands, one of my daughters should hold the basin, and the other hand her the towel." This and much more she said to the princess, who believed her, as children readily believe all that is told them is true.

Not a day now passed in which the king was free from the solicitations of his daughter, who incessantly besought him to marry the handsome waiting-woman; but he would not. Nevertheless, the princess would not desist from her entreaties, but spoke incessantly precisely as she had been taught by the false waiting-woman.

One day, when she was talking in the same strain, the king broke forth: "I see very well that it must at length be as you have resolved, greatly as it is against my wish; but it shall be only on one condition." "What is the condition?" asked the princess, overjoyed. "It is," said the king, "that, as it is for your sake if I marry again, you shall promise me that if at any future time you shall be discontented with your stepmother or your stepsisters, I shall not be troubled with your complaints and grievances." The princess made the promise, and it was settled that the king should marry the waiting-woman, and make her queen over all his realm.

As time passed on the king's daughter grew up to be the fairest maid in all the land; while the queen's daughters were as ugly in person as in disposition, so that no one had a good word for them. There could not, therefore, fail of being a number of young princes and knights, from both east and west, coming to demand the young princess; while not one vouchsafed to woo either of the queen's daughters. At this the stepmother was sorely vexed at heart, however she might conceal her feelings, being, to all outward appearance, as smooth and humble as before. Among the suitors there was a king's son from a distant country, who was both young and valorous, and as he passionately loved the princess, she listened to his addresses, and plighted her faith to him in return. The queen observed all this with a jaundiced eye; for she would fain have had the prince marry one of her own daughters, and, therefore, resolved that the young couple should never be united with each other.

From that moment her thoughts were solely bent on the destruction both of them and their love.

An opportunity soon offered itself to her; for just at that time intelligence was received that an enemy had invaded the country, so that the king was obliged to take the field. The princess was now soon made to learn what kind of a stepmother she had got; for hardly had the king departed before the queen began to show her true disposition, so that she now was as cruel and malignant as she had previously appeared to be friendly and obliging. Not a day passed on which the princess did not hear maledictions and hard words; nor did the queen's daughters yield to their mother in wickedness. But a lot still more cruel awaited the young prince, the lover of the princess. While engaged in the chase he had lost his way, and got separated from his companions. Availing herself of the opportunity, the queen practised on him her wicked arts, and transformed him into a werewolf, so that for the remainder of his days he should be a prowler of the forest. When evening drew on, and the prince did not appear, his men returned home; and the sorrow may be easily imagined with which the princess was overwhelmed when she was informed how the chase had terminated. She wept and mourned day and night, and would not be comforted. But the queen laughed at her affliction, and rejoiced in her false heart that everything had turned out so agreeably to her wishes.

As the princess was one day sitting alone in her maiden-bower, it entered her mind that she would visit the forest in which the young prince had disappeared.

She went, therefore, to her stepmother, and asked permission to go to the wood, that she might for a little while forget her heavy affliction. To her request the queen would hardly give her consent, as she was always more inclined to say no than yes; but the princess besought her so earnestly that at last her stepmother could no longer withhold her permission, only ordering one of her daughters to accompany and keep watch over her. A long dispute now arose between mother and daughters, neither of the stepsisters being willing to go with her, but excusing themselves, and asking what pleasure they could have in following her who did nothing but weep. The matter ended by the queen insisting that one of her daughters should go with the princess, however much it might be against her will. The maidens then strolled away from the palace and reached the forest, where the princess amused herself with wandering among the trees, and listening to the song of the little birds, and thinking on the friend she loved so dearly, and whom she now had lost; the queen's daughter following all the while, with a heart full of rancorous feeling for the princess and her grief.

After having wandered about for some time they came to a small cottage that stood far in the dark forest. At the same moment the princess was seized with a burning thirst, and entreated her stepsister to accompany her to the cottage, that she might get a draught of water. At this the queen's daughter became only more ill-humoured, and said, "Is it not enough that I follow you up and down in the wild wood? Now, because you are a princess, you require me to go into such a filthy nest. No, my foot shall never enter it. If you will go, go alone." The princess took no long time to consider, but did as her stepsister said, and entered the cabin. In the little apartment she saw an aged woman sitting on a bench, who appeared so stricken with years that her head shook. The princess saluted her, as was her wont, in a friendly tone, with "Good evening, good mother! may I ask you for a little drink of water?" "Yes, and right welcome," answered the old woman. "Who are you that come under my humble roof with so kind a greeting?" The princess told her that she was the king's daughter, and had come out to divert herself, with the hope, in some degree, of forgetting her heavy affliction. "What affliction have you, then?" asked the old woman. "Well may I grieve," answered the princess, "and never more feel joyful. I have lost my only friend, and God alone knows whether we shall ever meet again." She then related to the old woman all that had taken place, while the tears flowed from her eyes in such torrents that no one could have refrained from pitying her. When she had concluded, the old woman said, "It is well that you have made your grief known to me; I have experienced much, and can, perhaps, give you some advice. When you go from hence you will see a lily growing in the field. This lily is not like other lilies, but has many wonderful properties. Hasten, therefore, to pluck it. If you can do so, all will be well; for then there will come one who will tell you what you are to do." They then parted; the princess having thanked her, continued her walk, and the old woman remained sitting on her bench and shaking her head. But the queen's daughter had been standing during the whole time outside the door, murmuring and fretting that the princess staid so long.

When she came out she had to hear much chiding from her stepsister, as was to be expected; but to this she gave very little heed, thinking only how she should find the flower of which the old woman had spoken. She therefore proceeded further into the forest, and in the selfsame moment her eye fell on a spot where there stood a beautiful white lily in full bloom before her. On seeing it she was so glad, so glad, and instantly ran to gather it, but it vanished on a sudden and appeared again at some distance. The princess was now eager beyond measure, and no longer gave heed to the voice of her stepsister, but continued running; though every time she put forth her hand to take the flower it was already away, and immediately afterwards reappeared at a short distance farther off. Thus it continued for a considerable time, and the princess penetrated further and further into the dense forest, the lily all the while appearing and vanishing, and again showing itself, and every time looking taller and more beautiful than before. In this manner the princess at length came to a high mountain, when on casting her eyes up to the summit, there stood the flower on the very edge, as brilliant and fair as the brightest star. She now began to climb up the mountain, caring for neither the stocks nor the stones that lay in the way, so great was her ardour. When she at length had gained the mountain's top, lo! the lily no longer moved, but continued stationary. The princess then stooped and plucked it, and placed it in her bosom, and was so overjoyed that she forgot both stepsister and everything in the world besides. For a long time the princess could not sufficiently feast her eyes with the sight of the beautiful flower. It then on a sudden entered her mind, what her stepmother would say, when she returned home, for having staid out so long. She looked about her before returning to the palace, but on casting a glance behind her she saw that the sun had gone down, and that only a strip of day yet tarried on the mountain's summit; while down before her the forest appeared so dark and gloomy, that she did not trust herself to find the way through it. She was now exceedingly weary and exhausted, and saw no alternative but that she must remain for the night where she was. Sitting then down on the rock, she placed her hand under her cheek and wept, and thought on her wicked stepmother and stepsisters, and all the bitter words she must hear when she returned home, and on the king, her father, who was absent, and on the beloved of her heart, whom she should never see again; but abundantly as her tears flowed she noticed them not, so absorbing was her affliction. Night now drew on, all was shrouded in darkness, the stars rose and set, but the princess still continued sitting on the same spot, weeping without intermission. While thus sitting, lost in thought, she heard a voice greeting her with, "Good evening, fair maiden! Why do you sit here so lonely and sorrowful?"

She started and was greatly surprised, as may easily be imagined; and on looking back there stood a little, little old man, who nodded and looked so truly benevolent. She answered, "I may well be sorrowful, and never more be glad. I have lost my best beloved, and have, moreover, missed my path in the forest, so that I am fearful of being devoured by the wild beasts." "Oh," said the old man, "don't be disheartened for that. If you will obey me in all that I say, I will help you." To this the princess readily assented, seeing herself forsaken by the whole world besides. The old man then drew forth a flint and steel, and said, "Fair maiden! now, in the first place, you shall kindle a fire." The king's daughter did as she was desired, gathered moss, twigs, and dry wood, and kindled a fire on the mountain's brow. When she had done this the old man said to her, "Go now further on the mountain, and you will find a pot full of tar: bring it hither." The princess did so. The old man continued: "Now set the pot on the fire." The princess did so. "When, now, the tar begins to boil," said the old man, "cast your white lily into the pot." This seemed to the princess a very hard command, and she prayed earnestly that she might retain her lily; but the old man said: "Have you not promised to obey me in all that I desire, Do as I tell you; you will not repent." The princess then, with eyes averted, cast the lily into the boiling pot, although it grieved her to the heart; so dear to her was the beautiful flower.

At the same instant a hollow roaring was heard from the forest, like the cry of a wild beast, which came nearer and nearer, and passed into a hideous howl, so that the mountain re-echoed on every side. At the same time was heard a cracking and rustling among the trees, the bushes gave way, and the princess beheld a huge gray wolf come rushing out of the forest just opposite to the spot where they were sitting. In her terror she would gladly have fled from it; but the old man said, "Make haste, run to the brow of the mountain, and the moment the wolf comes before you, empty the tar-pot over him." The princess, although so terrified that she was hardly conscious of what she did, nevertheless followed the old man's direction, and poured the tar over the wolf, just as he came running towards her. But now a wonderful event took place, for scarcely had she done so when the wolf changed his covering, the great gray skin started off from him, and, instead of a ravenous wild beast, there stood a comely youth with eyes directed towards the brow of the mountain; and when the princess had so far recovered from her fright that she could look on him, whom did she behold before her but her own best beloved, who had been transformed into a werewolf!

Now let any one, who can, imagine what the feelings of the princess were at this moment. She stretched out her arms towards him, but could neither speak nor answer, so great were her surprise and joy. But the prince ran up the mountain and embraced her with all the ardour of the truest affection, and thanked her for having restored him. Nor did he forget the little old man, but thanked him in many kind words for his powerful aid. They then sat down on the mountain-top and conversed lovingly with each other. The prince related how he had been changed into a wolf, and all the privations he had suffered while he had to range about the forest; and the princess recounted to him her sorrow and all the tears she had shed during his absence. Thus they sat throughout the night, heedless of the passing hour, until the stars began gradually to retire before the daylight, so that the surrounding objects were visible. When the sun had risen they perceived that a wide road ran from the foot of the hill quite up to the royal palace. Then said the old man, "Fair maiden, turn about. Do you see anything yonder?" "Yes," answered the princess, "I see a horseman on a foaming horse; he rides along the road at full speed." "That," said the old man, "is a messenger from the king, your father. He will follow forthwith with his whole army." Now was the princess glad beyond measure, and wished instantly to descend to meet her father; but the old man held her back, saying: "Wait: it is yet too soon. Let us first see how things will turn out."

After some time the sun shone bright, so that its rays fell on the palace down before them. Then said the old man, "Fair maiden, turn about. Do you see anything yonder?" "Yes," answered the princess, "I see many persons coming out of my father's palace, some of whom proceed along the road, while others hasten towards the forest." The old man said, "They are your stepmother's servants. She has sent one party to meet the king and bid him welcome; but the other is going to the forest in search of you." At hearing this the princess was troubled, and was with difficulty induced to remain, but wished to go down to the queen's people: but the old man held her back, saying, "Wait yet a little while; we will first see how things turn out."

For some time the princess continued with her looks directed towards the road by which the king was to come. Then said the old man again, "Fair maiden, turn about. Do you observe anything yonder?" "Yes," answered the princess, "there is a great stir in my father's palace; and see! now they are busy in hanging the whole palace with black." The old man said, "That is your stepmother and her servants. They wish to make your father believe that you are dead." At this the princess was filled with anxiety, and prayed fervently, saying, "Let me go, let me go, that I may spare my father so great an affliction." But the old man detained her, saying, "No, wait. It is still too soon. We will first see how things turn out."

Again another interval passed, the sun rose high in the heaven, and the air breathed warm over field and forest; but the royal children and the little old man continued sitting on the mountain where we left them. They now observed a small cloud slowly rising in the horizon, which grew larger and larger, and came nearer and nearer along the road; and as it moved they saw that it glittered with weapons, and perceived helmets nodding and banners waving, heard the clanking of swords and the neighing of horses, and at length recognised the royal standard. Now it is easy to imagine that the joy of the princess exceeded all bounds, and that she only longed to go and greet her father. But the old man held her back, saying, "Turn about, fair maiden, do you see nothing at the king's palace?" "Yes," answered the princess, "I see my stepmother and my stepsisters coming out clad in deep mourning, and holding white handkerchiefs to their faces, and weeping bitterly." The old man said, "They are now pretending to mourn for your death; but wait awhile, we have yet to see how things will turn out."

Some time after, the old man asked again, "Fair maiden, turn about. Do you observe anything yonder?" "Yes," answered the princess, "I see them come bearing a black coffin. Now my father orders it to be opened. And see! the queen and her daughters fall on their knees, and my father threatens them with his sword." The old man said, "The king desired to see your corpse, and so your wicked stepmother has been forced to confess the truth." On hearing this, the princess entreated fervently: "Let me go, let me go, that I may console my father in his great affliction." But the old man still detained her, saying, "Attend to my counsel, and stay here a little while. We have not yet seen how everything will terminate."

Another interval passed, and the princess, and the prince, and the little old man, still continued sitting on the mountain. Then said the old man, "Turn about, fair maiden. Do you observe anything yonder?" "Yes," answered the princess, "I see my father, and my stepmother, and my stepsisters, coming this way with all their attendants." The old man continued, "They

45

have now set out in search of you. Go down now, and bring the wolfskin which is lying below." The king's daughter did so, and the old man then said, "Place yourself on the brink of the mountain." The princess did so, and at the same moment perceived the queen and her daughters coming along the road just beneath the mountain where they were sitting. "Now," said the old man, "cast the wolfskin straight down." The princess obeyed, and cast the wolfskin as the old man had directed. It fell exactly over the wicked queen and her two daughters. But now a wonderful event took place, for hardly had the skin touched the three women than they changed their guise, gave a hideous howl, and were transformed into three fierce werewolves, which at full speed rushed into the wild forest.

Scarcely had this taken place before the king himself with all his men came to the foot of the mountain. When he looked up and beheld the princess, he could not at first believe his eyes, but stood immovable, thinking it was a spectre. The old man then cried, "Fair maiden, hasten now down and gladden the heart of your father." The princess did not wait to be told a second time, but, taking her lover by the hand, was in an instant at the mountain's foot. When they reached the spot where the king was standing, the princess fell on her father's breast and wept for joy; the young prince also wept; even the king himself shed tears, and to every one present their meeting was a delightful spectacle. Great joy was there and many embracings, and the princess related all she had suffered from her stepmother and stepsisters, and all about her beloved prince, and the little old man who had so kindly assisted them. But when the king turned to thank him he had already vanished, and no one could ever say either who he was or whither he went.

The king and all his suite now returned to the palace, on their way towards which much was said both about the little old man and what the princess had undergone. On reaching home the king ordered a sumptuous banquet to be prepared, to which he invited all the most distinguished and exalted persons of his kingdom, and bestowed his daughter on the young prince; and their nuptials were celebrated with games and rejoicings for many days. And I, too, was at the feastings; and as I rode through the forest I was met by a wolf with two young ones; they were ravenous, and seemed to suffer much. I have since learned that they were no other than the wicked stepmother and her two daughters.

THE PRINCESS ON THE GLASS MOUNTAIN.

FROM SOUTH SMALAND.

THERE was once a king, who was so devoted to the chase that he knew of no greater pleasure than hunting the beasts of the forest. Early and late he would stay out in the field with hawk and hound, and always had good success. It nevertheless one day happened that he could start no game, though he sought on all sides from early morn. When evening was drawing on, and he was about to return home with his attendants, he suddenly perceived a dwarf, or "wild man," running before him in the forest. Putting spurs to his horse, the king instantly went in pursuit of him, and caught him. His extraordinary appearance caused no little surprise, for he was little and ugly as a Troll, and his hair resembled shaggy moss. To whatever the king said to him he would return no answer, good or bad. At this the king was angry, and the more so as he was already out of humour, in consequence of his bad luck at the chase. He therefore commanded his followers to keep a strict watch over the wild man, so that he might not escape, and then returned to his palace.

In those times it was an old-established custom for the king and his men to hold drinking meetings till a late hour in the night, at which much was said, and still more drunk. As they were sitting at one of these meetings, and making themselves merry, the king, taking up a large horn, said: "What think ye of our sport to-day? When could it before have been said of us, that we returned home without some game?" The men answered: "It is certainly true as you say, and yet, perhaps, there is not so good a sportsman as you to be found in the whole world. You must not, however, complain of our day's luck; for you have caught an animal, whose like was never before seen or heard of." This discourse pleased the king exceedingly, and he asked what they thought he had best to do with the dwarf. One of the courtiers answered: "You should keep him confined here in the palace, that it may be known far and near what a great hunter you are; provided that you can guard him so that he does not escape; for he is crafty and perverse withal." On hearing this, the king for some time sat silent; then raising the horn, said: "I will do as thou sayest, and it shall be through no fault of mine, if the wild man escapes. But this I vow, that if any one lets him loose, he shall die, even if it be my own son." Having said this, he emptied the horn, so that it was an inviolable oath. But the courtiers cast looks of doubt on each other; for they had never before heard the king so speak, and could plainly see that the mead had mounted to his head.

On the following morning, when the king awoke, he recollected the vow he had made at the drinking party; and accordingly sent for timber and other materials, and caused a small house or cage to be constructed close by the royal palace. The cage was formed of large beams, and secured by strong locks and bars, so that no one could break through. In the middle of the wall there was a little opening or window, for the purpose of conveying the food to the prisoner. When all was ready, the king had the wild man brought forth, placed him in the cage, and took the keys himself. There must the dwarf now sit day and night, both goers and comers stopping to gaze on him; but no one ever heard him complain, or even utter a single word.

Thus did a considerable time pass, when war broke out, and the king was obliged to take the field. When on the eve of departure, he said to his queen: "Thou shalt rule over my realm, and I will leave both land and people in thy care. But thou shalt promise me one thing, that thou wilt keep the wild man, so that he escape not while I am absent." The queen promised to do her best both in that and all things besides; and the king gave her the keys of the cage. He then pushed his barks from the shore, hoisted sail on the gilded yards, and went far, far away to distant countries; and to whatever place he came, he was there victorious. But the queen stood on the shore, looking after him as long as she could see his pendants waving over the ocean, and then, with her attendants, returned to the palace, there to sit sewing silk on her knee, awaiting her consort's return.

The king and queen had an only child, a prince, still of tender age, but who gave good promise of himself. After the king's departure, it one day happened that the boy, in his wanderings about the palace, came to the wild man's cage, and sat down close by it playing with his gold apple. While he was thus amusing himself, his apple chanced to pass through the window of the cage. The wild man instantly came forwards and threw it out. This the boy thought a pleasant pastime, and threw his apple in again, and the wild man cast it back, and thus they continued for some time. But at length pleasure was turned to sorrow, for the wild man kept the apple and would not throw it back. When neither threats nor prayers were of any avail, the little one burst into tears. Seeing this, the wild man said: "Thy father has acted wickedly towards me, in making me a prisoner, and thou shalt never get thy apple again, unless thou procurest my liberty." The boy answered: "How shall I procure thy liberty? Only give me my gold apple! my gold apple!" "Thou shalt do as I now tell thee," replied the wild man. "Go to the queen, thy mother, and desire her to comb thee. Be on the watch, and steal the keys from her girdle, then come and open the door. Thou canst afterwards restore the keys in the same manner, and no one will be the wiser." In short, the wild man succeeded in persuading the boy, who stole the keys from his mother, ran down to the cage, and let the wild man come out. At parting, the dwarf said: "Here is thy gold apple, as I promised, and thou hast my thanks for allowing me to escape. Another time, when thou art in trouble, I will help thee in return." He then ran off.

When it was known in the royal palace that the wild man had fled, there was a great commotion; the queen sent people on the roads and ways to trace him; but he was away and continued away. Thus some time passed, and the queen was more and more troubled, for she was in daily expectation of her consort's return. At last she descried his ships come dancing on the waves, and a multitude of people were assembled on the shore to bid him welcome. On landing, his first inquiry was, whether they had taken good care of the wild man; when the queen was obliged to confess what had taken place. At this intelligence the king was highly incensed, and declared he would punish the perpetrator, be he whoever he might. He then caused an investigation to be made throughout the palace and every man's child was called forth to bear witness; but no one knew anything. At last the little prince came forward. On appearing before his father he said: "I know that I have incurred my father's anger; nevertheless I cannot conceal the truth; for it was I who let the wild man escape." On hearing this the queen grew deadly pale, and every other with her; for the little prince was the favourite of all. At length the king spoke: "Never shall it be said of me that I broke my vow, even for my own flesh and blood; and thou shalt surely die as thou deservest." Thereupon he gave orders to his men to convey the young prince to the forest, and there slay him; but to bring his heart back, as a proof that his order had been fulfilled.

Now there was sorrow among the people such as the like had never before been experienced; every one interceded for the young prince, but the king's word was irrevocable. The young men had, therefore, no alternative; so taking the prince with them, they set out on their way. When they had penetrated very far into the forest, they met a man driving swine; whereupon one of the men said to his companion: "It seems to me not good to lay violent hands on a king's son: let us rather purchase a hog, and take its heart; for no one will know it not to be the prince's heart." This to the other seemed wisely said; so they bought a hog of the man, slaughtered it, and took out its heart. They then bade the prince go his way and never return.

The king's son did as they had directed him; he wandered on as far as he was able, and had no other sustenance than the nuts and wild berries, which grew in the forest. When he had thus travelled a long distance, he came to a mountain, on the summit of which stood a lofty fir. He then thought to himself: "I may as well climb up into this fir, and see whether there is any path." No sooner said than done. When he reached the top of the tree, and looked on all sides, he discerned a spacious palace lying at a great distance, and glittering in the sun. At this sight he was overjoyed, and instantly bent his steps thither. On his way he met with a boy following a plough, with whom he exchanged clothes. Thus equipped he at length reached the palace, entered it, and asked for employment; so was taken as a herd-boy, to watch the king's cattle. Now he ranged about the forest both late and early; and as time went on he forgot his sorrow, and grew, and became tall and vigorous, so that nowhere was to be found his like.

Our story now turns to the king, to whom the palace belonged. He had been married, and by his queen had an only daughter. She was much fairer than other damsels, and was both kind and courteous; so that he might be regarded as fortunate, who should one day possess her. When she had completed her fifteenth winter, she had an innumerable host of suitors, whose number, although she gave each a denial, was constantly increasing; so that the king at length knew not what answer to give them. He one day, therefore, went up to his daughter in her bower, and desired her to make a choice, but she would not. In his anger at her refusal he said: "As thou wilt not thyself make a choice, I will make one for thee, although it may happen not to be altogether to thy liking." He was then going away, but his daughter held him back, and said: "I am well convinced that it must be as you have resolved; nevertheless, you must not imagine that I will accept the first that is offered, as he alone shall possess me, who is able to ride to the top of the high glass mountain fully armed." This the king thought a good idea, and, yielding to his daughter's resolution, he sent a proclamation over the whole kingdom, that whosoever should ride fully armed to the top of the glass mountain, should have the princess to wife.

When the day appointed by the king had arrived, the princess was conducted to the glass mountain with great pomp and splendour. There she sat, the highest of all, on the summit of the mountain, with a golden crown on her head and a golden apple in her hand, and appeared so exquisitely beautiful, that there was no one present who would not joyfully have risked his life for her sake. Close at the mountain's foot were assembled all the suitors on noble horses and with splendid arms, which shone like fire in the sunshine; and from every quarter the people flocked in countless multitudes to witness the spectacle. When all was ready, a signal was given with horns and trumpets, and in the same instant the suitors galloped up the hill one after another. But the mountain was high, and slippery as ice, and was, moreover, exceedingly steep; so that there was no one, who, when he had ascended only a small portion, did not fall headlong to the bottom. It may, therefore, well be imagined there was no lack of broken legs and arms. Hence arose a noise of the neighing of horses, the outcry of people and the crash of armour that was to be heard at a considerable distance.

While all this was passing, the young prince was occupied in tending his cattle. On hearing the tumult and the rattling of arms, he sat on a stone, rested his head on his hand, and wept; for he thought of the beautiful princess, and it passed in his mind how gladly he would have been one of the riders. In the same moment he heard the sound of a footstep, and, on looking up, saw the wild man standing before him. "Thanks for the past," said he. "Why sittest thou here lonely and sad?" "I may well be sad," answered the prince. "For thy sake I am a fugitive from my native land, and have now not even a horse and arms, that I might ride to the glass mountain, and contend for the princess." "Oh," said the wild man, "if that's all, a remedy may easily be found. Thou hast helped me, I will now help thee in return." Thereupon taking the prince by the hand, he led him to his cave deep down in the earth, and showed a suit of armour hanging on the wall, forged of the hardest steel, and so bright that it shed a bluish light all around. Close by it stood a splendid steed, ready saddled and bridled, scraping the ground with his steel-shod hoofs, and champing his bit. The wild man then said to him: "Arm thyself quickly, and ride away, and try thy fortune. I will, in the mean time, tend thy cattle." The prince did not require a second bidding, but instantly armed himself with helm and harness, buckled spurs on his heels, and a sword by his side, and felt as light in his steel panoply as a bird in the air. Then vaulting into the saddle, he gave his horse the rein, and rode at full speed to the mountain.

The princess's suitors had just ceased from their arduous enterprise, in which none had won the prize, though each had well played his part, and were now standing and thinking that another time fortune might be more favourable, when on a sudden they see a young knight come riding forth from the verge of the forest directly towards the mountain. He was clad in steel from head to foot, with shield on arm and sword in belt, and bore himself so nobly in the saddle that it was a pleasure to behold him. All eyes were instantly directed towards the stranger knight, each asking another who he might be, for no one had seen him before. But they had no long time for asking; for scarcely had he emerged from the forest, when, raising himself in the stirrups, and setting spurs to his horse, he darted like an arrow straight up the glass mountain. Nevertheless, he did not reach the summit, but when about half way on the declivity, he suddenly turned his charger and rode down the hill, so that the sparks flew from his horse's hoofs. He then disappeared in the forest as a bird flies. Now, it is easy to imagine, there was a commotion among the assembled multitude, of whom there was not one that was not stricken with wonder at the stranger, who, I hardly need say it, was no other than the prince. At the same time all were unanimous that they had never seen a nobler steed or a more gallant rider. It was, moreover, whispered abroad that such was also the opinion of the princess herself, and that every night she dreamed of nothing but the venturous stranger.

The time had now arrived when the suitors of the princess should make a second trial. As on the first occasion, she was conducted to the glass mountain, the attempt to ascend which by the several competitors was attended with a result similar in every respect to what has been already related.

The prince in the meanwhile was watching his cattle, and silently bewailing his inability to join in the enterprise, when the wild man again appeared before him, who, after listening to his complaints, again conducted him to his subterranean abode, where there hung a suit of armour formed of the brightest silver, close by which stood a snow-white steed ready saddled and fully equipped, pawing the ground with his silver-shod hoofs and champing his bit. The prince, following the directions of the wild man, having put on the armour and mounted the horse, galloped away to the glass mountain.

As on the former occasion, the youth drew on him the gaze of every one present; he was instantly recognised as the knight who had already so distinguished himself; but he allowed them little time for observation, for setting spurs to his horse, he rode with an arrow's speed up the glassy mountain, when, having nearly reached the summit, he made an obeisance to the princess, turned his horse, rapidly rode down again, and again disappeared in the forest.

The same series of events took place a third time, excepting that on this occasion the prince received from the wild man a suit of golden armour, cased in which he, on the third day of trial, rode to the mountain's summit, bowed his knee before the princess, and from her hand received the golden apple. Then casting himself on his horse, he rode at full speed down the mountain, and again disappeared in the forest. Now arose an outcry on the mountain! The whole assemblage raised a shout of joy; horns and trumpets were sounded, weapons crashed, and the king caused it to be proclaimed aloud that the stranger knight, in the golden armour, had won the prize. What the princess herself thought on the occasion, we will leave unsaid; though we are told that she turned both pale and red, when she presented the young prince with the golden apple.

All that now remained was to discover the gold-clad knight, for no one knew him. For some time hopes were cherished that he would appear at court, but he came not. His absence excited the astonishment of all, the princess looked pale and was evidently pining away, the king became impatient, and the suitors murmured every day. When no alternative appeared, the king commanded a great assemblage to be held at his palace, at which every man's son, high or low, should be present, that the princess might choose among them. At this meeting there was not one who did not readily attend, both for the sake of the princess, and in obedience to the king's command, so that there was assembled an innumerable body of people. When all were gathered together, the princess issued from the royal palace in great state, and with her maidens passed among the whole throng; but although she sought in all directions, she found not what she sought. She was already surveying the outermost circle, when suddenly she caught sight of a man who was standing concealed amid the crowd. He wore a broad-brimmed hat, and was wrapped in a large gray cloak, like those worn by herdsmen, the hood of which was drawn up over his head, so that no one could discern his countenance. But the princess instantly ran towards him, pulled down his hood, clasped him in her arms and cried: "Here he is! here he is!" At this all the people laughed, for they saw that it was the king's herd-boy, and the king himself exclaimed: "Gracious heaven support me! What a son-in-law am I likely to have!" But the young man, with a perfectly unembarrassed air, said: "Let not that trouble you! You will get as good a king's son, as you yourself are a king." At the same moment he threw aside his cloak, and where were now the laughers, when, in place of the grey herdsman, they saw before them a comely young prince clad in gold from head to foot, and holding in his hand the princess's golden apple! All now recognized in him the youth who had ridden up the glass mountain.

Now, it is easy to imagine, there was joy, the like of which was never known. The prince clasped his beloved in his arms with the most ardent affection, and told her of his family and all he had undergone. The king allowed himself to rest, but instantly made preparations for the marriage, to which he invited all the suitors and all the people. A banquet was then given such as has never been heard of before or after. Thus did the prince gain the king's daughter and half the kingdom; and when the feastings had lasted about seven days, the prince took his fair young bride in great state to his father's kingdom, where he was received as may easily be conceived, both the king and the queen weeping for joy at seeing him again. They afterwards lived happily, each in his kingdom. But nothing more was heard of the wild man.

---

1. In "Runa, En skrift for Faderneslandets Fornvanner" utgifven af Richard Dybeck, Stockh. 1842, Haft i, p. 7, there is a similar tradition from Westmanland, which tells of a knight who captured an animal, the like of which had never been seen, it being overgrown with moss. It was kept in a tower, and released by the knight's young son, who was playing at ball close by. For this the boy was taken to the forest to be slain; but the servants, touched by his lamentations, killed a kid in his stead, the heart of which they showed for the boy's.

While wandering in the forest he meets with the animal he had liberated, and goes with him into the mountain, where he stays for some years. A proclamation is then sent through the country that the princess will accept for a husband him who shall be able to ride up a mountain, on which she will one day show herself. The knight's son now gets horse and clothing, and rides away to contend for the princess; but on reaching the middle of the mountain he is struck by a javelin cast from below. He, nevertheless, continues his course, and at length stands before the princess, who gives him a silk handkerchief to bind up his wound, and a day is fixed for the wedding.

When the day arrived, the wonderful animal, ugly as he is, desires to accompany the bridegroom, but contents himself with a place under the table. He there gives him a rusty sword, desiring him to touch him with it, when the old king's memory is drunk. The youth complies with his desire, when, to the astonishment of all, the old king, who, it was thought, had been carried off to the mount*, rises up. There was afterwards great rejoicing and tumult, and the king himself wishes the young couple joy.

2. According to an Upland version, a king one day lost his way in a forest, where he met with an old man who received him hospitably. The old man was immensely rich in gold and silver, which excited the king's avarice. The old man refuses to tell his name, and the king has him cast into a tower, telling him he should never be released unless he disclosed who he was.

Some time after, as the king's son was running about the court, he found a key, with which he opened the tower, and set the old man at liberty. At this the king was bitterly enraged, drove the prince from the country, and forbade him ever to return. On entering the forest, the boy met the old man, who desired him to follow him, which he did. They then took the old man's little gray horse, loaded it with gold and silver, and went to another kingdom. There the prince grew up, and became very tall and powerful; and his greatest pleasure was to ride on the gray horse over hill and dale.

It happened that the king who ruled the land had a daughter, who had a vast number of suitors. Her father, therefore, issued a proclamation, that whoever could ride up the glass mountain and take down a golden crown that was fixed on its summit, should possess the princess. When the prince received this intelligence, he went to the king's court and offered his services as a scullion; but when the suitors were to begin their competition, he ran home, got arms from his foster-father, together with the little gray horse, and rode at full speed up to the mountain's peak. Yet he did not take the golden crown, but rode down on the other side and away. On the second day he did the like; on the third day he took the crown, but rode away, so that no one knew who he was.

Some time after, as the princess was sitting in her maiden-bower, the door was opened, and in stepped the scullion. He had the golden crown in his hand, and told her that he had taken it; but that he was willing to give it back, that the prin-

*Berg-tagen (mount-taken) means carried off into a mountain by Trolls, concerning which see Thorpe, "Northern Mythology and Traditions," vol. ii. p. 67.

cess might exercise her own free will. This pleased the princess exceedingly, and she prayed her father to assemble all the men of his kingdom together at his court. The king did so.

When they were all assembled, the princess went forward to the scullion, gave him the golden crown, and chose him for her husband. At this there was a great wondering; but the prince, casting off his coarse grey cloak, stood there no longer a scullion, but a powerful king's son. He obtained the princess, and with her half the kingdom.

3. A variation from Gothland omits the introductory part about the wild man, and in its place tells of a poor peasant, whose youngest son was accustomed to sit in the chimney-corner, exposed to the insults of his brothers.

The king who ruled over the country had an only daughter, who had made a vow to marry no one who could not ride up a glass mountain. Whereupon the king issued a proclamation to that effect throughout his kingdom. When the day of trial came, the two elder sons of the peasant mounted their father's old jade and rode off to the glass mount; but the youngest boy might not accompany them, and therefore ran along the road weeping. Here he was met by a little old man, who asked him why he was so sorrowful. The boy told him the cause, when the old man replied: "Wait, I will help thee. Here is a pipe; take it, and place thyself under that tall pine yonder. When thou blowest in one end of the pipe, there shall come forth a charger with a suit of armour hanging on the pommel of his saddle; and when thou blowest in the other end, the whole shall disappear.' Hereupon the boy instantly ran to the tree, blew in the pipe, armed himself, and went his way. In passing his brothers, their old nag was so frightened that it ran with its two riders into a ditch, where we will for the present leave them.

The boy then rode on to the glass mountain, where he found an innumerable multitude of people, some with broken legs, others with broken arms, from their attempt to ascend the mountain. He did not, however, allow himself to be frightened, but galloped away, and reached the summit of the mountain, where the princess was sitting. She then threw to him her golden apple, which fastened itself to his knee, and he instantly rode back down the mountain, hastened home to the chimney-corner, and found great pleasure in hearing his two brothers relate about a strange prince who had frightened their horse into a ditch.

When the princess had long been waiting in vain for the successful rider, the king sent messengers over his whole kingdom, to ascertain whether any one had a golden apple on his knee. The messengers also came to the peasant's hut. When it was discovered that the youngest son had the apple, there was, it may easily be imagined, no small astonishment among them.

THE PRINCESS ON THE GLASS MOUNTAIN

The messengers desired the boy to accompany them to the king; but he would not, stole out of the hut, blew in his pipe, clad himself in complete armour, and rode alone to the royal palace, where he was instantly recognized, and obtained the princess. But the old peasant and his two elder sons have not recovered from their astonishment to this day.

4. In a version of the story from West Gothland, it is related how a poor peasant boy, as he was digging in a sand-pit, came to a hall, in which he found three horses and three suits of armour, one of silver, another of gold, and the third of precious stones.

The boy afterwards set out to wander about the world, and came at length to a royal palace, where he got employment as a scullion. The king, whose palace it was, had an only daughter, who had been carried away by a Troll, and could appear only on three successive Thursday evenings, on the summit of a high glass mountain; but if any one could ride up the mountain, and take the golden apple from her hand, she would be released. Hereupon the king, who was in great affliction, sent forth a proclamation, that whosoever would deliver the princess should have her to wife, together with half his kingdom.

When the first Thursday evening arrived, the boy ran to the sand-pit, clad himself in the silver armour, and rode half-way up the mountain. On the second Thursday evening he took the golden armour, and rode so high that his horse had one forefoot on the mountain's summit. On the third evening he took the armour of precious stones, rode up to the princess and got the golden apple. He then rode back to the sand-pit.

The king then issued an order that every male throughout the kingdom should appear at his court. The princess goes forth and recognizes her deliverer. The scullion casts off his rags, and stands in the armour of precious stones. The king gives him his daughter, and half the kingdom.

THE THREE DOGS.

THERE was once a miller who had three children, two girls and a boy. When the miller died, and the children divided the property, the daughters took the entire mill, and left their brother nothing but three sheep, that he tended in the forest. As he was one day wandering about, he met an old man, with whom he exchanged a sheep for a dog named *Snipp;* on the following day the same old man met him again, when he exchanged another sheep with him for a dog named *Snapp;* and on the third day his third sheep, for a dog named *Snorium.* The three dogs were large and strong, and obedient to their master in everything.

When the lad found there was no good to be done at home, he resolved to go out in the world and seek his fortune. After long wandering he came to a large city, in which the houses were hung with black, and everything betokened some great and universal calamity. The youth took up his quarters with an old fisherman, of whom he inquired the cause of this mourning. The fisherman informed him that there was a huge serpent named *Turenfax,* which inhabited an island out in the ocean; that every year a pure maiden must be given him to be devoured; and that the lot had now fallen on the king's only daughter. When the youth had heard this, he formed the resolution of venturing a contest with the serpent, and rescuing the princess, provided fortune would befriend him.

On the appointed day the youth sailed over to the island, and awaited whatever might happen. While he was sitting, he saw the young princess drawing near in a boat, accompanied by a number of people. The king's daughter stopped at the foot of the mountain and wept bitterly. The youth then approached her, greeted her courteously, and comforted her to the best of his power. When a short time had passed thus, he said: "Snipp! go to the mountain-cave, and see whether the serpent is coming." But the dog returned, wagged his tail, and said that the serpent had not yet made his appearance. When some time had elapsed, the youth said: "Snapp! go to the mountain-cave, and see whether the serpent is coming." The dog went, but soon returned without having seen the serpent. After a while the youth said: "Snorium! go to the mountain-cave, and see whether the serpent is coming." The dog went, but soon returned trembling violently. The youth could now easily guess that the serpent was approaching, and, consequently, made himself ready for the fight.

As Turenfax came hastening down the mountain, the youth set his dogs Snipp and Snapp on him. A desperate battle then ensued; but the serpent was so strong that the dogs were unable to master him. When the youth observed this, he set on his third dog, Snorium, and now the conflict became even fiercer; but the dogs got the mastery, and the game did not end until Turenfax received his death-wound.

When the serpent was dead the king's daughter thanked her deliverer with many affectionate expressions for her safety, and besought him to accompany her to the royal palace. But the youth would try his luck in the world for some time longer, and therefore declined her invitation. It was, however, agreed on between them that the youth should return in a year and woo the fair maiden. On parting the princess brake her gold chain in three, and bound a portion round the neck of each of the dogs. To the young man she gave her ring, and they promised ever to be faithful to each other.

The young man now travelled about in the wide world, as we have said, and the king's daughter returned home. On her way she was met by a courtier, who forced her to make oath that he and no other had slain Turenfax. This courtier was thenceforward looked upon as a most doughty champion, and got a promise of the princess. But the maiden would not break her faith to the youth, and deferred the marriage from day to day.

When the year was expired, the youth returned from his wandering, and came to the great city. But now the houses were hung with scarlet, and all things seemed to indicate a great and general rejoicing. The youth again took up his quarters with the old fisherman, and asked what might be the cause of all the joy. He was informed that a courtier had killed Turenfax, and was now about to celebrate his nuptials with the king's daughter. No one has heard what the miller's son said on receiving this intelligence; though it may easily be imagined that he was not generally delighted at it.

When dinner-time care, the youth felt a longing to partake of the king's fare, and his host was at a great loss how this could be brought to pass. But the youth said: "Snipp! go up to the palace, and bring me a piece of game from the king's table. Fondle the young princess; but strike the false courtier a blow that he may not soon forget." Snipp did as his master had commanded him; he went up to the palace, caressed the fair princess, but struck the courtier a blow that made him black and blue; then, seizing a piece of game, he ran off. Hereupon there arose a great uproar in the hall, and all were filled with wonder, excepting the king's daughter; for she had recognised her gold neck-chain, and thence divined who the dog's master was.

The next day a similar scene was enacted. The youth was inclined to eat some pastry from the king's own table, and the fisherman was at a loss how this could be brought about. But the youth said: "Snapp! go up to the palace, and bring me some pastry from the king's table. Fondle the young princess; but strike the false courtier a blow that he may not soon forget." Snapp did as his master had commanded him; he went up to the palace, broke through the sentinels, caressed the fair princess, but struck the false courtier a blow that made him see the sun both in the east and west; then, seizing a piece of pastry, he ran off. Now there was a greater uproar than on the preceding day, and every one wondered at what had taken place, excepting the king's daughter; for she again recognised her gold neck-chain, whereby she well knew who the dog's master was.

On the third day the youth wished to drink wine from the king's table and sent Snorium to fetch some. Everything now took place as before. The dog burst through the guard, entered the drinking apartment, caressed the princess, but struck the false courtier a blow that sent him tumbling head over heels on the floor; then, seizing a flask of wine, he ran off. The king was sorely vexed at all this, and sent the courtier with a number of people to seize the stranger who owned the three dogs. The courtier went, and came to where the young man dwelt with the poor fisherman. But there another game began; for the youth called to his three dogs: "Snipp! Snapp! Snorium! clear the house." In an instant the dogs rushed forward, and in a twinkling all the king's men lay on the ground.

The youth then caused the courtier to be bound hand and foot, and procceded to the apartment where the king was sitting at table with his men. When he entered, the princess ran to meet him with great affection, and began relating to her father how the courtier had deceived him. When the king heard all this, and recognised his daughter's gold chain and ring, he ordered the courtier to be cast to the three dogs; but the brave youth obtained the princess, and with her half the kingdom.

In another version from South Smaland, it is related that there was a peasant's son, who tended the cattle of the village in the forest, and who one day met a huntsman mounted on a tall horse, and accompanied by three very large dogs. The dogs were far more powerful than other dogs, and were named *Break-iron, Strikedown,* and *Hold-fast.* The boy becomes master of the three dogs; but it is a current story among the people, that the huntsman, who gave them to him, could be no other than Odin himself.

The youth then bids his employment farewell, and sets out in search of the king's daughter, who has been carried off. In his wanderings he meets with an aged crone, who directs him on the way. But the princess is confined in a large castle, that is well provided with locks and bars; and the lord of the castle has fixed his marriage with the fair damsel to be solemnized within a few days.

The youth is now at a loss how he can gain entrance into the castle. With this object he goes to the warders, and asks for employment to procure game for the feast. He is admitted, goes to the forest, and gets an abundance of game. Towards evening he returns, and in the night calls his dog, Break-iron, orders him to clear the way, and so, in spite of doors and bars, reaches the tower in which the princess is confined. The noise wakes the lord of the castle, who comes hurrying to the spot with weapons and attendans. But the youth calls his other two dogs, Strike-down and Hold-fast, and a bloody fight ensues, which ends in the youth's favour, who takes possession of the whole castle.

After the release of the princess the herd-boy sets out on his return to the old king, the damsel's father. On the way he has to engage in combat with a courtier, who would carry off the princess; but the youth is well seconded by his dogs, and comes off victor. The conclusion is the usual one, that the lad gets the king's daughter, and, after his father-in-law's death, becomes ruler over the whole realm.

THE WIDOW'S SON.

THERE was once a very poor woman who had only one son. She toiled for him till he was old enough to be confirmed by the priest, when she told him, that she could support him no longer, but that he must go out in the world and gain his own livelihood. So the youth set out, and, after wandering about for a day or two, he met a stranger. "Whither art thou going?" asked the man. "I am going out in the world to see if I can get an employment," answered the youth. "Wilt thou serve me?" "Yes, just as well serve you as anybody else," answered the youth. "Thou shalt be well cared for with me," said the man, "thou shalt only be my companion, and do little or nothing besides." So the youth resided with him, had plenty to eat and drink, and very little or nothing to do; but he never saw a living person in the man's house.

One day his master said to him: "I am going to travel, and shall be absent eight days, during that time thou wilt be here alone; but thou must not go into either of these four rooms; if thou dost I will kill thee when I return." The youth answered that he would not. When the man had been away three or four days, the youth could no longer refrain, but went into one of the rooms. He looked around, but saw nothing except a shelf over the door, with a whip made of briar on it. "This was well worth forbidding me so strictly from seeing," thought the youth. When the eight days had passed the man came home again. "Thou hast not, I hope, been into any of the rooms," said he. "No, I have not," answered the youth. "That I shall soon be able to see," said the man, going into the room the youth had entered. "But thou hast been in," said he, "and now thou shalt die." The youth cried and entreated to be forgiven, so that he escaped with his life, but had a severe beating; when that was over, they were as good friends as before.

Some time after this, the man took another journey; this time he would be away a fortnight, but first forbade the youth again from going into any of the rooms he had not already been in; but the one he had previously entered he might enter again. This time all took place just as before, the only difference being that the youth abstained for eight days before he entered the forbidden rooms. In one apartment he found only a shelf over the door, on which lay a huge stone and a water-bottle. "This is also something to be in such fear about," thought the youth again. When the man came home, he asked whether he had been in any of the rooms. "No, he had not," was the answer. "I shall soon see," said the man; and when he found that the youth had, nevertheless, been in, he said: "Now I will no longer spare thee, thou shalt die." But the youth cried and implored that his life might be spared, and thus again escaped with a beating; but this time he got as much as could be laid on him. When he had recovered from the effect of this beating he lived as well as ever, and he and the man were good friends as before.

Some time after this, the man again made a journey,

and now he was to be three weeks absent; he warned the youth anew not to enter the third room; if he did he must at once prepare to die. At the end of a fortnight, the youth had no longer any command over himself, and stole in; but here he saw nothing save a trap-door in the floor. He lifted it up and looked through; there stood a large copper kettle that boiled and bubbled, yet he could see no fire under it. "I should like to know if it is hot," thought the youth, dipping his finger down into it; but when he drew it up again, he found that all his finger was gilt. He scraped it and washed it, but the gilding was not to be removed; so he tied a rag over it, and when the man returned and asked him what was the matter with his finger, he answered, he had cut it badly. But the man, tearing the rag off, at once saw what ailed his finger. At first he was going to kill the youth, but as he cried and begged again, he merely beat him so that he was obliged to lie in bed for three days. The man then took a pot down from the wall and rubbed him with what it contained, so that the youth was as well as before.

After some time the man made another journey, and said he should not return for a month. He then told the youth that if he went into the fourth room, he must not think for a moment that his life would be spared. One, two, even three weeks the youth refrained from entering the forbidden room; but then having no longer any command over himself he stole in. There stood a large black horse in a stall, with a trough of burning embers at its head and a basket of hay at its tail. The youth thought this was cruel, and, therefore, changed their position, putting the basket of hay by the horse's head. The horse thereupon said: "As you have so kind a disposition that you enable me to get food, I will save you: should the Troll return and find you here, he will kill you. Now you must go up into the chamber above this, and take one of the suits of armour that hang there: but on no account take one that is bright; on the contrary, select the most rusty you can see, and take that; choose also a sword and saddle in like manner." The youth did so, but he found the whole very heavy for him to carry. When he came back the horse said, that now he should strip and wash himself well in the kettle, which stood boiling in the next apartment. "I feel afraid," thought the youth, but, nevertheless, did so. When he had washed himself, he became comely and plump, and as red and white as milk and blood, and much stronger than before. "Are you sensible of any change?" asked the horse. "Yes," answered the youth. "Try to lift me," said the horse. Aye that he could, and brandished the sword with ease. "Now lay the saddle on me," said the horse, "put on the armour, and take the whip of thorn, the stone, and the water-flask, and the pot with ointment, and then we will set out."

When the youth had mounted the horse, it started off at a rapid rate. After riding some time the horse said: "I think I hear a noise; look round, can you see anything?" "A great many are coming after us, certainly a score at least," answered the youth. "Ah! that is the Troll," said the horse, "he is coming with all his companions."

They travelled for a time until their pursuers were gaining on them. "Throw now the thorn whip over your shoulder," said the horse, "but throw it far away from me." The youth did so, and at the same moment there sprang up a large thick wood of briars. The youth now rode on a long way, while the Troll was obliged to go home for something wherewith to hew a road through the wood. After some time the horse again said: "Look back, can you see anything now?" "Yes, a whole multitude of people," said the youth, "like a church-congregation." "That is the Troll, he has got more with him; throw out the large stone, but throw it far from me."

When the youth had done what the horse desired, there arose a large stone mountain behind them. So the Troll was obliged to go home after something with which to bore through the mountain; and while he was thus employed, the youth rode on a considerable way. But now the horse again bade him look back; he then saw a multitude like a whole army, they were so bright that they glittered in the sun. "Well, that is the Troll with all his friends," said the horse. "Now throw the water-bottle behind you, but take good care to spill nothing on me!" The youth did so, but notwithstanding his caution he happened to spill a drop on the horse's loins. Immediately there rose a vast lake, and the spilling of the few drops caused the horse to stand far out in the water; nevertheless, he at last swam to the shore. When the Trolls came to the water they lay down to drink it all up, and they gulped and gulped it down till they burst. "Now we are quit of them," said the horse.

When they had travelled on a very long way they came to a green plain in a wood. "Take off your armour now," said the horse, "and put on your rags only, lift my saddle off and let me go loose, and hang everything up in that large hollow linden; make yourself then a wig of pine-moss, go to the royal palace which lies close by, and there ask for employment. When you desire to see me, come to this spot, shake the bridle, and I will instantly be with you."

The youth did as the horse told him; and when he put on the moss wig, he became so pale and miserable to look at, that no one would have recognised him. On reaching the palace, he only asked if he might serve in the kitchen to carry wood and water to the cook; but the cook-maid asked him, why he 'wore such an ugly wig? "Take it off," said she, "I will not have anybody here so frightful." "That I cannot," answered the youth; "for I am not very clean in the head." "Dost thou think then that I will have thee in the kitchen, if such be the case?" said she; "go to the master of the horse, thou are fittest to carry muck from the stables." When the master of the horse told him to take off his wig, he got the same answer, so he refused to have him. "Thou canst go to the gardener," said he, "thou art only fit to go and dig the ground." The gardener allowed him to remain, but none of the servants would sleep with him, so he was obliged to sleep alone under the stairs of the summer-house, which stood upon pillars and had a high staircase, under which he laid a quantity of moss for a bed, and there lay as well as he could.

When he had been some time in the royal palace, it happened one morning, just at sunrise, that the youth had taken off his moss wig and was standing washing himself, and appeared so handsome it was a pleasure to look on him. The princess saw from her window this comely gardener, and thought she had never before seen any one so handsome. She then asked the gardener why he lay out there under the stairs. "Because none of the other servants will lie with him," answered the gardener. "Let him come this evening and lie by the door in my room," said the princess; "they cannot refuse after that to let him sleep in the house."

The gardener told this to the youth. "Dost thou think I will do so?" said he. "If I do, all will say there is something between me and the princess." "Thou hast reason, forsooth, to fear such a suspicion," replied the gardener, "such a fine comely lad as thou art." "Well, if she has commanded it, I suppose I must comply," said the youth. In going up-stairs that evening he stamped and made such a noise that they were obliged to beg of him to go more gently lest it might come to the king's knowledge. When within the chamber, he lay down and began immediately to snore. The princess then said to her waiting-maid: "Go gently and pull off his moss wig." Creeping softly towards him, she was about to snatch it, but he held it fast with both hands, and said she should not have it. He then lay down again and began to snore. The princess again made a sign to the maid, and this time she snatched his wig off. There he lay so beautifully red and white, just as the princess had seen him in the morning sun. After this the youth slept every night in the princess's chamber.

But it was not long before the king heard that the garden-lad slept every night in the princess's chamber, at which he became so angry that he almost resolved on putting him to death. This, however, he did not do, but cast him into prison, and his daughter he confined to her room, not allowing her to go out, either by day or night. Her tears and prayers for herself and the youth were unheeded by the king, who only became the more incensed against her.

Some time after this, there arose a war and disturbances in the country, and the king was obliged to take arms and defend himself against another king, who threatened to deprive him of his throne. When the youth heard this he begged the gaoler would go to the king for him, and propose to let him have armour and a sword, and allow him to follow to the war. All the courtiers laughed, when the gaoler made known his errand to the king. They begged he might have some old trumpery for armour, that they might enjoy the sport of seeing the poor creature in the war. He got the armour and also an old jade of a horse, which limped on three legs, dragging the fourth after it.

Thus they all marched forth against the enemy, but they had not gone far from the royal palace before the youth stuck fast with his old jade in a swamp. Here he sat beating and calling to the jade, "Hie! wilt thou go? hie! wilt thou go?" This amused all the others, who laughed and jeered as they passed. But no sooner were they all gone, than, running to the linden, he put on his own armour, and shook the bridle, and immediately the horse appeared, and said: "Do thou do thy best and I will do mine."

When the youth arrived on the field, the battle had already begun, and the king was hardly pressed; but just at that moment the youth put the enemy to flight. The king and his attendants wondered who it could be that came to their help; but no one had been near enough to him to speak to him, and when the battle was over he was away. When they returned, the youth was still sitting fast in the swamp, beating and calling to his three-legged jade. They laughed as they passed, and said: "Only look, yonder sits the fool yet."

The next day when they marched out, the youth was still sitting there, and they again laughed and jeered at him; but no sooner had they all passed by than he ran again to the linden, and everything took place as on the previous day. Every one wondered who the stranger warrior was who had fought for them; but no one approached him so near that he could speak to him; of course no one ever imagined that it was the youth.

When they returned in the evening and saw him and his old jade still sticking fast in the swamp, they again made a jest of him; one shot an arrow at him and wounded him in the leg, and he began to cry and moan so that it was sad to hear, whereupon the king threw him his handkerchief that he might bind it about his leg. When they marched forth the third morning there sat the youth calling to his horse, "Hie! wilt thou go? hie!

wilt thou go?" "No, no! he will stay there till he starves," said the king's men as they passed by, and laughed so heartily at him that they nearly fell from their horses. When they had all passed, he again ran to the linden, and came to the battle just at the right moment. That day he killed the enemy's king, and thus the war was at an end.

When the fighting was over, the king observed his handkerchief tied round the leg of the strange warrior, and by this he easily knew him. They received him with great joy, and carried him with them up to the royal palace, and the princess, who saw them from her window, was so delighted no one could tell. "There comes my beloved also," said she. He then took the pot of ointment and rubbed his leg, and afterwards all the wounded, so that they were all well again in a moment.

After this the king gave him the princess to wife. On the day of his marriage he went down into the stable to see the horse, and found him dull, hanging his ears and refusing to eat. When the young king—for he was now king, having obtained the half of the realm—spoke to him and asked him what he wanted, the horse said: "I have now helped thee forward in the world, and I will live no longer; thou must take thy sword, and cut my head off." "No, that I will not do," said the young king, "thou shalt have whatever thou wilt, and always live without working." "If thou wilt not do as I say," answered the horse, "I shall find a way of killing thee." The king was then obliged to slay him; but when he raised the sword to give the stroke he was so distressed that he turned his face away; but no sooner had he struck his head off than there stood before him a handsome prince in the place of the horse.

"Whence in the name of Heaven didst thou come?" asked the king. "It was I who was the horse," answered the prince. "Formerly I was king of the country whose sovereign you slew yesterday; it was he who cast over me a horse's semblance, and sold me to the Troll. As he is killed, I shall recover my kingdom, and you and I shall be neighbouring kings; but we will never go to war with each other."

Neither did they; they were friends as long as they lived, and the one came often to visit the other.

THE THREE AUNTS.

THERE was once a poor man who lived in a hut far away in the forest, and supported himself on the game. He had an only daughter, who was very beautiful, and as her mother was dead and she was grown up, she said she would go out in the world and seek her own living. "It is true, my child," said her father, "that thou hast learnt nothing with me but to pluck and roast birds; but it is, nevertheless, well that thou shouldst earn thy bread." The young girl therefore went in search of work, and when she had gone some way, she came to the royal palace. There she remained, and the queen took such a liking to her that the other servants became quite jealous; they, therefore, contrived to tell the queen that the girl had boasted she could spin a pound of flax in twenty-four hours, knowing that the queen was very fond of all kinds of handiwork. "Well, if thou hast said it, thou shalt do it," said the queen to her. "But I will give thee a little longer time to do it in." The poor girl was afraid of saying she never had spun, but only begged she might have a room to herself. This was allowed, and the flax and spinning-wheel were carried up to it. Here she sat and cried, and was so unhappy she knew not what to do; she placed herself by the wheel and twisted and twirled at it without knowing how to use it; she had never even seen a spinning-wheel before.

But as she so sat, there came an old woman into the room. "What's the matter, my child?" said she. "Oh," answered the young girl, "it is of no use that I tell you, for I am sure you cannot help me!" "That thou dost not know," said the crone. "It might happen, however, that I could help thee." "I may as well tell her," thought the girl; and so she related to her, how her fellow-servants had reported that she had said she could spin a pound of flax in twenty-four hours. "And poor I," added she, "have never before in all my life seen a spinning-wheel; so far am I from being able to spin so much in one day." "Well, never mind," said the woman, "if thou wilt call me Aunt on thy wedding day, I will spin for thee, and thou canst lie down to sleep." That the young girl was quite willing to do, and went to bed.

In the morning when she awoke, all the flax was spun and lying on the table, and was so fine and delicate that no one had ever seen such even and beautiful thread.

The queen was delighted with the beautiful thread she had now got, and on that account felt more attached to the young girl than before. But the other servants were still more jealous of her, and told the queen she had boasted that in twenty-four hours she could weave all the thread she had spun. The queen again answered: "If she had said that, she should do it; but if it were not done within the exact time, she would allow her a little longer." The poor girl durst not say no, but begged she might have a room to herself, and then she would do her best. Now she again sat crying and lamenting, and knew not what to do, when another old woman came in, and asked: "What ails thee, my child?" The girl would not at first say, but at length told her what made her so sorrowful. "Well," answered the crone, "provided thou wilt call me Aunt upon thy wedding day I will weave for thee, and thou canst go to sleep." The young girl willingly agreed to do so, and went to bed.

When she awoke the piece of linen lay on the table woven, as fine and beautiful as it could be. The girl took it down to the queen, who was so delighted with the beautiful web which she had got, that she was fonder than ever of the young girl. At this the others were so exasperated that they thought of nothing but how they could injure her.

At length they told the queen, that she had boasted she could make the piece of linen into shirts in twenty-four hours. The girl was afraid to say she could not sew; and all took place as before: she was again put into a room alone, where she sat crying and unhappy. Now came another old woman to her, who promised to sew for her if she would call her Aunt upon her wedding day. This the young girl consented to do; she then did as the woman had desired her, and lay down to sleep. In the morning when she woke, she found that the linen was all made into shirts lying on the table, so beautiful that no one had ever seen the like; and they were all marked and completely finished. When the queen saw them she was so delighted with the work, that she clasped her hands together: "Such beautiful work," she said, "I have never owned nor seen before." And from that time she was as fond of the young girl as if she had been her own child. "If thou wouldst like to marry the prince, thou shalt have him," said she to the maiden, "for thou wilt never need to put out anything to be made, as thou canst both spin and weave and sew everything for thyself." As the young girl was very handsome, and the prince loved her, the wedding took place directly. Just as the prince was seated at the bridal table with her, an old woman entered who had an enormously long nose; it was certainly three ells long.

The bride rose from the table, curtsied, and said to her: "Good day, Aunt." "Is that my bride's aunt?" asked the prince. "Yes, she is." "Then she must sit down at the table with us," said he; though both the prince and the rest of the company thought it very disagreeable to sit at table with such a person.

At the same moment another very ugly old woman came in; she was so thick and broad behind that she could hardly squeeze herself through the door. Immediately the bride rose, and saluted her with a "Good day, Aunt;" and the prince asked again if she were his bride's aunt. They both answered "Yes:" the prince then said, if that were the case she must also take a place at the table with them.

She had hardly seated herself before there came in a third ugly old crone, whose eyes were as large as plates, and so red and running that it was shocking to look at. The bride rose again and said: "Good day, Aunt;" and the prince asked her also to sit down at table; but he was not well pleased, and thought within himself: "The Lord preserve me from my bride's aunts." After a short time he could not help asking: "How it came to pass that his bride, who was so beautiful, should have such ugly and deformed aunts." "That I will tell you," replied one of them. "I was as comely as your bride when at her age, but the reason of my having so long a nose is that I constantly and always sat jogging and nodding over the spinning-wheel, till my nose is become the length you see it." "And I," said the second, "ever since I was quite little, have sat upon the weaver's bench rocking to and fro; therefore am I become so broad and swelled as you see me." The third one said: "Ever since I was very young, I have sat poring over my work both night and day, therefore have my eyes become so red and ugly, and now there is no cure for them." "Ah! is that the case?" said the prince, "it is well that I know it; for if people become so ugly thereby, then my bride shall never spin, nor weave, nor work any more all her life."

SUCH WOMEN ARE; OR, THE MAN FROM RINGERIGE AND THE THREE WOMEN.

THERE was once a man and his wife who wanted to sow, but had no seed-corn, nor money to buy it. They had one cow, and this they agreed that the man should drive to the town and sell, to enable them to buy seed with the money. But when it came to the point, the woman was afraid to let her husband go with the cow, fearing he would spend the money in the town in drinking. "Hear now! father," said she, "I think it will be best for me to go, and then I can sell my old hen at the same time." "As thou wilt," answered the husband, "but act with discretion, and remember thou must have ten dollars for the cow." "Oh! that I shall," said the wife, and off she went with the cow and the hen.

Not far from the town she met a butcher. "Art thou going to sell thy cow, mother?" asked he. "Yes, that's what I am going to do," answered she. "How much dost thou want for it?" "I want a mark for my cow, and my hen you shall have for ten dollars."[1] "Well! that's cheap," said the butcher; "but I am not in want of the hen, and that thou canst always get rid of when thou comest to the town; but for the cow I am willing to give thee a mark." So they settled the bargain, and the woman got her mark; but when she came into the town, there was not a person who would give her ten dollars for an old lean hen. She therefore went back to the

---

[1] The rix dollar is equal to six marks, $1.44.

butcher, and said: "Hear, my good man, I cannot get rid of my hen, so thou must take that also, as thou hast got the cow, and then I can go home with the money."

"Well! well! I dare say we shall strike a bargain for that also," said he. Hereupon he invited her in, gave her something to eat, and as much brandy as she could drink. "This is a delightful butcher," thought she, and kept on drinking so long that at last she completely lost her senses.

What now did the butcher do? While the woman was sleeping herself sober, he dipped her into a tar barrel, then rolled her in a heap of feathers, and laid her down in a soft place, outside the house. When she awoke and found herself feathered from head to foot, she began to wonder, and said to herself: "What can be the matter with me? Is it I, or is it somebody else? No, this can never be me, this must be some strange, large bird. But what shall I do to know if it is really myself or not? Yes, now I know how I can find out whether it is myself. If the calves lick me and the dog does not bark at me, when I go home, then it is really myself."

The dog had hardly caught a glimpse of the strange animal that was entering the yard, before he set up a terrible barking; and the woman felt far from easy. "I begin to think it is not myself," said she; and when she went into the cattle-house, the calves would not lick her, as they smelt the strong tar. "No, I see now it cannot be me, it must be some wonderful strange bird, I may as well fly away." So creeping up on the top of the store-room she began to flap with her arms as if they were wings, and tried to rise in the air. When the man saw this he seized his rifle, went out into the yard and was just taking aim. "Oh! no," exclaimed the woman, "don't shoot me, father, it is I, indeed it is." "Is it thou?" said her husband; "then don't stand up there like a fool, but come down and give an account of the money." The woman crept down again, but no money could she give him, as she had got none. She looked for the mark the butcher had given her for her cow, but even this she had lost while she was drunk. When the husband heard the whole story, he was so angry that he swore he would leave her and everything, and never return, unless he could find three other women who were as great fools as herself.

He set out accordingly, and had not gone far on the road, before he saw a woman running in and out of a newly-built cottage with an empty sieve in her hand. Every time she ran in, she threw her apron over the sieve as if there were something in it. "What is it you are so busy about, mother?" said the man. "Oh! I am only carrying a little sunshine into my new house; but I know not how it is; when I am out of doors I have plenty of sun in my sieve, but when I come in it is all away. When I was in my old hut, I had sun enough; although I never carried any in. If I only knew of any one who would bring sunshine into my house, I would willingly give him a hundred dollars." "I think there must be a way for that," answered the man. "If you have got an axe, I will soon procure you sun enough." He got the axe and made a couple of windows in the house, which the carpenter had forgotten to do. Immediately the sun came in, and he got a hundred dollars. "There was *one,*" said the man as he again walked on.

Some time after, he came to a house and heard from the outside a terrible bellowing and noise within. He entered and saw a woman beating her husband about the head with a washerwoman's batlet. He had got a new shirt over his head, but could not get it on, because there was no slit made for the neck. "What's the matter here," cried the stranger at the door: "are you killing your husband, mother?" "No, Lord preserve us," said the woman, "I am only helping him to put on his new shirt." The man struggled and cried: "The Lord preserve and take pity upon all who put on a new shirt. If any one will only teach my wife to cut a slit in the proper place, I will give him a hundred dollars." "I think there must be a way for that; come bring a pair of scissors," said the stranger. The woman gave him the scissors, and he immediately cut a hole in the shirt, and got a hundred dollars. "There is the *second,*" said the man as he went on his way.

After walking on for some time he at length came to a farm-house where he thought of stopping to rest. When he entered the room the woman of the house asked him "Where he was from?" "I come from Ringerige," answered the man. "Oh, indeed! what, do you say you come from Himmerige (Heaven), then of course you know the second Peter, my poor late husband?" The woman, who was very deaf, had had three husbands, all named Peter. The first husband had used her ill, and therefore she thought that only the second, who had been kind to her, could be in heaven. "Know him, aye, and well too," answered the man from Ringerige. "How does he fare above?" asked the woman further. "Ah! but poorly," said the man. He goes wandering from one farm to another to get a little food, and has scarcely clothes to his back; and as to money, that is quite out of the question." "Oh God, be merciful to him!" exclaimed the poor woman, "I am sure he need not go so miserable, for there was plenty left after him. I have got a whole room full of his clothes, also a box of money, which I have taken care of, that belonged to my late husband. If you will take charge of all this for him, you shall have a cart and a horse to draw it. The horse he can keep up there, and the cart also; he then can sit in it and drive from one farm to another, for he was never so poor that he was obliged to walk." So the man from Ringerige got a whole cart-load of clothes, and a little box of bright silver-money, with as much provision as he liked to take. When he had filled the cart, he got up in it and drove away.

"That was the *third*," said he. But in the fields was the woman's third husband ploughing, who, when he saw a person he knew nothing of, coming from the yard with horse and cart, hurried home, and asked his wife who it was that was driving away with the dun horse. "Oh, that was a man from Himmerige (Heaven)," said she; "he told me that things went so badly with my second Peter, my poor husband; that he goes begging from one farm to another, and that he had neither food nor clothing; so I sent him a load of old things that were left after him."

But the box of silver-money she said nothing about. The man seeing how matters stood, saddled a horse, and set off at full gallop. It was not long before he was close behind the man in the cart, who, on observing him, turned off with the horse into a little wood, pulled out a handful of the horse's tail, ran up a small hill with it, and tied it to a birch tree; then laid himself down under the tree, and kept staring up at the clouds. "Well!" cried he, as the man on horseback approached him, "never have I seen such a thing before in my life——" Peter the third stood a while staring at him and wondering what he was about. At length he asked: "What art thou lying there for, gazing and gaping?" "No, never have I seen anything like it," said the other. "There is a man just gone up to heaven on a dun horse; here is some of the tail hanging in the birch, which he left behind, and there up in the clouds you can see the dun horse." Peter the third looked first at the man, then up at the clouds, and said: "I see nothing but some hair of a horse's tail hanging in the birch-tree." "No, you cannot see it where you stand," said the other, "but come and lie down here where I am, and look straight up, and you must continue gazing for some time, without turning your eyes from the clouds." While Peter lay quite still staring up at the clouds, the man from Ringerige sprang upon his horse and galloped off as fast as he could, both with that and the cart. When it began to rattle along the road, Peter jumped up, but he was at first so bewildered by this adventure, that he did not think of pursuing the man who had run off with his horse, until it was too late to overtake him. Peter then returned home to his wife quite chap-fallen. When she asked him what he had done with the other horse, he said: "I gave it to the man that he might take it to Peter the second; for I thought it was not becoming for him to sit in a cart and drive about from one farm to another up in heaven. Now he can sell the cart, buy a carriage, and drive a pair of horses." "How I thank you for that, Peter; never did I think you were so reasonable a man," said his wife.

When the man from Ringerige returned home with his two hundred dollars, a cart full of clothes, and a box of money, he saw that his land had been ploughed and sown. The first question he put to his wife was, where she had got the seed from to sow the fields with. "Oh!" exclaimed she, "I have always heard say, 'that what you sow, you shall reap,' so I took the salt we had left from the winter, and sowed that; and if we only get rain soon, I don't doubt but it will come up, and yield many a bushel." "A fool thou art, and a fool thou wilt be as long as thou livest," said her husband; "but there is no help, and others are no wiser than thou."

TOLLER'S NEIGHBOURS.

ONCE upon a time a young man and a young girl were in service together at a mansion down near Klode Mill, in the district of Lysgaard. They became attached to each other, and as they both were honest and faithful servants, their master and mistress had a great regard for them, and gave them a wedding dinner the day they were married. Their master gave them also a little cottage with a little field, and there they went to live.

This cottage lay in the middle of a wild heath, and the surrounding country was in bad repute; for in the neighbourhood were a number of old grave-mounds, which it was said were inhabited by the Mount-folk; though Toller, so the peasant was called, cared little for that. "When one only trusts in God," thought Toller, "and does what is just and right to all men, one need not be afraid of anything." They had now taken possession of their cottage and moved in all their little property. When the man and his wife, late one evening, were sitting talking together as to how they could best manage to get on in the world, they heard a knock at the door, and on Toller opening it, in walked a little little man, and wished them "Good evening." He had a red cap on his head, a long beard and long hair, a large hump on his back, and a leathern apron before him, in which was stuck a hammer. They immediately knew him to be a Troll; notwithstanding he looked so good-natured and friendly, that they were not at all afraid of him.

"Now hear, Toller," said the little stranger, "I see well enough that you know who I am, and matters stand thus: I am a poor little hill-man, to whom people have left no other habitation on earth than the graves of fallen warriors, or mounds, where the rays of the sun never can shine down upon us. We have heard that you are come to live here, and our king is fearful that you will do us harm, and even destroy us. He has, therefore, sent me up to you this evening, that I should beg of you, as amicably as I could, to allow us to hold our dwellings in peace. You shall never be annoyed by us, or disturbed by us in your pursuits."

"Be quite at your ease, good man," said Toller, "I have never injured any of God's creatures willingly, and the world is large enough for us all, I believe; and I think we can manage to agree, without the one having any need to do mischief to the other."

"Well, thank God!" exclaimed the little man, beginning in his joy to dance about the room, "that is excellent, and we will in return do you all the good in our power, and that you will soon discover; but now I must depart."

"Will you not first take a spoonful of supper with us?" asked the wife, setting a dish of porridge down on the stool near the window; for the Man of the Mount was so little that he could not reach up to the table. "No, I thank you," said the mannikin, "our king is impatient for my return, and it would be a pity to let him wait for the good news I have to tell him." Hereupon the little man bade them farewell and went his way.

From that day forwards, Toller lived in peace and concord with the little people of the Mount. They could see them go in and out of their mounds in daylight, and no one ever did anything to vex them. At length they became so familiar, that they went in and out of Toller's house, just as if it had been their own. Sometimes it happened that they would borrow a pot or a copper-kettle from the kitchen, but always brought it back again, and set it carefully on the same spot from which they had taken it. They also did all the service they could in return. When the spring came, they would come out of their mounds in the night, gather all the stones off the arable land, and lay them in a heap along the furrows. At harvest time they would pick up all the ears of corn, that nothing might be lost to Toller. All this was observed by the farmer, who, when in bed, or when he read his evening prayer, often thanked the Almighty for having given him the Mount-folk for neighbours. At Easter and Whitsuntide, or in the Christmas holidays, he always set a dish of nice milk-porridge for them, as good as it could be made, out on the mound.

Once, after having given birth to a daughter, his wife was so ill that Toller thought she was near her end. He consulted all the cunning people in the district, but no one knew what to prescribe for her recovery. He sat up every night and watched over the sufferer, that he might be at hand to administer to her wants. Once he fell asleep, and on opening his eyes again towards morning, he saw the room full of the Mount-folk: one sat and rocked the baby, another was busy in cleaning the room, a third stood by the pillow of the sick woman and made a drink of some herbs, which he gave his wife. As soon as they observed that Toller was awake they all ran out of the room; but from that night the poor woman began to mend, and before a fortnight was past she was able to leave her bed and go about her household work, well and cheerful as before.

Another time, Toller was in trouble for want of money to get his horses shod before he went to the town. He talked the matter over with his wife, and they knew not well what course to adopt. But when they were in bed his wife said: "Art thou asleep, Toller?" "No," he answered, "what is it?" "I think," said she, "there is something the matter with the horses in the stable, they are making such a disturbance." Toller rose, lighted his lantern, and went to the stable, and, on opening the door, found it full of the little Mount-folk. They had made the horses lie down, because the mannikins could not reach up to them. Some were employed in taking off the old shoes, some were filing the heads of the nails, while others were tacking on the new shoes; and the next morning, when Toller took his horses to water, he found them shod so beautifully that the best of smiths could not have shod them better. In this manner the Mount-folk and Toller rendered all the good services they could to each other, and many years passed pleasantly. Toller began to grow an old man, his daughter was grown up, and his circumstances were better every year. Instead of the little cottage in which he began the world, he now owned a large and handsome house, and the naked wild heath was converted into fruitful arable land.

One evening, just before bed-time, some one knocked at the door, and the Man of the Mount walked in. Toller and his wife looked at him with surprise; for the mannikin was not in his usual dress. He wore on his head a shaggy cap, a woollen kerchief round his throat, and a great sheep-skin cloak covered his body. In his hand he had a stick, and his countenance was very sorrowful. He brought a greeting to Toller from the king, who requested that he, his wife, and little Inger would come over to them in the Mount that evening, for the king had a matter of importance, about which he wished to talk with him. The tears ran down the little man's cheeks while he said this, and when Toller tried to comfort him, and inquired into the source of his trouble, the Man of the Mount only wept the more, but would not impart the cause of his grief.

Toller, his wife and daughter, then went over to the Mount. On descending into the cave, they found it decorated with bunches of sweet willow, crowfoots, and other flowers, that were to be found on the heath. A large table was spread from one end of the cave to the other. When the peasant and his family entered, they were placed at the head of the table by the side of the king. The little folk also took their places, and began to eat, but they were far from being as cheerful as usual; they sat and sighed and hung down their heads; and it was easy to see that something had gone amiss with them. When the repast was finished, the king said to Toller:

"I invited you to come over to us because we all wished to thank you for having been so kind and friendly to us, during the whole time we have been neighbours. But now there are so many churches built in the land, and all of them have such great bells, which ring so loud morning and evening, that we can bear it no longer; we are, therefore, going to leave Jutland and pass over to Norway, as the greater number of our people have done long ago. We now wish you farewell, Toller, as we must part."

When the king had said this, all the Mount-folk came and took Toller by the hand, and bade him farewell, and the same to his wife. When they came to Inger, they said: "To you, dear Inger, we will give a remembrance of us, that you may think of the little Mount-people when they are far away." And as they said this, each took up a stone from the ground and threw it into Inger's apron. They left the Mount one by one, with the king leading the way.

Toller and his family remained standing on the Mount as long as they could discern them. They saw the little Trolls wandering over the heath, each with a wallet on his back and a stick in his hand. When they had gone a good part of the way, to where the road leads down to the sea, they all turned round once more, and waved their hands, to say farewell. Then they disappeared, and Toller saw them no more. Sorrowfully he returned to his home.

The next morning Inger saw that all the small stones the Mount-folk had thrown into her apron shone and sparkled, and were real precious stones. Some were blue, others brown, white, and black, and it was the Trolls who had imparted the colour of their eyes to the stones, that Inger might remember them when they were gone; and all the precious stones which we now see, shine and sparkle only because the Mount-folk have given them the colour of their eyes, and it was some of these beautiful precious stones which they once gave to Inger.

THE MAGICIAN'S PUPIL.

THERE was once a peasant who had a son, whom, when of a proper age, his father apprenticed to a trade; but the boy, who had no inclination for work, always ran home again to his parents; at this the father was much troubled, not knowing what course to pursue. One day he entered a church, where, after repeating the Lord's Prayer, he said: "To what trade shall I apprentice my son? He runs away from every place."

The clerk, who happened at that moment to be standing behind the altar, hearing the peasant utter these words, called out in answer: "Teach him witchcraft; teach him witchcraft!"

The peasant, who did not see the clerk, thought it was our Lord who gave him this advice, and determined upon following it.

The next day he said to his son, that he should go with him, and he would find him a new situation. After walking a good way into the country, they met with a shepherd tending his flock.

"Where are you going to, good man?" inquired the shepherd.

"I am in search of a master, who can teach my son the black art," answered the peasant. "You may soon find him," said the shepherd: "keep straight on and you will come to the greatest wizard that is to be found in all the land." The peasant thanked him for this information, and went on. Soon after, he came to a large forest, in the middle of which stood the wizard's house. He knocked at the door, and asked the Troll-man whether he had any inclination to take a boy as a pupil. "Yes," answered the other; "but not for a less term than four years; and we will make this agreement, that at the end of that time, you shall come, and if you can find your son he shall belong to you, but should you not be able to discover him, he must remain in my house, and serve me for the rest of his life."

The peasant agreed to these conditions, and returned home alone. At the end of a week he began to look for his son's return; thinking that in this, as in all former cases, he would run away from his master. But he did not come back, and his mother began to cry, and say her husband had not acted rightly in giving their child into the power of the evil one, and that they should never see him more.

After four years had elapsed the peasant set out on a journey to the magician's, according to their agreement. A little before he reached the forest, he met the same shepherd, who instructed him how to act so as to get his son back. "When you get there," said he, "you must at night keep your eyes constantly turned towards the fireplace, and take care not to fall asleep, for then the Troll-man will convey you back to your own house, and afterwards say you did not come at the appointed time. To-morrow you will see three dogs in the yard, eating milk-porridge out of a dish. The middle one is your son, and he is the one you must choose."

The peasant thanked the shepherd for his information, and bade him farewell.

When he entered the house of the magician, everything took place as the shepherd had said. He was conducted into the yard, where he saw three dogs. Two of them were handsome with smooth skins, but the third was lean and looked ill. When the peasant patted the dogs, the two handsome ones growled at him, but the lean one, on the contrary, wagged his tail. "Canst thou now tell me which of these three dogs in thy son?" said the Troll-man; "if so thou canst take him with thee; if not, he belongs to me."

"Well then I will choose the one that appears the most friendly," answered the peasant; "although he looks less handsome than the others." "That is a sensible choice," said the Troll-man; "he knew what he was about who gave thee that advice."

The peasant was then allowed to take his son home with him. So, putting a cord round his neck, he went his way, bewailing that his son was changed into a dog. "Oh! why are you bewailing so?" asked the shepherd as he came out of the forest, "it appears to me you have not been so very unlucky."

When he had gone a little way, the dog said to him: "Now you shall see that my learning has been of some use to me. I will soon change myself into a little tiny dog, and then you must sell me to those who are coming past." The dog did as he said, and became a beautiful little creature. Soon after a carriage came rolling along with some great folks in it. When they saw the beautiful little dog that ran playing along the road, and heard that it was for sale, they bought it of the peasant for a considerable sum, and at the same moment the son changed his father into a hare, which he caused to run across the road, while he was taken up by those who had bought him. When they saw the hare they set the dog after it, and scarcely had they done so, than both hare and dog ran into the wood and disappeared. Now the boy changed himself again, and this time both he and his father assumed human forms. The old man began cutting twigs and his son helped him. When the people in the carriage missed the little dog, they got out to seek after it, and asked the old man and his son if they had seen anything of a little dog that had run away. The boy directed them further into the wood, and he and his father returned home, and lived well on the money they had received by selling the dog.

When all the money was spent, both father and son resolved upon going out again in search of adventures. "Now I will turn myself into a boar," said the youth, "and you must put a cord round my leg and take me to Horsens market for sale; but remember to throw the cord over my right ear at the moment you sell me, and then I shall be home again as soon as you." The peasant did as his son directed him, and went to market; but he set so high a price on the boar, that no one would buy it, so he continued standing in the market till the afternoon was far advanced. At length there came an old man who bought the boar of him. This was no other than the magician, who, angry that the father had got back his son, had never ceased seeking after them from the time they had left his house. When the peasant had sold his boar he threw the cord over its right ear as the lad had told him, and in the same moment the animal vanished; and when he reached his own door he again saw his son sitting at the table.

They now lived a pleasant merry life until all the money was spent, and then again set out on fresh adventures. This time the son changed himself into a bull, first reminding his father to throw the rope over his right ear as soon as he was sold. At the market he met with the same old man, and soon came to an agreement with him about the price of the bull. While they were drinking a glass together in the alehouse, the father threw the rope over the bull's right horn, and when the magician went to fetch his purchase it had vanished, and the peasant upon reaching home again found his son sitting by his mother at the table. The third time the lad turned himself into a horse, and the magician was again in the market and bought him. "Thou hast already tricked me twice," said he to the peasant; "but it shall not happen again." Before he paid down the money he hired a stable and fastened the horse in, so that it was impossible for the peasant to throw the rein over the animal's right ear. The old man, nevertheless, returned home, in the hope that this time also he should find his son; but he was disappointed, for no lad was there. The magician in the meantime mounted the horse and rode off. He well knew whom he had bought, and determined that the boy should pay with his life the deception he had practised upon him. He led the horse through swamps and pools, and galloped at a pace that, had he long continued it, he must have ridden the animal to death; but the horse was a hard trotter, and the magician being old he at last found he had got his master, and was therefore obliged to ride home.

When he arrived at his house he put a magic bridle on the horse and shut him in a dark stable without giving him anything either to eat or drink. When some time had elapsed, he said to the servant-maid: "Go out and see how the horse is." When the girl came into the stable the metamorphosed boy (who had been the girl's sweetheart while he was in the Troll's house) began to moan piteously, and begged her to give him a pail of water. She did so, and on her return told her master that the horse was well. Some time after he again desired her to go out and see if the horse were not yet dead. When she entered the stable the poor animal begged her to loose the rein and the girths, which were strapped so tight that the could hardly draw breath. The girl did as she was requested, and no sooner was it done than the boy changed himself into a hare and ran out of the stable. The magician, who was sitting in the window, was immediately aware of what had happened on seeing the hare go springing across the yard, and, instantly changing himself into a dog, went in pursuit of it. When they had run many miles over corn-fields and meadows, the boy's strength began to fail and the magician gained more and more upon him. The hare then changed itself into a dove, but the magician as quickly turned himself into a hawk and pursued him afresh.

In this manner they flew towards a palace where a princess was sitting at a window. When she saw a hawk in chase of a dove she opened the window, and immediately the dove flew into the room, and then changed itself into a gold ring. The magician now became a prince, and went into the apartment for the purpose of catching the dove. When he could not find it, he asked permission to see her gold rings. The princess showed them to him, but let one fall into the fire. The Troll-man instantly drew it out, in doing which he burnt his fingers, and was obliged to let it fall on the floor. The boy now knew of no better course than to change himself into a grain of corn.

At the same moment the magician became a hen, in order to eat the corn, but scarcely had he done so than the boy became a hawk and killed him.

He then went to the forest, fetched all the magician's gold and silver, and from that day lived in wealth and happiness with his parents.

TEMPTATIONS.

In Vinding, near Veile, lived once a poor cottager, who went out as day labourer; his son was employed by the priest at Skjærup to run on errands, for which he received his board and lodging. One day the boy was sent with a letter for the priest at Veile. It was in the middle of summer, and the weather was very hot; when he had walked some distance he became tired and drowsy, and lay down to sleep. On awaking he saw a willow, from the roots of which the water had washed away all the earth, whereby the tree was on the point of perishing. "I am but little, it is true," said John, for such was the boy's name, "and can do but little, still I can help thee." He then began to throw mould on the bare roots, and ceased not till they were quite covered and protected. When he had finished, he heard a soft voice proceeding from the tree, which said to him: "Thou shalt not have rendered me this good service for nothing; cut a pipe from my branches, and everything for which thou blowest shall befall thee."

Although the boy did not give much credit to this, he, nevertheless, cut off a twig for a pipe. "As such a fine promise has been made me," thought he to himself, "I will wish that I could blow myself into a good situation by Michaelmas, that I might be of some use to my poor old father." He blew, but saw nothing, and then, putting his pipe in his pocket, hurried on to make up for the time he had loitered away at the willow-tree. Not long after he found a pocket-book full of money lying in the road. Now John by keeping it, could at once have relieved both his own and his father's necessities, but such a thought never entered his mind; on the contrary, he ran back to the town, inquired of all that he met, whether they had not lost a pocket-book. At length there came a horseman galloping along the road, and when John also asked him, the stranger replied that he had that morning dropped his pocket-book on his way from home, at the same time giving a description of it.

John delivered the pocket-book to him, and the horseman, who was a proprietor from Ostedgaard, near Fredericia, was so gratified, that he immediately gave the boy a handsome reward, and asked him if he would like to enter his service. "Yes, I should indeed," answered John, quite pleased at the thought. He then parted from the gentleman with many thanks for his kindness, after having agreed between them that John should come down to Osted at Michaelmas. He then executed his errand for the priest, and felt convinced, that it was alone owing to the pipe that he had met with such a lucky adventure; he therefore concealed it carefully, and let no one know anything of the matter.

Now this gentleman was an adept in the black art, and had only offered to take the lad into his service that he might see how far his honesty would be proof against the temptations into which he purposed to lead him.

At the appointed time John went to Ostedgaard, and was summoned by the master, who inquired of him what he could do. "I am not fit for much," said John, "as I am so little; but I will do my best at all times to perform whatever my good master requires of me." "That is well, with that I am contented," answered the master; "I have twelve hares, these thou must take to the wood every morning, and if thou bringest back the full number every evening I will give thee house and home in remuneration; but if thou allowest them to run away, thou wilt have a reckoning to settle with me." "I will do my best," answered John.

The next morning his master came down to the inclosure, and counted the hares. As soon as he opened the door and gave the animals their liberty, away they all ran, one to the east, another to the west, and John remained standing alone; he was not, however, so disheartened as might be imagined; for he had his willow pipe in his pocket. As soon, therefore, as he came into a lonely part of the wood, he took out his pipe and began to blow, and no sooner had he put it to his mouth, than all the twelve hares came running and assembled round him. As John now felt he could rely on the virtues of his pipe, he let them all go again, and passed his time in amusing himself. In the evening he took out his pipe again, and as he walked up to the manor continued blowing it. All the hares then came forth and followed him one by one. The master was standing at the gate, to see what would take place. He could not recover from his astonishment, when he saw the little herd-boy blowing his pipe as he approached the house, and all the hares following him as gently and quietly as if it were a flock of sheep he was driving home. "Thou art more clever than thou appearest," said the master; "the number is right, go in and get some food; for to-day thou hast done a good piece of work: we shall now see whether thou art as fortunate to-morrow."

The next day everything passed in exactly the same manner. As soon as the inclosure was opened, all the hares ran out in different directions, and the boy let them enjoy their liberty, as he now felt certain that he could bring them back whenever he wished. But this time his master had prepared a harder trial for him.

At noon he desired his daughter to disguise herself in a peasant's dress, and to go and ask the boy to give her a hare. The young maiden was so beautiful that he did not think John could refuse her request.

When the daughter had thus disguised herself, she went into the field and began talking to John, asking him what he was doing there. "I am taking care of hares," answered the boy.

"What has become of thy hares?" said the maiden, "I see nothing of them." "Oh, they are only gone a little way into the wood," said he; "but as soon as I call them they will all come back again." When the young girl pretended to doubt this, he blew on his pipe, and instantly all the twelve came running towards him. She now begged and prayed him to give her one of them. The boy at first refused, but as she was very importunate, he at length told her that she should have a hare for a kiss. In short, the maiden got the hare, and carried it up to the manor; but when John thought she must be near home, he blew on his pipe, and immediately the hare came bounding back to him, and so he brought all the twelve home that evening.

On the third day, the lord of Osted was determined to try whether he could not trick the boy. He therefore dressed himself like a peasant and went in search of John. When they had conversed some time, he requested him to call his hares together, and when they came, he wished to purchase one of them, but the boy answered, that he did not dare to sell what did not belong to him. As the lord continued to entreat him most urgently, John promised him a hare, if he would give him the ring that was on his finger. The lord, it must be observed, had forgotten to take off his ring when he put on the peasant's dress, and now found that he was known. He, nevertheless, gave the boy the ring and got one of the hares. When he had nearly reached Osted, John blew on his pipe, and, although the master held the hare as firmly as he could, it got away and ran back, just as on the preceding day. When the master found he could not get the better of the boy by fair means, he had recourse to the black art, and ascertained that the willow pipe was the cause of the hares always obeying John.

When the boy returned on the fourth evening, his master gave him plenty of food and strong drink, and being unaccustomed to such things, he soon fell asleep, so that it was no difficult matter to steal his pipe from him. The next day the hares were turned out as usual; but this time John could not bring them back; he, consequently, durst not show himself at Osted, but continued wandering about the wood, crying and sobbing. His master had now gained his point. When it began to grow dark, he went to seek for John, and asked him why he remained away so long that evening. John scarcely ventured to confess his misfortune; but as his master continued urging him to tell him, he at length acknowledged that the hares had run away, and that it was not in his power to get them back again. The lord took pity on him and told him to return home, for the loss was not very great. "A house and home I see thou wilt not get at present," said he as they walked back, "unless thou canst fulfil a condition, which I will propose to-morrow." John was glad to hear these words; for his sorrow was less at losing what his master had promised him than at forfeiting his benefactor's favour, and being turned out of the house. The next day there were guests at Ostedgaard, and when they were all assembled, the lord of the manor, calling John, told him he should have what had been promised him, if he could relate a bagful of untruths. "No," replied John, "to untruths I have never been addicted; but, if my good master pleases, I can, perhaps, tell him a bagful of truths."

"Well then," said his master, "here is a bag, and now begin thy story."

John began to recite about his lot as a little boy, how he had passed all his life in indigence and misery. Then he recited about his adventure with the willow-tree, how he had obtained his pipe, and had afterwards found the pocket-book, which was the cause of his master taking him into his service. Lastly, he recited how a maiden had come to him and given him a kiss for a hare. As he was continuing his master called out (as he did not wish his own fruitless attempt should be known): "Stop, John, thou hast kept thy word—the bag is full." He then let the boy go out of the room, and told his guests how faithfully and honourably John had always conducted himself, adding, that it was not possible to seduce him to deceive or to tell an untruth."

"Still I think it is to be done," said the proprietor of Nebbegaard. "I will answer for it that he will not be able to withstand, if he is seriously tempted."

His host felt offended by this doubting, and immediately offered to lay as large a wager as his neighbour pleased, that he could not get John either to deceive him or to tell an untruth. The challenge was accepted, and their estates were pledged for and against the boy.

The proprietor of Nebbegaard wrote a letter to his daughter, in which he explained to her what had taken place, and how important it was for him to win the wager. He desired her, therefore, to entertain John in the best manner possible, and to appear as affable and friendly towards him as she could, with the view of prevailing on him to give her the horse on which he rode.

The lad was then sent to Nebbegaard with this letter. His master lent him a horse, that he might the more expeditiously perform his errand; but warned him not to ride too fast, or by any means to lose the horse, which was the finest and most valuable animal he had in his stable. John promised to follow his instructions, and rode away. When he had ridden a short way from home, he dismounted, and led the horse, in order to comply, as much as possible, with his master's wish. In this manner he proceeded but slowly, and it was evening before he reached Nebbegaard.

When the young lady had read her father's letter, she sent for John, and behaved in the kindest and most friendly manner towards him. The maiden was very handsome, and treated the young lad as her equal in condition and rank. She entertained him sumptuously, and said not a word about the horse till he had drunk much more than he could bear. Without knowing what he did, John promised (after she had long entreated him in vain) that he would give her the horse, and the young girl behaved yet more friendly towards him; so the next morning John finding he had no longer a horse, took the saddle and bridle and wandered back to Ostedgaard. As he walked along it struck him how wrongly he had acted, and he began to repent bitterly of what he had done. "What shall I now say when I reach home, and my master finds that the horse is gone?" said he to himself, as he hung the saddle and bridle on the hedge. " 'Well, John,' master will say, 'hast thou executed my errand?' Then I shall answer, 'Yes.' 'But what then is become of my horse, with which I entrusted thee?' Then I will say, 'that I met a band of robbers on the way, and they took the horse from me.' No, that will never do," continued he, "never have I told a lie yet, and I will not do it now." Not long after another thought rose to his mind: "I can say that the horse fell, and that I buried it in a ditch. That won't do either—Lord knows what I, poor fellow, had best do." When he had gone on a little further, he resolved within himself that he would say that the horse had run away, and had shaken off his saddle and bridle.

Long before he reached Ostedgaard, the guests saw him approaching with the saddle on his head and the bridle on his arm.

"Here comes our truthful boy," exclaimed the proprietor of Nebbegaard, "look only how slowly he approaches, who do you now think has won the wager?"

The lord of Osted had already recognised John, and was highly incensed at seeing him return without the horse. As soon as the boy entered the house, he was called up where all the guests were assembled, and his master said: "Well, John, hast thou executed my errand?" "Yes, I have, gracious master," answered the boy, trembling with fear. "What then is become of my good horse, which I ordered thee to take such care of?"

John did not dare to meet the look of his master, but cast his eyes on the ground and said, in a whimpering voice:—

"Dainty the fare, sweet was the mead,
The lady's arm was soft and round,
The sparkling cup my senses drown'd,
And thus I lost my master's steed."

When he had recited this, his master embraced him in his joy, and exclaimed: "See now! I knew well enough that he would speak the truth. Which of us two has won the wager?"

John did not comprehend the meaning of these words, and continued sorrowful, till his master said to him:

"Be of good heart, my boy! as thou hast always kept to truth and right, I will give thee both house and land, and when thou art old enough, I will give thee my daughter to wife."

The following day John was allowed to fetch his old father to live with him, and some years after he was married to his master's daughter.

THE OUTLAW.

AT Palsgaard, in the district of Bjerge, lived once a knight, whose name was Eisten Brink. He was addicted to the belief in supernatural agency, and kept an astrologer in his house, that he might foretell him his fate. As Eisten had been many years a widower, he resolved to marry again, and with that object courted the daughter of Jens Grib of Barritskov. Although the young maiden was not very favourably inclined towards her old suitor, her father forced her to give the consenting "Yes" to his proposals.

Two nights before the wedding was to take place, Eisten went up to the Astrologer's tower, and requested him to foretell what his fate would be in the married state.

The Astrologer took out his instruments, and after having for some time consulted the heavens, he told the knight, "that there always appeared a little black spot upon his star, which signified some secret, and with this he must become acquainted before he could possibly foretell his future."

At first Eisten would divulge nothing; but as the Astrologer refused to proceed before he made a full confession, the knight was at last obliged to acknowledge that Palsgaard had unjustly come into his possession in the following manner. His brother-in-law a knight named Palle, had, many years ago, made him the superintendent of the castle, and, at the same time, committed to his care his little son, while he went to join in the war. A few years after this, Eisten received intelligence of Palle's death, and a year later his son also disappeared one day, when he had been seen playing near the lake. The people in the neighbourhood believed that the boy had fallen into the water and been drowned; but the truth was, that Eisten Brink had got an old woman to kidnap the child, and conceal him, so that he might be no impediment in the way of his becoming master of Palsgaard.

When Eisten had related this tale, the Astrologer asked him, if he had never since heard what had become of Palle's son. "Yes," replied the knight, "old Trude (so the woman was called) sent him first to Sleswig, to live with a sister of hers, but at her death he returned to Trude, and she got him placed as huntsman to my future father-in-law."

"And is he there now?" asked the Astrologer.

"No, that he is not; for a day or two ago, as Grib observed that Abel was paying too much attention to Inger, who is to be my wife to-morrow, he turned him out of doors, and forbade him ever to appear again at Barritskov."

When the Astrologer had heard all he wished to know, he predicted much happiness to Eisten in the married state. The next day the knight, richly attired, and attended by a numerous retinue, rode over to Jens Grib's at Barritskov. Jens immediately told his son-in-law in confidence, that Abel, although forbidden the house and grounds, was still lingering about, and that Inger did not appear to be unfavourably disposed towards him. He therefore advised Eisten to have all his eyes about him when they were married, and to be cautious whom he admitted to Palsgaard. Eisten smiled at this warning, and thought that he could very well manage matters.

In the afternoon of that day, he rode down to Rosenvold, or Staxesvold, as it was then called. This place belonged at that time to a noted freebooter who roamed about in Middlefart Sound, and plundered all the vessels he could master. Eisten, through good words and good pay, got a promise that two of the freebooters would waylay and murder Abel, whom they knew by sight, having often met him, as Jens Grib's wood reached down to theirs. They agreed to do their work the following night, so that the knight should never more be troubled with the huntsman. With regard to Abel, Jens Grib's suspicions were well founded. Inger and he had been attached to each other for some time, long, in fact, before Eisten thought of becoming her suitor. The young lover was, therefore, much grieved at finding himself suddenly dismissed from Barritskov, and knew not how to find an opportunity of speaking to Inger.

In his distress he went in the evening down to the

wood, where old Trude, his foster-mother, lived. He confided to her his secret, and asked her what course she thought he had best pursue. After they had had some conversation together, the old woman advised him to accompany her into the wood, to a mount in which lived a Troll, and if he could be brought to interest himself in the matter, Abel need have no fear, either for the father or lover of Inger. The young huntsman felt no great inclination to follow this advice; yet what else could he do? He at length consented, and they set out together, taking the road that led to the Troll's Mount.

The real cause why Trude was desirous of inducing Abel to go with her to the Troll was, that she had sold herself to him, body and soul, after a certain period, unless she could find another willing to enter into the same conditions. This period expired on the very evening of Abel's visit, and the wicked woman resolved in her evil heart to save herself by the sacrifice of her fosterson. When they came to the spot the old woman began to summon forth the Troll. She made a circle of human bones about the hill, within which she placed herself and Abel. A noise was then heard around them; the mount rose on four pillars of fire, and the Troll appeared.

The woman made known her errand, and presented Abel to him. The Troll was just laying hold of the young man, when a loud cry was heard in the wood, and the Astrologer from Palsgaard rushed towards Abel, but could not enter the circle which the crone had made. He cried again with all his might: "This boy is mine, take him not from me, he is my only son."

To this appeal the Troll gave little heed, and it would have fared ill with the huntsman, had not the Astrologer again cried with a powerful voice: "In the name of our Lord, I conjure you to spare my son!" No sooner had he uttered these words, than the Troll gave a horrible scream, and, seizing old Trude round the waist, disappeared with her in the mount, which immediately closed upon them and sank down again; but Abel remained behind and was saved.

The Astrologer was no other than the old knight Palle, the brother-in-law of Eisten Brink. He had been outlawed for having joined the king's enemies, hence the reason of his living in concealment at Palsgaard. No sooner had Eisten informed him how he had acted towards his son than he went down to Trude's cottage. Not finding her at home, he wandered into the wood, where he fortunately came to the Troll's Mount, just as Abel was in the greatest danger. When he had made himself known to his son, and they had embraced each other, and thanked God for their happy deliverance, they consulted together as to the course they should pursue, then lay down in the wood to sleep.

That same night the two freebooters left Staxesvold in quest of Abel, as had been agreed between them and Eisten Brink. They first took the road to old Trude's house, then proceeded further along the same path which the Astrologer had taken just before. On the same day, it happened that the king had been out hunting from a neighbouring manor. He had found a white hind, and pursued it throughout the day, over hill and through dale, until it reached the wood of Palsgaard. He thus became separated from his followers, and as the evening was drawing on, he could neither find his way out of the wood, nor any path through it. He rode about for some time at a venture, when the voices of Abel and his father talking together attracted his attention. He went in the direction of the sound, and came to the spot where they had lain down to rest.

Here he was met by the freebooters, who, believing they had found the man they were in search of, entered into discourse with the king, who did not dream of any mischief. Abel looked up on hearing voices, and saw one of the miscreants draw forth a knife and steal softly behind the king. He immediately saw that murder was intended, and sprang up, exclaiming: "Defend yourself, sir! for your life is threatened."

Old Palle rushed to the assistance of his son, and it cost them but little trouble to overpower the two freebooters. One was killed in the fray, the other threw away his weapon and begged for mercy. The king ordered him immediately to confess what inducement he had for making this murderous attack; when the assassin, without reserve, acknowledged how Eisten had instigated them to murder Abel.

The king now turned to the Astrologer, and asked him who he was. The old man laid his sword at the king's feet, and said: "Kneel down with me, my son, for you stand before Denmark's king." Hereupon he related his history, and also the manner in which Eisten Brink had acted towards him and his son Abel.

The king pardoned him; and when he heard that Eisten's wedding was to be celebrated at Barritskov on the following day, he determined on being present at the festival, taking with him the captured robber. Palle and his son also accompanied him to the castle.

At Barritskov all was mirth and glee; the bridesmaids were adorning Inger and twining the bridal wreath in her hair. Jens Grib was busied in receiving the congratulations of his neighbours. But Eisten had not yet made his appearance; he was sitting alone in his chamber, impatiently waiting to hear tidings from the two assassins, who had undertaken to murder Abel.

At once he thought he heard a great and unusual noise in the castle-yard. He approached the door to ascertain the cause, when his future father-in-law burst into the room with the intelligence, that the king had arrived at the castle, in company with Abel, the Astrologer, and a prisoner.

Eisten Brink could scarcely believe his own ears, but still more astounded was he upon finding that the king had suspended all the festivities, and commanded every one to meet him in the knights' hall.

Here the king related to the astonished company how Eisten had acted towards his brother-in-law, the old Palle, and requested the assembled guests to pass judgment upon such a criminal.

Eisten was deprived of his honours. Palle was restored to his power and dignity; but the best of all was, that Abel was wedded to Inger, and lived with her many years in splendour and felicity.

THE BLUE RIBAND.

FROM MARNE.

THERE was once a man, who was very poor, and sick into the bargain. When he felt that his end was drawing nigh, he summoned his wife to his bedside, and said to her: "My dear wife, I feel that my end approaches, but I should die tranquil and free from solicitude, if I only knew that all would go well with thee and our Hans, when I shall be no more. I can leave you nothing to protect you from want; but when I am dead, go with our son to my brother, who dwells in a village on the other side of the great forest. He is wealthy and has always cherished brotherly feelings towards me, and will, I doubt not, provide for you." He then died. After his burial, the widow and her son set out on their way to her brother-in-law, as her husband had recommended. Now it must be observed that the mother hated her son, and was hostile to him in every way possible, though Hans was a good youth and approaching to manhood. When they had been journeying for some time, they observed a blue riband lying in the path. Hans stooped to take it up, but his mother said: "Let the old riband lie; what dost thou want with it?" But Hans thought within himself: "Who knows what it may be good for? It would be a real pity to let so pretty a riband lie here;" so he took it up, and bound it, without his mother's knowledge, under his jacket round his arm. He now became so strong, that no one, as long as he wore that riband, could prevail against him, and every one must stand in awe of him.

When they had proceeded some way further, and had entered the large forest, after having wandered about for a long time, they came to a cave, in which stood a covered table, loaded with a profusion of the daintiest viands in silver dishes. Hans said: "We are come just in the right moment. I have been hungry a long while; I will now make a hearty meal." So they sat down and ate and drank to their hearts' content. They had scarcely finished when the giant, to whom the cave belonged, returned home; but he was quite friendly, and said: "You were right to help yourselves and not wait for me; if you find it pleasant, you can remain always here in the cave with me." To the woman he said that she might be his wife. To his proposal they both agreed, and now for a while lived content in the cave with the giant.

From day to day the giant became more and more attached to Hans; but his mother's hatred to him increased every hour, and when she observed how strong he was become, she was still more embittered, and said one day to the giant: "Dost thou notice how strong Hans is? He may become dangerous to us the older he grows and the more he increases in strength, and may one day easily strike us both dead, that he may possess the cave alone; or he may drive us from it. It would be well and prudent on thy part, if thou wert to provide in time, and take an opportunity of getting rid of him." But the giant answered: "Never again speak to me in that strain. Hans is a good youth, and will do us no harm; I will not hurt a hair of his head."

When the woman found that the giant would not lend himself to her purpose, she lay in bed on the following day and pretended to be ill. She then called her son, and said: "My dear Hans, I am so ill that I shall certainly die. There is, nevertheless, one remedy that may save me. I dreamed that if I could get a draught of the milk of the lioness that has her den not far from here, I should surely recover. If thou lovest me, thou canst help me; thou art so strong and fearest nothing; thou couldst go and fetch me some of the milk." "Certainly, dear mother," answered Hans; "that I will most readily do, if I only knew that it would do you good." So he took a bowl and went to the den of the lioness. There she lay suckling her young ones; but Hans, laying the young ones aside, began to milk, which the lioness allowed quite quietly; but then in came the old lion roaring, and attacked Hans from behind, who, turning round, took the lion's neck under his arm and squeezed him so firmly that he began to whine most piteously, and became quite tame. Hans then released him, and he went and lay in the corner, and Hans proceeded with his milking, until the basin was full. When he left the den, the lioness sprang after him with her young ones, and were soon followed by the old lion. Hans then carried the milk to his mother, who was so terrified at the sight of the lions that she cried: "Hans, send the savage beasts away, or I shall die of fright." The lions thereupon went away of their own accord and lay down before the door, and when Hans came out they ran to him and appeared glad.

When this attempt of the wicked mother had thus failed, she again said to the giant: "If thou hadst directly followed my counsel, we should now have nothing more to fear; but now it is wore than before, and as he has got the wild beasts we cannot so easily do anything to harm him." The giant answered: "I know not why we should do anything to injure him. Hans is a good youth, and the animals are tame. I would on no account lay a hand on him." To this the mother replied: "It may, notwithstanding, easily enter his mind either to drive us from the cave, or even destroy us outright, in order to become its master. I cannot feel happy so long as I must live in fear."

After a time the woman again lay in bed, saying she was sick, and again called to her son and said: "I have had another dream, that if I could get a few of the apples that grow in the garden of the three giants, I should again be well; otherwise I feel that I must die." Hans said: "My dear mother, as you have such great need of them, I will go to the giants and fetch you some." So, taking a sack, he was instantly on his way, and the lions after him. But the wicked mother thought that this time he would surely never return. Hans went straight into the garden and gathered a sackful of apples; and having so done, ate a few himself; immediately after which he fell into a deep sleep and sank down under one of the trees. This was caused by the apples, which possessed that property. Had the faithful lions now not been with him, he must have perished; for instantly there rushed a huge giant through the garden, crying: "Who has stolen our apples?" But Hans slept on and answered not. On perceiving Hans, the giant ran fiercely at him, and would have finished him, but then up sprang the lions, fell upon the giant, and in a short time tore him in pieces. Now came the second giant, also crying out: "Who has stolen our apples?" and when he was about to rush on Hans, the lions again sprang up, and in like manner despatched him. Lastly came the third giant, and cried: "Who is stealing our apples here?" Hans slept on, but the lions seized this giant also and killed him. Hans then opened his eyes and went wandering about the garden. When he came near the castle, in which the giants had dwelt, he heard, from a deep underground chamber, a voice of lamentation. He descended and found a princess of exquisite beauty, whom the giants had carried away from her father, and here confined, loaded with heavy chains. But Hans had scarcely touched the chains, when they flew in fragments, and he conducted the beautiful princess up into the most magnificent apartment of the castle, that she might recover herself, and wait until he returned. She entreated him to accompany her to her father's court, but he answered: "I must first go and carry the apples to my mother, who is sick to death." He then left the princess in the castle, took his sack of apples, and returned to the cave to his mother. When she saw him coming she could scarcely believe her eyesight, so great was her astonishment at seeing him unscathed and bearing a sackful of apples. She instantly asked him how he had been able to accomplish his errand. "My dear mother," said he, "since I wear the blue riband, that you would not have had me take with me, I am so strong that nothing can prevail against me. On this occasion my lions killed all the giants, and now you shall go with me and leave this old den. Henceforth we will live at the castle in joy and splendour; I have found there a most beautiful princess, who shall remain with us." The mother and the giant now went with Hans to the castle; but when the former saw all the magnificence there, and how beautiful the princess was, she grudged Hans his good fortune more than ever, and was constantly on the watch for an opportunity to destroy him; for she now knew whence he derived his strength. So one day, as Hans was lying at rest on his bed, with his riband hanging by him on a nail, she stole softly in, and, before he was aware, pierced out both his eyes; then took the riband, and as Hans was now blind and helpless, thrust him out of the castle, and said, that henceforward she would be sole mistress there. Poor Hans would soon have perished, had not the faithful lions conducted the princess to him. She attended him and led him; for she would proceed to her father's kingdom, hoping there to find a cure for her deliverer. But the way was long, and long they wandered about; at length, however, they arrived in the neighbourhood of the city in which the father of the princess resided. Here she observed a blind hare running in the road before her, which, on coming to a brook that flowed by, dived thrice under the water, and ran, with its sight restored, away. She then led Hans to the water, who, when he had plunged into it three times, could see as before.

Full of joy they now entered the city, and when the old king was informed that Hans was the deliverer of his daughter, he would have no other son-in-law but him, nor could the princess have chosen a husband more agreeable to her than Hans. But when his mother had learned that Hans was restored to sight and had married the princess, she became suddenly ill through spite, and this time in earnest, and she died. Shortly after the giant also died. When looking under their pillow, Hans found the blue riband, which he wore as long as he lived, never laying it aside. He afterwards succeeded his father-in-law in the kingdom, and as king was feared by all his enemies far and near, and regarded as a true protector of his people.

THE MAN WITHOUT A HEART.

FROM MELDORF.

THERE was once seven brothers, who had neither father nor mother. They lived together in one house, and had to do all the household work themselves, to wash, cook, sweep, and whatever else was to be done; for they had no sisters. Of this kind of housekeeping they soon grew tired, and one of them said: "Let us set out, and each of us get a wife." This idea pleased the other brothers, and they made themselves ready for travelling, all excepting the youngest, who preferred to remain at home and keep house, his six brothers promising to bring him a wife with them. The brothers then set out, and all six went forth merrily in the wide world. They soon came into a large, wild forest, where, after wandering about for some time, they found a small house, at the door of which an old man was standing. On seeing the brothers passing by and appearing so gay, he called to them: "For what place are you bound that you pass my door so merrily?" "We are going each of us to fetch a handsome young bride," answered they, "and therefore are we so merry. We are all brothers, but have left one at home, for whom we are also to bring a bride." "I wish you then success in your undertaking," replied the old man; "you see, however, very plainly that I am so lonely that I too have need of a wife, and so I advise you to bring me one also with you." To this the brothers made no answer, but continued their way, thinking the old man spoke only in jest, and that he could have no occasion for a wife.

They soon arrived in a city, where they found seven young and handsome sisters, of whom each of the brothers chose one, and took the seventh with them for their youngest brother.

When they again arrived in the forest, there stood the old man at his door, apparently awaiting their coming. He even called to them at a distance: "Well, have you brought me a wife with you as I desired you?" "No," answered them, "we could not find one for thee, old man; we have only brought brides for ourselves, and one for our youngest brother." "You must leave her for me," said the old man, "for you must keep to your promise." This the brothers refused to do. The old man then took a little white staff from a shelf over the door, with which when he had touched the six brothers and their brides, they were all turned into gray stones. These, together with the staff, he laid on the shelf above the door, but kept the seventh young bride for himself.

The young woman had now to attend to all that was to be done in the house; and she did it all cheerfully, for what would resistance have availed her? She had, moreover, every comfort with him, the only thought that gave her uneasiness being that he might soon die; for what was she then to do alone in the great wild forest, and how was she to release her six poor enchanted sisters and their betrothed husbands? The longer she lived with him the more dreadful did this thought become; she wept and wailed the whole livelong day, and was incessantly crying in the old man's ear: "Thou art old, and mayest die suddenly, and what am I then to do? I shall be left alone here in this great forest." The old man would then appear sad, and at length said: "Thou hast no cause to be uneasy; I cannot die, for I have no heart in my breast; but even if I should die, the twelve gray stones lie over the house-door, and with them a little white staff. If thou strikest the stones with that staff, thy sisters and their betrothed will again be living." The young woman now appeared contented, and asked him, that as his heart was not in his breast, where he kept it. "My child," answered the old man, "be not so inquisitive; thou canst not know everything." But she never ceased her importunities, until he at last said somewhat peevishly, "Well, in order to make you easy, I tell thee that my heart lies in the coverlet."

Now it was the old man's custom to go every morning into the forest and not return till the evening, when his young housekeeper had to prepare supper for him. One evening on his return, finding his coverlet adorned with all kinds of beautiful feathers and flowers, he asked the young woman the meaning of it. "Oh, father," answered she, "I sit here the whole day alone and can do nothing for thy gratification, and so thought I would do something for the delight of thy heart, which, as thou sayest, is in the coverlet!" "My child," said the old man, laughing, "that was only a joke of mine; my heart is not in the coverlet, it is in a very different place." She then began again to weep and lament, and said: "Thou hast then a heart in thy breast and canst die; what am I then to do, and how shall I recover my friends when thou art dead?" "I tell thee," answered the old man, "that I cannot die, and have positively no heart in my breast; but even if I should die, which is not possible, there lie the gray stones over the door together with a little white stick, with which thou hast only, as I have already told thee, to strike the stones, and thou wilt have all thy friends again!" She then prayed and implored him so long to inform her where he kept his heart, that he at length said: "It is in the room-door."

On the following day she decorated the room-door with variegated feathers and flowers from top to bottom, and when the old man came home in the evening and inquired the cause, she answered: "Oh, father, I sit here the whole day, and can do nothing for thy pleasure, and wished therefore to give some delight to thy heart." But the old man answered as before: "My heart is not in the room-door; it is in a very different place." Then, as on the previous day, she began to weep and implore, and said: "Thou hast then a heart and canst die; thou wilt only deceive me." The old man answered: "Die I cannot; but as thou wilt positively know where my heart is, I will tell thee, that thou mayest be at ease. Far, very far, from here, in a wholly unknown solitary place, there is a large church; this church is well secured by thick iron doors; around it there runs a wide, deep moat; within the church there flies a bird, and in that bird is my heart. So long as that bird lives, I also live. Of itself it will not die, and no one can catch it. Hence I cannot die, and thou mayest be without apprehension."

In the meantime the youngest brother had waited and waited at home; but as his brothers did not return, he supposed that some mishap had befallen them, and therefore set out in quest of them. After traveling for some days he arrived at the house of the old man. He was not at home, but the young woman, his bride, received him. He related to her how he had six brothers, who had all left home to get themselves wives, but that some mischance must have befallen them, as they had never returned. He had, therefore, set out in search of them. The young woman then instantly knew him for her bridegroom, and informed him who she was, and what had become of his brothers and their brides. Both were overjoyed at having thus met; she gave him to eat, and when he had recruited his strength he said: "Tell me now, my dear bride, how I can release my brothers." She then related to him all about the old man, whose heart was not in his breast, but in a far distant church, of which she gave him every particular, according to the old man's narrative. "I will at all events try," said the young man, "whether I cannot get hold of the bird. It is true that the way is long and unknown to me, and the church is well secured; but by God's help I may succeed." "Do so," said the young woman, "seek the bird; for as long as that lives thy brothers cannot be released. This night thou must hide thyself under the bedstead, that the old man may not find thee: to-morrow thou canst continue thy journey." Accordingly he crept under the bed just before the old man's return, and on the following morning, as soon as the old man was gone out, the young woman drew her bridegroom forth from his hiding-place, gave him a whole basketful of provisions, and after a tender farewell, he resumed his journey. He had proceeded a considerable way, when feeling hungry he sat down, placed his basket before him and opened it. While in the act of taking forth some bread and meat, he said: "Let come now every one that desires to eat with me!" At the instant there came a huge red ox, and said: "If thou didst say that every one should come that desires to eat with thee, I would gladly eat with thee." "Very well," said the young man, "I did say so, and thou shalt partake with me." They then began to eat, and when they were satisfied, the red ox, when about to depart, said: "If at any time thou art in difficulty and requirest my aid, thou hast only to utter the wish, and I will come and help thee." He then disappeared among the trees, and the young man recommenced his journey.

When he had proceeded a considerable way farther, he was again hungry, so sat down, opened his basket, and said as before: "Let those come that desire to eat with me!" In a moment there came from the thicket a large wild boar and said: "Thou hast said that whoever desired to eat with thee should come; now I would gladly eat with thee." The bridegroom answered: "Thou art quite right, comrade; so just fall to." When they had eaten, the boar said: "If thou art ever in difficulty and needest my aid, thou hast only to utter the wish, and I will help thee." He then disappeared in the forest, and the young man pursued his journey.

On the third day, when about to eat, he said again:

"Let all that desire to eat with me come!" At the instant a rattling was heard among the trees and a large griffon descended and placed himself by the side of the traveller, saying: "If thou didst say that all who desired to eat with thee might come, I would gladly eat with thee." "With all my heart," answered the bridegroom; " 'tis far more pleasant to eat in company than alone; so just fall to." Both then began to eat. When their hunger was satisfied, the griffon said: "If ever thou art in difficulty, thou hast only to call me and I will aid thee." He then disappeared in the air, and the young man went his way.

After travelling a while longer he perceived the church at a distance; so redoubling his pace, he was soon close by it. But now there was the moat in his way, which was too deep for him to wade through, and he could not swim. Now the red ox occurred to his recollection: "He could help thee," thought he, "if he were to drink a green path through the water. Oh, that he were here!" Hardly had he expressed the wish when the red ox was there, laid himself on his knees and drank until there was a dry green path through the water. The young man now passed through the moat and stood before the church, the iron doors of which were so strong that he could not force one open, and the walls many feet thick, without an opening in any part. Knowing no other means, he endeavoured to break some stones, one by one out of the wall, and after great labour succeeded in extracting a few. It then occurred to him that the wild boar could help him; and he cried: "Oh, if the wild boar were here!" In an instant it came rushing up, and ran with such force against the wall, that in one moment a large hole was broken through it, and the young man entered the church. Here he saw the bird flying about. "Thou canst not catch it thyself," thought he, "but if the griffon were here——!" Scarcely had he uttered the thought, when the griffon was there; but it cost even the griffon a great deal of trouble to catch the little bird; at last, however, he seized it, gave it into the young man's hand and flew away. Overjoyed, he placed his prize in the basket, and set forth on his way back to the house in which his bride was.

When he reached the house and informed her that he had the bird in his basket, she was overjoyed, and said: "Now thou shalt first eat something in haste, and then creep again under the bed with the bird, so that the old man may know nothing of the matter." This was done, and just as he had crept under the bed, the old man returned home, but felt ill and complained. The young woman then again began to weep, and said: "Ah, now father will die, that I can well see, and he has a heart in his breast!" "Ah, my child," answered the old man, "be still only; I cannot die; it will soon pass over." The bridegroom under the bed now gave the bird a little pinch, and the old man felt quite ill and sat down, and when the young man squeezed it yet harder, he fell to the earth in a swoon. The bride then cried out: "Squeeze it quite to death." The young man did so, and the old man lay dead on the ground. The young woman then drew her bridegroom from under the bed, and afterwards went and took the stones and the little white staff from the shelf over the door, struck every stone with the staff, and in one instant there stood all her sisters and the brothers before her. "Now," said she, "we will set out for home, and celebrate our marriage and be happy; for the old man is dead, and there is nothing more to fear from him." They did so, and lived many years in harmony and happily together.

THE SEVEN RAVENS.

As many strange things come to pass in the world, so there was a poor woman who had seven sons at a birth, all of whom lived and throve. After some years, the same woman had a daughter. Her husband was a very industrious and active man, on which account people in want of a handicraftsman were very willing to take him into their service, so that he could not only support his numerous family in an honest manner, but earned so much that, by prudent economy, his wife was enabled to lay by a little money for a rainy day. But this good father died in the prime of life, and the poor widow soon fell into poverty; for she could not earn enough to support and clothe her eight children. Her seven boys grew bigger, and daily required more and more, besides which they were a great grief to their mother, for they were wild and wicked. The poor woman could hardly stand against all the afflictions that weighed so heavily upon her. She wished to bring up her children in the paths of virtue, but neither mildness nor severity availed anything: the boys' hearts were hardened. One day, when her patience was quite exhausted, she spoke thus to them: "Oh, you wicked young ravens! would that you were seven black ravens, and would fly away, so that I might never see you again!" and the seven boys immediately became seven ravens, flew out of the window, and disappeared.

The mother now lived with her little daughter in peace and contentment, and was able to earn more than she spent. And the young girl grew up handsome, modest, and good. But after some years had passed, both mother and daughter began to long after the seven boys; they often talked about them and wept; they thought, that could only the seven brothers return and be good lads, how well they could all live by their work and have so much pleasure in one another. And as this longing in the heart of the young maiden increased daily, she one day said to her mother: "Dear mother, let me wander in the world in quest of my brothers, that I may turn them from their wicked ways, and make them a comfort and a blessing to you in your old age." The mother answered: "Thou good girl! I will not restrain thee from accomplishing this pious deed. Go, my child! and may God guide thee." She then gave her a small gold ring which she had formerly worn when a child, at the time the brothers were changed into ravens.

The young girl set out, and wandered far, very far away, and for a very long time found no traces of her brothers; but at length she came to the foot of a very high mountain, on the top of which stood a small dwelling. At the mountain's foot she sat down to rest, all the while looking up in deep thought at the little habitation. It appeared at first to her like a bird's nest, for it was of a grayish hue, as if built of small stones and mud; then it looked like a human dwelling. She thought within herself: "Can that be my brothers' habitation?" And when she at length saw seven ravens flying out of the house, she was confirmed in her conjecture. Full of joy, she began to ascend the mountain, but the road that led to the summit was paved with such curious glass-like stones, that every time she had with the greatest caution proceeded but a few paces, her feet slipped and she fell down to the bottom. At this she was sadly disheartened, and felt completely at a loss how to get up, when she chanced to see a beautiful white goose, and thought: "If I had only thy wings, I could soon be at the top." She then thought again: "But can I not cut thy wings off? yes, they would help me." So she caught the beautiful goose, and cut off its wings, also its legs, and sewed them on to herself; and see! when she attempted to fly, she succeeded to perfection; and when she was tired of flying, she walked a little on the goose's feet, and did not slip down again. She arrived at length safely at the desired spot. When at the top of the mountain, she entered the little dwelling; it was very small; within stood seven tiny tables, seven little chairs, seven little beds, and in the room were seven little windows, and in the oven seven little dishes, in which were little baked birds and seven eggs. The good sister was weary after her long journey, and rejoiced that she could once again take some rest and appease her hunger. So she took the seven little dishes out of the oven and ate a little from each, and sat down for a while on each of the seven little chairs, and lay down on each of the little beds, but on the last she fell fast asleep, and there remained until the seven brothers came back. They flew through the seven windows into the room, took their dishes out of the oven, and began to eat; but instantly saw that a part of their fare had disappeared. They then went to lie down, and found their beds rumpled, when one of the brothers uttered a loud cry, and said: "Oh! what a beautiful young girl there is on my bed!" The other brothers flew quickly to see, and with amazement beheld the sleeping maiden. Then the one said to the other: "Oh, if only she were our sister!" Then they again cried out to each other with joy: "Yes, it is our sister; oh yes, it is, just such hair she had, and just such a mouth, and just such a little gold ring she wore on her middle finger as she now has on her little one." And they all danced for joy, and all kissed their sister, but she continued to sleep so soundly, that it was a long time before she awoke.

At length the maiden opened her eyes, and saw her seven black brothers standing about the bed. She then said: "Oh happy meeting, my dear brothers; God be praised that I have at length found you! I have had a long and tedious journey on your account, in the hope of fetching you back from your banishment, provided your hearts are inclined never more to vex and trouble your good mother; that you will work with us diligently, and

139

be the honour and comfort of your old affectionate parent." During this discourse the brothers wept bitterly, and answered: "Yes, dearest sister, we will be better, never will we offend our mother again. Alas! as ravens we have led a miserable life, and before we built this hut we almost perished with hunger and cold. Then came repentance, which racked us day and night; for we were obliged to live on the bodies of poor executed criminals, and were thereby always reminded of the sinner's end."

The sister shed tears of joy at her brothers' repentance, and on hearing them utter such pious sentiments: "Oh!" exclaimed she, "all will be well. When you return home, and your mother sees how penitent you are, she will forgive you from her heart, and restore you to your human form."

When the brothers were about to return home with their sister, they said, while opening a small box: "Dear sister, take these beautiful gold rings and shining stones, which we have from time to time found abroad: put them in your apron and carry them home with you, for with them we shall be rich as men. As ravens we collected them only on account of their brilliancy." The sister did as her brothers requested her, and was pleased with the beautiful ornaments. As they journeyed home, first one of the ravens and then another bore their sister on their pinions, until they reached their mother's dwelling, when they flew in at the window and implored her forgiveness, and promised that in future they would be dutiful children. Their sister also prayed and supplicated for them, and the mother was full of joy and love, and

forgave her seven sons. They then became human beings again, and were fine blooming youths, each one as
large and graceful as the other. With heartfelt gratitude
they kissed their dear mother and darling sister; and soon
after, all the seven brothers married young discreet maidens, built themselves a large beautiful house (for they
had sold their jewels for a considerable sum of money),
and the house-warming was the wedding of all the seven
brothers. Their sister was also married to an excellent
man, and, at the earnest desire of her brothers, she and
her husband took up their abode with them.

The good mother had great joy and pleasure in her
children in her old age, and as long as she lived was
loved and honoured by them.

THE LITTLE CUP OF TEARS.

THERE was once a mother and a child, and the mother
loved this her only child with her whole heart, and
thought she could not live without it; but the Almighty
sent a great sickness among children, which also seized
this little one, who lay on its bed sick even to death.
Three days and three nights the mother watched, and
wept, and prayed by the side of her darling child; but it
died. The mother, now left alone in the wide world,
gave way to the most violent and unspeakable grief; she
ate nothing and drank nothing, and wept, wept, wept
three long days and three long nights without ceasing,
calling constantly upon her child. The third night, as
she thus sat overcome with suffering in the place where

her child had died, her eyes bathed in tears, and faint from grief, the door softly opened, and the mother started, for before her stood her departed child. It had become a heavenly angel, and smiled sweetly as innocence, and was beautiful like the blessed. It had in its hand a small cup, that was almost running over, so full it was. And the child spoke: "O! dearest mother, weep no more for me; the angel of mourning has collected in this little cup the tears which you have shed for me. If for me you shed but one tear more, it will overflow, and I shall have no more rest in the grave, and no joy in heaven. Therefore, O dearest mother! weep no more for your child; for it is well and happy, and angels are its companions." It then vanished.

The mother shed no more tears, that she might not disturb her child's rest in the grave and its joys in heaven. For the sake of her infant's happiness, she controlled the anguish of her heart. So strong and self-sacrificing is a mother's love.

THE MAN IN THE MOON.[1]

VERY, very long ago there was a man who went into the forest one Sunday to cut wood. Having chopped a large quantity of brushwood, he tied it together, thrust a stick through the bundle, threw it over his shoulder, and was on his way home, when there met him on the road a comely man, dressed in his Sunday clothes, who was going to church. He stopped, and, accosting the wood-

---

[1] See Chaucer, Testament of Cresseide, 260-263, Shakspeare, Tempest, ii. 2. Mids. Night's Dream, i. 3; also Grimm, Deutsche Mythologie, p. 679.

cutter, said: "Dost thou not know that on earth this is Sunday, the day on which God rested from his works, after he had created the world, with all the beasts of the field, and also man? Dost thou not know what is written in the fourth commandment, 'Thou shalt keep holy the Sabbath-day?'" The questioner was our Lord himself. The wood-cutter was hardened, and answered: "Whether it is Sunday on earth or Monday (Moonday) in heaven, what does it concern me or thee?"

"For this thou shalt for ever bear thy bundle of wood," said the Lord; "and because the Sunday on earth is profaned by thee, thou shalt have an everlasting Monday, and stand in the moon, a warning to all such as break the Sunday by work."

From that time the man stands in the moon, with his faggot of brushwood, and will stand there to all eternity.

LORA, THE GODDESS OF LOVE.

THE mountain-fortress of Lora is so called from a goddess of that name. Before Charles, the conqueror of Saxony, and his missionary, Winfrid,[1] had baptized the subjugated inhabitants of the Harz, Lora was held in great veneration by the Saxons of those parts. To her was consecrated a large awe-inspiring forest, the remains of which, even at the present day, almost involuntarily, and as it were by enchantment, transport our thoughts

---

[1]The apostle of Germany, better known by his ecclesiastical name of Boniface. He was born at Crediton in the year 680, and was murdered by the Pagan Frisians in 755. Boniface placed the crown on the head of Pepin, the first monarch of the Carlovingian race, and, besides many monasteries in Germany, founded the sees of Erfurt, Buraburg, Eichstadt, and Wurzburg. He died archbishop of Mentz.

back to ages long passed away. The only memorial of it, at the present day, is a wood of small extent, the abode of numberless flocks of birds, called the Ruhensburg, between the Reinhartsberg, Bleicherode, and the fortress of Lora, together with some detached woods, among which well-built villages, watered by the Wipper, now enliven the delightful landscape, to which the distant Brocken serves as a background.

From this forest the youths, in time of old, offered to the goddess Lora, in the autumn, the first-fruits of the chase; and in the spring, the young maidens, singing joyful songs, brought wreaths of flowers to the goddess. With the finest wreath the high priest of Lora solemnly adorned the head of that maiden who had most distinguished herself by the feminine virtues: by constancy in love, and by unshaken fidelity to her beloved.

In the middle of the mountain on which Lora was principally worshiped there gushed forth a spring, to which a pilgrimage was made by unhappy lovers, especially young maidens, whom death had bereft of their beloved, in the hope that, by drinking of those waters, they might obtain peace and forgetfulness. On the summit of this mountain a noble Saxon lady, whose lover had fallen in a battle with the Franks, built the Ruhensburg,[1] from which the wood derives its present name. She called the spot the Ruhensburg, because in the wood the goddess sent her a new lover worthy of her, whose love comforted the mourner, and gave back to her heart its long-lost peace.

But terrible was this sacred forest to the faithless

---

[1] From ruhe, peace of mind, quiet, and burg, castle.

lover. There Hermtrud expiated her crime with her life. She was betrothed to Eilgern, a noble Saxon youth. The defence of his country tore him from her. At parting, she swore to him, with hypocritical tears, eternal fidelity; but in a few days after, Lora saw the violator of faith and duty in the arms of Herrman. The culprits had concealed themselves in the Buchen, a wood not far from the Ruhensburg. Here Lora startled them by a deer that came rushing through the thicket; and Hermtrud fled, and entered, without reflection, Lora's sacred grove. The mountain trembled, and the earth darted forth flames, which consumed the false-hearted fair one. The priests hastened to the spot, collected Hermtrud's ashes, and buried them in a little valley at the foot of the mountain. Here may still be heard at twilight the mournful wail of the false one, a warning to all faithless lovers not to enter the sacred grove.

Winfrid, the terror of Saxon gods, together with his companions, destroyed the Ruhensburg; for Lora's might had then fled. The following act of revenge exhausted her last remaining powers. Not far from the Reinhartsberg she overtook Winfrid, exulting in his spiritual victories. His carriage and horses suddenly stuck fast in the mire; and he would have been instantly swallowed up, had not his prayers to the Holy Virgin saved him. In memory of this danger he erected three crosses, which are yet to be seen, on the spot where the abyss opened its jaws to receive him, and in his misery dedicated, in Lora's wood, a chapel to the Virgin. From this event the place is still called Elend (Misery).

THE GOATHERD.

(THE STORY WHICH SUGGESTED TO WASHINGTON IRVING THE LEGEND OF SLEEPY HOLLOW—RIP VAN WINKLE.)

PETER CLAUS, a goatherd from Sittendorf, who led his herd to pasture on the Kyffhauser, was accustomed in the evening to stop and let them rest in a place inclosed by old walls, and there to count them.

He had observed for several days that one of his finest goats, as soon as they came to this place, disappeared, and did not follow the herd till quite late. He watched it more closely, and saw that it crept through a rent in the wall. He followed and found it in a cave comfortably enjoying some oats which were falling from the roof. He looked up at seeing the rain of oats, but with all his peering, was unable to solve the mystery. At length he heard the neighing and stamping of horses overhead, from whose cribs the oats must have fallen.

While the goatherd was thus standing, lost in astonishment at hearing the sound of horses in such an uninhabited mountain, a young man suddenly appeared, who silently beckoned Peter to follow him. The goatherd ascended some steps, and came through a walled courtyard to a deep dell, inclosed by steep craggy precipices, down into which a dim light penetrated through the dense foliage of the overhanging branches. Here he found, on a well-levelled, cool grass-plot, twelve grave knightly personages playing at skittles, not one of them uttering a word. Peter was silently directed to set up the fallen skittles.

He began his task with trembling knees, when with a stolen glance he viewed the long beards and slashed doublets of the noble knights. By degrees, however, use made him bolder; he gazed around him with a more observing eye, and at length ventured to drink from a can that stood near him, the wine in which exhaled towards him a delicious fragrance. He felt as if inspired with new life, and as often as he was fatigued, he drew fresh strength from the inexhaustible wine-can. But at length he was overpowered by sleep.

When he awoke, he found himself again on the inclosed plain, where his goats had been accustomed to rest. He rubbed his eyes, but could see neither dog nor goats; he was astonished at the height of the grass, and at the sight of shrubs and trees which he had never before observed. Shaking his head, he walked on through all the ways and paths, along which he had been in the daily habit of wandering with his herd; but nowhere could he find a trace of his goats. At his feet he saw Sittendorf, and with quickened steps began to descend the mountain, for the purpose of inquiring in the village after his herd. The people he met coming from the village were all strangers to him, and differently clad, and did not even speak like his acquaintances; every one stared at him, when he inquired after his goats, and stroked their chins; he unconsciously did the same, and found, to his astonishment, that his beard was more than a foot long. He began to think that both himself and all around were bewitched;

nevertheless, he recognised the mountain he had just descended as the Kyffhauser; the houses also with their gardens were familiar to him; some boys, too, when asked by a traveller the name of the place, answered: "Sittendorf."

He now walked up the village towards his own hut. He found it in a very ruinous condition: before it lay a strange herd-boy, in a ragged jacket, and by him a half-famished dog, which showed its teeth and snarled when he called to it.

He passed through an opening where once had been a door; when he entered he found all void and desolate. Like a drunken man he reeled out at the back-door, calling on wife and children by name. But no one heard—no voice answered. Soon many women and children collected round the old graybeard, all eagerly asking him what he sought. To ask before his own house after his wife and children, or after himself, appeared to him so extraordinary, that, in order to get rid of his questioners, he named the first one that recurred to his memory, "Kurt Steffen!" All were now silent and looked at each other. At length an aged woman said: "For more than twelve years he has dwelt under the Sachsenburg, but you will not get so far to-day." "Where is Velter Meier?" "God be merciful to him," answered an old crone, leaning on her crutches, "for more than fifteen years he has lain in that house, which he will never leave." Shuddering, he now recognised a neighbour, though, as it seemed to him, grown suddenly old; but he had lost all desire to make further inquiries. There now pressed forward through the inquisitive crowd, a young comely woman with a boy in her arms about a year old, and a little fellow of four years holding by her hand; they were all three the image of his wife. "What is your name?" asked he with astonishment. "Maria." "And your father's?" "God be merciful to him, Peter Claus. It is now twenty years and more that we searched for him a whole day and night upon the Kyffhauser, the herd having come back without him. I was then seven years old."

No longer could the goatherd dissemble: "I am Peter Claus," he exclaimed, "and no other," taking the boy out of his daughter's arms. Every one stood as if petrified, until first one voice and then another exclaimed: "Yes, that is Peter Claus! Welcome, neighbour, welcome after twenty years!"

THE DWELLER IN THE ILSENSTEIN.

HAST thou never seen the beautiful maiden sitting on the Ilsenstein? Every morning with the first beams of the sun, she opens the rock and goes down to the Ilse to bathe in its clear cold waters. True, the power of seeing her is not granted to every one, but those who have seen her, praise her beauty and benevolence. She often dispenses the treasures contained in the Ilsenstein; and many families owe their prosperity to the lovely maiden.

Once, very early in the morning, a charcoal-burner, proceeding to the forest, saw the maiden sitting on the Ilsenstein. He greeted her in a friendly tone, and she beckoned to him to follow her. He went, and they soon stood before the great rock. She knocked thrice, and the Ilsenstein opened. She entered, and brought him back his wallet filled, but strictly enjoined him not to open it till he reached his hut. He took it with thanks. As he proceeded, he was struck by the weight of the wallet, and would gladly have seen what it contained. At length, when he came to the bridge across the Ilse, he could no longer withstand his curiosity. He opened it, and saw in it acorns and fir-cones. Indignant he shook the cones and acorns from the bridge down into the swollen stream, when he instantly heard a loud jingling as the acorns and cones touched the stones of the Ilse, and found to his dismay that he had shaken out gold. He then very prudently wrapped up the little remnant that he had found in the corners of the wallet, and carried them carefully home; and even this was enough to enable him to purchase a small house and garden.

But who is this maiden? Listen to what our fathers and mothers have told us. At the Deluge, when the waters of the North Sea overflowed the valleys and plains of Lower Saxony, a youth and a maiden, who had been long attached to each other, fled from the North country towards the Harz mountains, in the hope of saving their lives. As the waters rose they also mounted higher and higher, continually approaching the Brocken, which in the distance appeared to offer them a safe retreat. At length they stood upon a vast rock, which reared its head far above the raging waters. From this spot they saw the whole surrounding country covered by the flood, and houses, and animals, and men had disappeared. Here they stood alone and gazed on the foaming waves, which dashed against the foot of the rock.

The waters rose still higher, and already they thought of fleeing farther over a yet uncovered ridge of rock, and climbing to the summit of the Brocken, which appeared like a large island rising above the billowy sea.

At this moment the rock on which they stood trembled under their feet and split asunder, threatening every instant to separate the lovers. On the left side towards the Brocken stood the maiden, on the right the youth; their hands were firmly clasped in each other's; the precipice inclined right and left outwards; the maiden and the youth sank into the flood.

The maiden was called Ilse, and she gave her name to the beautiful Ilsenthal, to the river which flows through it, and to the Ilsenstein, in which she still dwells.

THE ROSSTRAPPE; OR, HORSE'S FOOT-MARK.

THE Rosstrappe, or Horse's Foot-mark, is the name of a rock in the lofty projection of the Harz behind Thale, with an oval cavity bearing some resemblance to the impression of a gigantic horse's hoof, which many passengers ascend, on account of the beautiful romantic Swiss-like view from its summit.

Popular tradition gives the following account of the cavity.

More than a thousand years ago, before the robber-knights had erected the surrounding castles of Hoymburg, Leuenburg, Steckelnburg, and Winzenburg, the whole country round the Harz was inhabited by giants, who were heathens and sorcerers. They knew no other pleasure than murder, rapine, and violence. If in want of weapons, they tore up the nearest sexagenarian oak, and fought with it. Whatever stood in their way they beat down with their clubs, and the women who pleased them they carried off by force, to be either their servants or wives.

In the Bohemian forest there lived at that time a giant named Bohdo, of vast stature and strength, and the terror of the whole country; every giant in Bohemia and Franconia crouched before him; but he could not prevail on Emma, the daughter of the king of the Riesengebirge,[1] to return his love. Here neither strength nor stratagem availed him aught; for she stood in compact with a mighty spirit. One day Bohdo caught sight of his beloved as she was hunting on the Schneekoppe, and instantly saddled his horse, which could spring over the plains at the rate of five miles a minute, and swore by all the powers of darkness to obtain Emma this time or perish in the attempt. Quicker than the hawk flies he darted forward, and had almost overtaken her before she was aware that her enemy was so near. But when she saw him only nine miles behind, and knew him by the gates of a destroyed town, which served him as a shield, she hastily urged on her horse. And it flew, impelled by her spurs, from mountain to mountain, from cliff to cliff, through valleys, morasses and forests, so that the beeches

[1]Or Giant-mountains, a chain of mountains which separate Silesia from Bohemia, the highest of which is the Schneekoppe.

and oaks were scattered like so much stubble by the force of her horse's hoofs. Thus she fled through the country of Thuringia, and came to the mountains of the Harz. From time to time she heard behind her the snorting of Bohdo's horse, and then pushed on her yet unwearied steed to new exertions.

Her horse now stood snorting and panting on the frightful rock which, from the evil one holding his revels there, is called the Devil's Dancing-place. Emma cast a fearful glance around, her horse trembled as it looked into the abyss, for the precipice was perpendicular as a tower, and more than a thousand feet down to the yawning gulf below. She heard the hollow rushing of the water under her feet, which here formed a frightful whirlpool. The opposite rock, on the other side of the precipice, appeared to her even more distant than the abyss, and hardly to afford space enough for one of her horse's fore-feet.

Here she stood, anxious and doubtful. Behind her was an enemy whom she dreaded more than death itself. Before her was the abyss, which opened its jaws towards her. Emma now again heard the snorting of Bohdo's panting horse. In her terror she called upon the spirits of her fathers for help, and without reflection pressed the ell-long spurs into the sides of her steed; and she sprang! sprang across over the abyss, and happily reached the opposite rock; but it struck its hoofs four feet deep into the hard stone, so that the flying sparks illumined the whole country around like lightning. This is the *horse's foot-mark*. Time has made the hollow less, but no rains can entirely efface it.

Emma was saved! but the gold crown which she wore, and which weighed a hundred pounds, fell into the abyss as the horse sprang across it. Bohdo, who saw only Emma and not the abyss, sprang after the fugitive, and fell with his horse into the vortex of the stream, to which he gave its name.[1]

Here, changed into a black dog, he guards the princess's golden crown, that no thirster after gold may raise it up from the foaming gulf. A diver once, induced by large promises, tried to obtain it. He descended into the abyss, found the crown, and raised it so high, that all the assembled people could see the rays of it. Twice it fell from his hands, and the spectators called to him to descend a third time. He did so, and—a stream of blood rose high up in the air. The diver never appeared again.

With fear and horror the traveller now approaches the gulf, which is covered with the darkness of night. The stillness of the grave reigns over the abyss. No birds fly over it, and, in the dead of the night, may often be heard in the distance the hollow dog-like howl of the heathen

At the present day the whirlpool where the dog guards the golden crown is called the Kreetpfuhl,[2] and the rock where Emma implored the aid of the spirits of her fathers, the Devil's Dancing-place.

---

[1] The Bode, which, with the Emme and the Saale, flows into the Elbe.
[2] That is, the devil's pool. So Kreetkind, the devil's child, in the dialect of those parts.

KING WALDEMAR.[1]

NOT far from Bau there stood formerly the hunting-seat of Waldemarstoft, where King Waldemar was accustomed to pass the summer and autumn, that he might enjoy his favourite diversion of the chase. The king once, accompanied by many huntsmen and dogs, rode early in the morning to the forest. The hunt was good, but the more game they found, the stronger grew his desire to continue the chase. The day ended, the sun went down, yet still he did not give in. But when dark night set it, and it was no longer possible to continue the sport, the king exclaimed: "Oh! that I could hunt for ever!" A voice was then heard in the air, saying: "Thy wish shall be granted, King Waldemar, from this hour thou shalt hunt for ever." Soon after the king died, and from the day of his death he rides every night, on a snow-white horse, through the air, in furious chase, surrounded by his huntsmen and dogs. It is only on St. John's night that he is to be heard; but in the city-ditch at Flensborg he has been also heard in the autumn. The air then resounds with the echo of the horn and the baying of dogs, with whistling and calling, as if a whole party were in motion. People then say, "There goes King Waldemar!"

The old hunting-place is now converted into an inn; but one of the rooms still remains in the same state it was

[1]This was Waldemar IV., king of Denmark. He reigned from 1334 to 1375. He is distinguished by the sobriquet of Atterdag, given him, it is said, in consequence of a phrase he was constantly using: "Morgen er atter en dag," To-morrow is again a day.

in when inhabited by King Waldemar. The walls are covered with old pictures; in one corner is a canopy-bed over which is a dark red velvet coverlet, bordered with gold fringe, in very tolerable preservation. There is also an old organ, on which the king was in the habit of playing. In this room he was once shot at. The murderer fired through the door, but missed his aim, and hit the wall where the king's picture hung. There is a hole in the picture through which the bullet passed before it entered the wall, where the mark is still visible.

WHY THE SEA IS SALT.

ONCE on a time, but it was a long, long time ago, there were two brothers, one rich and one poor. Now, one Christmas eve, the poor one hadn't so much as a crumb in the house, either of meat or bread, so he went to his brother to ask him for something to keep Christmas with, in God's name. It was not the first time his brother had been forced to help him, and you may fancy he wasn't very glad to see his face, but he said—

"If you will do what I ask you to do, I'll give you a whole flitch of bacon."

So the poor brother said he would do anything, and was full of thanks.

"Well, here is the flitch," said the rich brother, "and now go straight to Hell."

"What I have given my word to do, I must stick to," said the other; so he took the flitch and set off. He

walked the whole day, and at dusk he came to a place
where he saw a very bright light.

"Maybe this is the place," said the man to himself. So
he turned aside, and the first thing he saw was an old,
old man, with a long white beard, who stood in an out-
house, hewing wood for the Christmas fire.

"Good even," said the man with the flitch.

"The same to you; whither are you going so late?"
said the man.

"Oh! I'm going to Hell, if I only knew the right way,"
answered the poor man.

"Well, you're not far wrong, for this is Hell," said the
old man; "when you get inside they will be all for buying
your flitch, for meat is scarce in Hell; but mind, you
don't sell it unless you get the hand-quern which stands
behind the door for it. When you come out, I'll teach
you how to handle the quern, for it's good to grind almost
anything."

So the man with the flitch thanked the other for his
good advice, and gave a great knock at the Devil's door.

When he got in, everything went just as the old man
had said. All the devils, great and small, came swarm-
ing up to him like ants round an anthill, and each tried to
outbid the other for the flitch.

"Well!" said the man, "by rights my old dame and I
ought to have this flitch for our Christmas dinner; but
since you have all set your hearts on it, I suppose I must
give it up to you; but if I sell it at all, I'll have for it
that quern behind the door yonder."

At first the Devil wouldn't hear of such a bargain, and

chaffered and haggled with the man; but he stuck to what he said, and at last the Devil had to part with his quern. When the man got out into the yard, he asked the old woodcutter how he was to handle the quern; and after he had learned how to use it, he thanked the old man and went off home as fast as he could, but still the clock had struck twelve on Christmas eve before he reached his own door.

"Wherever in the world have you been?" said his old dame; "here have I sat hour after hour waiting and watching, without so much as two sticks to lay together under the Christmas brose."

"Oh!" said the man, "I couldn't get back before, for I had to go a long way first for one thing, and then for another; but now you shall see what you shall see."

So he put the quern on the table, and bade it first of all grind lights, then a table-cloth, then meat, then ale, and so on till they had got everything that was nice for Christmas fare. He had only to speak the word, and the quern ground out what he wanted. The old dame stood by blessing her stars, and kept on asking where he had got this wonderful quern, but he wouldn't tell her.

"It's all one where I got it from; you see the quern is a good one, and the mill-stream never freezes, that's enough."

So he ground meat and drink and dainties enough to last out till Twelfth Day, and on the third day he asked all his friends and kin to his house, and gave a great feast. Now, when his rich brother saw all that was on the table, and all that was behind in the larder, he grew quite spite-

ful and wild, for he couldn't bear that his brother should
have anything.

" 'Twas only on Christmas eve," he said to the rest,
"he was in such straits, that he came and asked for a
morsel of food in God's name, and now he gives a feast
as if he were count or king;" and he turned to his brother
and said,—

"But whence, in Hell's name, have you got all this
wealth?"

"From behind the door," answered the owner of the
quern, for he didn't care to let the cat out of the bag.
But later on the evening, when he had got a drop too
much, he could keep his secret no longer, and brought
out the quern and said—

"There, you see what has gotten me all this wealth;"
and so he made the quern grind all kind of things.
When his brother saw it, he set his heart on having the
quern, and, after a deal of coaxing, he got it; but he had
to pay three hundred dollars for it, and his brother bar-
gained to keep it till hay-harvest, for he thought, if I keep
it till then, I can make it grind meat and drink that will
last for years. So you may fancy the quern didn't grow
rusty for want of work, and when hay-harvest came, the
rich brother got it, but the other took care not to teach
him how to handle it.

It was evening when the rich brother got the quern
home, and next morning he told his wife to go out into
the hay-field and toss, while the mowers cut the grass,
and he would stay at home and get the dinner ready.
So, when dinner-time drew near, he put the quern on the
kitchen table and said,— 159

"Grind herrings and broth, and grind them good and fast."

So the quern began to grind herrings and broth; first of all, all the dishes full, then all the tubs full, and so on till the kitchen floor was quite covered. Then the man twisted and twirled at the quern to get it to stop, but for all his twisting and fingering the quern went on grinding, and in a little while the broth rose so high that the man was like to drown. So he threw open the kitchen door and ran into the parlour, but it wasn't long before the quern had ground the parlour full too, and it was only at the risk of his life that the man could get hold of the latch of the house door through the stream of broth. When he got the door open, he ran out and set off down the road, with the stream of herrings and broth at his heels, roaring like a waterfall over the whole farm.

Now, his old dame, who was in the field tossing hay, thought it a long time to dinner, and at last she said—

"Well! though the master doesn't call us home, we may as well go. Maybe he finds it hard work to boil the broth, and will be glad of my help."

The men were willing enough, so they sauntered homewards; but just as they had got a little way up the hill, what should they meet but herrings, and broth, and bread, all running and dashing, and splashing together in a stream, and the master himself running before them for his life, and as he passed them he bawled out,—"Would to heaven each of you had a hundred throats! but take care you're not drowned in the broth."

Away he went, as though the Evil One were at his

heels, to his brother's house, and begged him for God's sake to take back the quern that instant; for, said he—

"If it grinds only one hour more, the whole parish will be swallowed up by herrings and broth."

But his brother wouldn't hear of taking it back till the other paid him down three hundred dollars more.

So the poor brother got both the money and the quern, and it wasn't long before he set up a farm-house far finer than the one in which his brother lived, and with the quern he ground so much gold that he covered it with plates of gold; and as the farm lay by the sea-side, the golden house gleamed and glistened far away over the sea. All who sailed by put ashore to see the rich man in the golden house, and to see the wonderful quern, the fame of which spread far and wide, till there was nobody who hadn't heard tell of it.

So one day there came a skipper who wanted to see the quern; and the first thing he asked was if it could grind salt.

"Grind salt!" said the owner; "I should just think it could. It can grind anything."

When the skipper heard that, he said he must have the quern, cost what it would; for if he only had it, he thought he should be rid of his long voyage across stormy seas for a lading of salt. Well, at first the man wouldn't hear of parting with the quern; but the skipper begged and prayed so hard, that at last he let him have it, but he had to pay many, many thousand dollars for it. Now, when the skipper had got the quern on his back, he soon made off with it, for he was afraid lest the man should change his mind; so he had no time to ask how to handle the quern, but got on board his ship as fast as he could, and set sail. When he had sailed a good way off, he brought the quern on deck and said—

"Grind salt, and grind both good and fast."

Well, the quern began to grind salt so that it poured out like water; and when the skipper had got the ship full, he wished to stop the quern, but whichever way he turned it, and however much he tried, it was no good; the quern kept grinding on, and the heap of salt grew higher and higher, and at last down sunk the ship.

There lies the quern at the bottom of the sea, and grinds away at this very day, and that's why the sea is salt.

THE TWELVE WHITE PEACOCKS.

ONCE on a time there was a Queen who was out driving, when there had been a new fall of snow in the winter; but when she had gone a little way, she began to bleed at the nose, and had to get out of her sledge. And so, as she stood there, leaning against the fence, and saw the red blood on the white snow, she fell a-thinking how she had twelve sons and no daughter, and she said to herself,

"If I only had a daughter as white as snow and as red as blood, I shouldn't care what became of all my sons."

But the words were scarce out of her mouth before an old witch of the Trolls came up to her.

"A daughter you shall have," she said, "and she shall be as white as snow, and as red as blood; but your sons shall be mine, though you may keep them till the babe is christened."

So when the time came the Queen had a daughter, and she was as white as snow, and as red as blood, just as the Troll had promised, and so they called her "Snow-white and Rosy-red." Well, there was great joy at the King's court, and the Queen was as glad as glad could be; but when what she had promised to the old witch came into her mind, she sent for a silversmith, and bade him make twelve silver spoons, one for each prince, and after that she bade him make one more, and that she gave to Snow-white and Rosy-red. But as soon as ever the Princess was christened, the Princes were turned into twelve white peacocks, and flew away. They never saw them again,—away they went, and away they stayed.

So the Princess grew up, and she was both tall and fair, but she was often so strange and sorrowful, and no one could understand what it was that ailed her. But one evening the Queen was also sorrowful, for she had many strange thoughts when she thought of her sons. She said to Snow-white and Rosy-red,

"Why are you so sorrowful, my daughter? Is there anything you want? if so, only say the word, and you shall have it."

"Oh, it seems so dull and lonely here," said Snow-white and Rosy-red; "every one else has brothers and sisters, but I am all alone; I have none; and that's why I'm so sorrowful."

"But you *had* brothers, my daughter," said the Queen; "I had twelve sons who were your brothers, but I gave them all away to get you;" and so she told her the whole story.

So when the Princess heard that, she had no rest; for, in spite of all the Queen could say or do, and all she wept and prayed, the lassie would set off to seek her brothers, for she thought it was all her fault; and at last she got leave to go away from the palace. On and on she walked into the wide world, so far, you would never have thought a young lady could have strength to walk so far.

So, once, when she was walking through a great, great wood, one day she felt tired, and sat down on a mossy tuft and fell asleep. Then she dreamt that she went deeper and deeper into the wood, till she came to a little wooden hut, and there she found her brothers; just then she woke, and straight before her she saw a worn path in the green moss, and this path went deeper into the wood; so she followed it, and after a long time she came to just such a little wooden house as that she had seen in her dream.

Now, when she went into the room there was no one at home, but there stood twelve beds, and twelve chairs, and twelve spoons—a dozen of everything, in short. So when she saw that she was so glad, she hadn't been so glad for many a long year, for she could guess at once that her brothers lived here, and that they owned the beds, and chairs, and spoons. So she began to make up the fire, and sweep the room, and make the beds, and cook the dinner, and to make the house as tidy as she could; and when she had done all the cooking and work, she ate her own dinner, and crept under her youngest brother's bed, and lay down there, but she forgot her spoon upon the table.

So she had scarcely laid herself down before she heard something flapping and whirring in the air, and so all the twelve white peacocks came sweeping in; but as soon as ever they crossed the threshold they became Princes.

"Oh, how nice and warm it is in here," they said. "Heaven bless him who made up the fire, and cooked such a good dinner for us."

And so each took up his silver spoon and was going to eat. But when each had taken his own, there was one still left lying on the table, and it was so like the rest that they couldn't tell it from them.

"This is our sister's spoon," they said; "and if her spoon be here, she can't be very far off herself."

"If this be our sister's spoon, and she be here," said the eldest, "she shall be killed, for she is to blame for all the ill we suffer."

And this she lay under the bed and listened to.

"No," said the youngest, "'twere a shame to kill her for that. She has nothing to do with our suffering ill; for if any one's to blame, it's our own mother."

So they set to work hunting for her both high and low, and at last they looked under all the beds, and so when they came to the youngest Prince's bed, they found her, and dragged her out. Then the eldest Prince wished again to have her killed, but she begged and prayed so prettily for herself.

"Oh! gracious goodness! don't kill me, for I've gone

165

about seeking you these three years, and if I could only set you free, I'd willingly lose my life."

"Well!" said they, "if you will set us free, you may keep your life; for you can if you choose."

"Yes; only tell me," said the Princess, "how it can be done, and I'll do it, whatever it be."

"You must pick thistle-down," said the Princes, "and you must card it, and spin it, and weave it; and after you have done that, you must cut out and make twelve coats, and twelve shirts, and twelve neckerchiefs, one for each of us, and while you do that, you must neither talk, nor laugh, nor weep. If you can do that, we are free."

"But where shall I ever get thistle-down enough for so many neckerchiefs, and shirts, and coats?" asked Snow-white and Rosy-red.

"We'll soon show you," said the Princes; and so they took her with them to a great wide moor, where there stood such a crop of thistles, all nodding and nodding in the breeze, and the down all floating and glistening like gossamers through the air in the sunbeams. The Princess had never seen such a quantity of thistle-down in her life, and she began to pluck and gather it as fast and as well as he could; and when she got home at night she set to work carding and spinning yarn from the down. So she went on a long long time, picking, and carding, and spinning, and all the while keeping the Princes' house, cooking, and making their beds. At evening home they came, flapping and whirring like wild birds, and all night they were Princes, but in the morning off they flew again, and were white peacocks the whole day.

But now it happened once, when she was out on the moor to pick thistle-down,—and if I don't mistake, it was the very last time she was to go thither,—it happened that the young King who ruled that land was out hunting, and came riding across the moor, and saw her. So he stopped there and wondered who the lovely lady could be that walked along the moor picking thistle-down, and he asked her her name, and when he could get no answer, he was still more astonished; and at last he liked her so much, that nothing would do but he must take her home to his castle and marry her. So he ordered his servants to take her and put her up on his horse. Snow-white and Rosy-red, she wrung her hands, and made signs to them, and pointed to the bags in which her work was, and when the King saw she wished to have them with her, he told his men to take up the bags behind them. When they had done that the Princess came to herself, little by little, for the King was both a wise man and a handsome man too, and he was as soft and kind to her as a doctor. But when they got home to the palace, and the old Queen, who was his stepmother, set eyes on Snow-white and Rosy-red, she got so cross and jealous of her because she was so lovely, that she said to the king,—

"Can't you see now, that this thing whom you have picked up, and whom you are going to marry, is a witch. Why? she can't either talk, or laugh, or weep!"

But the King didn't care a pin for what she said, but held on with the wedding, and married Snow-white and Rosy-red, and they lived in great joy and glory; but she didn't forget to go on sewing at her shirts.

So when the year was almost out, Snow-white and Rosy-red brought a Prince into the world; and then the old Queen was more spiteful and jealous than ever, and at dead of night, she stole in to Snow-white and Rosy-red, while she slept, and took away her babe, and threw it into a pit full of snakes. After that she cut Snow-white and Rosy-red in her finger, and smeared the blood over her mouth, and went straight to the King.

"Now come and see," she said, "what sort of a thing you have taken for your Queen; here she has eaten up her own babe."

Then the King was so downcast, he almost burst into tears, and said,—

"Yes, it must be true, since I see it with my own eyes; but she'll not do it again, I'm sure, and so this time I'll spare her life."

So before the next year was out she had another son, and the same thing happened. The King's stepmother got more and more jealous and spiteful. She stole into the young Queen at night while she slept, took away the babe, and threw it into a pit full of snakes, cut the young Queen's finger, and smeared the blood over her mouth, and then went and told the King she had eaten up her own child. Then the King was so sorrowful, you can't think how sorry he was, and he said,—

"Yes, it must be true, since I see it with my own eyes; but she'll not do it again, I'm sure, and so this time too I'll spare her life."

Well, before the next year was out, Snow-white and Rosy-red brought a daughter into the world, and her, too, the old Queen took and threw into the pit full of snakes, while the young Queen slept. Then she cut her finger, smeared the blood over her mouth, and went again to the King and said, —

"Now you may come and see if it isn't as I say; she's a wicked, wicked witch, for here she has gone and eaten up her third babe too."

Then the King was so sad, there was no end to it, for now he couldn't spare her any longer, but had to order her to be burnt alive on a pile of wood. But just when the pile was all a-blaze, and they were going to put her on it, she made signs to them to take twelve boards and lay them round the pile, and on these she laid the neckerchiefs, and the shirts, and the coats for her brothers, but the youngest brother's shirt wanted its left arm, for she hadn't had time to finish it. And as soon as ever she had done that, they heard such a flapping and whirring in the air, and down came twelve white peacocks flying over the forest, and each of them snapped up his clothes in his bill and flew off with them.

"See now!" said the old Queen to the King, "wasn't I right when I told you she was a witch; but make haste and burn her before the pile burns low."

"Oh!" said the King, "we've wood enough and to spare, and so I'll wait a bit, for I have a mind to see what the end of all this will be."

As he spoke, up came the twelve princes riding along, as handsome well-grown lads as you'd wish to see; but the youngest prince had a peacock's wing instead of his left arm.

"What's all this about?" asked the Princes.

"My Queen is to be burnt," said the King, "because she's a witch, and because she has eaten up her own babes."

"She hasn't eaten them at all," said the Princes. "Speak now, sister; you have set us free and saved us, now save yourself."

Then Snow-white and Rosy-red spoke, and told the whole story; how every time she was brought to bed, the old Queen, the King's stepmother, had stolen into her at night, had taken her babes away, and cut her little finger, and smeared the blood over her mouth; and then the Princes took the King, and showed him the snake-pit where three babes lay playing with adders and toads, and lovelier children you never saw.

So the King had them taken out at once, and went to his stepmother, and asked her what punishment she thought that woman deserved who could find it in her heart to betray a guiltless Queen and three such blessed little babes.

"She deserves to be fast bound between twelve unbroken steeds, so that each may take his share of her," said the old Queen.

"You have spoken your own doom," said the King, "and you shall suffer it at once."

So the wicked old Queen was fast bound between twelve unbroken steeds, and each got his share of her. But the King took Snow-white and Rosy-red, and their three children, and the twelve Princes; and so they all went home to their father and mother, and told all that had befallen them, and there was joy and gladness over the whole kingdom, because the Princess was saved and set free, and because she had set free her twelve brothers.

THE MASTER-SMITH.

ONCE on a time, in the days when our Lord and St. Peter used to wander on earth, they came to a smith's house. He had made a bargain with the Devil, that the fiend should have him after seven years, but during that time he was to be the master of all masters in his trade, and to this bargain both he and the Devil had signed their names. So he had stuck up in great letters over the door of his forge,—

"Here dwells the Master over all Masters."

Now when our Lord passed by and saw that, he went in.

"Who are you?" he said to the Smith.

"Read what's written over the door," said the Smith; "but maybe you can't read writing. If so, you must wait till some one comes to help you."

Before our Lord had time to answer him, a man came with his horse, which he begged the Smith to shoe.

"Might I have leave to shoe it?" asked our Lord.

"You may try if you like," said the Smith; "you can't do it so badly that I shall not be able to make it right again."

So our Lord went out and took one leg off the horse, and laid it in the furnace, and made the shoe red-hot;

171

after that, he turned up the ends of the shoe, and filed down the heads of the nails, and clenched the points; and then he put back the leg safe and sound on the horse again. And when he was done with that leg, he took the other fore-leg and did the same with it; and when he was done with that, he took the hind-legs—first, the off, and then the near leg, and laid them in the furnace, making the shoes red-hot, turning up the ends, filing the heads of the nails, and clenching the points; and after all was done, putting the legs on the horse again. All the while, the Smith stood by and looked on.

"You're not so bad a smith after all," said he.

"Oh, you think so, do you?" said our Lord.

A little while after came the Smith's mother to the forge, and called him to come home and eat his dinner; she was an old, old woman with an ugly crook on her back, and wrinkles in her face, and it was as much as she could do to crawl along.

"Mark now, what you see," said our Lord.

Then he took the woman and laid her in the furnace, and smithied a lovely young maiden out of her.

"Well," said the Smith, "I say now, as I said before, you are not such a bad smith after all. There it stands over my door. *Here dwells the Master over all Masters;* but for all that, I say right out, one learns as long as one lives;" and with that he walked off to his house and ate his dinner.

So after dinner, just after he had got back to his forge, a man came riding up to have his horse shod.

"It shall be done in the twinkling of an eye," said the

Smith, "for I have just learnt a new way to shoe; and a very good way it is when the days are short."

So he began to cut and hack till he had got all the horse's legs off, for he said, "I don't know why one should go pottering backwards and forwards—first, with one leg, and then with another."

Then he laid the legs in the furnace, just as he had seen our Lord lay them, and threw on a great heap of coal, and made his mates work the bellows bravely; but it went as one might suppose it would go. The legs were burnt to ashes, and the Smith had to pay for the horse.

Well, he didn't care much about that, but just then an old beggar-woman came along the road, and he thought to himself, "better luck next time;" so he took the old dame and laid her in the furnace, and though she begged and prayed hard for her life, it was no good.

"You're so old, you don't know what is good for you," said the Smith; "now you shall be a lovely young maiden in half no time, and for all that, I'll not charge you a penny for the job."

But it went no better with the poor old woman than with the horse's legs.

"That was ill done, and I say it," said our Lord.

"Oh! for that matter," said the Smith, "there's not many who'll ask after her, I'll be bound; but it's a shame of the Devil, if this is the way he holds to what is written up over the door."

"If you might have three wishes from me," said our Lord, "what would you wish for?"

"Only try me," said the Smith, "and you'll soon know."

So our Lord gave him three wishes.

"Well," said the Smith, "first and foremost, I wish that any one whom I ask to climb up into the pear-tree that stands outside by the wall of my forge, may stay sitting there till I ask him to come down again. The second wish I wish is, that any one whom I ask to sit down in my easy chair which stands inside the workshop yonder, may stay sitting there till I ask him to get up. Last of all, I wish that any one whom I ask to creep into the steel purse which I have in my pocket, may stay in it till I give him leave to creep out again."

"You have wished as a wicked man," said St. Peter; "first and foremost, you should have wished for God's grace and good will."

"I durst n't look so high as that," said the Smith; and after that our Lord and St. Peter bade him "good-by," and went on their way.

Well, the years went on and on, and when the time was up, the Devil came to fetch the Smith, as it was written in their bargain.

"Are you ready?" he said, as he stuck his nose in at the door of the forge.

"Oh," said the Smith, "I must just hammer the head of this tenpenny nail first; meantime, you can just climb up into the pear-tree, and pluck yourself a pear to gnaw at; you must be both hungry and thirsty after your journey."

So the Devil thanked him for his kind offer, and climbed up into the pear-tree.

"Very good," said the Smith; "but now, on thinking

the matter over, I find I shall never be able to have done hammering the head of this nail till four years are out at least, this iron is so plaguy hard; down you can't come in all that time, but may sit up there and rest your bones."

When the Devil heard this, he begged and prayed till his voice was as thin as a silver penny that he might have leave to come down; but there was no help for it. There he was, and there he must stay. At last he had to give his word of honour not to come again till the four years were out, which the Smith had spoken of, and then the Smith said, "Very well, now you may come down."

So when the time was up, the Devil came again to fetch the Smith.

"You're ready now, of course," said he; "you've had time enough to hammer the head of that nail, I should think."

"Yes, the head is right enough now," said the Smith; "but still you have come a little tiny bit too soon, for I haven't quite done sharpening the point; such plaguy hard iron I never hammered in all my born days. So while I work at the point, you may just as well sit down in my easy chair and rest yourself; I'll be bound you're weary after coming so far."

"Thank you kindly," said the Devil, and down he plumped into the easy chair; but just as he had made himself comfortable, the Smith said, on second thoughts, he found he couldn't get the point sharp till four years were out. First of all, the Devil begged so prettily to be let out of the chair, and afterwards, waxing wroth, he began to threaten and scold; but the Smith kept on, all the while excusing himself, and saying it was all the iron's fault, it was so plaguy hard, and telling the Devil he was not so badly off to have to sit quietly in an easy chair, and that he would let him out to the minute when the four years were over. Well, at last there was no help for it, and the Devil had to give his word of honour not to fetch the Smith till the four years were out; and then the Smith said,—

"Well now, you may get up and be off about your business," and away went the Devil as fast as he could lay legs to the ground.

When the four years were over, the Devil came again to fetch the Smith, and he called out, as he stuck his nose in at the door of the forge,—

"Now, I know you must be ready."

"Ready, aye, ready," answered the Smith; "we can go now as soon as you please; but hark ye, there is one thing I have stood here and thought, and thought, I would ask you to tell me. Is it true what people say, that the Devil can make himself as small as he pleases?"

"God knows, it is the very truth," said the Devil.

"Oh!" said the Smith; "it *is* true, is it? then I wish you would just be so good as to creep into this steel-purse of mine, and see whether it is sound at the bottom, for to tell you the truth, I'm afraid my travelling money will drop out."

"With all my heart," said the Devil, who made himself small in a trice, and crept into the purse; but he was scarce in when the Smith snapped to the clasp.

"Yes," called out the Devil inside the purse; "it's right and tight everywhere."

176

"Very good," said the Smith; "I'm glad to hear you say so, but 'more haste the worse speed,' says the old saw, and 'forewarned is forearmed,' says another; so I'll just weld these links a little together, just for safety's sake;" and with that he laid the purse in the furnace, and made it red-hot.

"AU! AU!" screamed the Devil, "are you mad? don't you know I'm inside the purse?"

"Yes, I do!" said the Smith; "but I can't help you, for another old saw says, 'one must strike while the iron is hot;'" and as he said this, he took up his sledge hammer, laid the purse on the anvil, and let fly at it as hard as he could.

"AU! AU! AU!" bellowed the Devil, inside the purse. "Dear friend, do let me out, and I'll never come near you again."

"Very well!" said the Smith; "now, I think, the links are pretty well welded, and you may come out;" so he unclasped the purse, and away went the Devil in such a hurry that he didn't once look behind him.

Now, some time after, it came across the Smith's mind that he had done a silly thing in making the Devil his enemy, for, he said to himself,—

"If, as is like enough, they won't have me in the kingdom of Heaven, I shall be in danger of being houseless, since I've fallen out with him who rules over Hell."

So he made up his mind it would be best to try to get either into Hell or Heaven, and to try at once, rather than to put it off any longer, so that he might know how things really stood. Then he threw his sledge-hammer over his shoulder and set off; and when he had gone a good bit of the way, he came to a place where two roads met, and where the path to the kingdom of Heaven parts from the path that leads to Hell, and here he overtook a tailor, who was pelting along with his goose in his hand.

"Good day," said the Smith; "whither are you off to?"

"To the kingdom of Heaven," said the Tailor, "if I can only get into it;—but whither are you going yourself?"

"Oh, our ways don't run together," said the Smith; "for I have made up my mind to try first in Hell, as the Devil and I know something of one another, from old times."

So they bade one another "Good bye," and each went his way; but the Smith was a stout, strong man, and got over the ground far faster than the tailor, and so it wasn't long before he stood at the gates of Hell. Then he called the watch, and bade him go and tell the Devil there was some one outside who wished to speak a word with him.

"Go out," said the Devil to the watch, "and ask him who he is?" So that when the watch came out and told him that, the Smith answered,—

"Go and greet the Devil in my name, and say it is the Smith who owns the purse he wots of; and beg him prettily to let me in at once, for I worked at my forge till noon, and I have had a long walk since."

But when the Devil heard who it was, he charged the watch to go back and lock up all the nine locks on the gates of Hell.

"And, besides," he said, "you may as well put on a

padlock, for if he only once gets in, he'll turn Hell topsy-turvy!"

"Well!" said the Smith to himself, when he saw them busy bolting up the gates, "there's no lodging to be got here, that's plain; so I may as well try my luck in the kingdom of Heaven;" and with that he turned round and went back till he reached the cross-roads, and then he went along the path the tailor had taken. And now, as he was cross at having gone backwards and forwards so far for no good, he strode along with all his might, and reached the gate of Heaven just as St. Peter was opening it a very little, just enough to let the half-starved tailor slip in. The Smith was still six or seven strides off the gate, so he thought to himself, "Now there's no time to be lost;" and, grasping his sledge-hammer, he hurled it into the opening of the door just as the tailor slunk in; and if the Smith didn't get in then, when the door was ajar, why I don't know what has become of him.

GUDBRAND ON THE HILL-SIDE.

ONCE on a time there was a man whose name was Gudbrand; he had a farm which lay far, far away upon a hill-side, and so they called him Gudbrand on the Hill-side.

Now, you must know this man and his good wife lived so happily together, and understood one another so well, that all the husband did the wife thought so well done there was nothing like it in the world, and she was always glad whatever he turned his hand to. The farm was their own land, and they had a hundred dollars lying at the bottom of their chest, and two cows tethered up in a stall in their farm-yard.

So one day his wife said to Gudbrand,—

"Do you know, dear, I think we ought to take one of our cows into town and sell it; that's what I think; for then we shall have some money in hand, and such well-to-do people as we ought to have ready money like the rest of the world. As for the hundred dollars at the bottom of the chest yonder, we can't make a hole in them, and I'm sure I don't know what we want with more than one cow. Besides, we shall gain a little in another way, for then I shall get off with only looking after one cow, instead of having, as now, to feed and litter and water two."

Well, Gudbrand thought his wife talked right good sense, so he set off at once with the cow on his way to town to sell her; but when he got to the town, there was no one who would buy his cow.

"Well! well! never mind," said Gudbrand, "at the worst, I can only go back home again with my cow. I've both stable and tether for her, I should think, and the road is no farther out than in;" and with that he began to toddle home with his cow.

But when he had gone a bit of the way, a man met him who had a horse to sell, so Gudbrand thought 'twas better to have a horse than a cow, so he swopped with the man. A little farther on he met a man walking along and driving a fat pig before him, and he thought it better to have a fat pig than a horse, so he swopped with the man. After that he went a little farther, and a man met him with a goat; so he thought it better to have a goat than a pig, and he swopped with the man that owned the goat. Then he went on a bit till he met a man who had a sheep, and he swopped with him too, for he thought it always better to have a sheep than a goat. After a while he met a man with a goose, and he swopped away the sheep for the goose; and when he had walked a long, long time, he met a man with a cock, and he swopped with him, for he thought in this wise, " 'Tis surely better to have a cock than a goose." Then he went on till the day was far spent, and he began to get very hungry, so he sold the cock for a shilling, and bought food with the money, for, thought Gudbrand on the Hill-side, " 'Tis always better to save one's life than to have a cock."

After that he went on home till he reached his nearest neighbour's house, where he turned in.

"Well," said the owner of the house, "how did things go with you in town?"

"Rather so so," said Gudbrand, "I can't praise my luck, nor do I blame it either," and with that he told the whole story from first to last.

"Ah!" said his friend, "you'll get nicely called over the coals, that one can see, when you get home to your wife. Heaven help you, I wouldn't stand in your shoes for something."

"Well!" said Gudbrand on the Hill-side, "I think things might have gone much worse with me; but now, whether I have done wrong or not, I have so kind a good-wife, she never has a word to say against anything that I do."

"Oh!" answered his neighbour, "I hear what you say, but I don't believe it for all that."

"Shall we lay a bet upon it?" asked Gudbrand on the Hill-side. "I have a hundred dollars at the bottom of my chest at home; will you lay as many against them?"

Yes! the friend was ready to bet; so Gudbrand stayed there till evening, when it began to get dark, and then they went together to his house, and the neighbour was to stand outside the door and listen, while the man went in to see his wife.

"Good evening!" said Gudbrand on the Hill-side.

"Good evening!" said the goodwife, "Oh! is that you? now God be praised."

Yes! it was he. So the wife asked how things had gone with him in town?

"Oh! only so so," answered Gudbrand; "not much to brag of. When I got to the town there was no one who would buy the cow, so you must know I swopped it away for a horse."

"For a horse," said hs wife; "well that is good of you; thanks with all my heart. We are so well to do that we may drive to church, just as well as other people; and if we choose to keep a horse we have a right to get one, I should think. So run out, child, and put up the horse."

"Ah!" said Gudbrand, "but you see I've not got the horse after all; for when I got a bit farther on the road, I swopped it away for a pig."

"Think of that, now!" said the wife; "you did just as I should have done myself; a thousand thanks! Now I can have a bit of bacon in the house to set before people when they come to see me, that I can. What do we want with a horse? People would only say we had got so proud that we couldn't walk to church. Go out, child, and put up the pig in the stye."

"But I've not got the pig either," said Gudbrand; "for when I got a little farther on, I swopped it away for a milch goat."

"Bless us!" cried his wife, "how well you manage every thing! Now I think it over, what should I do with a pig? People would only point at us and say, 'Yonder they eat up all they have got.' No! now I have got a goat, and I shall have milk and cheese, and keep the goat too. Run out, child, and put up the goat."

"Nay, but I haven't got the goat either," said Gudbrand, "for a little farther on I swopped it away, and got a fine sheep instead."

"You don't say so!" cried his wife; "why, you do everything to please me, just as if I had been with you;

what do we want with a goat? If I had it I should lose half my time in climbing up the hills to get it down. No! if I have a sheep, I shall have both wool and clothing, and fresh meat in the house. Run out, child, and put up the sheep."

"But I haven't got the sheep any more than the rest," said Gudbrand; "for when I had gone a bit farther, I swopped it away for a goose."

"Thank you! thank you! with all my heart," cried his wife; "what should I do with a sheep? I have no spinning-wheel, nor carding-comb, nor should I care to worry myself with cutting, and shaping, and sewing clothes. We can buy clothes now, as we have always done; and now I shall have roast goose, which I have longed for so often; and, besides, down to stuff my little pillow with. Run out, child, and put up the goose."

"Ah!" said Gudbrand, "but I haven't the goose either; for when I had gone a bit farther I swopped it away for a cock."

"Dear me!" cried his wife, "how you think of everything! just as I should have done myself. A cock! think of that! why it's as good as an eight-day clock, for every morning the cock crows at four o'clock, and we shall be able to stir our stumps in good time. What should we do with a goose? I don't know how to cook it; and as for my pillow, I can stuff it with cotton-grass. Run out, child, and put up the cock."

"But, after all, I haven't got the cock," said Gudbrand; "for when I had gone a bit farther, I got as hungry as a hunter, so I was forced to sell the cock for a shilling, for fear I should starve."

184

"Now, God be praised that you did so!" cried his wife; "whatever you do, you do it always just after my own heart. What should we do with the cock? We are our own masters, I should think, and can lie a-bed in the morning as long as we like. Heaven he thanked that I have got you safe back again; you who do everything so well that I want neither cock nor goose; neither pigs nor kine."

Then Gudbrand opened the door and said,—

"Well, what do you say now? Have I won the hundred dollars?" and his neighbour was forced to allow that he had.

THE BLUE BELT.

ONCE on a time there was an old beggar-woman, who had gone out to beg. She had a little lad with her, and when she had got her bag full, she struck across the hills towards her own home. So when they had gone a bit up the hill-side, they came upon a little blue belt, which lay where two paths met, and the lad asked his mother's leave to pick it up.

"No," said she, "may be there's witchcraft in it;" and so with threats she forced him to follow her. But when they had gone a bit further, the lad said he must turn aside a moment out of the road, and meanwhile his mother sat down on a tree-stump. But the lad was a long time gone, for as soon as he got so far into the wood, that the old dame could not see him, he ran off to where the belt lay, took it up, tied it round his waist, and

185

lo! he felt as strong as if he could lift the whole hill. When he got back, the old dame was in a great rage, and wanted to know what he had been doing all that while. "You don't care how much time you waste, and yet you know the night is drawing on, and we must cross the hill before it is dark!" So on they tramped; but when they had got about half-way, the old dame grew weary, and said she must rest under a bush.

"Dear mother," said the lad, "mayn't I just go up to the top of this high crag while you rest, and try if I can't see some sign of folk hereabouts?"

Yes! he might do that; so when he had got to the top, he saw a light shining from the north. So he ran down and told his mother.

"We must get on, mother; we are near a house, for I see a bright light shining quite close to us in the north." Then she rose and shouldered her bag, and set off to see; but they hadn't gone far, before there stood a steep spur of the hill, right across their path.

"Just as I thought!" said the old dame; "now we can't go a step farther; a pretty bed we shall have here!"

But the lad took the bag under one arm, and his mother under the other, and ran straight up the steep crag with them.

"Now, don't you see! don't you see that we are close to a house! don't you see the bright light?"

But the old dame said those were no Christian folk, but Trolls, for she was at home in all that forest far and near, and knew there was not a living soul in it, until you were well over the ridge, and had come down on the

186

other side. But they went on, and in a little while they came to a great house which was all painted red.

"What's the good?" said the old dame, "we daren't go in, for here the Trolls live."

"Don't say so; we must go in. There must be men where the lights shine so," said the lad. So in he went, and his mother after him, but he had scarce opened the door before she swooned away, for there she saw a great stout man, at least twenty feet high, sitting on the bench.

"Good evening, grandfather!" said the lad.

"Well, here I've sat three hundred years," said the man who sat on the bench, "and no one has ever come and called me grandfather before." Then the lad sat down by the man's side, and began to talk to him as if they had been old friends.

"But what's come over your mother?" said the man, after they had chattered a while. "I think she swooned away; you had better look after her."

So the lad went and took hold of the old dame; and dragged her up the hall along the floor. That brought her to herself, and she kicked, and scratched, and flung herself about, and at last sat down upon a heap of firewood in the corner; but she was so frightened that she scarce dared to look one in the face.

After a while, the lad asked if they could spend the night there.

"Yes, to be sure," said the man.

So they went on talking again, but the lad soon got hungry, and wanted to know if they could get food as well as lodging.

"Of course," said the man, "that might be got too." And after they had sat a while longer, he rose up and threw six loads of dry pitch-pine on the fire. This made the old hag still more afraid.

"Oh! now he's going to roast us alive," she said, in the corner where she sat.

And when the wood had burned down to glowing embers, up got the man and strode out of his house.

"Heaven bless and help us! what a stout heart you have got," said the old dame; "don't you see we have got amongst Trolls?"

"Stuff and nonsense!" said the lad; "no harm if we have."

In a little while back came the man with an ox so fat and big, the lad had never seen its like, and he gave it one blow with his fist under the ear, and down it fell dead on the floor. When that was done, he took it up by all the four legs, and laid it on the glowing embers, and turned it and twisted it about till it was burnt brown outside. After that, he went to a cupboard and took out a great silver dish, and laid the ox on it; and the dish was so big that none of the ox hung over on any side. This he put on the table, and then he went down into the cellar, and fetched a cask of wine, knocked out the head, and put the cask on the table, together with two knives, which were each six feet long. When this was done, he bade them go and sit down to supper and eat. So they went, the lad first and the old dame after, but she began to whimper and wail, and to wonder how she should ever use such knives. But her son seized one, and began to

cut slices out of the thigh of the ox, which he placed
before his mother. And when they had eaten a bit, he
took up the cask with both hands, and lifted it down to
the floor; then he told his mother to come and drink, but
it was still so high she couldn't reach up to it; so he
caught her up, and held her up to the edge of the cask
while she drank; as for himself, he clambered up and
hung down like a cat inside the cask while he drank.
So when he had quenched his thirst, he took up the cask
and put it back on the table, and thanked the man for the
good meal, and told his mother to come and thank him
too, and a-feared though she was, she dared do nothing
else but thank the man. Then the lad sat down again
alongside the man and began to gossip, and after they had
sat a while, the man said—

"Well! I must just go and get a bit of supper too;" and
so he went to the table and ate up the whole ox—hoofs,
and horns, and all—and drained the cask to the last drop,
and then went back and sat on the bench.

"As for beds," he said, "I don't know what's to be
done. I've only got one bed and a cradle; but we could
get on pretty well if you would sleep in the cradle, and
then your mother might lie in the bed yonder."

"Thank you kindly, that'll do nicely," said the lad; and
with that he pulled off his clothes and lay down in the
cradle; but, to tell you the truth, it was quite as big as a
four-poster. As for the old dame, she had to follow the
man who showed her to bed, though she was out of her
wits for fear.

"Well!" thought the lad to himself; "'twill never do

to go to sleep yet. I'd best lie awake and listen how things go as the night wears on."

So after a while the man began to talk to the old dame, and at last he said—

"We two might live here so happily together, could we only be rid of this son of yours."

"But do you know how to settle him? Is that what you're thinking of?" said she.

"Nothing easier," said he; at any rate he would try. He would just say he wished the old dame would stay and keep house for him a day or two, and then he would take the lad out with him up the hill to quarry corner-stones, and roll down a great rock on him. All this the lad lay and listened to.

Next day the Troll—for it was a Troll as clear as day—asked if the old dame would stay and keep house for him a few days; and as the day went on he took a great iron crowbar, and asked the lad if he had a mind to go with him up the hill and quarry a few corner-stones. With all his heart, he said, and went with him; and so, after they had split a few stones, the Troll wanted him to go down below and look after cracks in the rock; and while he was doing this, the Troll worked away, and wearied himself with his crowbar till he moved a whole crag out of its bed, which came rolling right down on the place where the lad was; but he held it up till he could get on one side, and then let it roll on.

"Oh!" said the lad to the Troll, "now I see what you mean to do with me. You want to crush me to death;

so just go down yourself and look after the cracks and rifts in the rock, and I'll stand up above."

The Troll did not dare to do otherwise than the lad bade him, and the end of it was that the lad rolled down a great rock, which fell upon the Troll, and broke one of his thighs.

"Well! you *are* in a sad plight," said the lad, as he strode down, lifted up the rock, and set the man free. After that he had to put him on his back and carry him home; so he ran with him as fast as a horse, and shook him so that the Troll screamed and screeched as if a knife were run into him. And when he got home, they had to put the Troll to bed, and there he lay in a sad pickle.

When the night wore on the Troll began to talk to the old dame again, and to wonder how ever they could be rid of the lad.

"Well," said the old dame, "if you can't hit on a plan to get rid of him, I'm sure I can't."

"Let me see," said the Troll; "I've got twelve lions in a garden; if they could only get hold of the lad they'd soon tear him to pieces."

So the old dame said it would be easy enough to get him there. She would sham sick, and say she felt so poorly, nothing would do her any good but lion's milk. All that the lad lay and listened to; and when he got up in the morning his mother said she was worse than she looked, and she thought she should never be right again unless she could get some lion's milk.

"Then I'm afraid you'll be poorly a long time, mother," said the lad, "for I'm sure I don't know where any is to be got."

"Oh! if that be all," said the Troll, "there's no lack of lion's milk, if we only had the man to fetch it;" and then he went on to say how his brother had a garden with twelve lions in it, and how the lad might have the key if he had a mind to milk the lions. So the lad took the key and a milking pail, and strode off; and when he unlocked the gate and got into the garden, there stood all the twelve lions on their hind-paws, rampant and roaring at him. But the lad laid hold of the biggest, and led him about by the fore-paws, and dashed him against the stocks and stones, till there wasn't a bit of him left but the two paws. So when the rest saw that, they were so afraid that they crept up and lay at his feet like so many curs. After that they followed him about wherever he went, and when he got home, they laid down outside the house, with their fore-paws on the door sill.

"Now, mother, you'll soon be well," said the lad, when he went in, "for here is the lion's milk."

He had just milked a drop in the pail.

But the Troll, as he lay in bed, swore it was all a lie. He was sure the lad was not the man to milk lions.

When the lad heard that, he forced the Troll to get out of bed, threw open the door, and all the lions rose up and seized the Troll, and at last the lad had to make them leave their hold.

That night the Troll began to talk to the old dame again. "I'm sure I can't tell how to put this lad out of the way—he is so awfully strong; can't you think of some way?"

"No," said the old dame, "if you can't tell, I'm sure I can't."

"Well!" said the Troll, "I have two brothers in a castle; they are twelve times as strong as I am, and that's why I was turned out and had to put up with this farm. They hold that castle, and round it there is an orchard with apples in it, and whoever eats those apples sleeps for three days and three nights. If we could only get the lad to go for the fruit, he wouldn't be able to keep from tasting the apples, and as soon as ever he fell asleep my brothers would tear him in pieces."

The old dame said she would sham sick, and say she could never be herself again unless she tasted those apples; for she had set her heart on them.

All this the lad lay and listened to.

When the morning came the old dame was so poorly that she couldn't utter a word but groans and sighs. She was sure she should never be well again, unless she had some of those apples that grew in the orchard near the castle where the man's brothers lived; only she had no one to send for them.

Oh! the lad was ready to go that instant; but the eleven lions went with him. So when he came to the orchard, he climbed up into the apple tree and ate as many apples as he could, and he had scarce got down before he fell into a deep sleep; but the lions all lay round him in a ring. The third day came the Troll's brothers, but they did not come in man's shape. They came snorting like man-eating steeds, and wondered who it was that dared to be there, and said they would tear him to pieces, so small that there should not be a bit of him left. But up rose the lions and tore the Trolls into small pieces, so that the place looked as if a dungheap had been tossed about it; and when they had finished the Trolls they lay down again. The lad did not wake till late in the afternoon, and when he got on his knees and rubbed the sleep out of his eyes, he began to wonder what had been going on, when he saw the marks of hoofs. But when he went towards the castle, a maiden looked out of a window who had seen all that had happened, and she said,—

"You may thank your stars you wern't in that tussle, else you must have lost your life."

"What! I lose my life! No fear of that, I think," said the lad.

So she begged him to come in, that she might talk with him, for she hadn't seen a Christian soul ever since she came there. But when she opened the door the lions wanted to go in too, but she got so frightened, that she began to scream, and so the lad let them lie outside. Then the two talked and talked, and the lad asked how it came that she, who was so lovely, could put up with those ugly Trolls. She never wished it, she said; 'twas quite against her will. They had seized her by force, and she was the King of Arabia's daughter. So they talked on, and at last she asked him what he would do; whether she should go back home, or whether he would have her to wife. Of course he would have her, and she shouldn't go home.

After that they went round the castle, and at last they came to a great hall, where the Trolls' two great swords hung high up on the wall.

"I wonder if you are man enough to wield one of these," said the Princess. 194

"Who?—I?" said the lad. " 'Twould be a pretty thing if I couldn't wield one of these."

With that he put two or three chairs one a-top of the other, jumped up, and touched the biggest sword with his finger tips, tossed it up in the air, and caught it again by the hilt; leapt down, and at the same time dealt such a blow with it on the floor, that the whole hall shook. After he had thus got down, he thrust the sword under his arm and carried it about with him.

So, when they had lived a little while in the castle, the Princess thought she ought to go home to her parents, and let them know what had become of her; so they loaded a ship, and she set sail from the castle.

After she had gone, and the lad had wandered about a little, he called to mind that he had been sent on an errand thither, and had come to fetch something for his mother's health; and though he said to himself, "After all, the old dame was not so bad but she's all right by this time,"—still he thought he ought to go and just see how she was. So he went and found both the man and his mother quite fresh and hearty.

"What wretches you are to live in this beggarly hut," said the lad. "Come with me up to my castle, and you shall see what a fine fellow I am."

Well! they were both ready to go, and on the way his mother talked to him, and asked, "How it was he had got so strong?"

"If you must know, it came of that blue belt which lay on the hill-side that time when you and I were out begging," said the lad.

"Have you got it still?" asked she.

"Yes,"—he had.   It was tied round his waist.

"Might she see it?"

"Yes, she might;" and with that he pulled open his waistcoat and shirt to show it to her.

Then she seized it with her hands, tore it off, and twisted it round her fist.

"Now," she cried, "what shall I do with such a wretch as you?   I'll just give you one blow, and dash your brains out!"

"Far too good a death for such a scamp," said the Troll.   "No! let's first burn out his eyes, and then turn him adrift in a little boat."

So they burned out his eyes and turned him adrift, in spite of his prayers and tears; but, as the boat drifted, the lions swam after, and at last they laid hold of it and dragged it ashore on an island, and placed the lad under a fir tree.   They caught game for him, and they plucked the birds and made him a bed of down; but he was forced to eat his meat raw, and he was blind.   At last, one day the biggest lion was chasing a hare which was blind, for it ran straight over stock and stone, and the end was, it ran right up against a fir-stump and tumbled head over heels across the field right into a spring; but lo! when it came out of the spring it saw its way quite plain, and so saved its life.

"So, so!" thought the lion, and went and dragged the lad to the spring, and dipped him over head and ears in it.   So, when he had got his sight again, he went down to the shore and made signs to the lions that they should all lie close together like a raft; then he stood upon their backs while they swam with him to the mainland. When he had reached the shore he went up into a birchen copse, and made the lions lie quiet. Then he stole up to the castle, like a thief, to see if he couldn't lay hands on his belt; and when he got to the door, he peeped through the keyhole, and there he saw his belt hanging up over a door in the kitchen. So he crept softly in across the floor, for there was no one there; but as soon as he had got hold of the belt, he began to kick and stamp about as though he were mad. Just then his mother came rushing out,—

"Dear heart, my darling little boy! do give me the belt again," she said.

"Thank you kindly," said he. "Now you shall have the doom you passed on me," and he fulfilled it on the spot. When the old Troll heard that, he came in and begged and prayed so prettily that he might not be smitten to death.

"Well, you may live," said the lad, "but you shall undergo the same punishment you gave me;" and so he burned out the Troll's eyes, and turned him adrift on the sea in a little boat, but he had no lions to follow him.

Now the lad was all alone, and he went about longing and longing for the Princess; at last he could bear it no longer; he must set out to seek her, his heart was so bent on having her. So he loaded four ships and set sail for Arabia. For some time they had fair wind and fine weather, but after that they lay wind-bound under a rocky island. So the sailors went ashore and strolled about to spend the time, and there they found a huge egg, almost as big as a little house. So they began to knock it about with large stones, but, after all, they couldn't crack the shell. Then the lad came up with his sword to see what all the noise was about, and when he saw the egg, he thought it a trifle to crack it; so he gave it one blow and the egg split, and out came a chicken as big as an elephant.

"Now we have done wrong," said the lad; "this can cost us all our lives;" and then he asked his sailors if they were men enough to sail to Arabia in four-and-twenty hours, if they got a fine breeze. Yes! they were good to do that, they said, so they set sail with a fine breeze, and got to Arabia in three-and-twenty hours. As soon as they landed, the lad ordered all the sailors to go and bury themselves up to the eyes in a sandhill, so that they could barely see the ships. The lad and the captains climbed a high crag and sat down under a fir. In a little while came a great bird flying with an island in its claws, and let it fall down on the fleet, and sunk every ship. After it had done that, it flew up to the sandhill and flapped its wings, so that the wind nearly took off the heads of the sailors, and it flew past the fir with such force that it turned the lad right about, but he was ready with his sword, and gave the bird one blow and brought it down dead.

After that he went to the town, where every one was glad because the king had got his daughter back; but now the king had hidden her away somewhere himself, and promised her hand as a reward to any one who could find her, and this though she was betrothed before. Now as the lad went along he met a man who had white bear-skins for sale, so he bought one of the hides and put it on; and one of the captains was to take an iron chain and lead him about, and so he went into the town and began to play pranks. At last the news came to the king's ears, that there never had been such fun in the town before, for here was a white bear that danced and cut capers just as it was bid. So a messenger came to say the bear must come to the castle at once, for the king wanted to see its tricks. So when it got to the castle every one was afraid, for such a beast they had never seen before; but the captain said there was no danger unless they laughed at it. They mustn't do that, else it would tear them to pieces. When the king heard that, he warned all the court not to laugh. But while the fun was going on, in came one of the king's maids, and began to laugh and make game of the bear, and the bear flew at her and tore her, so that there was scarce a rag of her left. Then all the court began to bewail, and the captain most of all.

"Stuff and nonsense," said the king; "she's only a maid, besides it's more my affair than yours."

When the show was over, it was late at night. "It's no good your going away, when it's so late," said the king. "The bear had best sleep here."

"Perhaps it might sleep in the ingle by the kitchen fire," said the captain.

"Nay," said the king, "it shall sleep up here, and it shall have pillows and cushions to sleep on." So a whole heap of pillows and cushions was brought, and the captain had a bed in a side-room. 199

But at midnight the king came with a lamp in his hand and a big bunch of keys, and carried off the white bear. He passed along gallery after gallery, through doors and rooms, up-stairs and down-stairs, till at last he came to a pier which ran out into the sea. Then the king began to pull and haul at posts and pins, this one up and that one down, till at last a little house floated up to the water's edge. There he kept his daughter, for she was so dear to him that he had hid her, so that no one could find her out. He left the white bear outside while he went in and told her how it had danced and played its pranks. She said she was afraid, and dared not look at it; but he talked her over, saying there was no danger, if she only wouldn't laugh. So they brought the bear in, and locked the door, and it danced and played its tricks; but just when the fun was at its height, the Princess's maid began to laugh. Then the lad flew at her and tore her to bits, and the Princess began to cry and sob.

"Stuff and nonsense," cried the king; "all this fuss about a maid! I'll get you just as good a one again. But now I think the bear had best stay here till morning, for I don't care to have to go and lead it along all those galleries and stairs at this time of night."

"Well!" said the Princess, "if it sleeps here, I'm sure I won't."

But just then the bear curled himself up and lay down by the stove; and it was settled at last that the Princess should sleep there too, with a light burning. But as soon as the king was well gone, the white bear came and begged her to undo his collar. The Princess was so scared she almost swooned away; but she felt about till she found the collar, and she had scarce undone it before the bear pulled his head off. Then she knew him again, and was so glad there was no end to her joy, and she wanted to tell her father at once that her deliverer was come. But the lad would not hear of it; he would earn her once more, he said. So in the morning when they heard the king rattling at the posts outside, the lad drew on the hide, and lay down by the stove.

"Well, has it lain still?" the king asked.

"I should think so," said the Princess; "it hasn't so much as turned or stretched itself once."

When they got up to the castle again, the captain took the bear and led it away, and then the lad threw off the hide, and went to a tailor and ordered clothes fit for a prince; and when they were fitted on he went to the king, and said he wanted to find the Princess.

"You're not the first who has wished the same thing," said the king, "but they have all lost their lives; for if any one who tries can't find her in four-and-twenty hours his life is forfeited."

Yes; the lad knew all that. Still he wished to try, and if he couldn't find her, 'twas his look-out. Now in the castle there was a band that played sweet tunes, and there were fair maids to dance with, and so the lad danced away. When twelve hours were gone, the king said,—

"I pity you with all my heart. You're so poor a hand at seeking; you will surely lose your life."

"Stuff!" said the lad; "while there's life there's hope! So long as there's breath in the body there's no fear;

we have lots of time;" and so he went on dancing till there was only one hour left.

Then he said he would begin to search.

"It's no use now," said the king; "time's up."

"Light your lamp; out with your big bunch of keys." said the lad, "and follow me whither I wish to go. There is still a whole hour left."

So the lad went the same way which the king had led him the night before, and he bade the king unlock door after door till they came down to the pier which ran out into the sea.

"It's all no use, I tell you," said the king; "time's up, and this will only lead you right out into the sea."

"Still five minutes more," said the lad, as he pulled and pushed at the posts and pins, and the house floated up.

"Now the time is up," bawled the king; "come hither, headsman, and take off his head."

"Nay, nay!" said the lad; "stop a bit, there are still three minutes! Out with the key, and let me get into this house."

But there stood the king and fumbled with his keys, to draw out the time. At last he said he hadn't any key.

"Well, if you haven't, I *have*," said the lad, as he gave the door such a kick that it flew to splinters inwards on the floor.

At the door the Princess met him, and told her father this was her deliverer, on whom her heart was set. So she had him; and this was how the beggar boy came to marry the king's daughter of Arabia.

THE THREE PRINCESSES OF WHITELAND.

ONCE on a time there was a fisherman who lived close by a palace, and fished for the king's table. One day when he was out fishing he just caught nothing. Do what he would—however he tried with bait and angle—there was never a sprat on his hook. But when the day was far spent a head bobbed up out of the water, and said, —

"If I may have what your wife bears under her girdle, you shall catch fish enough."

So the man answered boldly, "Yes;" for he did not know that his wife was going to have a child. After that, as was like enough, he caught plenty of fish of all kinds. But when he got home at night and told his story, how he had got all that fish, his wife fell a-weeping and moaning, and was beside herself for the promise which her husband had made, for she said, "I bear a babe under my girdle."

Well, the story soon spread, and came up to the castle; and when the king heard the woman's grief and its cause, he sent down to say he would take care of the child, and see if he couldn't save it.

So the months went on and on, and when her time came the fisher's wife had a boy; so the king took it at once, and brought it up as his own son, until the lad grew up. Then he begged leave one day to go out fishing with his father; he had such a mind to go, he said. At first the king wouldn't hear of it, but at last the lad had his way, and went. So he and his father were out the whole day, and all went right and well till they landed at night. Then the lad remembered he had left his handkerchief, and went to look for it; but as soon as ever he got into the boat, it began to move off with him at such speed that the water roared under the bow, and all the lad could do in rowing against it with the oars was no use; so he went and went the whole night, and at last he came to a white strand, far far away.

There he went ashore, and when he had walked about a bit, an old, old man met him, with a long white beard.

"What's the name of this land?" asked the lad.

"Whiteland," said the man, who went on to ask the lad whence he came, and what he was going to do. So the lad told him all.

"Aye, aye!" said the man; "now when you have walked a little farther along the strand here, you'll come to three Princesses, whom you will see standing in the earth up to their necks, with only their heads out. Then the first—she is the eldest—will call out and beg you so prettily to come and help her; and the second will do the same; to neither of these shall you go; make haste past them, as if you neither saw nor heard anything. But the third you shall go to, and do what she asks. If you do this, you'll have good luck—that's all."

When the lad came to the first Princess, she called out to him, and begged him so prettily to come to her, but he passed on as though he saw her not. In the same way he passed by the second; but to the third he went straight up.

"If you'll do what I bid you," she said, "you may have which of us you please."

"Yes;" he was willing enough; so she told him how three Trolls had set them down in the earth there; but before they had lived in the castle up among the trees.

"Now" she said, "you must go into that castle, and let the Trolls whip you each one night for each of us. If you can bear that, you'll set us free."

Well, the lad said he was ready to try.

"When you go in," the Princess went on to say, "you'll see two lions standing at the gate; but if you'll only go right in the middle between them they'll do you no harm. Then go straight on into a little dark room, and make your bed. Then the Troll will come to whip you; but if you take the flask which hangs on the wall, and rub yourself with the ointment that's in it, wherever his lash falls, you'll be as sound as ever. Then grasp the sword that hangs by the side of the flask and strike the Troll dead."

Yes, he did as the Princess told him; he passed in the midst between the lions, as if he hadn't seen them, and went straight into the little room, and there he lay down to sleep. The first night there came a Troll with three heads and three rods, and whipped the lad soundly; but he stood it till the Troll was done; then he took the flask and rubbed himself, and grasped the sword and slew the Troll.

So, when he went out next morning the Princesses stood out of the earth up to their waists.

The next night 'twas the same story over again, only

this time the Troll had six heads and six rods, and he whipped him far worse than the first; but when he went out next morning, the Princesses stood out of the earth as far as the knee.

The third night there came a Troll that had nine heads and nine rods, and he whipped and flogged the lad so long that he fainted away; then the Troll took him up and dashed him against the wall; but the shock brought down the flask, which fell on the lad, burst, and spilled the ointment all over him, and so he became as strong and sound as ever again. Then he wasn't slow; he grasped the sword and slew the Troll; and next morning when he went out of the castle the Princesses stood before him with all their bodies out of the earth. So he took the youngest for his Queen, and lived well and happily with her for some time.

At last he began to long to go home for a little to see his parents. His Queen did not like this; but at last his heart was so set on it, and he longed and longed so much, there was no holding him back, so she said,—

"One thing you must promise me. This.—Only to do what your father begs you to do, and not what your mother wishes;" and that he promised.

Then she gave him a ring, which was of that kind that any one who wore it might wish two wishes. So he wished himself home, and when he got home his parents could not wonder enough what a grand man their son had become.

Now, when he had been at home some days, his mother wished him to go up to the palace and show the king what a fine fellow he had come to be. But his father said—

"No! don't let him do that; if he does, we shan't have any more joy of him this time."

But it was no good, the mother begged and prayed so long, that at last he went. So when he got up to the palace, he was far braver, both in clothes and array, than the other king, who didn't quite like this, and at last he said—

"All very fine; but here you can see my queen, what like she is, but I can't see yours, that I can't. Do you know, I scarce think she's so good looking as mine."

"Would to Heaven," said the young king, "she were standing here, then you'd see what she was like." And that instant there she stood before them.

But she was very woeful, and said to him—

"Why did you not mind what I told you; and why did you not listen to what your father said? Now, I must away home, and as for you, you have had both your wishes."

With that she knitted a ring among his hair with her name on it, and wished herself home, and was off.

Then the young king was cut to the heart, and went, day out day in, thinking and thinking how he should get back to his queen. "I'll just try," he thought, "if I can't learn where Whiteland lies;" and so he went out into the world to ask. So when he had gone a good way, he came to a high hill, and there he met one who was lord over all the beasts of the wood, for they all came home to him when he blew his horn; so the king asked if he knew where Whiteland was?

"No, I don't," said he, "but I'll ask my beasts." Then he blew his horn and called them, and asked if any of them knew where Whiteland lay? but there was no beast that knew.

So the man gave him a pair of snow-shoes.

"When you get on these," he said, "you'll come to my brother, who lives hundreds of miles off; he is lord over all the birds of the air. Ask him. When you reach his house, just turn the shoes, so that the toes point this way, and they'll come home of themselves." So when the king reached the house, he turned the shoes as the lord of the beasts had said, and away they went home of themselves.

So he asked again after Whiteland, and the man called all the birds with a blast of his horn, and asked if any of them knew where Whiteland lay; but none of the birds knew. Now, long, long after the rest of the birds, came an old eagle, which had been away ten round years, but he couldn't tell any more than the rest.

"Well! well!" said the man, "I'll lend you a pair of snow-shoes, and when you get them on, they'll carry you to my brother, who lives hundreds of miles off; he's lord of all the fish in the sea; you'd better ask him. But don't forget to turn the toes of the shoes this way."

The king was full of thanks, got on the shoes, and when he came to the man who was lord over the fish of the sea, he turned the toes round, and so off they went home like the other pair. After that, he asked again after Whiteland.

So the man called the fish with a blast, but no fish

could tell where it lay. At last came an old pike, which they had great work to call home, he was such a way off. So when they asked him he said—

"Know it! I should think I did. I've been cook there ten years, and to-morrow I'm going there again; for now, the queen of Whiteland, whose king is away, is going to wed another husband."

"Well!" said the man, "as this is so, I'll give you a bit of advice. Hereabouts, on a moor, stand three brothers, and here they have stood these hundred years, fighting about a hat, a cloak and a pair of boots. If any one has these three things he can make himself invisible, and wish himself anywhere he pleases. You can tell them you wish to try the things, and after that, you'll pass judgment between them whose they shall be."

Yes! the king thanked the man, and went and did as he told him.

"What's all this?" he said to the brothers. "Why do you stand here fighting for ever and a day? Just let me try these things, and I'll give judgment whose they shall be."

They were very willing to do this; but as soon as he had got the hat, cloak and boots, he said—

"When we meet next time I'll tell you my judgment," and with these words he wished himself away.

So as he went along up in the air, he came up with the North Wind.

"Whither away?" roared the North Wind.

"To Whiteland," said the king; and then he told him all that had befallen him.

"Ah," said the North Wind, "you go faster than I— you do; for you can go straight, while I have to puff and blow round every turn and corner. But when you get there, just place yourself on the stairs by the side of the door, and then I'll come storming in, as though I were going to blow down the whole castle. And then when the prince, who is to have your queen, comes out to see what's the matter, just you take him by the collar and pitch him out of doors; then I'll look after him, and see if I can't carry him off."

Well—the king did as the North Wind said. He took his stand on the stairs, and when the North Wind came, storming and roaring, and took hold of the castle wall, so that it shook again, the prince came out to see what was the matter. But as soon as ever he came, the king caught him by the collar and pitched him out of doors, and then the North Wind caught him up and carried him off. So when there was an end of him, the king went into the castle, and at first his queen didn't know him, he was so wan and thin, through wandering so far and being so woeful; but when he showed her the ring, she was as glad as glad could be; and so the rightful wedding was held, and the fame of it spread far and wide.

RICH PETER THE PEDLAR.

ONCE on a time there was a man whom they called Rich Peter the Pedlar, because he used to travel about with a pack, and got so much money, that he became quite rich. This Rich Peter had a daughter, whom he held so dear that all who came to woo her, were sent about their business, for no one was good enough for her he thought. Well, this went on and on, and at last no one came to woo her, and as years rolled on, Peter began to be afraid that she would die an old maid.

"I wonder now," he said to his wife, "why suitors no longer come to woo our lass, who is so rich. 'Twould be odd if nobody cared to have her, for money she has, and more she shall have. I think I'd better just go off to the Stargazers, and ask them whom she shall have, for not a soul comes to us now."

"But how," asked the wife, "can the Stargazers answer that?"

"Can't they?" said Peter; "why! they read all things in the stars."

So he took with him a great bag of money, and set off to the Stargazers, and asked them to be so good as to look at the stars, and tell him the husband his daughter was to have.

Well! the Stargazers looked and looked, but they said they could see nothing about it. But Peter begged them to look better, and to tell him the truth; he would pay them well for it. So the Stargazers looked better, and at last they said that his daughter's husband was to be the miller's son, who was only just born, down at the mill below Rich Peter's house. Then Peter gave the Stargazers a hundred dollars, and went home with the answer he had got.

Now he thought it too good a joke that his daughter should wed one so newly born, and of such poor estate. He said this to his wife, and added—

"I wonder now if they would sell me the boy; then I'd soon put him out of the way?"

"I daresay they would," said his wife; "you know they're very poor."

So Peter went down to the mill and asked the miller's wife whether she would sell him her son; she should get a heap of money for him?

"No!" that she wouldn't.

"Well!" said Peter, "I'm sure I can't see why you shouldn't; you've hard work enough as it is to keep hunger out of the house, and the boy won't make it easier, I think."

But the mother was so proud of the boy she couldn't part with him. So when the miller came home, Peter said the same thing to him, and gave his word to pay six hundred dollars for the boy, so that they might buy themselves a farm of their own, and not have to grind other folks' corn, and to starve when they ran short of water. The miller thought it was a good bargain, and he talked over his wife; and the end was, that Rich Peter got the boy. The mother cried and sobbed, but Peter comforted her by saying the boy should be well cared for; only they had to promise never to ask after him, for he said he meant to send him far away to other lands, so that he might learn foreign tongues.

So when Peter the Pedlar got home with the boy, he sent for a carpenter, and had a little chest made, which was so tidy and neat, 'twas a joy to see. This he made water-tight with pitch, put the miller's boy into it, locked it up, and threw it into the river, where the stream carried it away.

"Now, I'm rid of him," thought Peter the Pedlar.

But when the chest had floated ever so far down the stream, it came into the mill-head of another mill, and ran down and hampered the shaft of the wheel, and stopped it. Out came the miller to see what stopped the mill, found the chest, and took it up. So when he came home to dinner to his wife, he said,—

"I wonder now whatever there can be inside this chest which came floating down the mill-head, and stopped our mill to-day?"

"That we'll soon know," said his wife; "see, there's the key in the lock, just turn it."

So they turned the key and opened the chest, and lo! there lay the prettiest child you ever set eyes on. So they were both glad, and were ready to keep the child, for they had no children of their own, and were so old they could now hope for none.

Now, after a little while, Peter the Pedlar began to wonder how it was no one came to woo his daughter, who was so rich in land, and had so much ready money. At last, when no one came, off he went again to the

Stargazers, and offered them a heap of money if they could tell him whom his daughter was to have for a husband.

"Why! we have told you already that she is to have the miller's son down yonder," said the Stargazers.

"All very true, I daresay," said Peter the Pedlar; "but it so happens he's dead; but if you can tell me whom she's to have, I'll give you two hundred dollars and welcome."

So the Stargazers looked at the stars again, but they got quite cross, and said—

"We told you before, and we tell you now, she is to have the miller's son, whom you threw into the river, and wished to make an end of; for he is alive, safe and sound, in such and such a mill, far down the stream."

So Peter the Pedlar gave them two hundred dollars for this news, and thought how he could best be rid of the miller's son. The first thing Peter did when he got home, was to set off for the mill. By that time the boy was so big that he had been confirmed, and went about the mill and helped the miller. Such a pretty boy you never saw.

"Can't you spare me that lad yonder?" said Peter the Pedlar to the miller.

"No! that I can't," he answered; "I've brought him up as my own son, and he has turned out so well, that now he's a great help and aid to me in the mill, for I'm getting old and past work."

"It's just the same with me," said Peter the Pedlar; "that's why I'd like to have some one to learn my trade.

Now, if you'll give him up to me, I'll give you six hundred dollars, and then you can buy yourself a farm, and live in peace and quiet the rest of your days."

Yes! when the miller heard that, he let Peter the Pedlar have the lad.

Then the two travelled about far and wide, with their packs and wares, till they came to an inn, which lay by the edge of a great wood. From this Peter the Pedlar sent the lad home with a letter to his wife, for the way was not so long if you took the short cut across the wood, and told him to tell her she was to be sure and do what was written in the letter as quickly as she could. But it was written in the letter, that she was to have a great pile made there and then, fire it, and cast the miller's son into it. If she didn't do that, he'd burn her alive himself when he came back. So the lad set off with the letter across the wood, and when evening came on he reached a house far, far away in the wood, into which he went; but inside he found no one. In one of the rooms was a bed ready made, so he threw himself across it and fell asleep. The letter he had stuck into his hat-band, and the hat he pulled over his face. So when the robbers came back—for in that house twelve robbers had their abode—and saw the lad lying on the bed, they began to wonder who he could be, and one of them took the letter and broke it open, and read it.

"Ho! ho!" said he; "this comes from Peter the Pedlar does it? Now we'll play him a trick. It would be a pity if the old niggard made an end of such a pretty lad."

So the robbers wrote another letter to Peter the Pedlar's wife, and fastened it under his hat-band while he slept; and in that they wrote that as soon as ever she got it she was to make a wedding for her daughter and the miller's boy, and give them horses and cattle, and household stuff, and set them up for themselves in the farm which he had under the hill; and if he didn't find all this done by the time he came back, she'd smart for it—that was all.

Next day the robbers let the lad go, and when he came home and delivered the letter, he said he was to greet her kindly from Peter the Pedlar, and to say that she was to carry out what was written in the letter as soon as ever she could.

"You must have behaved very well then," said Peter the Pedlar's wife to the miller's boy, "if he can write so about you now, for when you set off, he was so mad against you, he didn't know how to put you out of the way." So she married them on the spot, and set them up for themselves, with horses and cattle and household stuff, in the farm under the hill.

No long time after Peter the Pedlar came home, and the first thing he asked was if she had done what he had written in his letter.

"Aye! aye!" she said; "I thought it rather odd, but I dared not do anything else;' and so Peter asked where his daughter was.

"Why, you know well enough where she is," said his wife. "Where should she be but up at the farm under the hill, as you wrote in the letter."

So when Peter the Pedlar came to hear the whole story, and came to see the letter, he got so angry he was ready to burst with rage, and off he ran up to the farm to the young couple.

"It's all very well, my son, to say you have got my daughter," he said to the miller's lad; "but if you wish to keep her, you must go to the Dragon of Deepferry, and get me three feathers out of his tail; for he who has them may get anything he chooses."

"But where shall I find him?" said his son-in-law.

"I'm sure I can't tell," said Peter the Pedlar; "that's your lookout, not mine."

So the lad set off with a stout heart, and after he had walked some way, he came to a king's palace.

"Here I'll just step in and ask," he said to himself; "for such great folk know more about the world than others, and perhaps I may here learn the way to the Dragon."

Then the King asked him whence he came, and whither he was going?

"Oh!" said the lad, "I'm going to the Dragon of Deepferry to pluck three feathers out of his tail, if I only knew where to find him."

"You must take luck with you, then,' said the King, "for I never heard of any one who came back from that search. But if you find him, just ask him from me why I can't get clear water in my well; for I've dug it out time after time, and still I can't get a drop of clear water."

"Yes, I'll be sure to ask him," said the lad. So he lived on the fat of the land at the palace, and got money and food when he left it. 217

At even he came to another king's palace; and when he went into the kitchen, the King came out of the parlour, and asked whence he came, and on what errand he was bound?

"Oh!" said the lad, "I'm going to the Dragon of Deepferry to pluck three feathers out of his tail."

"Then you must take luck with you," said the King, "for I never yet heard that any one came back who went to look for him. But if you find him, be so good as to ask him from me where my daughter is, who has been lost so many years. I have hunted for her, and had her name out in every church in the country, but no one can tell me anything about her."

"Yes, I'll mind and do that," said the lad; and in that palace too he lived on the best, and when he went away he got both money and food.

So when evening drew on again he came at last to another king's palace. Here who should come out into the kitchen but the Queen, and she asked him whence he came, and on what errand he was bound?

"I'm going to the Dragon of Deepferry to pluck three feathers out of his tail," said the lad.

"Then you'd better take a good piece of luck with you," said the Queen, "for I never heard of any one that came back from him. But if you find him, just be good enough to ask him from me where I shall find my gold keys which I have lost."

"Yes! I'll be sure to ask him," said the lad.

Well! when he left the palace he came to a great broad river; and while he stood there and wondered whether he should cross it, or go down along the bank, an old hunchbacked man came up, and asked whither he was going?

"Oh, I'm going to the Dragon of Deepferry, if I could only find any one to tell where I can find him."

"I can tell you that," said the man; "for here I go backwards and forwards, and carry those over who are going to see him. He lives just across, and when you climb the hill you'll see his castle; but mind, if you come to talk with him, to ask him from me how long I'm to stop here and carry folk over."

"I'll be sure to ask him," said the lad.

So the man took him on his back and carried him over the river; and when he climbed the hill, he saw the castle, and went in.

He found there a Princess who lived with the Dragon all alone; and she said,—

"But, dear friend, how can Christian folk dare to come hither? None have been here since I came, and you'd best be off as fast as you can; for as soon as the Dragon comes home, he'll smell you out, and gobble you up in a trice, and that'll make me so unhappy."

"Nay! nay!' said the lad; "I can't go before I've got three feathers out of his tail."

"You'll never get them," said the Princess; "you'd best be off."

But the lad wouldn't go; he would wait for the Dragon and get the feathers and an answer to all his questions.

"Well, since you're so steadfast I'll see what I can do to help you," said the Princess; "just try to lift that sword that hangs on the wall yonder."

No; the lad could not even stir it.

"I thought so," said the Princess; "but just take a drink out of this flask."

So when the lad had sat a while, he was to try again; and then he could just stir it.

"Well! you must take another drink," said the Princess; "and then you may as well tell me your errand hither."

So he took another drink, and then he told her how one king had begged him to ask the Dragon how it was he couldn't get clean water in his well?—how another had bidden him ask what had become of his daughter, who had been lost many years since?—and how a queen had begged him to ask the Dragon what had become of her gold keys?—and, last of all, how the ferryman had begged him to ask the Dragon how long he was to stop there and carry folk over? When he had done his story, and took hold of the sword, he could lift it; and when he had taken another drink, he could brandish it

"Now," said the Princess, "if you don't want the Dragon to make an end of you, you'd best creep under the bed, for night is drawing on, and he'll soon be home, and then you must lie as still as you can, lest he should find you out. And when we have gone to bed, I'll ask him, but you must keep your ears open, and snap up all that he says; and under the bed you must lie till all is still, and the Dragon falls asleep; then creep out softly and seize the sword, and as soon as he rises, look out to hew off his head at one stroke, and at the same time pluck out the three feathers, for else he'll tear them out himself, that no one may get any good by them."

So the lad crept under the bed, and the Dragon came home.

"What a smell of Christian flesh," said the Dragon.

"Oh, yes," said the Princess, "a raven came flying with a man's bone in his bill, and perched on the roof. No doubt it's that you smell."

"So it is, I daresay," said the Dragon.

So the Princess served supper, and after they had eaten, they went to bed. But after they had lain a while, the Princess began to toss about, and all at once she started up and said,—

"Ah! ah!"

"What's the matter?" said the Dragon.

"Oh," said the Princess, "I can't rest at all, and I've had such a strange dream."

"What did you dream about? Let's hear?" said the Dragon.

"I thought a king came here, and asked you what he must do to get clear water in his well."

"Oh," said the Dragon, "he might just as well have found that out for himself. If he dug the well out, and took out the old rotten stump which lies at the bottom, he'd get clean water fast enough. But be still now, and don't dream any more."

When the Princess had lain a while, she began to toss about, and at last she started up with her

"Ah! ah!"

"What's the matter now?" said the Dragon.

"Oh! I can't get any rest at all, and I've had such a strange dream," said the Princess.

"Why, you seem full of dreams to-night," said the Dragon; "what was your dream now?"

"I thought a king came here, and asked you what had become of his daughter who had been lost many years since," said the Princess.

"Why, you are she." said the Dragon; "but he'll never set eyes on you again. But now, do pray be still, and let me get some rest, and don't let's have any more dreams, else I'll break your ribs."

Well, the Princess hadn't lain much longer before she began to toss about again. At last she started up with her

"Ah! ah!"

"What! Are you at it again?" said the Dragon. "What's the matter now?" for he was wild and sleep-surly, so that he was ready to fly to pieces.

"Oho, don't be angry," said the Princess; "but I've had such a strange dream."

"The deuce take your dreams," roared the Dragon; "what did you dream this time?"

"I thought a queen came here, who asked you to tell her where she would find her gold keys, which she has lost."

"Oh," said the Dragon, "she'll find them soon enough if she looks among the bushes where she lay that time she wots of. But do now let me have no more dreams, but sleep in peace.'

So they slept a while; but then the Princess was just as restless as ever, and at last she screamed out—

"Ah! ah!"

"You'll never behave till I break your neck," said the Dragon, who was now so wroth that sparks of fire flew out of his eyes. "What's the matter now?"

"Oh, don't be so angry," said the Princess; "I can't bear that; but I've had such a strange dream."

"Bless me!" said the Dragon, "if I ever heard the like of these dreams—there's no end to them. And pray, what did you dream now?"

"I thought the ferryman down at the ferry came and asked how long he was to stop there and carry folk over," said the Princess.

"The dull fool!" said the Dragon; "he'd soon be free, if he chose. When any one comes who wants to go across, he has only to take and throw him into the river, and say, 'Now, carry folk over yourself till some one sets you free.' But now, pray let's have an end of these dreams, else I'll lead you a pretty dance."

So the Princess let him sleep on. But as soon as all was still, and the miller's lad heard that the Dragon snored, he crept out. Before it was light the Dragon rose; but he had scarce set both his feet on the floor before the lad cut off his head, and plucked three feathers out of his tail. Then came great joy, and both the lad and the Princess took as much gold and silver and money and precious things as they could carry; and when they came down to the ford, they so puzzled the ferryman with all they had to tell, that he quite forgot to ask what the Dragon had said about him till they had got across.

"Halloa, you sir," he said, as they were going off, "did you ask the Dragon what I begged you to ask?"

"Yes I did," said the lad, "and he said, 'When any one comes and wants to go over, you must throw him into the midst of the river, and say, 'Now carry folk over yourself till some one comes to set you free,' and then you'll be free."

"Ah, bad luck to you," said the ferryman; "had you told me that before, you might have set me free yourself."

So, when they got to the first palace, the Queen asked if he had spoken to the Dragon about her gold keys?

"Yes," said the lad, and whispered in the Queen's ear, "he said you must look among the bushes where you lay the day you wot of."

"Hush! hush! Don't say a word," said the Queen, and gave the lad a hundred dollars.

When they came to the second palace, the King asked if he had spoken to the Dragon of what he begged him?

"Yes,'" said the lad, "I did; and see, here is your daughter."

At that the King was so glad he would gladly have given the Princess to the miller's lad to wife, and half the kingdom beside; but as he was married already, he gave him two hundred dollars, and coaches and horses, and as much gold and silver as he could carry away.

When he came to the third King's palace, out came the King and asked if he had asked the Dragon of what he begged him?

"Yes," said the lad, "and he said you must dig out the well, and take out the rotten old stump which lies at the bottom, and then you'll get plenty of clear water."

Then the King gave him three hundred dollars, and

he set out home; he was so loaded with gold and silver, and so grandly clothed, that it gleamed and glistened from him, and he was now far richer than Peter the Pedlar.

When Peter got the feathers he hadn't a word more to say against the wedding; but when he saw all that wealth, he asked if there was much still left at the Dragon's castle.

"Yes, I should think so," said the lad; "there was much more than I could carry with me—so much, that you might load many horses with it; and if you choose to go, you may be sure there'll be enough for you.'

So his son-in-law told him the way so clearly, that he hadn't to ask it of any one.

"But the horses," said the lad, "you'd best leave this side of the river; for the old ferryman, he'll carry you over safe enough."

So Peter set off, and took with him great store of food and many horses; but these he left behind him on the river's brink, as the lad had said. And the old ferryman took him upon his back; but when they had come a bit out into the stream, he cast him into the midst of the river, and said,—

"Now you may go backwards and forwards here, and carry folk over till you are set free."

And unless some one has set him free, there goes Rich Peter the Pedlar backwards and forwards, and carries folk across this very day.

THE BEST WISH.

ONCE on a time there were three brothers; I don't quite know how it happened, but each of them had got the right to wish one thing, whatever he chose. So the two elder were not long a-thinking, they wished that every time they put their hands in their pockets they might pull out a piece of money; for, said they,—

"The man who has as much money as he wishes for is always sure to get on in the world."

But the youngest wished something better still. He wished that every woman he saw might fall in love with him as soon as he saw him; and you shall soon hear how far better this was than gold and goods.

So, when they had all wished their wishes, the two elder were for setting out to see the world; and Boots, their youngest brother, asked if he mightn't go along with them, but they wouldn't hear of such a thing.

"Wherever we go," they said, "we shall be treated as counts and kings; but you, you starveling wretch, who haven't a penny, and never will have one, who do you think will care a bit about you?"

"Well, but in spite of that, I'd like to go with you," said Boots; "perhaps a dainty bit may fall to my share too off the plates of such high and mighty lords."

At last, after begging and praying, he got leave to go with them, if he would be their servant, else they wouldn't hear of it.

So, when they had gone a day or so, they came to an

inn, where the two who had the money alighted, and called for fish and flesh and fowl, and brandy and mead, and everything that was good; but Boots, poor fellow, had to look after their luggage and all that belonged to the two great people. Now, as he went to and fro outside, and loitered about in the inn-yard, the innkeeper's wife looked out of window and saw the servant of the gentlemen up stairs; and, all at once, she thought she had never set eyes on such a handsome chap. So she stared and stared, and the longer she looked the handsomer he seemed.

"Why what, by the Deil's skin and bones, is it that you are standing there gaping at out of the window?" said her husband. "I think 'twould be better if you just looked how the sucking pig is getting on, instead of hanging out of window in that way. Don't you know what grand folk we have in the house to-day?"

"Oh!" said his old dame, "I don't care a farthing about such a pack of rubbish; if they don't like it they may lump it, and be off; but just do come and look at this lad out in the yard, so handsome a fellow I never saw in all my born days; and, if you'll do as I wish, we'll ask him to step in and treat him a little, for, poor lad, he seems to have a hard fight of it."

"Have you lost the little brains you had, Goody?" said the husband, whose eyes glistened with rage; "into the kitchen with you, and mind the fire; but don't stand there glowering after strange men."

So the wife had nothing left for it but to go into the kitchen, and look after the cooking; as for the lad outside, she couldn't get leave or ask him in, or to treat him either; but just as she was about spitting the pig in the kitchen, she made an excuse for running out into the yard, and then and there she gave Boots a pair of scissors, of such a kind that they cut of themselves out of the air the loveliest clothes any one ever saw, silk and satin, and all that was fine.

"This you shall have because you are so handsome," said the innkeeper's wife.

So when the two elder brothers had crammed themselves with roast and boiled, they wished to be off again, and Boots had to stand behind their carriage, and be their servant; and so they travelled a good way, till they came to another inn.

There the two brothers again alighted and went indoors, but Boots, who had no money, they wouldn't have inside with them; no, he must wait outside and watch the luggage.

"And mind," they said, "if any one asks whose servant you are, say we are two foreign Princes."

But the same thing happened now as it happened before; while Boots stood hanging about out in the yard, the innkeeper's wife came to the window and saw him, and she too fell in love with him, just like the first innkeeper's wife; and there she stood and stared, for she thought she could never have her fill of looking at him. Then her husband came running through the room with something the two Princes had ordered.

"Don't stand there staring like a cow at a barn-door, but take this into the kitchen, and look after your fish-kettle, Goody," said the man; "don't you see what grand people we have in the house to-day?"

"I don't care a farthing for such a pack of rubbish," said the wife "if they don't like what they get they may lump it, and eat what they brought with them. But just do come here, and see what you shall see! Such a handsome fellow as walks here, out in the yard, I never saw in all my born days. Shan't we ask him in and treat him a little; he looks as if he needed it, poor chap?" and then she went on,—

"Such a love! such a love!"

"You never had much wit, and the little you had is clean gone, I can see," said the man, who was much more angry than the first innkeeper, and chased his wife back, neck and crop, into the kitchen.

"Into the kitchen with you, and don't stand glowering after lads," he said.

So she had to go in and mind her fish-kettle, and she dared not treat Boots, for she was afraid of her old man but as she stood there making up the fire, she made an excuse for running out into the yard, and then and there she gave Boots a tablecloth, which was such that it covered itself with the best dishes you could think of, as soon as it was spread out.

"This you shall have," she said, "because you're so handsome."

So when the two brothers had eaten and drunk of all that was in the house, and had paid the bill in hard cash, they set off again, and Boots stood up behind their carriage. But when they had gone so far that they grew hungry again, they turned into a third inn, and called for the best and dearest they could think of.

"For," said they, "we are two kings on our travels, and as for our money, it grows like grass."

Well, when the innkeeper heard that, there was such a roasting, and baking and boiling; why! you might smell the dinner at the next neighbour's house, though it wasn't so very near; and the innkeeper was at his wit's end to find all he wished to put before the two kings. But Boots, he had to stand outside here too, and look after the things in the carriage.

So it was the same story over again. The innkeeper's wife came to the window and peeped out, and there she saw the servant standing by the carriage. Such a handsome chap she had never set eyes on before; so she looked and looked, and the more she stared the handsomer he seemed to the innkeeper's wife. Then out came the innkeeper, scampering through the room, with some dainty which the travelling kings had ordered, and he wasn't very soft-tongued when he saw his old dame standing and glowering out of the window.

"Don't you know better than to stand gaping and staring there, when we have such great folk in the house," he said; "back into the kitchen with you this minute, to your custards."

"Well! well!" she said, "as for them, I don't care a pin. If they can't wait till the custards are baked, they may go without—that's all. But do, pray, come here, and you'll see such a lovely lad standing out here in the yard. Why I never saw such a pretty fellow in my life.

Shan't we ask him in now, and treat him a little, for he looks as if it would do him good. Oh! what a darling! What a darling!

"A wanton gadabout you've been all your days, and so you are still," said her husband, who was in such a rage he scarce knew which leg to stand on; "but if you don't be off to your custards this minute, I'll soon find out how to make you stir your stumps; see if I don't."

So the wife had off to her custards as fast as she could, for she knew that her husband would stand no nonsense; but as she stood there over the fire she stole out into the yard, and gave Boots a tap.

"If you only turn this tap," she said; "you'll get the finest drink of whatever kind you choose, both mead and wine and brandy; and this you shall have because you are so handsome."

So when the two brothers had eaten and drunk all they could, they started from the inn, and Boots stood up behind again as their servant, and thus they drove far and wide, till they came to a king's palace. There the two elder gave themselves out for two emperor's sons, and as they had plenty of money, and were so fine that their clothes shone again ever so far off, they were well treated. They had rooms in the palace, and the king couldn't tell how to make enough of them. But Boots, who went about in the same rags he stood in when he left home, and who had never a penny in his pocket, he was taken up by the king's guard, and put across to an island, whither they used to row over all the beggars and rogues that came to the palace. This the king had ordered, because he wouldn't have the mirth at the palace spoilt by those dirty blackguards; and thither, too, only just as much food as would keep body and soul together was sent over every day. Now Boots' brothers saw very well that the guard was rowing him over to the island, but they were glad to be rid of him, and didn't pay the least heed to him.

But when Boots got over there, he just pulled out his scissors and began to snip and cut in the air; so the scissors cut out the finest clothes any one would wish to see; silk and satin both, and all the beggars on the island were soon dressed far finer than the king and all his guests in the palace. After that, Boots pulled out his tablecloth, and spread it out, and so they got food too, the poor beggars. Such a feast had never been seen at the king's palace, as was served that day at the Beggars' Isle.

"Thirsty, too, I'll be bound you all are," said Boots, and out with his tap, gave it a turn, and so the beggars got all a drop to drink; and such ale and mead the king himself had never tasted in all his life.

So, next morning, when those who were to bring the beggars their food on the island, came rowing over with the scrapings of the porridge-pots and cheese-parings—that was what the poor wretches had—the beggars wouldn't so much as taste them, and the king's men fell to wondering what it could mean; but they wondered much more when they got a good look at the beggars, for they were so fine the guard thought they must be Emperors or Popes at least, and that they must have rowed to a wrong island; but when they looked better about them, they saw they were come to the old place.

Then they soon found out it must be he whom they had rowed out the day before who had brought the beggars on the island all this state and bravery; and as soon as they got back to the palace, they were not slow to tell how the man, whom they had rowed over the day before, had dressed out all the beggars so fine and grand that precious things fell from their clothes.

"And as for the porridge and cheese we took, they wouldn't even taste them, so proud have they got," they said.

One of them, too, had smelt out that the lad had a pair of scissors which he cut out the clothes with.

"When he only snips with those scissors up in the air he snips and cuts out nothing but silk and satin," said he.

So, when the Princess heard that, she had neither peace nor rest till she saw the lad and his scissors that cut out silk and satin from the air; such a pair was worth having, she thought, for with its help she would soon get all the finery she wished for. Well, she begged the king so long and hard, he was forced to send a messenger for the lad who owned the scissors; and when he came to the palace, the Princess asked him if it were true that he had such and such a pair of scissors, and if he would sell it to her. Yes, it was all true he had such a pair, said Boots, but sell it he wouldn't; and with that he took the scissors out of his pocket, and snipped and snipped with them in the air till strips of silk and satin flew all about him.

233

"Nay, but you must sell me these scissors," said the Princess. "You may ask what you please for them, but have them I must."

No, such a pair of scissors he wouldn't sell at any price, for he could never get such a pair again; and while they stood and haggled for the scissors, the Princess had time to look better at Boots, and she too thought with the innkeepers' wives that she had never seen such a handsome fellow before. So she began to bargain for the scissors over again, and begged and prayed Boots to let her have them; he might ask many, many hundred dollars for them, 'twas all the same to her, so she got them.

"No! sell them I won't," said Boots; "but all the same, if I can get leave to sleep one night on the floor of the Princess' bed-room, close by the door, I'll give her the scissors. I'll do her no harm, but if she's afraid, she may have two men to watch inside the room."

Yes! the Princess was glad enough to give him leave, for she was ready to grant him anything if she only got the scissors. So Boots lay on the floor inside the Princess' bed-room that night, and two men stood watch there too; but the Princess didn't get much rest after all; for when she ought to have been asleep, she must open her eyes to look at Boots, and so it went on the whole night. If she shut her eyes for a minute, she peeped out at him again the next, such a handsome fellow he seemed to her to be.

Next morning Boots was rowed over to the Beggars' isle again; but when they came with the porridge scrap-

234

ings and cheese parings from the palace, there was no
one who would taste them that day either, and so those
who had brought the food were more astonished than
ever. But one of those who brought the food contrived
to smell out that the lad who had owned the scissors
owned also a tablecloth, which he only needed to spread
out, and it was covered with all the good things he could
wish for. So when he got back to the palace, he wasn't
long before he said,—

"Such hot joints and such custards I never saw the
like of in the king's palace."

And when the Princess heard that, she told it to the
king, and begged and prayed so long, that he was forced
to send a messenger out to the island to fetch the lad
who owned the table-cloth; and so Boots came back to
the palace. The Princess must and would have the
cloth of him, and offered him gold and green woods for
it, but Boots wouldn't sell it at any price.

"But if I may have leave to lie on the bench by the
Princess' bed-side to-night, she shall have the cloth; but
if she's afraid, she is welcome to set four men to watch
inside the room."

Yes! the Princess agreed to this, so Boots lay down
on the bench by the bed-side, and the four men watched;
but if the Princess hadn't much sleep the night before,
she had much less this, for she could scarce get a wink
of sleep; there she lay wide awake looking at the lovely
lad the whole night through, and after all, the night
seemed too short.

Next morning Boots was rowed off again to the Beggars' island, though sorely against the Princess' will, so happy was she to be near him; but it was past praying for; to the island he must go, and there was an end of it. But when those who brought the food to the beggars came with the porridge scrapings and cheese parings, there wasn't one of them who would even look at what the king sent, and those who brought it didn't wonder either; though they all thought it strange that none of them were thirsty. But just then, one of the king's guard smelled out that the lad who had owned the scissors and the table-cloth had a tap besides, which, if one only turned it a little, gave out the rarest drink, both ale and mead and wine. So when he came back to the palace, he couldn't keep his mouth shut this time any more than before; he went about telling high and low about the tap, and how easy it was to draw all sorts of drink out of it.

"And as for that mead and ale, I've never tasted the like of them in the king's palace; honey and syrup are nothing to them for sweetness."

So when the Princess heard that, she was all for getting the tap, and was nothing loath to strike a bargain with the owner either. So she went again to the king, and begged him to send a messenger to the Beggars' isle after the lad who had owned the scissors and cloth, for now he had another thing worth having, she said; and when the king heard it was a tap, that was good to give the best ale and wine any one could drink, when one gave it a turn, he wasn't long in sending the messenger, I should think.

236

So when Boots came up to the palace, the Princess asked whether it were true he had a tap which could do such and such things? "Yes! he had such a tap in his waistcoat pocket," said Boots; but when the Princess wished with all her might to buy it, Boots said, as he had twice before, he wouldn't sell it, even if the Princess gave half the kingdom for it.

"But all the same," said Boots; "if I may have leave to sleep on the Princess' bed to-night, outside the quilt, she shall have my tap. I'll not do her any harm; but, if she's afraid, she may set eight men to watch in her room."

"Oh, no!" said the Princess, "there was no need of that, she knew him now so well;" and so Boots lay outside the Princess' bed that night. But if she hadn't slept much the two nights before, she had less sleep that night; for she couldn't shut her eyes the livelong night, but lay and looked at Boots, who lay alongside her outside the quilt.

So, when she got up in the morning, and they were going to row Boots back to the island, she begged them to hold hard a little bit; and in she ran to the king, and begged him so prettily to let her have Boots for a husband, she was so fond of him, and, unless she had him, she did not care to live.

"Well, well!" said the king, "you shall have him if you must; for he who has such things is just as rich as you are."

So Boots got the Princess and half the kingdom—the other half he was to have when the king died; and so everything went smooth and well; but as for his brothers, who had always been so bad to him, he packed them off to the Beggars' island.

"There," said Boots, "perhaps they may find out which is best off, the man who has his pockets full of money, or the man whom all women fall in love with."

Nor, to tell you the truth, do I think it would help them much to wander about upon the Beggars' island pulling pieces of money out of their pockets; and so, if Boots hasn't taken them off the island, there they are still walking about to this very day, eating cheese-parings and the scrapings of the porridge-pots.

THE HUSBAND WHO WAS TO MIND THE HOUSE.

ONCE on a time there was a man, so surly and cross, he never thought his wife did anything right in the house. So, one evening, in hay-making time, he came home, scolding and swearing, and showing his teeth and making a dust.

"Dear love, don't be so angry; there's a good man," said his goody; "to-morrow let's change our work. I'll go out with the mowers and mow, and you shall mind the house at home."

Yes! the husband thought that would do very well. He was quite willing, he said.

So, early next morning, his goody took a scythe over her neck, and went out into the hay-field with the mow-

ers, and began to mow; but the man was to mind the
house, and do the work at home.

First of all, he wanted to churn the butter; but when
he had churned a while, he got thirsty, and went down
to the cellar to tap a barrel of ale. So, just when he
had knocked in the bung, and was putting the tap into
the cask, he heard overhead the pig come into the kitchen.
Then off he ran up the cellar steps, with the tap in his
hand, as fast as he could, to look after the pig, lest it
should upset the churn; but when he got up, and saw
the pig had already knocked the churn over, and stood
there, routing and grunting amongst the cream which
was running all over the floor, he got so wild with rage
that he quite forgot the ale-barrel, and ran at the pig as
hard as he could. He caught it, too, just as it ran out
of doors, and gave it such a kick, that piggy lay for dead
on the spot. Then all at once he remembered he had the
tap in his hand; but when he got down to the cellar,
every drop of ale had run out of the cask.

Then he went into the dairy and found enough cream
left to fill the churn again, and so he began to churn, for
butter they must have at dinner. When he had churned
a bit, he remembered that their milking cow was still
shut up in the byre, and hadn't had a bit to eat or a
drop to drink all the morning, though the sun was high.
Then all at once he thought 'twas too far to take her
down to the meadow, so he'd just get her up on the
house top—for the house, you must know, was thatched
with sods, and a fine crop of grass was growing there.
Now their house lay close up against a steep down, and

he thought if he laid a plank across to the thatch at the back he'd easily get the cow up.

But still he couldn't leave the churn, for there was his little babe crawling about on the floor, and "if I leave it," he thought, "the child is safe to upset it." So he took the churn on his back, and went out with it; but then he thought he'd better first water the cow before he turned her out on the thatch; so he took up a bucket to draw water out of the well; but, as he stooped down at the well's brink, all the cream ran out of the churn over his shoulders, and so down into the well.

Now it was near dinner-time, and he hadn't even got the butter yet; so he thought he'd best boil the porridge, and filled the pot with water, and hung it over the fire. When he had done that, he thought the cow might perhaps fall off the thatch and break her legs or her neck. So he got up on the house to tie her up. One end of the rope he made fast to the cow's neck, and the other he slipped down the chimney and tied round his own thigh; and he had to make haste, for the water now began to boil in the pot, and he had still to grind the oatmeal.

So he began to grind away; but while he was hard at it, down fell the cow off the house-top after all, and as she fell, she dragged the man up the chimney by the rope. There he stuck fast; and as for the cow, she hung half way down the wall, swinging between heaven and earth, for she could neither get down nor up.

And now the goody had waited seven lengths and seven breadths for her husband to come and call them home to dinner; but never a call they had. At last she thought she'd waited long enough, and went home. But when she got there and saw the cow hanging in such an ugly place, she ran up and cut the rope in two with her scythe. But as she did this, down came her husband out of the chimney; and so when his old dame came inside the kitchen, there she found him standing on his head in the porridge pot.

———

FARMER WEATHERSKY.

ONCE on a time there was a man and his wife, who had an only son, and his name was Jack. The old dame thought it high time for her son to go out into the world to learn a trade, and bade her husband be off with him.

"But all you do," she said, "mind you bind him to some one who can teach him to be master above all masters;" and with that she put some food and a roll of tobacco into a bag, and packed them off.

Well! they went to many masters; but one and all said they could make the lad as good as themselves, but better they couldn't make him. So when the man came home again to his wife with that answer, she said,—

"I don't care what you make of him; but this I say and stick to, you must bind him to some one where he can learn to be master above all masters;" and with that she packed up more food and another roll of tobacco, and father and son had to be off again.

Now when they had walked a while they got upon the ice, and there they met a man who came whisking along in a sledge, and drove a black horse.

"Whither away?" said the man.

"Well!" said the father, "I'm going to bind my son to some one who is good to teach him a trade; but my old dame comes of such fine folk, she will have him taught to be master above all masters."

"Well met then," said the driver; "I'm just the man for your money, for I'm looking out for such an apprentice. Up with you behind!" he added to the lad, and whisk! off they went, both of them, and sledge and horse, right up into the air.

"Nay, nay!" cried the lad's father, "you haven't told me your name, nor where you live."

"Oh!" said the master, "I'm at home alike north and south, and east and west, and my name's *Farmer Weathersky*. In a year and a day you may come here again, and then I'll tell you if I like him." So away they went through the air, and were soon out of sight.

So when the man got home, his old dame asked what had become of her son.

"Well," said the man, "Heaven knows, I'm sure I don't. They went up aloft;" and so he told her what had happened. But when the old dame heard that her husband couldn't tell at all when her son's apprenticeship would be out, nor whither he had gone, she packed him off again, and gave him another bag of food and another roll of tobacco.

So, when he had walked a bit, he came to a great wood, which stretched on and on all day as he walked through it. When it got dark he saw a great light, and he went towards it. After a long, long time he came to a little hut under a rock, and outside stood an old hag drawing water out of a well with her nose, so long was it.

"Good evening, mother!" said the man.

"The same to you," said the old hag. "It's hundreds of years since any one called me mother."

"Can I have lodging here to-night?" asked the man.

"No! that you can't," said she.

But then the man pulled out his roll of tobacco, lighted his pipe, and gave the old dame a whiff, and a pinch of snuff. Then she was so happy she began to dance for joy, and the end was, she gave the man leave to stop the night.

So next morning he began to ask after Farmer Weathersky. "No! she never heard tell of him, but she ruled over all the four-footed beasts; perhaps some of them might know him." So she played them all home with a pipe she had, and asked them all, but there wasn't one of them who knew anything about Farmer Weathersky.

"Well!" said the old hag, "there are three sisters of us; maybe one of the other two know where he lives. I'll lend you my horse and sledge, and then you'll be at her house by night; but it's at least three hundred miles off, the nearest way."

Then the man started off, and at night reached the house, and when he came there, there stood another old hag before the door, drawing water out of the well with her nose.

"Good evening, mother!" said the man.

"The same to you," said she; "it's hundreds of years since any one called me mother."

"Can I lodge here to-night?" asked the man.

"No!" said the old hag.

But he took out his roll of tobacco, lighted his pipe, and gave the old dame a whiff, and a good pinch of snuff besides, on the back of her hand. Then she was so happy that she began to jump and dance for joy, and so the man got leave to stay the night. When that was over, he began to ask after Farmer Weathersky. "No! she had never heard tell of him; but she ruled all the fish in the sea; perhaps some of them might know something about him." So she played them all home with a pipe she had, and asked them, but there wasn't one of them who knew anything about Farmer Weathersky.

"Well, well!" said the old hag, "there's one sister of us left; maybe she knows something about him. She lives six hundred miles off, but I'll lend you my horse and sledge, and then you'll get there by nightfall."

Then the man started off, and reached the house by nightfall, and there he found another old hag who stood before the grate, and stirred the fire with her nose, so long and tough it was.

"Good evening, mother!" said the man.

"The same to you," said the old hag; "it's hundreds of years since any one called me mother."

"Can I lodge here to-night?" asked the man.

"No," said the old hag.

Then the man pulled out his roll of tobacco again, and lighted his pipe, and gave the old hag such a pinch of snuff it covered the whole back of her hand. Then she got so happy she began to dance for joy, and so the man got leave to stay.

But when the night was over, he began to ask after Farmer Weathersky. She never heard tell of him she said; but she ruled over all the birds of the air, and so she played them all home with a pipe she had, and when she had mustered them all, the Eagle was missing. But a little while after he came flying home, and when she asked him, he said he had just come straight from Farmer Weathersky. Then the old hag said he must guide the man thither; but the eagle said he must have something to eat first, and besides he must rest till the next day; he was so tired with flying that long way, he could scarce rise from the earth.

So when he had eaten his fill and taken a good rest, the old hag pulled a feather out of the Eagle's tail, and put the man there in its stead; so the Eagle flew off with the man, and flew, and flew, but they didn't reach Farmer Weathersky's house before midnight.

So when they got there, the Eagle said,—

"There are heaps of dead bodies lying about outside, but you mustn't mind them. Inside the house every man Jack of them all are so sound asleep, 'twill be hard work to wake them; but you must go straight to the table drawer, and take out of it three crumbs of bread, and when you hear some one snoring loud, pull three feathers out of his head; he won't wake for all that."

So the man did as he was told, and after he had taken the crumbs of bread, he pulled out the first feather.

"OOF!" growled Farmer Weathersky, for it was he who snored.

So the man pulled out another feather.

"OOF!" he growled again.

But when he pulled out the third, Farmer Weathersky roared so, the man thought roof and wall would have flown asunder, but for all that the snorer slept on.

After that the Eagle told him what he was to do. He went to the yard, and there at the stable-door he stumbled against a big gray stone, and that he lifted up; underneath it lay three chips of wood, and those he picked up too; then he knocked at the stable-door, and it opened of itself. Then he threw down the three crumbs of bread, and a hare came and ate them up; that hare he caught and kept. After that the Eagle bade him pull three feathers out of his tail, and put the hare, the stone, the chips, and himself there instead, and then he would fly away home with them all.

So when the Eagle had flown a long way, he lighted on a rock to rest.

"Do you see anything?" it asked.

"Yes," said the man, "I see a flock of crows coming flying after us."

"We'd better be off again, then," said the Eagle, who flew away.

After a while it asked again,—

"Do you see anything now?"

"Yes," said the man; "now the crows are close behind us."

"Drop now the three feathers you pulled out of his head," said the Eagle.

Well, the man dropped the feathers, and as soon as ever he dropped them they became a flock of ravens which drove the crows home again. Then the Eagle flew on far away with the man, and at last it lighted on another stone to rest.

"Do you see anything?" it said.

"I'm not sure," said the man; "I fancy I see something coming far far away."

"We'd better get on then," said the Eagle; and after a while it said again—

"Do you see anything?"

"Yes," said the man, "now he's close at our heels."

"Now, you must let fall the chips of wood which you took from under the gray stone at the stable door," said the Eagle.

Yes! the man let them fall, and they grew at once up into tall thick wood, so that Farmer Weathersky had to go back home to fetch an axe to hew his way through. While he did this, the Eagle flew ever so far, but when it got tired, it lighted on a fir to rest.

"Do you see anything?" it said.

"Well! I'm not sure," said the man; "but I fancy I catch a glimpse of something far away."

"We'd best be off then," said the Eagle; and off it flew as fast as it could. After a while it said—

"Do you see anything now?"

"Yes! now he's close behind us," said the man.

"Now, you must drop the big stone you lifted up at the stable door," said the Eagle.

The man did so, and as it fell, it became a great high mountain, which Farmer Weathersky had to break his way through. When he had got half through the mountain, he tripped and broke one of his legs, and so he had to limp home again and patch it up.

But while he was doing this, the Eagle flew away to the man's house with him and the hare, and as soon as they got home, the man went into the churchyard and sprinkled Christian mould over the hare, and lo! it turned into "Jack," his son.

Well, you may fancy the old dame was glad to get her son again, but still she wasn't easy in her mind about his trade, and she wouldn't rest till he gave her a proof that he was "master above all masters."

So when the fair came round, the lad changed himself into a bay horse, and told his father to lead him to the fair.

"Now, when any one comes," he said, "to buy me, you may ask a hundred dollars for me; but mind you don't forget to take the headstall off me; if you do, Farmer Weathersky will keep me for ever, for he it is who will come to deal with you."

So it turned out. Up came a horse-dealer, who had a great wish to deal for the horse, and he gave a hundred dollars down for him; but when the bargain was struck, and Jack's father had pocketed the money, the horse-dealer wanted to have the headstall. "Nay, nay!" said the man, "there's nothing about that in the bargain; and besides, you can't have the headstall, for I've other horses at home to bring to town to-morrow."

So each went his way; but they hadn't gone far before Jack took his own shape and ran away, and when his father got home, there sat Jack in the ingle.

Next day he turned himself into a brown horse, and told his father to drive him to the fair.

"And when any one comes to buy me, you may ask two hundred dollars for me—he'll give that and treat you besides; but whatever you do, and however much you drink, don't forget to take the headstall off me, else you'll never set eyes on me again."

So all happened as he had said: the man got two hundred dollars for the horse and a glass of drink besides, and when the buyer and seller parted, it was as much as he could do to remember to take off the headstall. But the buyer and the horse hadn't got far on the road before Jack took his own shape, and when the man got home, there sat Jack in the ingle

The third day, it was the same story over again: the lad turned himself into a black horse, and told his father some one would come and bid three hundred dollars for him, and fill his skin with meat and drink besides; but however much he ate or drank, he was to mind and not forget to take the headstall off, else he'd have to stay with Farmer Weathersky all his life long.

"No, no; I'll not forget, never fear," said the man.

So when he came to the fair, he got three hundred dollars for the horse, and as it wasn't to be a dry bargain, Farmer Weathersky made him drink so much that he quite forgot to take the headstall off, and away went Farmer Weathersky with the horse. Now when he had gone a little way, Farmer Weathersky thought he would just stop and have another glass of brandy; so he put a barrel of red hot nails under his horse's nose, and a sieve of oats under his tail, hung the halter upon a hook, and went into the inn. So the horse stood there, and stamped and pawed, and snorted and reared. Just then out came a lassie, who thought it a shame to treat a horse so.

"Oh, poor beastie," she said, "what a cruel master you must have to treat you so," and as she said this she pulled the halter off the hook, so that the horse might turn round and taste the oats.

"*I'm after you,*" roared Farmer Weathersky, who came rushing out of the door.

But the horse had already shaken off the headstall, and jumped into a duck-pond, where he turned himself into a tiny fish. In went Farmer Weathersky after him, and turned himself into a great pike. Then Jack turned himself into a dove, and Farmer Weathersky made himself into a hawk, and chased and struck at the dove. But just then a Princess stood at the window of the palace and saw the struggle.

"Ah! poor dove," she cried, "if you only knew what I know, you'd fly to me through this window."

So the dove came flying in through the window, and turned itself into Jack again, who told his own tale.

"Turn yourself into a gold ring, and put yourself on my finger," said the Princess.

"Nay, nay!" said Jack, "that'll never do, for then Farmer Weathersky will make the king sick, and then there'll be no one who can make him well again till Farmer Weathersky comes and cures him, and then, for his fee, he'll ask for that gold ring."

"Then I'll say I had it from my mother, and can't part with it," said the Princess.

Well, Jack turned himself into a gold ring, and put himself on the Princess' finger, and so Farmer Weathersky couldn't get at him. But then followed what the lad had foretold; the king fell sick, and there wasn't a doctor in the kingdom who could cure him till Farmer Weathersky came, and he asked for the ring off the Princess' finger for his fee. So the king sent a messenger to the Princess for the ring; but the Princess said she wouldn't part with it, her mother had left it her. When the king heard that, he flew into a rage, and said he would have the ring, whoever left it to her.

"Well," said the Princess, "it's no good being cross about it. I can't get it off, and if you must have the ring, you must take my finger too."

"If you'll let me try, I'll soon get the ring off," said Farmer Weathersky.

"No, thanks, I'll try myself," said the Princess, and flew off to the grate and put ashes on her finger. Then the ring slipped off and was lost among the ashes. So Farmer Weathersky turned himself into a cock, who scratched and pecked after the ring in the grate, till he was up to the ears in ashes. But while he was doing this, Jack turned himself into a fox, and bit off the cock's head; and so if the Evil One was in Farmer Weathersky, it is all over with him now.

LORD PETER.

ONCE on a time there was a poor couple, and they had nothing in the world but three sons. What the names the two elder had I can't say, but the youngest he was called Peter. So when their father and mother died, the sons were to share what was left, but there was nothing but a porridge-pot, a griddle, and a cat.

The eldest, who was to have first choice, he took the pot; "for," said he, "whenever I lend the pot to any one to boil porridge, I can always get leave to scrape it."

The second took the griddle; "for," said he, "whenever I lend it to any one, I'll always get a morsel of dough to make a bannock."

But the youngest, he had no choice left him; if he was to choose anything it must be the cat.

"Well!" said he, "if I lend the cat to any one I shan't get much by that; for if pussy gets a drop of milk, she'll want it all herself. Still, I'd best take her along with me; I shouldn't like her to go about here and starve."

So the brothers went out into the world to try their luck, and each took his own way; but when the youngest had gone a while, the cat said,—

"Now you shall have a good turn, because you wouldn't let me stay behind in the old cottage and starve. Now I'm off to the wood to lay hold of a fine fat head of game, and then you must go up to the king's palace that you see yonder, and say you are come with a little present for the king; and when he asks who sends it, you must say, 'Why, who should it be from but Lord Peter.'"

Well! Peter hadn't waited long before back came the cat with a reindeer from the wood; she had jumped up on the reindeer's head, between his horns, and said, "If you don't go straight to the king's palace I'll claw your eyes out."

So the reindeer had to go whether he liked it or no.

And when Peter got to the palace he went into the kitchen with the deer, and said,—"Here I'm come with a little present for the King, if he won't despise it."

Then the King went out into the kitchen, and when he saw the fine plump reindeer, he was very glad.

"But, my dear friend," he said, "who in the world is it that sends me such a fine gift?"

"Oh!" said Peter. "who should send it but Lord Peter."

"Lord Peter! Lord Peter!" said the King. "Pray tell me where he lives;" for he thought it a shame not to know so great a man. But that was just what the lad wouldn't tell him; he daren't do it, he said, because his master had forbidden him.

So the King gave him a good bit of money to drink his health, and bade him be sure and say all kind of pretty things, and many thanks for the present to his master when he got home.

Next day the Cat went again into the wood, and jumped up on a red deer's head, and sat between his horns, and forced him to go to the palace. Then Peter went again into the kitchen, and said he was come with a little present for the King, if he would be pleased to take it. And the King was still more glad to get the red deer than he had been to get the reindeer, and asked again who it was that sent so fine a present.

"Why, it's Lord Peter, of course," said the lad; but when the King wanted to know where Lord Peter lived, he got the same answer as the day before; and this day, too, he gave Peter a good lump of money to drink his health with.

The third day the Cat came with an elk. And so when Peter got into the palace-kitchen, and said he had a little present for the King, if he'd be pleased to take it, the King came out at once into the kitchen; and when he saw the grand big elk, he was so glad he scarce knew which leg to stand on; and this day, too, he gave Peter many more dollars—at least a hundred. He wished now, once for all, to know where this Lord Peter lived, and asked and asked about this thing and that, but the lad said he daren't say, for his master's sake, who had strictly forbidden him to tell.

"Well, then," said the King, "beg Lord Peter to come and see me."

Yes, the lad would take that message; but when Peter got out into the yard again, and met the Cat, he said,

"A pretty scrape you've got me into now, for here's the King, who wants me to come and see him, and you know I've nothing to go in but these rags I stand and walk in."

"Oh, don't be afraid about that," said the Cat; "in three days you shall have coach and horses, and fine clothes, so fine that the gold falls from them, and then you may go and see the king very well. But mind, whatever you see in the king's palace, you must say you have far finer and grander things of your own. Don't forget that."

No, no, Peter would bear that in mind, never fear.

So when three days were over, the Cat came with a coach and horses, and clothes, and all that Peter wanted, and altogether it was as grand as anything you ever set eyes on; so off he set, and the Cat ran alongside the coach. The King met him well and graciously; but whatever the King offered him, and whatever he showed him, Peter said, 'twas all very well, but he had far finer and better things in his own house. The King seemed not quite to believe this, but Peter stuck to what he said, and at last the King got so angry, he couldn't bear it any longer.

"Now I'll go home with you," he said, "and see if it be true what you've been telling me, that you have far finer and better things of your own. But if you've been telling a pack of lies, Heaven help you, that's all I say."

"Now, you've got me into a fine scrape," said Peter to the Cat, "for here's the King coming home with me; but my home, that's not so easy to find, I think."

"Oh! never mind," said the Cat; "only do you drive after me as I run before."

So off they set; first Peter, who drove after his Cat, and then the King and all his court.

But when they had driven a good bit, they came to a great flock of fine sheep, that had wool so long it almost touched the ground.

"If you'll only say," said the Cat to the Shepherd, "this flock of sheep belongs to Lord Peter, when the King asks you, I'll give you this silver spoon," which she had taken with her from the King's palace.

Yes! he was willing enough to do that. So when the king came up, he said to the lad who watched the sheep,—

"Well, I never saw so large and fine a flock of sheep in my life! Whose is it? my little lad."

"Why," said the lad, "whose should it be but Lord Peter's."

A little while after they came to a great, great herd of fine brindled kine, who were all so sleek the sun shone from them.

"If you'll only say," said the Cat to the neat-herd, "this herd is Lord Peter's, when the King asks you, I'll give you this silver ladle;" and the ladle too she had taken from the King's palace.

"Yes! with all my heart," said the neat-herd.

So when the King came up, he was quite amazed at the fine fat herd, for such a herd he had never seen before, and so he asked the neat-herd who owned those brindled kine.

"Why! who should own them but Lord Peter," said the neat-herd.

So they went on a little further, and came to a great, great drove of horses, the finest you ever saw, six of each colour, bay, and black, and brown, and chestnut.

"If you'll only say this drove of horses is Lord Peter's when the King asks you," said the Cat, "I'll give you this silver stoop;" and the stoop too she had taken from the palace.

Yes! the lad was willing enough; and so when the King came up, he was quite amazed at the grand drove of horses, for the matches of such horses he had never yet set eyes on, he said.

So he asked the lad who watched them, whose all these blacks, and bays, and browns, and chestnuts were?

"Whose should they be," said the lad, "but Lord Peter's."

So when they had gone a good bit farther, they came to a castle; first there was a gate of tin, and next there was a gate of silver, and next a gate of gold. The castle itself was of silver, and so dazzling white, that it quite hurt one's eyes to look at in the sunbeams which fell on it just as they reached it.

So they went into it, and the Cat told Peter to say this was his house. As for the castle inside, it was far finer than it looked outside, for every thing was pure gold,—chairs, and tables, and benches, and all. And when the King had gone all over it, and seen everything high and low, he got quite shameful and downcast.

"Yes," he said at last; "Lord Peter has everything far finer than I have, there's no gainsaying that," and so he wanted to be off home again.

But Peter begged him to stay to supper, and the King stayed, but he was sour and surly the whole time.

So as they sat at supper, back same the Troll who owned the castle, and gave such a great knock at the door.

"Who's this eating my meat and drinking my mead like swine in here," roared out the Troll.

As soon as the Cat heard that, she ran down to the gate.

"Stop a bit," she said, "and I'll tell you how the farmer sets to work to get in his winter rye."

And so she told him such a long story about the winter rye.

"First of all, you see, he ploughs his field, and then he dungs it, and then he ploughs it again, and then he harrows it;" and so she went on till the sun rose.

"Oh, do look behind you, and there you'll see such a lovely lady," said the Cat to the Troll.

So the Troll turned round, and, of course, as soon as he saw the sun he burst.

"Now all this is yours," said the Cat to Lord Peter. "Now, you must cut off my head; that's all I ask for what I have done for you."

"Nay, nay," said Lord Peter, "I'll never do any such thing, that's flat."

"If you don't," said the Cat, "see if I don't claw your eyes out."

Well! so Lord Peter had to do it, though it was sore against his will. He cut off the Cat's head, but there and then she became the loveliest Princess you ever set eyes on, and Lord Peter fell in love with her at once.

"Yes! all this greatness was mine first," said the Princess, "but a Troll bewitched me to be a Cat in your father's and mother's cottage. Now you may do as you please, whether you take me as your queen or not, for you are now king over all this realm."

Well, well; there was little doubt Lord Peter would

be willing enough to have her as his queen, and so there
was a wedding that lasted eight whole days, and a feast
besides; and after it was over, I stayed no longer with
Lord Peter and his lovely queen, and so I can't say anything more about them.

BOOTS AND HIS BROTHERS.

ONCE on a time there was a man who had three sons,
Peter, Paul, and John. John was Boots, of course, because he was the youngest. I can't say the man had
anything more than these three sons, for he hadn't one
penny to rub against another; and so he told his sons
over and over again they must go out into the world and
try to earn their bread, for there at home there was
nothing to be looked for but starving to death.

Now, a bit off the man's cottage was the king's palace,
and you must know, just against the king's windows a
great oak had sprung up, which was so stout and big that
it took away all the light from the king's palace. The
King had said he would give many, many dollars to the
man who could fell the oak, but no one was man enough
for that, for as soon as ever one chip of the oak's trunk
flew off, two grew in its stead. A well, too, the King
had dug, which was to hold water for the whole year;
for all his neighbours had wells, but he hadn't any, and
that he thought a shame. So the King said he would
give any one who could dig him such a well as would
hold water for a whole year round, both money and

goods; but no one could do it, for the King's palace lay
high, high up on a hill, and they hadn't dug a few inches
before they came upon the living rock.

But as the King had set his heart on having these two
things done, he had it given out far and wide, in all the
churches of his kingdom, that he who could fell the big
oak in the king's court-yard, and get him a well that
would hold water the whole year round, should have the
Princess and half the kingdom. Well! you may easily
know there was many a man who came to try his luck;
but for all their hacking and hewing, and all their digging and delving, it was no good. The oak got bigger
and stouter at every stroke, and the rock didn't get softer
either. So one day those three brothers thought they'd
set off and try too, and their father hadn't a word against
it; for even if they didn't get a Princess and half the
kingdom, it might happen they might get a place somewhere with a good master; and that was all he wanted.
So when the brothers said they thought of going to the
palace, their father said "yes" at once. So Peter, Paul,
and Jack went off from their home.

Well! they hadn't gone far before they came to a fir
wood, and up along one side of it rose a steep hillside,
and as they went, they heard something hewing and hacking away up on the hill among the trees.

"I wonder now what it is that is hewing away up
yonder?" said Jack.

"You're always so clever with your wonderings," said
Peter and Paul both at once. "What wonder is it, pray,
that a woodcutter should stand and hack up on a hill-
side?"

260

"Still, I'd like to see what it is, after all," said Jack; and up he went.

"Oh, if you're such a child, 'twill do you good to go and take a lesson," bawled out his brothers after him.

But Jack didn't care for what they said; he climbed the steep hillside towards where the noise came, and when he reached the place, what do you think he saw? why, an axe that stood there hacking and hewing, all of itself, at the trunk of a fir.

"Good day!" said Jack. "So you stand here all alone and hew, do you?"

"Yes; here I've stood and hewed and hacked a long long time, waiting for you," said the Axe.

"Well, here I am at last," said Jack, as he took the axe, pulled it off its haft, and stuffed both head and haft into his wallet.

So when he got down again to his brothers, they began to jeer and laugh at him.

"And now, what funny thing was it you saw up yonder on the hillside?" they said.

"Oh, it was only an axe we heard," said Jack.

So when they had gone a bit farther, they came under a steep spur of rock, and up there they heard something digging and shovelling.

"I wonder now," said Jack, "what it is digging and shovelling up yonder at the top of the rock."

"Ah, you're always so clever with your wonderings," said Peter and Paul again, "as if you'd never heard a woodpecker hacking and pecking at a hollow tree."

"Well, well," said Jack, "I think it would be a piece of fun just to see what it really is."

And so off he set to climb the rock, while the others laughed and made game of him. But he didn't care a bit for that; up he clomb, and when he got near the top, what do you think he saw? Why, a spade that stood there digging and delving.

"Good day!" said Jack. "So you stand here all alone, and dig and delve!"

"Yes, that's what I do," said the Spade, "and that's what I've done this many a long day, waiting for you."

"Well, here I am," said Jack again, as he took the spade and knocked it off its handle, and put it into his wallet, and then down again to his brothers.

"Well, what was it, so rare and strange," said Peter and Paul, "that you saw up there at the top of the rock?"

"Oh," said Jack, "nothing more than a spade; that was what we heard."

So they went on again a good bit, till they came to a brook. They were thirsty, all three, after their long walk, and so they lay down beside the brook to have a drink.

"I wonder now," said Jack, "where all this water comes from."

"I wonder if you're right in your head," said Peter and Paul, in one breath. "If you're not mad already, you'll go mad very soon, with your wonderings. Where the brook comes from, indeed! Have you never heard how water rises from a spring in the earth?"

"Yes! but still I've a great fancy to see where this brook comes from," said Jack.

So up alongside the brook he went, in spite of all that his brothers bawled after him. Nothing could stop him. On he went. So, as he went up and up, the brook got smaller and smaller, and at last, a little way farther on, what do you think he saw? Why, a great walnut, and out of that the water trickled.

"Good-day!" said Jack again. "So you lie here, and trickle and run down all alone?"

"Yes, I do," said the Walnut; "and here have I trickled and run this many a long day, waiting for you."

"Well, here I am," said Jack, as he took up a lump of moss, and plugged up the hole, that the water mightn't run out. Then he put the walnut into his wallet, and ran down to his brothers.

"Well now," said Peter and Paul, "have you found out where the water comes from? A rare sight it must have been!"

"Oh, after all, it was only a hole it ran out of," said Jack; and so the others laughed and made game of him again, but Jack didn't mind that a bit.

"After all, I had the fun of seeing it," said he.

So when they had gone a bit farther, they came to the king's palace; but as every one in the kingdom had heard how they might win the Princess and half the realm, if they could only fell the big oak and dig the king's well, so many had come to try their luck that the oak was now twice as stout and big as it had been at first, for two chips grew for every one they hewed out with their axes, as I daresay you all bear in mind. So the King had now laid it down as a punishment, that if any one tried and couldn't fell the oak, he should be put on a barren island, and both his ears were to be clipped off. But the two brothers didn't let themselves be scared by that; they were quite sure they could fell the oak, and Peter, as he was the eldest, was to try his hand first; but it went with him as with all the rest who had hewn at the oak; for every chip he cut out, two grew in its place. So the king's men seized him, and clipped off both his ears, and put him out on the island.

Now Paul, he was to try his luck, but he fared just the same; when he had hewn two or three strokes, they began to see the oak grow, and so the king's men seized him too, and clipped his ears, and put him out on the island; and his ears they clipped closer, because they said he ought to have taken a lesson from his brother.

So now Jack was to try.

"If you *will* look like a marked sheep, we're quite ready to clip your ears at once, and then you'll save yourself some bother," said the King, for he was angry with him for his brothers' sake.

"Well, I'd just like to try first," said Jack, and so he got leave. Then he took his axe out of his wallet and fitted it to its haft.

"Hew away!" said he to his axe; and away it hewed, making the chips fly again, so that it wasn't long before down came the oak.

When that was done, Jack pulled out his spade, and fitted it to its handle.

"Dig away!" said he to the spade; and so the spade began to dig and delve till the earth and rock flew out in splinters, and so he had the well soon dug out, you may think.

And when he had got it as big and deep as he chose, Jack took out his walnut and laid it in one corner of the well, and pulled the plug of moss out.

"Trickle and run," said Jack; and so the nut trickled and ran, till the water gushed out of the hole in a stream, and in a short time the well was brimfull.

Then Jack had felled the oak which shaded the king's palace, and dug a well in the palace-yard, and so he got the Princess and half the kingdom, as the King had said; but it was lucky for Peter and Paul that they had lost their ears, else they had heard each hour and day, how every one said, "Well, after all, Jack wasn't so much out of his mind when he took to wondering."

TATTERHOOD.

ONCE on a time there was a king and a queen who had no children, and that gave the queen much grief; she scarce had one happy hour. She was always bewailing and bemoaning herself, and saying how dull and lonesome it was in the palace.

"If we had children there'd be life enough," she said.

Wherever she went in all her realm she found God's blessing in children, even in the vilest hut; and wherever she came she heard the Goodies scolding the bairns, and saying how they had done that and that wrong. All this the queen heard, and thought it would be so nice to do as other women did. At last the king and queen took into their palace a stranger lassie to rear up, that they might have her always with them, to love her if she did well, and scold her if she did wrong, like their own child.

So one day the little lassie whom they had taken as their own, ran down into the palace yard, and was playing with a gold apple. Just then an old beggar wife came by, who had a little girl with her, and it wasn't long before the little lassie and the beggar's bairn were great friends, and began to play together, and to toss the gold apple about between them. When the Queen saw this, as she sat at a window in the palace, she tapped on the pane for her foster-daughter to come up. She went at once, but the beggar-girl went up too; and as they went into the Queen's bower, each held the other by the hand.

Then the Queen began to scold the little lady, and to say—

"You ought to be above running about and playing with a tattered beggar's brat."

And so she wanted to drive the lassie down stairs.

"If the Queen only knew my mother's power, she'd not drive me out," said the little lassie; and when the Queen asked what she meant more plainly, she told her how her mother could get her children if she chose. The Queen wouldn't believe it, but the lassie held her own, and said every word of it was true, and bade the Queen only to try and make her mother do it. So the Queen sent the lassie down to fetch up her mother.

"Do you know what your daughter says?" asked the Queen of the old woman, as soon as ever she came into the room.

No; the beggar-wife knew nothing about it.

"Well, she says you can get me children if you will," answered the Queen.

"Queens shouldn't listen to beggar lassies' silly stories," said the old wife, and strode out of the room.

Then the Queen got angry, and wanted again to drive out the little lassie; but she declared it was true every word that she had said.

"Let the Queen only give my mother a drop to drink," said the lassie; "when she gets merry she'll soon find out a way to help you."

The Queen was ready to try this; so the beggar wife was fetched up again once more, and treated both with wine and mead as much as she chose; and so it was not long before her tongue began to wag. Then the Queen came out again with the same question she had asked before.

"One way to help you perhaps I know," said the beggar wife. "Your Majesty must make them bring in two pails of water some evening before you go to bed. In each of them you must wash yourself, and afterwards throw away the water under the bed. When you look under the bed next morning, two flowers will have sprung up, one fair and one ugly. The fair one you must eat, the ugly one you must let stand; but mind you don't forget the last."

That was what the beggar wife said.

Yes; the Queen did what the beggar wife advised her to do; she had the water brought up in two pails, washed herself in them, and emptied them under the bed; and lo! when she looked under the bed next morning, there stood two flowers; one was ugly and foul, and had black leaves; but the other was so bright, and fair, and lovely, she had never seen its like; so she ate it up at once. But the pretty flower tasted so sweet, that she couldn't help herself. She ate the other up too, for, she thought, "it can't hurt or help one much either way, I'll be bound."

Well, sure enough, after a while the Queen was brought to bed. First of all, she had a girl who had a wooden spoon in her hand, and rode upon a goat; loathly and ugly she was, and the very moment she came into the world, she bawled out "Mamma."

"If I'm your mamma," said the Queen, "God give me grace to mend my ways."

"Oh, don't be sorry," said the girl, who rode on the goat, "for one will soon come after me who is better looking."

So, after a while, the Queen had another girl, who was so fair and sweet, no one had ever set eyes on such a lovely child, and with her you may fancy the Queen was very well pleased. The elder twin they called "Tatterhood," because she was always so ugly and ragged, and because she had a hood which hung about her ears in tatters. The Queen could scarce bear to look at her, and the nurses tried to shut her up in a room by herself, but it was all no good; where the younger twin was, there she must also be, and no one could ever keep them apart.

Well, one Christmas eve, when they were half grown up, there rose such a frightful noise and clatter in the gallery outside the Queen's bower. So Tatterhood asked what it was that dashed and crashed so out in the passage.

"Oh!" said the Queen, "it isn't worth asking about."

But Tatterhood wouldn't give over till she found out all about it; and so the Queen told her it was a pack of Trolls and witches who had come there to keep Christmas. So Tatterhood said she'd just go out and drive them away; and in spite of all they could say, and however much they begged and prayed her to let the Trolls alone, she must and would go out to drive the witches off; but she begged the Queen to mind and keep all the doors close shut, so that not one of them came so much as the least bit ajar. Having said this, off she went with her wooden spoon, and began to hunt and sweep away the hags; and all this while there was such a pother out in the gallery, the like of it was never heard. The whole Palace creaked and groaned as if every joint and beam were going to be torn out of its place. Now, how it was, I'm sure I can't tell; but somehow or other one door did get the least bit a-jar, then her twin sister just peeped out to see how things were going with Tatterhood, and put her head a tiny bit through the opening. But, POP! up came an old witch, and whipped off her head, and stuck a calf's head on her shoulders instead; and so the Princess ran back into the room on all-fours, and began to "moo" like a calf. When Tatterhood came back and saw her sister, she scolded them all round, and was very angry because they hadn't kept better watch, and asked them what they thought of their heedlessness now, when her sister was turned into a calf.

"But still I'll see if I can't set her free," she said.

Then she asked the King for a ship in full trim, and well fitted with stores; but captain and sailors she wouldn't have. No; she would sail away with her sister all alone; and as there was no holding her back, at last they let her have her own way.

Then Tatterhood sailed off, and steered her ship right under the land where the witches dwelt, and when she came to the landing-place, she told her sister to stay quite still on board the ship; but she herself rode on her goat up to the witches' castle. When she got there, one of the windows in the gallery was open, and there she saw her sister's head hung up on the window frame; so she leapt her goat through the window into the gallery, snapped up the head, and set off with it. After her came

the witches to try to get the head again, and they flocked
about her as thick as a swarm of bees or a nest of ants;
but the goat snorted, and puffed, and butted with his
horns, and Tatterhood beat and banged them about with
her wooden spoon; and so the pack of witches had to
give it up. So Tatterhood got back to her ship, took the
calf's head off her sister, and put her own on again, and
then she became a girl as she had been before. After
that she sailed a long, long way, to a strange king's realm.

Now the king of that land was a widower, and had
an only son. So when he saw the strange sail, he sent
messengers down to the strand to find out whence it
came, and who owned it; but when the king's men came
down there, they saw never a living soul on board but
Tatterhood, and there she was, riding round and round
the deck on her goat at full speed, till her elf locks
streamed again in the wind. The folk from the palace
were all amazed at this sight, and asked, were there not
more on board. Yes, there were; she had a sister with
her, said Tatterhood. Her, too, they wanted to see, but
Tatterhood said "No,"—

"No one shall see her, unless the king comes himself," she said; and so she began to gallop about on her
goat till the deck thundered again.

So when the servants got back to the palace, and told
what they had seen and heard down at the ship, the king
was for setting out at once, that he might see the lassie
that rode on the goat. When he got down, Tatterhood
led out her sister, and she was so fair and gentle, the
king fell over head and ears in love with her as he stood.

He brought them both back with him to the Palace, and wanted to have the sister for his queen; but Tatterhood said "No;" the king couldn't have her in any way, unless the king's son chose to have Tatterhood. That you may fancy the prince was very loath to do, such an ugly hussy as Tatterhood was; but at last the king and all the others in the palace talked him over, and he yielded, giving his word to take her for his queen; but it went sore against the grain, and he was a doleful man.

Now they set about the wedding, both with brewing and baking; and when all was ready, they were to go to church; but the prince thought it the weariest churching he had ever had in all his life. First, the king drove off with his bride, and she was so lovely and so grand, all the people stopped to look after her all along the road, and they stared at her till she was out of sight. After them came the prince on horseback by the side of Tatterhood, who trotted along on her goat with her wooden spoon in her fist, and to look at him, it was more like going to a burial than a wedding, and that his own; so sorrowful he seemed, and with never a word to say.

"Why don't you talk?" asked Tatterhood, when they had ridden a bit.

"Why, what should I talk about?" answered the prince.

"Well, you might at least ask me why I ride upon this ugly goat," said Tatterhood.

"Why do you ride on that ugly goat?" asked the prince.

"Is it an ugly goat? why, it's the grandest horse bride

ever rode on," answered Tatterhood; and in a trice the goat became a horse, and that the finest the prince had ever set eyes on.

Then they rode on again a bit, but the prince was just as woeful as before, and couldn't get a word out. So Tatterhood asked him again why he didn't talk, and when the Prince answered, he didn't know what to talk about, she said,—

"You can at least ask me why I ride with this ugly spoon in my fist."

"Why do you ride with that ugly spoon?" asked the prince.

"Is it an ugly spoon? why, it's the loveliest silver wand bride ever bore," said Tatterhood; and in a trice it became a silver wand, so dazzling bright, the sunbeams glistened from it.

So they rode on another bit, but the Prince was just as sorrowful, and said never a word. In a little while, Tatterhood asked him again why he didn't talk, and bade him ask why she wore that ugly grey hood on her head.

"Why do you wear that ugly grey hood on your head?" asked the Prince.

"Is it an ugly hood? why, it's the brightest golden crown bride ever wore," answered Tatterhood, and it became a crown on the spot.

Now, they rode on a long while again, and the Prince was so woeful, that he sat without sound or speech just as before. So his bride asked him again why he didn't talk, and bade him ask now, why her face was so ugly and ashen-grey?

"Ah!" asked the Prince, "why is your face so ugly and ashen-grey?"

"I ugly," said the bride; "you think my sister pretty, but I am ten times prettier;" and lo! when the Prince looked at her, she was so lovely, he thought there never was so lovely a woman in all the world. After that, I shouldn't wonder if the Prince found his tongue, and no longer rode along hanging down his head.

So they drank the bridal cup both deep and long, and, after that, both Prince and King set out with their brides to the Princess's father's palace, and there they had another bridal feast, and drank anew, both deep and long. There was no end to the fun; and, if you make haste and run to the King's palace, I dare say you'll find there's still a drop of the bridal ale left for you.

KATIE WOODENCLOAK.

ONCE on a time there was a King who had become a widower. By his Queen he had one daughter, who was so clever and lovely, there wasn't a cleverer or lovelier Princess in all the world. So the King went on a long time sorrowing for the Queen, whom he had loved so much, but at last he got weary of living alone, and married another Queen, who was a widow, and had, too, an only daughter; but this daughter was just as bad and ugly as the other was kind, and clever, and lovely. The stepmother and her daughter were jealous of the Princess, because she was so lovely; but so long as the King was at home, they dared n't do her any harm, he was so fond of her.

Well, after a time he fell into war with another King, and went out to battle with his host, and then the stepmother thought she might do as she pleased; and so she both starved and beat the Princess, and was after her in every hole and corner of the house. At last she thought everything too good for her, and turned her out to herd cattle. So there she went about with the cattle, and herded them in the woods and on the fells. As for food, she got little or none, and she grew thin and wan, and was always sobbing and sorrowful. Now in the herd there was a great dun bull, which always kept himself so neat and sleek, and often and often he came up to the Princess, and let her pat him. So one day when she sat there, sad, and sobbing, and sorrowful, he came up to her

275

and asked her outright why she was always in such grief.
She answered nothing, but went on weeping.

"Ah!" said the Bull, "I know all about it quite well,
though you won't tell me; you weep because the Queen
is bad to you, and because she is ready to starve you to
death. But food you've no need to fret about, for in my
left ear lies a cloth, and when you take and spread it out,
you may have as many dishes as you please."

So she did that, took the cloth and spread it out on
the grass, and lo! it served up the nicest dishes one could
wish to have; there was wine too, and mead, and sweet
cake. Well, she soon got up her flesh again, and grew
so plump, and rosy, and white, that the Queen and her
scrawny chip of a daughter turned blue and yellow for
spite. The Queen couldn't at all make out how her stepdaughter got to look so well on such bad fare, so she
told one of her maids to go after her in the wood, and
watch and see how it all was, for she thought some of
the servants in the house must give her food. So the
maid went after her, and watched in the wood, and then
she saw how the stepdaughter took the cloth out of the
Bull's ear, and spread it out, and how it served up the
nicest dishes which the stepdaughter ate and made good
cheer over. All this the maid told the Queen when she
went home.

And now the King came home from war, and had won
the fight against the other king with whom he went out
to battle. So there was great joy throughout the palace,
and no one was gladder than the king's daughter. But
the Queen shammed sick, and took to her bed, and paid

the doctor a great fee to get him to say she could **never** be well again unless she had some of the Dun Bull's flesh to eat. Both the king's daughter and the folk in the palace asked the doctor if nothing else would help her, and prayed hard for the Bull, for every one was fond of him, and they all said there wasn't that Bull's match in all the land. But, no; he must and should be slaughtered, nothing else would do. When the king's daughter heard that, she got very sorrowful, and went down into the byre to the Bull. There, too, he stood and hung down his head, and looked so downcast that she began to weep over him.

"What are you weeping for?" asked the Bull.

So she told him how the King had come home again, and how the Queen had shammed sick and got the doctor to say she could never be well and sound again unless she got some of the Dun Bull's flesh to eat, and so now he was to be slaughtered.

"If they get me killed first," said the Bull, "they'll soon take your life too. Now, if you're of my mind, we'll just start off, and go away to-night."

Well, the Princess thought it bad, you may be sure, to go and leave her father, but she thought it still worse to be in the house with the Queen; and so she gave her word to the Bull to come to him.

At night, when all had gone to bed, the Princess stole down to the byre to the Bull, and so he took her on his back, and set off from the homestead as fast as ever he could. And when the folk got up at cockrow next morning to slaughter the Bull, why, he was gone; and when the King got up and asked for his daughter, she was gone too. He sent out messengers on all sides to hunt for them, and gave them out in all the parish churches; but there was no one who had caught a glimpse of them. Meanwhile, the Bull went through many lands with the King's daughter on his back, and so one day they came to a great copper-wood, where both the trees, and branches, and leaves, and flowers, and everything, were nothing but copper.

But before they went into the wood, the Bull said to the King's daughter,—

"Now, when we get into this wood, mind you take care not to touch even a leaf of it, else it's all over both with me and you, for here dwells a Troll with three heads who owns this wood."

No, bless her, she'd be sure to take care not to touch anything. Well, she was very careful, and leant this way and that to miss the boughs, and put them gently aside with her hands; but it was such a thick wood, 'twas scarce possible to get through; and so, with all her pains, somehow or other she tore off a leaf, which she held in her hand.

"*AU! AU!* what have you done now?" said the Bull; "there's nothing for it now but to fight for life or death; but mind you keep the leaf safe."

Soon after they got to the end of the wood, and a Troll with three heads came running up,—

"Who is this that touches my wood?" said the Troll.

"It's just as much mine as yours," said the Bull.

"Ah!" roared the Troll, "we'll try a fall about that."

"As you choose," said the Bull.

So they rushed at one another, and fought; and the Bull he butted, and gored, and kicked with all his might and main; but the Troll gave him as good as he brought, and it lasted the whole day before the Bull got the mastery; and then he was so full of wounds, and so worn out, he could scarce lift a leg. Then they were forced to stay there a day to rest, and then the Bull bade the King's daughter to take the horn of ointment which hung at the Troll's belt, and rub him with it. Then he came to himself again, and the day after they trudged on again. So they travelled many, many days, until, after a long, long time, they came to a silver wood, where both the trees, and branches, and leaves, and flowers, and everything, were silvern.

Before the Bull went into the wood, he said to the King's daughter,—

"Now, when we get into this wood, for heaven's sake mind you take good care; you mustn't touch anything, and not pluck off so much as one leaf, else it is all over both with me and you; for here is a Troll with six heads who owns it, and him I don't think I should be able to master.

"No," said the King's daughter; "I'll take good care and not touch anything you don't wish me to touch."

But when they got into the wood, it was so close and thick, they could scarce get along. She was as careful as careful could be, and leant to this side and that to miss the boughs, and put them on one side with her hands, but every minute the branches struck her across the eyes,

279

and in spite of all her pains, it so happened she tore off a leaf.

"*AU! AU!* what have you done now?" said the Bull. "There's nothing for it now but to fight for life and death, for this Troll has six heads, and is twice as strong as the other, but mind you keep the leaf safe, and don't lose it."

Just as he said that, up came the Troll,—

"Who is this," he said, "that touches my wood?"

"It's as much mine as yours," said the Bull.

"That we'll try a fall about that," roared the Troll.

"As you choose," said the Bull, and rushed at the Troll, and gored out his eyes, and drove his horns right through his body, so that the entrails gushed out; but the Troll was almost a match for him, and it lasted three whole days before the Bull got the life gored out of him. But then he, too, was so weak and wretched, it was as much as he could do to stir a limb, and so full of wounds, that the blood streamed from him. So he said to the King's daughter she must take the horn of ointment that hung at the Troll's belt, and rub him with it. Then she did that, and he came to himself; but they were forced to stay there a week to rest before the Bull had strength enough to go on.

At last they set off again, but the Bull was still poorly, and they went rather slow at first. So, to spare time, the King's daughter said, as she was young and light of foot, she could very well walk, but she couldn't get leave to do that. No; she must seat herself up on his back again. So on they travelled through many lands a long time, and the King's daughter did not know in the least whither they went; but after a long, long time they came to a gold wood. It was so grand, the gold dropped from every twig, and all the trees, and boughs, and flowers, and leaves, were of pure gold. Here, too, the same thing happened as had happened in the silver wood and copper wood. The Bull told the King's daughter she mustn't touch it for anything, for there was a Troll with nine heads who owned it, and he was much bigger and stouter than both the others put together, and he didn't think he could get the better of him. No; she'd be sure to take heed not to touch it; that he might know very well. But when they got into the wood, it was far thicker and closer than the silver wood, and the deeper they went into it, the worse it got. The wood went on, getting thicker and thicker, and closer and closer; and at last she thought there was no way at all to get through it. She was in such an awful fright of plucking off anything, that she sat, and twisted, and turned herself this way and that, and hither and thither, to keep clear of the boughs, and she put them on one side with her hands; but every moment the branches struck her across the eyes, so that she couldn't see what she was clutching at; and lo! before she knew how it came about, she had a gold apple in her hand. Then she was so bitterly sorry, she burst into tears, and wanted to throw it away; but the Bull said, she must keep it safe and watch it well, and comforted her as well as he could; but he thought it would be a hard tussle, and he doubted how it would go.

Just then up came the Troll with the nine heads, and

he was so ugly, the King's daughter scarcely dared to look at him.

"*Who is this that touches my wood?*" he roared.

"It's just as much mine as yours," said the Bull.

"That we'll try a fall about," roared the Troll again.

"Just as you choose," said the Bull; and so they rushed at one another, and fought, and it was such a dreadful sight, the King's daughter was ready to swoon away. The Bull gored out the Troll's eyes, and drove his horns through and through his body, till the entrails came tumbling out; but the Troll fought bravely; and when the Bull got one head gored to death, the rest breathed life into it again, and so it lasted a whole week before the Bull was able to get the life out of them all. But then he was utterly worn out and wretched. He couldn't stir a foot, and his body was all one wound. He couldn't so much as ask the King's daughter to take the horn of ointment which hung at the Troll's belt, and rub it over him. But she did it all the same, and then he came to himself by little and little; but they had to lie there and rest three weeks before he was fit to go on again.

Then they set off at a snail's pace, for the Bull said they had still a little further to go, and so they crossed over many high hills and thick woods. So after a while they got upon the fells.

"Do you see anything?" asked the Bull.

"No, I see nothing but the sky and the wild fell," said the King's daughter.

So when they clomb higher up, the fell got smoother, and they could see further off.

"Do you see anything now?" asked the Bull.

"Yes, I see a castle far, far away," said the Princess.

"That's not so little though," said the Bull.

After a long, long time, they came to a great cairn, where there was a spur of the fell that stood sheer across the way.

"Do you see anything now?" asked the Bull.

"Yes, now I see the castle close by," said the King's daughter, "and now it is much, much bigger."

"Thither you're to go," said the Bull. "Right underneath the castle is a pig-stye, where you are to dwell. When you come thither you'll find a wooden cloak, all made of strips of lath; that you must put on, and go up to the castle and say your name is 'Katie Woodencloak,' and ask for a place. But before you go, you must take your penknife and cut my head off, and then you must flay me, and roll up the hide, and lay it under the wall of rock yonder, and under the hide you must lay the copper leaf, and the silvern leaf, and the golden apple. Yonder, up against the rock, stands a stick; and when you want anything, you've only got to knock on the wall of rock with that stick."

At first she wouldn't do anything of the kind; but when the Bull said it was the only thanks he would have for what he had done for her, she couldn't help herself. So, however much it grieved her heart, she hacked and cut away with her knife at the big beast till she got both his head and his hide off, and then she laid the hide up under the wall of rock, and put the copper leaf, and the silvern leaf, and the golden apple inside it.

So when she had done that, she went over to the pig-stye, but all the while she went she sobbed and wept. There she put on the wooden cloak, and so went up to the palace. When she came into the kitchen she begged for a place, and told them her name was Katie Wooden-cloak. Yes, the cook said she might have a place—she might have leave to be there in the scullery, and wash up, for the lassie who did that work before had just gone away.

"But as soon as you get weary of being here, you'll go your way too, I'll be bound."

No; she was sure she wouldn't do that.

So there she was, behaving so well, and washing up so handily. The Sunday after there were to be strange guests at the palace, so Katie asked if she might have leave to carry up water for the Prince's bath; but all the rest laughed at her, and said,—

"What should you do there? Do you think the Prince will care to look at you, you who are such a fright!"

But she wouldn't give it up, and kept on begging and praying; and at last she got leave. So when she went up the stairs, her wooden cloak made such a clatter, the Prince came out and asked,—

"Pray who are you?"

"Oh! I was just going to bring up water for your Royal Highness's bath," said Katie.

"Do you think now," said the Prince, "I'd have any-thing to do with the water you bring?" and with that he threw the water over her.

So she had to put up with that, but then she asked

leave to go to church; well, she got that leave too, for the church lay close by. But, first of all, she went to the rock, and knocked on its face with the stick which stood there, just as the Bull had said. And straightway out came a man, who said,—

"What's your will?"

So the Princess said she had got leave to go to church and hear the priest preach, but she had no clothes to go in. So he brought out a kirtle, which was as bright as the copper wood, and she got a horse and saddle beside. Now, when she got to the church, she was so lovely and grand, all wondered who she could be, and scarce one of them listened to what the priest said, for they looked too much at her. As for the Prince, he fell so deep in love with her, he didn't take his eyes off her for a single moment.

So, as she went out of church, the Prince ran after her, and held the church door open for her; and so he got hold of one of her gloves, which was caught in the door. When she went away and mounted her horse, the Prince went up to her again, and asked whence she came.

"Oh! I'm from Bath," said Katie; and while the Prince took out the glove to give it to her, she said,—

> "Bright before and dark behind,
> Clouds come rolling on the wind;
> That this Prince may never see
> Where my good steed goes with me."

The Prince had never seen the like of that glove, and went about far and wide asking after the land whence the proud lady, who rode off without her glove, said she came; but there was no one who could tell where "Bath" lay.

Next Sunday some one had to go up to the Prince with a towel.

"Oh! may I have leave to go up with it?" said Katie.

"What's the good of your going?" said the others; "you saw how it fared with you last time."

But Katie wouldn't give in; she kept on begging and praying, till she got leave; and then she ran up the stairs, so that her wooden cloak made a great clatter. Out came the Prince, and when he saw it was Katie, he tore the towel out of her hand, and threw it into her face.

"Pack yourself off, you ugly Troll," he cried; "do you think I'd have a towel which you have touched with your smutty fingers?"

After that the Prince set off to church, and Katie begged for leave to go too. They all asked what business she had at church—she who had nothing to put on but that wooden cloak, which was so black and ugly. But Katie said the priest was such a brave man to preach, what he said did her so much good; and so at last she got leave. Now she went again to the rock and knocked, and so out came the man, and gave her a kirtle far finer than the first one; it was all covered with silver, and it shone like the silver wood; and she got besides a noble steed, with a saddle-cloth broidered with silver, and a silver bit.

So when the King's daughter got to the church, the

folk were still standing about in the churchyard. And all wondered and wondered who she could be, and the Prince was soon on the spot, and came and wished to hold her horse for her while she got off. But she jumped down, and said there was no need, for her horse was so well broke, it stood still when she bid it, and came when she called it. So they all went into church, but there was scarce a soul that listened to what the priest said, for they looked at her a deal too much; and the Prince fell still deeper in love than the first time.

When the sermon was over, and she went out of church, and was going to mount her horse, up came the Prince again, and asked her whence she came.

"Oh! I'm from Towelland," said the King's daughter; and as she said that, she dropped her riding-whip, and when the Prince stooped to pick it up, she said,—

> "Bright before and dark behind,
> Clouds come rolling on the wind;
> That this Prince may never see
> Where my good steed goes with me."

So away she was again; and the Prince couldn't tell what had become of her. He went about far and wide asking after the land whence she said she came, but there was no one who could tell him where it lay; and so the Prince had to make the best he could of it.

Next Sunday some one had to go up to the Prince with a comb. Katie begged for leave to go up with it, but the others put her in mind how she had fared the last time, and scolded her for wishing to go before the

Prince—such a black and ugly fright as she was in her wooden cloak. But she wouldn't leave off asking till they let her go up to the Prince with his comb. So, when she came clattering up the stairs again, out came the Prince, and took the comb, and threw it at her, and bade her be off as fast as she could. After that the Prince went to church, and Katie begged for leave to go too. They asked again what business she had there, she who was so foul and black, and who had no clothes to show herself in. Might be the Prince or some one else would see her, and then both she and all the others would smart for it; but Katie said they had something else to do than to look at her; and she wouldn't leave off begging and praying till they gave her leave to go.

So the same thing happened now as had happened twice before. She went to the rock and knocked with the stick, and then the man came out and gave her a kirtle which was far grander than either of the others. It was almost all pure gold, and studded with diamonds; and she got besides a noble steed, with a gold broidered saddle-cloth and a golden bit.

Now when the King's daughter got to the church, there stood the priest and all the people in the church-yard waiting for her. Up came the Prince running, and wanted to hold her horse, but she jumped off, and said,—

"No; thanks—there's no need, for my horse is so well broke, it stands still when I bid him."

So they all hastened into church, and the priest got into the pulpit, but no one listened to a word he said; for they all looked too much at her, and wondered whence she came; and the Prince, he was far deeper in love than either of the former times. He had no eyes, or ears, or sense for anything, but just to sit and stare at her.

So when the sermon was over, and the King's daughter was to go out of the church, the Prince had got a firkin of pitch poured out in the porch, that he might come and help her over it; but she didn't care a bit—she just put her foot right down into the midst of the pitch, and jumped across it; but then one of her golden shoes stuck fast in it, and as she got on her horse, up came the Prince running out of the church, and asked whence she came.

"I'm from Combland," said Katie. But when the Prince wanted to reach her the gold shoe, she said,—

> "Bright before and dark behind,
> Clouds come rolling on the wind;
> That this Prince may never see
> Where my good steed goes with me."

So the Prince couldn't tell still what had become of her, and he went about a weary time all over the world asking for "Combland;" but when no one could tell him where it lay, he ordered it to be given out everywhere that he would wed the woman whose foot could fit the gold shoe.

So many came of all sorts from all sides, fair and ugly alike; but there was no one who had so small a foot as to be able to get on the gold shoe. And after a long, long time, who should come but Katie's wicked stepmother, and her daugnter, too, and her the gold shoe fitted; but ugly she was, and so loathly she looked, the Prince only kept his word sore against his will. Still they got ready the wedding-feast, and she was dressed up and decked out as a bride; but as they rode to church, a little bird sat upon a tree and sang,—

> "A bit off her heel,
> And a bit off her toe;
> Katie Woodencloak's tiny shoe
> Is full of blood—that's all I know."

And sure enough, when they looked to it the bird told the truth, for blood gushed out of the shoe.

Then all the maids and women who were about the palace had to go up to try on the shoe, but there was none of them whom it would fit at all.

"But where's Katie Woodencloak?" asked the Prince, when all the rest had tried the shoe, for he understood the song of birds very well, and bore in mind what the little bird had said.

"Oh! she think of that!" said the rest; "it's no good her coming forward. Why, she's legs like a horse."

"Very true, I daresay," said the Prince; "but since all the others have tried, Katie may as well try too."

"Katie," he bawled out through the door; and Katie came trampling up stairs, and her wooden cloak clattered as if a whole regiment of dragoons were charging up.

"Now, you must try the shoe on, and be a Princess, you too," said the other maids, and laughed and made game of her.

So Katie took up the shoe, and put her foot into it like nothing, and threw off her wooden cloak; and so there she stood in her gold kirtle, and it shone so that the sunbeams glistened from her; and lo! on her other foot she had the fellow to the gold shoe.

So when the Prince knew her again, he grew so glad, he ran up to her and threw his arms round her, and gave her a kiss; and when he heard she was a King's daughter, he got gladder still, and then came the wedding-feast; and so

"Snip, snip, snover,
This story's over."

SORIA MORIA CASTLE.

ONCE on a time there was a poor couple who had a son whose name was Halvor. Ever since he was a little boy he would turn his hand to nothing, but just sat there and groped about in the ashes. His father and mother often put him out to learn this trade or that, but Halvor could stay nowhere; for, when he had been there a day or two, he ran away from his master, and never stopped till he was sitting again in the ingle, poking about in the cinders.

Well, one day a skipper came and asked Halvor if he hadn't a mind to be with him, and go to sea, and see strange lands. Yes, Halvor would live that very much; so he wasn't long in getting himself ready.

How long they sailed I'm sure I can't tell; but the

end of it was, they fell into a great storm, and when it was blown over, and it got still again, they couldn't tell where they were; for they had been driven away to a strange coast, which none of them knew anything about.

Well, as there was just no wind at all, they stayed lying wind-bound there, and Halvor asked the skipper's leave to go on shore and look about him; he would sooner go, he said, than lie there and sleep.

"Do you think now you're fit to show yourself before folk," said the skipper, "why, you've no clothes than those rags you stand in?"

But Halvor stuck to his own, and so at last he got leave, but he was to be sure and come back as soon as ever it began to blow. So off he went and found a lovely land; wherever he came there were fine large flat corn-fields and rich meads, but he couldn't catch a glimpse of a living soul. Well, it began to blow, but Halvor thought he hadn't seen enough yet, and he wanted to walk a little farther just to see if he couldn't meet any folk. So after a while he came to a broad high road, so smooth and even, you might easily roll an egg along it. Halvor followed this, and when evening drew on he saw a great castle ever so far off, from which the sunbeams shone. So as he had now walked the whole day and hadn't taken a bit to eat with him, he was as hungry as a hunter, but still the nearer he came to the castle, the more afraid he got.

In the castle kitchen a great fire was blazing, and Halvor went into it, but such a kitchen he had never seen in all his born days. It was so grand and fine;

there were vessels of silver and vessels of gold, but still never a living soul. So when Halvor had stood there a while and no one came out, he went and opened a door, and there inside sat a Princess who spun upon a spinning-wheel.

"Nay, nay, now!" she called out, "dare Christian folk come hither? But now you'd best be off about your business, if you don't want the Troll to gobble you up; for here lives a Troll with three heads."

"All one to me," said the lad, "I'd be just as glad to hear he had four heads beside; I'd like to see what kind of fellow he is. As for going, I won't go at all. I've done no harm; but meat you must get me, for I'm almost starved to death."

When Halvor had eaten his fill, the Princess told him to try if he could brandish the sword that hung against the wall; no, he couldn't brandish it, he couldn't even lift it up.

"Oh!" said the Princess, "now you must go and take a pull of that flask that hangs by its side; that's what the Troll does every time he goes out to use the sword."

So Halvor took a pull, and in the twinkling of an eye he could brandish the sword like nothing; and now he thought it high time the Troll came; and lo! just then up came the Troll puffing and blowing. Halvor jumped behind the door.

"*Hutetu,*" said the Troll, as he put his head in at the door, "what a smell of Christian man's blood!"

"Aye," said Halvor, "you'll soon know that to your cost," and with that he hewed off all his heads.

Now the Princess was so glad that she was free, she both danced and sang, but then all at once she called her sisters to mind, and so she said,—

"Would my sisters were free too!"

"Where are they?" asked Halvor.

"Well, she told him all about it; one was taken away by a Troll to his Castle which lay fifty miles off, and the other by another Troll to his Castle which was fifty miles further still.

"But now," she said, "you must first help me to get this ugly carcass out of the house."

Yes, Halvor was so strong he swept everything away, and made it all clean and tidy in no time. So they had a good and happy time of it, and next morning he set off at peep of gray dawn; he could take no rest by the way, but ran and walked the whole day. When he first saw the Castle he got a little afraid; it was far grander than the first, but here too there wasn't a living soul to be seen. So Halvor went into the kitchen, and didn't stop there either, but went straight further on into the house.

"Nay, nay," called out the Princess, "dare Christian folk come hither? I don't know I'm sure how long it is since I came here, but in all that time I haven't seen a Christian man. 'Twere best you saw how to get away as fast as you came; for here lives a Troll, who has six heads."

"I shan't go," said Halvor, "if he had six heads besides."

"He'll take you up and swallow you down alive," said the Princess.

But it was no good, Halvor wouldn't go; he wasn't at all afraid of the Troll, but meat and drink he must have, for he was half starved after his long journey. Well, he got as much of that as he wished, but then the Princess wanted him to be off again.

"No," said Halvor, "I won't go, I've done no harm, and I've nothing to be afraid about."

"He won't stay to ask that," said the Princess, "for he'll take you without law or leave; but as you won't go, just try if you can brandish that sword yonder, which the Troll wields in war."

He couldn't brandish it, and then the Princess said he must take a pull at the flask which hung by its side, and when he had done that he could brandish it.

Just then back came the Troll, and he was both stout and big, so that he had to go sideways to get through the door. When the Troll got his first head in he called out,—

"*Hutetu*, what a smell of Christian man's blood!"

But that very moment Halvor hewed off his first head, and so on all the rest as they popped in. The Princess was overjoyed, but just then she came to think of her sisters, and wished out loud they were free. Halvor thought that might easily be done, and wanted to be off at once; but first he had to help the Princess to get the Troll's carcass out of the way, and so he could only set out next morning.

It was a long way to the Castle, and he had to walk fast and run hard to reach it in time; but about night-fall he saw the Castle, which was far finer and grander than either of the others. This time he wasn't the least afraid, but walked straight through the kitchen, and into the Castle. There sat a Princess who was so pretty, there was no end to her loveliness. She, too, like the others told him there hadn't been Christian folk there ever since she came thither, and bade him go away again, else the Troll would swallow him alive, and do you know, she said, he has nine heads.

"Aye, aye," said Halvor, "if he had nine other heads, and nine other heads still, I won't go away," and so he stood fast before the stove. The Princess kept on begging him so prettily to go away, lest the Troll should gobble him up, but Halvor said,—

"Let him come as soon as he likes."

So she gave him the Troll's sword, and bade him take a pull at the flask, that he might be able to brandish and wield it.

Just then back came the Troll puffing and blowing and tearing along. He was far stouter and bigger than the other two, and he too had to go on one side to get through the door. So when he got his first head in, he said as the others had said,—

"*Hutetu,* what a smell of Christian man's blood!"

That very moment Halvor hewed off the first head and then all the rest; but the last was the toughest of them all, and it was the hardest bit of work Halvor had to do to get it hewn off, although he knew very well he had strength enough to do it.

So all the Princesses came together to that Castle, which was called *Soria Moria Castle,* and they were glad and happy as they had never been in all their lives before, and they were fond of Halvor and Halvor of them, and he might choose the one he liked best for his bride; but the youngest was fondest of him of all the three.

But after a while, Halvor went about, and was so strange and dull and silent. Then the Princesses asked him what he lacked, and if he didn't like to live with them any longer? Yes, he did, for they had enough and to spare, and he was well off in every way, but still somehow or other he did so long to go home, for his father and mother were alive, and them he had such a great wish to see.

Well, they thought that might be done easily enough.

"You shall go thither and come back hither, safe and unscathed, if you will only follow our advice," said the Princesses.

Yes, he'd be sure to mind all they said. So they dressed him up till he was as grand as a king's son, and then they set a ring on his finger, and that was such a ring, he could wish himself thither and hither with it; but they told him to be sure not to take it off, and not to name their names, for there would be an end of all his bravery, and then he'd never see them more.

"If I only stood at home I'd be glad," said Halvor; and it was done as he had wished. Then stood Halvor at his father's cottage door before he knew a word about it. Now it was about dusk at even, and so, when they saw such a grand stately lord walk in, the old couple got so afraid they began to bow and scrape. Then Halvor asked if he couldn't stay there, and have a lodging there that night. No; that he couldn't.

"We can't do it at all," they said, "for we haven't this thing or that thing which such a lord is used to have; 'twere best your lordship went up to the farm, no long way off, for you can see the chimneys, and there they have lots of everything."

Halvor wouldn't hear of it—he wanted to stop; but the old couple stuck to their own, that he had better go to the farmer's; there he would get both meat and drink; as for them, they hadn't even a chair to offer him to sit down on.

"No," said Halvor, "I won't go up there till to-morrow early, but let me just stay here to-night; worst come to worst, I can sit in the chimney-corner."

Well, they couldn't say anything against that; so Halvor sat down by the ingle, and began to poke about in the ashes, just as he used to do when he lay at home in old days, and stretched his lazy bones.

Well, they chattered and talked about many things; and they told Halvor about this thing and that; and so he asked them if they had never had any children.

"Yes, yes, they had once a lad whose name was Halvor, but they didn't know whither he had wandered; they couldn't even tell whether he were dead or alive."

"Couldn't it be me now?" said Halvor.

"Let me see; I could tell him well enough," said the old wife, and rose up. "Our Halvor was so lazy and dull, he never did a thing; and besides, he was so ragged, that one tatter took hold of the next tatter on him. No;

there never was the making of such a fine fellow in him as you are, master."

A little while after the old wife went to the hearth to poke up the fire, and when the blaze fell on Halvor's face, just as when he was at home of old poking about in the ashes, she knew him at once.

"Ah! but is it you after all, Halvor?" she cried; and then there was much joy for the old couple, there was no end to it; and he was forced to tell how he had fared, and the old dame was so fond and proud of him, nothing would do but he must go up at once to the farmer's, and show himself to the lassies, who had always looked down on him. And off she went first, and Halvor followed after. So, when she got up there, she told them all how her Halvor had come home again, and now they should only just see how grand he was, for, she said, "he looks like nothing but a king's son."

"All very fine," said the lassies, and tossed up their heads. "We'll be bound he's just the same beggarly ragged boy he always was."

Just then in walked Halvor, and then the lassies were all so taken aback, they forgot their sarks in the ingle, where they were sitting darning their clothes, and ran out in their smocks. Well, when they were got back again, they were so shamefaced they scarce dared look at Halvor, towards whom they had always been proud and haughty.

"Aye, aye," said Halvor, "you always thought yourselves so pretty and neat, no one could come near you; but now you should just see the eldest Princess I have set free; against her you look just like milk-maids, and the midmost is prettier still; but the youngest, who is my sweetheart, she's fairer than both sun and moon. Would to Heaven she were only here," said Halvor, "then you'ld see what you would see."

He had scarce uttered these words before there they stood, but then he felt so sorry, for now what they had said came into his mind. Up at the farm there was a great feast got ready for the Princesses, and much was made of them, but they wouldn't stop there.

"No; we want to go down to your father and mother," they said to Halvor; "and so we'll go out now and look about us."

So he went down with them, and they came to a great lake just outside the farm. Close by the water was such a lovely green bank; here the Princesses said they would sit and rest a while; they thought it so sweet to sit down and look over the water.

So they sat down there, and when they had sat a while, the youngest Princess said,—

"I may as well comb your hair a little, Halvor."

Yes, Halvor laid his head on her lap, and so she combed his bonny locks, and it wasn't long before Halvor fell fast asleep. Then she took the ring from his finger, and put another in its stead; and so she said,—

"Now hold me all together! and now would we were all in *Soria Moria Castle.*"

So when Halvor woke up, he could very well tell that he had lost the Princesses, and began to weep and wail; and he was so downcast, they couldn't comfort him at all. In spite of all his father and mother said, he wouldn't stop there, but took farewell of them, and said he was safe not to see them again; for if he couldn't find the Princesses, he thought it not worth while to live.

Well, he had still three hundred dollars left, so he put them into his pocket, and set out on his way. So, when he had walked a while, he met a man with a tidy horse, and he wanted to buy it, and began to chaffer with the man.

"Aye," said the man, "to tell the truth, I never thought of selling him; but if we could strike a bargain, per-haps—"

"What do you want for him," asked Halvor.

"I didn't give much for him, nor is he worth much; he's a brave horse to ride, but he can't draw at all; still he's strong enough to carry your knapsack and you too, turn and turn about," said the man.

At last they agreed on the price, and Halvor laid the knapsack on him, and so he walked a bit, and rode a bit, turn and turn about. At night he came to a green plain where stood a great tree, at the roots of which he sat down. There he let the horse loose, but he didn't lie down to sleep, but opened his knapsack and took a meal. At peep of day off he set again, for he could take no rest. So he rode and walked and walked and rode the whole day through the wide wood, where there were so many green spots and glades that shone so bright and lovely between the trees. He didn't know at all where he was or whither he was going, but he gave himself no more time to rest, than when his horse cropped a bit of grass, and he took a snack out of his knapsack when they came to one of those green glades. So he went on walking and riding by turns, and as for the wood there seemed to be no end to it.

But at dusk the next day he saw a light gleaming away through the trees.

"Would there were folk hereaway," thought Halvor, "that I might warm myself a bit and get a morsel to keep body and soul together."

When he got up to it, he saw the light came from a wretched little hut, and through the window he saw an old couple inside. They were as grey headed as a pair of doves, and the old wife had such a nose! why, it was so long she used it for a poker to stir the fire as she sat in the ingle.

"Good evening," said Halvor.

"Good evening," said the old wife.

"But what errand can you have in coming hither?" she went on, "for no Christian folk have been here these hundred years and more."

Well, Halvor told her all about himself, and how he wanted to get to *Soria Moria Castle,* and asked if she knew the way thither.

"No," said the old wife, "that I don't, but see now, here comes the Moon, I'll ask her, she'll know all about it, for doesn't she shine on everything."

So when the Moon stood clear and bright over the tree-tops, the old wife went out.

"*Thou Moon, thou Moon,*" she screamed, "canst thou tell me the way to *Soria Moria Castle?*"

302

"No," said the Moon, "that I can't, for the last time I shone there a cloud stood before me."

"Wait a bit still," said the old wife to Halvor, "by and bye comes the West Wind; he's sure to know it, for he puffs and blows round every corner."

"Nay, nay," said the old wife when she went out again, "you don't mean to say you've got a horse too; just turn the poor beastie loose in our 'toun,' and don't let him stand there and starve to death at the door."

Then she ran on,—

"But won't you swop him away to me; we've got an old pair of boots here, with which you can take twenty miles at each stride; those you shall have for your horse, and so you'll get all the sooner to *Soria Moria Castle.*"

That Halvor was willing to do at once; and the old wife was so glad at the horse, she was ready to dance and skip for joy.

"For now," she said, "I shall be able to ride to church. I too, think of that."

As for Halvor, he had no rest, and wanted to be off at once, but the old wife said there was no hurry.

"Lie down on the bench with you and sleep a bit, for we've no bed to offer you, and I'll watch and wake you when the West Wind comes."

So after a while up came the West Wind, roaring and howling along till the walls creaked and groaned again.

Out ran the old wife.

"Thou West Wind, thou West Wind! Canst thou tell me the way to *Soria Moria Castle?* Here's one who wants to get thither."

"Yes, I know it very well," said the West Wind, "and now I'm just off thither to dry clothes for the wedding that's to be; if he's swift of foot he can go with me."

Out ran Halvor.

"You'll have to stretch your legs if you mean to keep up," said the West Wind.

So off he set over field and hedge, and hill and fell, and Halvor had hard work to keep up.

"Well," said the West Wind, "now I've no time to stay with you any longer, for I've got to go away yonder and tear down a strip of spruce wood first before I go to the bleaching-ground to dry the clothes; but if you go alongside the hill you'll come to a lot of lassies standing washing clothes, and then you've not far to go to *Soria Moria Castle*."

In a little while Halvor came upon the lassies who stood washing, and they asked if he had seen anything of the West Wind who was to come and dry the clothes for the wedding.

"Aye, aye, that I have," said Halvor, "he's only gone to tear down a strip of spruce wood. It'll not be long before he's here," and then he asked them the way to *Soria Moria Castle*.

So they put him into the right way, and when he got to the Castle it was full of folk and horses; so full it made one giddy to look at them. But Halvor was so ragged and torn from having followed the West Wind through brush and brier and bog, that he kept on one side, and wouldn't show himself till the last day when the bridal feast was to be.

So when all, as was then right and fitting, were to drink the bride and bridegroom's health and wish them luck, and when the cupbearer was to drink to them all again, both knights and squires, last of all he came in turn to Halvor. He drank their health, but let the ring which the Princess had put upon his finger as he lay by the lake fall into the glass, and bade the cupbearer go and greet the bride and hand her the glass.

Then up rose the Princess from the board at once.

"Who is most worthy to have one of us," she said, "he that has set us free, or he that here sits by me as bridegroom."

Well they all said there could be but one voice and will as to that, and when Halvor heard that he wasn't long in throwing off his beggar's rags, and arraying himself as bridegroom.

"Aye, aye, here is the right one after all," said the youngest Princess as soon as she saw him, and so she tossed the other one out of the window, and held her wedding with Halvor.

THE LAD WHO WENT TO THE NORTH WIND.

ONCE on a time there was an old widow who had one son; and as she was poorly and weak, her son had to go up into the safe to fetch meal for cooking; but when he got outside the safe, and was just going down the steps, there came the North Wind, puffing and blowing, caught up the meal, and so away with it through the air. Then the lad went back into the safe for more; but when he came out again on the steps, if the North Wind didn't come again and carry off the meal with a puff; and, more than that, he did so the third time. At this the lad got very angry; and as he thought it hard that the North Wind should behave so, he thought he'd just look him up, and ask him to give up his meal.

So off he went, but the way was long, and he walked and walked; but at last he came to the North Wind's house.

"Good day!" said the lad, "and thank you for coming to see us yesterday."

"Good day!" answered the North Wind, for his voice was loud and gruff, "and thanks for coming to see me. What do you want?"

"Oh!" answered the lad, "I only wished to ask you to be so good as to let me have back that meal you took from me on the safe steps, for we haven't much to live on; and if you're to go on snapping up the morsel we have, there'll be nothing for it but to starve."

"I haven't got your meal," said the North Wind; "but if you are in such need, I'll give you a cloth which will get you everything you want, if you only say, 'Cloth, spread yourself, and serve up all kind of good dishes!'"

With this the lad was well content. But, as the way was so long he couldn't get home in one day, so he turned into an inn on the way; and when they were going to sit down to supper he laid the cloth on a table which stood in the corner, and said,—

"Cloth, spread yourself, and serve up all kinds of good dishes."

He had scarce said so before the cloth did as it was bid; and all who stood by thought it a fine thing, but most of all the landlady. So, when all were fast asleep, at dead of night, she took the lad's cloth, and put another in its stead, just like the one he had got from the North Wind, but which couldn't so much as serve up a bit of dry bread.

So, when the lad woke, he took his cloth and went off with it, and that day he got home to his mother.

"Now," said he, "I've been to the North Wind's house, and a good fellow he is, for he gave me this cloth, and when I only say to it, 'Cloth, spread yourself, and serve up all kind of good dishes,' I get any sort of food I please."

"All very true, I dare say," said his mother; "but seeing is believing, and I shan't believe it till I see it."

So the lad made haste, drew out a table, and laid the cloth on it, and said,—

"Cloth, spread yourself, and serve up all kind of good dishes."

307

But never a bit of dry bread did the cloth serve up.

"Well!" said the lad, "there's no help for it but to go to the North Wind again;" and away he went

So he came to where the North Wind lived late in the afternoon.

"Good evening!" said the lad.

"Good evening!" said the North Wind.

"I want my rights for that meal of ours which you took," said the lad; "for, as for that cloth I got, it isn't worth a penny."

"I've got no meal," said the North Wind; "but yonder you have a ram which coins nothing but golden ducats as soon as you say to it,—

"Ram, ram! make money!"

So the lad thought this a fine thing; but as it was too far to get home that day, he turned in for the night to the same inn where he had slept before.

Before he called for anything, he tried the truth of what the North Wind had said of the ram, and found it all right; but, when the landlord saw that, he thought it was a famous ram, and, when the lad had fallen asleep, he took another which couldn't coin gold ducats, and changed the two.

Next morning off went the lad; and when he got home to his mother, he said,—

"After all, the North Wind is a jolly fellow; for now he has given me a ram which can coin golden ducats if I only say, 'Ram, ram! make money.'"

"All very true, I dare say," said his mother; "but I shan't believe any such stuff until I see the ducats made."

"Ram, ram! make money!" said the lad; but if the ram made anything, it wasn't money.

So the lad went back again to the North Wind, and blew him up, and said the ram was worth nothing, and he must have his rights for the meal.

"Well!" said the North Wind; "I've nothing else to give you but that old stick in the corner yonder; but it's a stick of that kind if you say,—

" 'Stick, stick! lay on!' it lays on till you say,—

" 'Stick, stick! now stop!' "

So, as the way was long, the lad turned in this night too to the landlord; but as he could pretty well guess how things stood as to the cloth and the ram, he lay down at once on the bench and began to snore, as if he were asleep.

Now the landlord, who easily saw that the stick must be worth something, hunted up one which was like it, and when he heard the lad snore, was going to change the two; but, just as the landlord was about to take it, the lad bawled out,—

"Stick, stick! lay on!"

So the stick began to beat the landlord, till he jumped over chairs, and tables, and benches, and yelled and roared,—

"Oh my! oh my! bid the stick be still, else it will beat me to death, and you shall have back both your cloth and your ram."

When the lad thought the landlord had got enough, he said,

"Stick, stick! now stop!"

Then he took his cloth and put it into his pocket, and went home with his stick in his hand, leading the ram by a cord round its horns; and so he got his rights for the meal he had lost.

THE CAT ON THE DOVREFELL.

ONCE on a time there was a man up in Finnmark who had caught a great white bear, which he was going to take to the king of Denmark. Now, it so fell out, that he came to the Dovrefell just about Christmas Eve, and there he turned into a cottage where a man lived, whose name was Halvor, and asked the man if he could get house-room there, for his bear and himself.

"Heaven never help me, if what I say isn't true!" said the man; "but we can't give any one house-room just now, for every Christmas Eve such a pack of Trolls come down upon us, that we are forced to flit, and haven't so much as a house over our own heads, to say nothing of lending one to any one else."

"Oh!" said the man, "if that's all, you can very well lend me your house; my bear can lie under the stove yonder, and I can sleep in the side-room."

Well, he begged so hard, that at last he got leave to stay there; so the people of the house flitted out, and before they went, everything was got ready for the Trolls; the tables were laid, and there was rice porridge, and fish boiled in lye, and sausages, and all else that was good, just as for any other grand feast.

So, when everything was ready, down came the Trolls. Some were great, and some were small; some had long tails, and some had no tails at all; some, too, had long, long noses; and they ate and drank, and tasted everything. Just, then, one of the little Trolls caught sight of the white bear, who lay under the stove; so he took a piece of sausage and stuck it on a fork, and went and poked it up against the bear's nose, screaming out—

"Pussy, will you have some sausage?"

Then the white bear rose up and growled, and hunted the whole pack of them out of doors, both great and small.

Next year Halvor was out in the wood, on the afternoon of Christmas Eve, cutting wood before the holidays, for he thought the Trolls would come again; and just as he was hard at work, he heard a voice in the wood calling out,—

"Halvor! Halvor!"

"Well," said Halvor, "here I am."

"Have you got your big cat with you still?"

"Yes, that I have," said Halvor; "she's lying at home under the stove, and what's more, she has now got seven kittens, far bigger and fiercer than she is herself."

"Oh, then, we'll never come to see you again," bawled out the Troll away in the wood, and he kept his word; for since that time the Trolls have never eaten their Christmas brose with Halvor on the Dovrefell.

THE THREE SISTERS WHO WERE EN-TRAPPED INTO A MOUNTAIN.

THERE was once an old widow who lived far from any inhabited spot, under a mountain ridge, with her three daughters. She was so poor that all she possessed was a hen, and this was as dear to her as the apple of her eye; she petted and fondled it from morning till night. But one day it so happened that the hen was missing. The woman looked everywhere about her room, but the hen was away, and remained away. "Thou must go out and search for our hen," said the woman to her eldest daughter, "for have it back again we must, even if we have to get it out of the mountain." So the daughter went in search of the hen. She went about in all directions, and searched and coaxed, yet no hen could she find; but all at once she heard a voice from a mountain-side saying:—

"The hen trips in the mountain!
The hen trips in the mountain!"

She went naturally to see whence it proceeded; but just as she came to the spot, she fell through a trap-door, far, far down into a vault under the earth. Here she walked through many rooms, every one more beautiful than the other; but in the last a great ugly Troll came to her, and asked her if she would be his wife. "No," she answered, she would not on any account, she would go back again directly, and look after her hen which had wandered away. On hearing this, the Troll was so angry, that he seized her and wrung her head off, and then threw her head and body down into a cellar.

The mother in the meantime sat at home expecting and expecting, but no daughter came back. After waiting a long time, and neither hearing nor seeing anything more of her, she said to the second daughter, that she must go out and look after her sister and at the same time "coax back the hen."

Now the second daughter went out, and it happened to her just as it had to her sister; she looked and looked about, and all at once, she also heard a voice from a mountain-side say :—

> "The hen trips in the mountain!
> The hen trips in the mountain!"

This she thought very strange, and she would go and see whence it proceeded, and so she fell also through the trap-door, deep, deep down into the vault. Here she went through all the rooms, and in the innermost the Troll came to her and asked her if she would be his wife. "No," she would not on any account, she would go up again instantly and search for her hen, which had gone astray. Thereupon the Troll was so exasperated that, catching hold of her, he wrung her head off and threw both head and body into the cellar.

When the mother had waited a long time for the other daughter, and no daughter was to be seen or heard of, she said to the youngest: "Now thou must set out and seek after thy sisters. Bad enough it was that the hen strayed away, but worse will it be, if we cannot find thy sisters again, and the hen thou canst also coax back at the same time." So the youngest was now to go out; she went in all directions, and looked and coaxed, but she neither saw the hen nor her sisters. After wandering about for some time, she came at length to the mountain-side and heard the same voice saying:—

"The hen trips in the mountain!
The hen trips in the mountain!"

This seemed to her extraordinary, but she would go and see whence it came, and so she also fell through the trap-door, deep, deep down into the vault. Here she went through many rooms, every one finer than the other; but she was not terrified, and gave herself time to look at this and at that, and then cast her eyes on the trap-door to the cellar; on looking down she immediately saw her two sisters, who lay there dead. Just as she had shut the trap-door again, the Troll came to her. "Wilt thou be my wife?" asked the Troll. "Yes, willingly," said the girl, for she saw well enough how it had fared with her sisters. When the Troll heard this, he gave her splendid clothes, the most beautiful she could wish for, and everything she desired, so delighted was he that somebody would be his mate.

When she had been there some time, she was one day more sad and silent than usual; whereupon the Troll asked her what it was that grieved her. "Oh!" answered she, "it is because I cannot go home again to my mother, I am sure she both hungers and thirsts, and she has no one with her." "Thou canst not be allowed to go to her," said the Troll, "but put some food in a sack, and I will carry it to her." For this she thanked him, and would do so, she said; but at the bottom of the sack she stuffed in a great deal of gold and silver, and then laid a little food on the top, telling the Troll the sack was ready, but that he must on no account look into it; and he promised that he would not. As soon as the Troll was gone, she watched him through a little hole there was in the door. When he had carried it some way, he said: "This sack is so heavy, I will see what is in it," and was just about to untie the strings, when the girl cried out: "I see you, I see you." "What sharp eyes thou hast got in thy head," said the Troll, and durst not repeat the attempt. On reaching the place where the widow dwelt, he threw the sack in through the door of the room, saying: "There's food for thee from thy daughter, she wants for nothing."

When the young girl had been for some time in the mountain, it happened one day that a goat fell through the trap-door. "Who sent for thee, thou long-bearded beast!" said the Troll, and fell into a violent passion; so, seizing the goat, he wrung its head off, and threw it into the cellar. "Oh! why did you do that?" said the girl; "he might have been some amusement to me down here." "Thou needst not put on such a fast-day face," said the Troll, "I can soon put life into the goat again." Saying this he took a flask, which hung against the wall, set the goat's head on again, rubbed it with what was in the flask, and the animal was as sound as ever. "Ha, ha!" thought the girl, "that flask is worth something." When she had been some time longer with the Troll, and he was one day gone out, she took the eldest of her sisters, set her head on, and rubbed her with what was in the flask, just as she had seen the Troll do with the goat, and her sister came instantly to life again. The girl then put her into a sack with a little food at the top; and as soon as the Troll came home, she said to him: "Dear friend, you must go again to my mother, and carry her a little food; I am sure she both hungers and thirsts, poor thing! and she is so lonely; but do not look into the sack." He promised to take the sack, and also that he would not look into it. When he had gone some distance, he thought the sack very heavy, and going on a little further, he said: "This sack is so heavy, I must see what is in it; for of whatever her eyes may be made, I am sure she can't see me now." But just as he was going to untie the sack, the girl who was in it cried out: "I can see you, I can see you." "What sharp eyes thou must have in thy head," said the Troll; for he thought it was the girl in the mountain that spoke, and therefore did not dare to look again, but carried it as fast as he could to the mother; and when he came to the door, he threw it inside, saying: "There is some food for thee from thy daughter, she wants for nothing."

Some time after this the girl in the mountain performed a like operation on her second sister; she set her head on again, rubbed her with what was in the flask, and put her into a sack; but this time she put as much gold and silver into the sack as it would hold, and only a very little food on the top. "Dear friend," said she to the Troll, "you must go home again to my mother with a little more food, but do not look into the sack." The

Troll was quite willing to please her, and promised he would not look into the sack. But when he had gone a good way, the sack was so insufferably heavy that he was obliged to sit down and rest awhile, being quite unable to carry it any further; so he thought he would untie the string and look into it; but the girl in the sack called out: "I can see you, I can see you!" "Then thou must have sharp eyes indeed, in thy head," said the Troll quite frightened, and taking up the sack, made all the haste he could to the mother's. When he came to the door of the room, he threw it in, saying: "There is some food from thy daughter for thee, she is in want of nothing."

When the young girl had been some time longer in the mountain, the Troll having occasion one day to go out, she pretended to be ill and sick, and complained. "It is of no use that you come home before twelve o'clock," said she to the Troll, "for I feel so sick and ill that I cannot get the dinner ready before that time;" so the Troll promised he would not come back.

When the Troll was gone she stuffed her clothes out with straw, and set the straw girl in the chimney-corner with a ladle in her hand, so that she looked exactly as if she were standing there herself. She then stole home clandestinely, and took with her a gamekeeper, whom she met, to be at home with her mother. When the clock struck twelve the Troll returned. "Give me something to eat," said he to the straw girl; but she made him no answer.

"Give me something to eat, I say," said the Troll

again; "for I am hungry." But still there was no answer.

"Give me something to eat," screamed the Troll a third time; "I advise thee to do so, I say dost thou hear? otherwise I will try to wake thee."

But the girl stood stock still, whereupon he became so furious, that he gave her a kick that made the straw fly about in all directions. On seeing that, he found there was something wrong, and began to look about, and at last went down into the cellar; but both the girl's sisters were gone, and he was now at no loss to know how all this had happened.

"Ah! thou shalt pay dearly for this," said he, taking the road to her mother's house; but when he came to the door, the gamekeeper fired, and the Troll durst not venture in, for he believed that it thundered; so he turned about to go home with all possible speed, but just as he got to the trap-door, the sun rose, and the Troll burst.

There is plenty of gold and silver still in the mountains, if one only knew how to find the trap-door.

THE BOY THAT STOLE THE GIANT'S TREASURE.

1. THE SWORD, THE GOLDEN FOWLS, THE GOLDEN LANTERN, AND THE GOLDEN HARP.

From South Smaland.

THERE was once a poor peasant, who had three sons. The eldest two accompanied their father to field and forest, and aided him in his labour; but the youngest lad stayed at home with his mother, and helped her in her occupations. Hence he was slighted by his brothers, who treated him wrongfully whenever they had an opportunity.

After a time the father and mother died, and the three sons were to divide the inheritance; on which occasion, as may easily be imagined, the elder brothers took for their share all that was of any value, leaving nothing for their young brother. When everything else had been appropriated, there remained only an old split kneading-trough that neither of the two would have. One of the brothers thereupon said, "The old trough is exactly the thing for our young brother, he is so fond of baking and coddling." The lad, as he well might, thought this was but a poor inheritance; but he had no remedy, and from that time he was convinced there was no good to be got by staying at home. So, bidding his brothers farewell, he went out into the world to try his luck. On coming to the water-side he caulked his trough with oakum, and so made a little boat of it, using two sticks for oars. He then rowed away.

Having crossed the water, he came to a spacious palace, into which he entered, and demanded to speak with the king. The king said, "What is thy family and thy errand?" The lad answered, "I am a poor peasant's son, who has nothing in the world but an old kneading-trough. I come hither in search of employment." When the king heard this he laughed, and said, "Thou hast, indeed, but a small inheritance; but luck often takes a wonderful turn." The boy was then received among the king's under-servants, and was well liked by all for his courage and activity.

We must now relate that the king, to whom the palace belonged, had an only daughter. She was both beautiful and discreet, so that her beauty and understanding were the subject of discourse throughout the whole realm, and wooers, from the east and west, came to demand her; but the princess said *nay* to all of them, unless they could bring her, as a bridal present, four precious things that were possessed by a giant on the other side of the water. These were—a golden sword, two gold fowls, a golden lantern, and a harp of gold. Many warriors and sons of kings had gone forth to gain these treasures, but not one had returned, for the giant had seized and eaten them all. This was a cause of grief to the king; he was fearful that his daughter would never get a husband, nor himself a son-in-law, who should inherit his kingdom.

When the lad heard talk of this, he thought to himself that it would be well worth while to make an attempt to win the king's fair daughter. So, full of these thoughts, he one day appeared before the king and told his errand; but the king was incensed, and said, "How canst thou, who art a poor peasant, think of performing that which no warrior has hitherto been able to accomplish?" Nevertheless, the boy persisted in his design, and begged for leave to try his luck. When the king saw his resolution, his anger ceased, and he gave him permission, adding, "Thy life is at stake, and I would not willingly lose thee." They then separated.

The lad then went down to the water, found his trough, which he carefully examined on all sides, after which he again rowed over the water, and lay on the watch near the giant's dwelling, where he stayed during the night. In the morning, before it was light, the giant went to his barn and began threshing, so that it resounded through the mountain. On hearing this the lad gathered a number of small stones into his pouch, crept on to the roof and made a little hole, through which he could look down into the barn. The giant was wont at all times to wear his golden sword by his side, which possessed the extraordinary property of ringing loudly whenever its owner was angry. While the giant was threshing with might and main, the boy cast a small stone, so that it fell on the sword, at which the weapon gave forth a loud clank. "Why dost thou clank?" asked the giant, peevishly; "I am not angry with thee." He resumed his threshing; but at the same moment the sword clanked again. The giant went on threshing, and

the sword clanked for the third time. The giant then
lost his patience, unclasped his belt, and cast the sword
out at the door of the barn. "Lie there," said he, "until
I have done my threshing." The lad, however, did not
wait for that, but, creeping down from the roof, he
seized the sword, ran to his boat, and rowed across the
water. There he concealed his booty, and rejoiced that
his enterprise had ended so favourably.

The next day the boy filled his scrip with corn, laid a
bundle of bast in the boat, and again betook himself to
the giant's habitation. After lying on the watch for a
while he perceived where the giant's three golden fowls
were spreading out their wings by the water's edge, so
that they glittered beautifully in the bright sunshine.
He was instantly at hand, and began softly enticing the
birds, at the same time giving them corn from his scrip.
All the time they were engaged in eating the lad kept
drawing nearer and nearer to the water, till at last all
the three golden fowls were assembled in his little boat.
He then sprang in himself, and having tied the fowls with
the bast, pushed off the boat, and rowed away with all
speed, to conceal his booty on the opposite side.

On the third day the lad put some lumps of salt into
his scrip, and again crossed the water. When night
drew near, he remarked how the smoke rose from the
giant's dwelling; and thence concluded that the giant's
wife was busied in preparing food; so creeping up on
the roof, he looked down the chimney, and saw where a
huge pot was boiling on the fire. Taking then the lumps
of salt from his scrip, he let them fall one by one into

the pot. He then stole down from the roof, and waited to see what would happen.

In a little while the giantess lifted the pot from the fire, poured out the porridge, and placed the bowl on the table. The giant was hungry, and instantly began to eat; but no sooner had he tasted the porridge and found it was both salt and bitter, than he started up overcome with anger. The crone excused herself, and thought the porridge was good; but the giant bade her taste it herself; he, for his part, would eat no more of her mess. The crone now tasted the porridge, but having so done, grinned most fearfully; for such nauseous stuff she had never before tasted.

The giantess had now no alternative but to boil some fresh porridge for her husband. For this purpose she took the pail, reached the gold lantern down from the wall, and ran to the well to fetch water. Having set the lantern down on the edge of the well, she stooped forwards to draw up the water, when the lad rushed towards her, and seizing her by the feet, pitched her headlong into the well, and possessed himself of the golden lantern. He then ran off and crossed the water in safety. In the meanwhile the giant sat wondering why his wife stayed so long away, and at length went in search of her; but nothing of her could he see, only a dull plashing was audible from the well. The giant was now aware that his wife was in the water, and with great difficulty helped her out. "Where is my golden lantern?" was his first question, as soon as the crone began a little to recover herself. "I don't know," answered she, "but it seemed to me that some one seized me by the feet and cast me into the well." The giant was highly incensed at this intelligence, and said: "Three of my most precious things have now disappeared, and I have nothing left save my gold harp; but the thief, whoever he may be, shall not get that. I will secure it under twelve locks."

While this was passing at the giant's, the lad was sitting on the opposite side rejoicing that all had turned out so well; but the most difficult task still remained to be performed—to steal the giant's golden harp. He meditated for a long time how this was to be effected; but could hit on no plan, and, therefore, resolved to cross over to the giant's, and there wait for an opportunity.

No sooner said than done. The boy rowed over and stationed himself on the watch. But the giant was now on the look-out, got sight of the boy, and, rushing quickly forth, seized him. "So, I have caught thee at last, thou thief," said the giant, almost bursting with rage. "It is no other than thou who has stolen my sword, my three golden fowls, and my golden lantern." The lad was now terrified, thinking that his last hour was come; and he answered meekly: "Let me have my life, dear father; I will never come again." "No," replied the giant, "it shall go with thee as it has gone with the others. No one passes alive out of my hands." The giant then caused the boy to be shut up in a sty, and gave him nuts and milk, that he might grow fat, previous to slaughtering him, and eating him up.

The lad was now a prisoner, but ate and drank and

made himself comfortable. After some time had passed, the giant was desirous of ascertaining whether he were yet sufficiently fattened: he went, therefore, to the sty, bored a hole in the wall, and ordered the boy to put one of his fingers through. But the lad, being aware of his object, instead of a finger, put forth a peg of peeled alder. The giant made an incision in it, so that the red sap dropped from the wood; whence he concluded that the boy must still be very lean, seeing that his flesh was so hard; and therefore caused a larger allowance to be given him of milk and nuts than before.

After another interval had elapsed the giant went again to the sty and ordered the boy to put his finger through the hole in the wall. The lad this time put forth a cabbage-stalk, and the giant made a cut in it with his knife. He now thought his captive must be sufficiently plump, as his flesh seemed so soft.

When it was morning, the giant said to his wife: "Mother, the boy seems now fat enough; take him, therefore, and bake him in the oven. I will in the meanwhile go and invite our kinsmen to the feast." The crone promised to do as her husband had commanded; so having made the oven very hot, she laid hold on the boy for the purpose of baking him. "Place thyself on the peel," said the giantess. The boy did so; but when the crone raised the handle of the peel, he contrived to fall off, and thus it happened at least ten times. At length the crone became very angry, and scolded him for his awkwardness; but the boy excused himself by saying that he did not know exactly how to sit. "Wait,

I will show thee," said the giantess, placing herself on the peel, with crooked back and drawn-up knees. But scarcely had she so done when the boy, seizing hold of the handle, shoved the beldam into the oven and closed the mouth. He then took the crone's fur cloak, stuffed it with straw, and laid it on the bed; seized the giant's great bunch of keys, opened the twelve locks, snatched up the golden harp and hurried down to his boat.

When the giant returned home, "Where can my wife be?" thought he to himself, not seeing her anywhere in the house. "Ah, she is no doubt lying down awhile to rest; that I can well imagine." But long as the crone had slept, she, nevertheless, would not wake up, although the guests were every moment expected. So the giant went to wake her, crying aloud: "Wake up! wake up, mother!" But no one answered. He called a second time, but still without an answer. The giant now lost his temper, and gave the fur cloak a violent shake; and now discovered that it was not his old woman, but a bundle of straw over which her clothes had been laid. At this discovery the giant began to suspect mischief, and ran off to look after his golden harp. But the bunch of keys was away, the twelve locks had been opened, and the golden harp had also vanished. And when at length he went to the mouth of the oven, to look after his festal repast, lo!—there sat his own wife, baked in the oven and grinning horribly at him.

The giant was now beside himself with grief and rage, and rushed out to take vengeance on the author of all this evil. On reaching the water's edge, he saw the boy sitting in his boat, and playing on the harp, the tones of which resounded over the water, and the golden strings glittered beautifully in the bright sunshine. The giant sprang into the water to seize the boy; but finding it too deep, he laid himself down on the shore and began to drink, for the purpose of draining off the water. As he drank with all his might, he caused such a current that the little boat was borne nearer and nearer to the shore; but just as he was in the act of seizing it, he had drunk too much and burst.

The giant now lay dead on the land; but the boy rowed back over the water with great exultation and glee. On reaching the opposite shore, he combed his golden locks, arrayed himself in costly garments, girded the giant's golden sword by his side, took the golden harp in one hand and the golden lantern in the other, enticed the golden fowls after him, and, thus equipped, entered the hall where the king was sitting at table with his courtiers. When the king saw the youth, he was overjoyed at heart, and beheld him with friendly eyes. But the youth, approaching the king's fair daughter, greeted her courteously, and laid the giant's treasures at her feet. There was now great joy throughout the royal palace, that the princess had obtained the giant's treasures, and also a bridegroom so comely and so valorous. The king shortly after caused his daughter's nuptials to be solemnized with great pomp and rejoicing; and when the old king died, the boy was chosen king of the country, and lived there both long and happy. Since that time I was no longer with them.

A CATALOG OF SELECTED DOVER
BOOKS IN ALL FIELDS OF INTEREST

CONCERNING THE SPIRITUAL IN ART, Wassily Kandinsky. Pioneering work by father of abstract art. Thoughts on color theory, nature of art. Analysis of earlier masters. 12 illustrations. 80pp. of text. 5⅜ x 8½. 23411-8 Pa. $4.95

ANIMALS: 1,419 Copyright-Free Illustrations of Mammals, Birds, Fish, Insects, etc., Jim Harter (ed.). Clear wood engravings present, in extremely lifelike poses, over 1,000 species of animals. One of the most extensive pictorial sourcebooks of its kind. Captions. Index. 284pp. 9 x 12. 23766-4 Pa. $14.95

CELTIC ART: The Methods of Construction, George Bain. Simple geometric techniques for making Celtic interlacements, spirals, Kells-type initials, animals, humans, etc. Over 500 illustrations. 160pp. 9 x 12. (Available in U.S. only.) 22923-8 Pa. $9.95

AN ATLAS OF ANATOMY FOR ARTISTS, Fritz Schider. Most thorough reference work on art anatomy in the world. Hundreds of illustrations, including selections from works by Vesalius, Leonardo, Goya, Ingres, Michelangelo, others. 593 illustrations. 192pp. 7⅛ x 10¼. 20241-0 Pa. $9.95

CELTIC HAND STROKE-BY-STROKE (Irish Half-Uncial from "The Book of Kells"): An Arthur Baker Calligraphy Manual, Arthur Baker. Complete guide to creating each letter of the alphabet in distinctive Celtic manner. Covers hand position, strokes, pens, inks, paper, more. Illustrated. 48pp. 8¼ x 11. 24336-2 Pa. $3.95

EASY ORIGAMI, John Montroll. Charming collection of 32 projects (hat, cup, pelican, piano, swan, many more) specially designed for the novice origami hobbyist. Clearly illustrated easy-to-follow instructions insure that even beginning papercrafters will achieve successful results. 48pp. 8¼ x 11. 27298-2 Pa. $3.50

THE COMPLETE BOOK OF BIRDHOUSE CONSTRUCTION FOR WOOD-WORKERS, Scott D. Campbell. Detailed instructions, illustrations, tables. Also data on bird habitat and instinct patterns. Bibliography. 3 tables. 63 illustrations in 15 figures. 48pp. 5¼ x 8½. 24407-5 Pa. $2.50

BLOOMINGDALE'S ILLUSTRATED 1886 CATALOG: Fashions, Dry Goods and Housewares, Bloomingdale Brothers. Famed merchants' extremely rare catalog depicting about 1,700 products: clothing, housewares, firearms, dry goods, jewelry, more. Invaluable for dating, identifying vintage items. Also, copyright-free graphics for artists, designers. Co-published with Henry Ford Museum & Greenfield Village. 160pp. 8¼ x 11. 25780-0 Pa. $12.95

HISTORIC COSTUME IN PICTURES, Braun & Schneider. Over 1,450 costumed figures in clearly detailed engravings–from dawn of civilization to end of 19th century. Captions. Many folk costumes. 256pp. 8⅜ x 11¾. 23150-X Pa. $12.95

STICKLEY CRAFTSMAN FURNITURE CATALOGS, Gustav Stickley and L. & J. G. Stickley. Beautiful, functional furniture in two authentic catalogs from 1910. 594 illustrations, including 277 photos, show settles, rockers, armchairs, reclining chairs, bookcases, desks, tables. 183pp. 6½ x 9¼.   23838-5 Pa. $11.95

AMERICAN LOCOMOTIVES IN HISTORIC PHOTOGRAPHS: 1858 to 1949, Ron Ziel (ed.). A rare collection of 126 meticulously detailed official photographs, called "builder portraits," of American locomotives that majestically chronicle the rise of steam locomotive power in America. Introduction. Detailed captions. xi+ 129pp. 9 x 12.   27393-8 Pa. $13.95

AMERICA'S LIGHTHOUSES: An Illustrated History, Francis Ross Holland, Jr. Delightfully written, profusely illustrated fact-filled survey of over 200 American light-houses since 1716. History, anecdotes, technological advances, more. 240pp. 8 x 10¾.
25576-X Pa. $12.95

TOWARDS A NEW ARCHITECTURE, Le Corbusier. Pioneering manifesto by founder of "International School." Technical and aesthetic theories, views of industry, eco-nomics, relation of form to function, "mass-production split" and much more. Profusely illustrated. 320pp. 6⅛ x 9¼. (Available in U.S. only.)   25023-7 Pa. $10.95

HOW THE OTHER HALF LIVES, Jacob Riis. Famous journalistic record, expos-ing poverty and degradation of New York slums around 1900, by major social reformer. 100 striking and influential photographs. 233pp. 10 x 7⅞.
22012-5 Pa. $11.95

FRUIT KEY AND TWIG KEY TO TREES AND SHRUBS, William M. Harlow. One of the handiest and most widely used identification aids. Fruit key covers 120 deciduous and evergreen species; twig key 160 deciduous species. Easily used. Over 300 photographs. 126pp. 5⅜ x 8½.   20511-8 Pa. $3.95

COMMON BIRD SONGS, Dr. Donald J. Borror. Songs of 60 most common U.S. birds: robins, sparrows, cardinals, bluejays, finches, more–arranged in order of increasing complexity. Up to 9 variations of songs of each species.
Cassette and manual 99911-4 $8.95

ORCHIDS AS HOUSE PLANTS, Rebecca Tyson Northen. Grow cattleyas and many other kinds of orchids–in a window, in a case, or under artificial light. 63 illus-trations. 148pp. 5⅜ x 8½.   23261-1 Pa. $7.95

MONSTER MAZES, Dave Phillips. Masterful mazes at four levels of difficulty. Avoid deadly perils and evil creatures to find magical treasures. Solutions for all 32 exciting illustrated puzzles. 48pp. 8¼ x 11.   26005-4 Pa. $2.95

MOZART'S DON GIOVANNI (DOVER OPERA LIBRETTO SERIES), Wolfgang Amadeus Mozart. Introduced and translated by Ellen H. Bleiler. Standard Italian libretto, with complete English translation. Convenient and thoroughly portable–an ideal companion for reading along with a recording or the performance itself. Introduction. List of characters. Plot summary. 121pp. 5¼ x 8½.
24944-1 Pa. $3.95

TECHNICAL MANUAL AND DICTIONARY OF CLASSICAL BALLET, Gail Grant. Defines, explains, comments on steps, movements, poses and concepts. 15-page pictorial section. Basic book for student, viewer. 127pp. 5⅜ x 8½.
21843-0 Pa. $4.95

THE CLARINET AND CLARINET PLAYING, David Pino. Lively, comprehensive work features suggestions about technique, musicianship, and musical interpretation, as well as guidelines for teaching, making your own reeds, and preparing for public performance. Includes an intriguing look at clarinet history. "A godsend," *The Clarinet,* Journal of the International Clarinet Society. Appendixes. 7 illus. 320pp. 5⅜ x 8½. 40270-3 Pa. $9.95

HOLLYWOOD GLAMOR PORTRAITS, John Kobal (ed.). 145 photos from 1926-49. Harlow, Gable, Bogart, Bacall; 94 stars in all. Full background on photographers, technical aspects. 160pp. 8⅜ x 11¼. 23352-9 Pa. $12.95

THE ANNOTATED CASEY AT THE BAT: A Collection of Ballads about the Mighty Casey/Third, Revised Edition, Martin Gardner (ed.). Amusing sequels and parodies of one of America's best-loved poems: Casey's Revenge, Why Casey Whiffed, Casey's Sister at the Bat, others. 256pp. 5⅜ x 8½. 28598-7 Pa. $8.95

THE RAVEN AND OTHER FAVORITE POEMS, Edgar Allan Poe. Over 40 of the author's most memorable poems: "The Bells," "Ulalume," "Israfel," "To Helen," "The Conqueror Worm," "Eldorado," "Annabel Lee," many more. Alphabetic lists of titles and first lines. 64pp. 5$\frac{3}{16}$ x 8¼. 26685-0 Pa. $1.00

PERSONAL MEMOIRS OF U. S. GRANT, Ulysses Simpson Grant. Intelligent, deeply moving firsthand account of Civil War campaigns, considered by many the finest military memoirs ever written. Includes letters, historic photographs, maps and more. 528pp. 6⅛ x 9¼. 28587-1 Pa. $12.95

ANCIENT EGYPTIAN MATERIALS AND INDUSTRIES, A. Lucas and J. Harris. Fascinating, comprehensive, thoroughly documented text describes this ancient civilization's vast resources and the processes that incorporated them in daily life, including the use of animal products, building materials, cosmetics, perfumes and incense, fibers, glazed ware, glass and its manufacture, materials used in the mummification process, and much more. 544pp. 6⅛ x 9¼. (Available in U.S. only.) 40446-3 Pa. $16.95

RUSSIAN STORIES/PYCCKNE PACCKA3bl: A Dual-Language Book, edited by Gleb Struve. Twelve tales by such masters as Chekhov, Tolstoy, Dostoevsky, Pushkin, others. Excellent word-for-word English translations on facing pages, plus teaching and study aids, Russian/English vocabulary, biographical/critical introductions, more. 416pp. 5⅜ x 8½. 26244-8 Pa. $9.95

PHILADELPHIA THEN AND NOW: 60 Sites Photographed in the Past and Present, Kenneth Finkel and Susan Oyama. Rare photographs of City Hall, Logan Square, Independence Hall, Betsy Ross House, other landmarks juxtaposed with contemporary views. Captures changing face of historic city. Introduction. Captions. 128pp. 8¼ x 11. 25790-8 Pa. $9.95

AIA ARCHITECTURAL GUIDE TO NASSAU AND SUFFOLK COUNTIES, LONG ISLAND, The American Institute of Architects, Long Island Chapter, and the Society for the Preservation of Long Island Antiquities. Comprehensive, well-researched and generously illustrated volume brings to life over three centuries of Long Island's great architectural heritage. More than 240 photographs with authoritative, extensively detailed captions. 176pp. 8¼ x 11. 26946-9 Pa. $14.95

NORTH AMERICAN INDIAN LIFE: Customs and Traditions of 23 Tribes, Elsie Clews Parsons (ed.). 27 fictionalized essays by noted anthropologists examine religion, customs, government, additional facets of life among the Winnebago, Crow, Zuni, Eskimo, other tribes. 480pp. 6⅛ x 9¼. 27377-6 Pa. $10.95

FRANK LLOYD WRIGHT'S DANA HOUSE, Donald Hoffmann. Pictorial essay of residential masterpiece with over 160 interior and exterior photos, plans, elevations, sketches and studies. 128pp. 9¼ x 10¾.　　　　29120-0 Pa. $14.95

THE MALE AND FEMALE FIGURE IN MOTION: 60 Classic Photographic Sequences, Eadweard Muybridge. 60 true-action photographs of men and women walking, running, climbing, bending, turning, etc., reproduced from rare 19th-century masterpiece. vi + 121pp. 9 x 12.　　　　24745-7 Pa. $12.95

1001 QUESTIONS ANSWERED ABOUT THE SEASHORE, N. J. Berrill and Jacquelyn Berrill. Queries answered about dolphins, sea snails, sponges, starfish, fishes, shore birds, many others. Covers appearance, breeding, growth, feeding, much more. 305pp. 5¼ x 8¼.　　　　23366-9 Pa. $9.95

ATTRACTING BIRDS TO YOUR YARD, William J. Weber. Easy-to-follow guide offers advice on how to attract the greatest diversity of birds: birdhouses, feeders, water and waterers, much more. 96pp. 5³⁄₁₆ x 8¼.　　　　28927-3 Pa. $2.50

MEDICINAL AND OTHER USES OF NORTH AMERICAN PLANTS: A Historical Survey with Special Reference to the Eastern Indian Tribes, Charlotte Erichsen-Brown. Chronological historical citations document 500 years of usage of plants, trees, shrubs native to eastern Canada, northeastern U.S. Also complete identifying information. 343 illustrations. 544pp. 6½ x 9¼.　　　　25951-X Pa. $12.95

STORYBOOK MAZES, Dave Phillips. 23 stories and mazes on two-page spreads: Wizard of Oz, Treasure Island, Robin Hood, etc. Solutions. 64pp. 8¼ x 11.
　　　　23628-5 Pa. $2.95

AMERICAN NEGRO SONGS: 230 Folk Songs and Spirituals, Religious and Secular, John W. Work. This authoritative study traces the African influences of songs sung and played by black Americans at work, in church, and as entertainment. The author discusses the lyric significance of such songs as "Swing Low, Sweet Chariot," "John Henry," and others and offers the words and music for 230 songs. Bibliography. Index of Song Titles. 272pp. 6½ x 9¼.　　　　40271-1 Pa. $10.95

MOVIE-STAR PORTRAITS OF THE FORTIES, John Kobal (ed.). 163 glamor, studio photos of 106 stars of the 1940s: Rita Hayworth, Ava Gardner, Marlon Brando, Clark Gable, many more. 176pp. 8⅜ x 11¼.　　　　23546-7 Pa. $14.95

BENCHLEY LOST AND FOUND, Robert Benchley. Finest humor from early 30s, about pet peeves, child psychologists, post office and others. Mostly unavailable elsewhere. 73 illustrations by Peter Arno and others. 183pp. 5⅜ x 8½. 22410-4 Pa. $6.95

YEKL and THE IMPORTED BRIDEGROOM AND OTHER STORIES OF YIDDISH NEW YORK, Abraham Cahan. Film Hester Street based on *Yekl* (1896). Novel, other stories among first about Jewish immigrants on N.Y.'s East Side. 240pp. 5⅜ x 8½.　　　　22427-9 Pa. $7.95

SELECTED POEMS, Walt Whitman. Generous sampling from *Leaves of Grass*. Twenty-four poems include "I Hear America Singing," "Song of the Open Road," "I Sing the Body Electric," "When Lilacs Last in the Dooryard Bloom'd," "O Captain! My Captain!"–all reprinted from an authoritative edition. Lists of titles and first lines. 128pp. 5³⁄₁₆ x 8¼.　　　　26878-0 Pa. $1.00

THE BEST TALES OF HOFFMANN, E. T. A. Hoffmann. 10 of Hoffmann's most important stories: "Nutcracker and the King of Mice," "The Golden Flowerpot," etc. 458pp. 5⅜ x 8½. 21793-0 Pa. $9.95

FROM FETISH TO GOD IN ANCIENT EGYPT, E. A. Wallis Budge. Rich detailed survey of Egyptian conception of "God" and gods, magic, cult of animals, Osiris, more. Also, superb English translations of hymns and legends. 240 illustrations. 545pp. 5⅜ x 8½. 25803-3 Pa. $13.95

FRENCH STORIES/CONTES FRANÇAIS: A Dual-Language Book, Wallace Fowlie. Ten stories by French masters, Voltaire to Camus: "Micromegas" by Voltaire; "The Atheist's Mass" by Balzac; "Minuet" by de Maupassant; "The Guest" by Camus, six more. Excellent English translations on facing pages. Also French-English vocabulary list, exercises, more. 352pp. 5⅜ x 8½. 26443-2 Pa. $9.95

CHICAGO AT THE TURN OF THE CENTURY IN PHOTOGRAPHS: 122 Historic Views from the Collections of the Chicago Historical Society, Larry A. Viskochil. Rare large-format prints offer detailed views of City Hall, State Street, the Loop, Hull House, Union Station, many other landmarks, circa 1904-1913. Introduction. Captions. Maps. 144pp. 9⅜ x 12¼. 24656-6 Pa. $12.95

OLD BROOKLYN IN EARLY PHOTOGRAPHS, 1865-1929, William Lee Younger. Luna Park, Gravesend race track, construction of Grand Army Plaza, moving of Hotel Brighton, etc. 157 previously unpublished photographs. 165pp. 8⅞ x 11¾. 23587-4 Pa. $13.95

THE MYTHS OF THE NORTH AMERICAN INDIANS, Lewis Spence. Rich anthology of the myths and legends of the Algonquins, Iroquois, Pawnees and Sioux, prefaced by an extensive historical and ethnological commentary. 36 illustrations. 480pp. 5⅜ x 8½. 25967-6 Pa. $10.95

AN ENCYCLOPEDIA OF BATTLES: Accounts of Over 1,560 Battles from 1479 B.C. to the Present, David Eggenberger. Essential details of every major battle in recorded history from the first battle of Megiddo in 1479 B.C. to Grenada in 1984. List of Battle Maps. New Appendix covering the years 1967-1984. Index. 99 illustrations. 544pp. 6½ x 9¼. 24913-1 Pa. $16.95

SAILING ALONE AROUND THE WORLD, Captain Joshua Slocum. First man to sail around the world, alone, in small boat. One of great feats of seamanship told in delightful manner. 67 illustrations. 294pp. 5⅜ x 8½. 20326-3 Pa. $6.95

ANARCHISM AND OTHER ESSAYS, Emma Goldman. Powerful, penetrating, prophetic essays on direct action, role of minorities, prison reform, puritan hypocrisy, violence, etc. 271pp. 5⅜ x 8½. 22484-8 Pa. $8.95

MYTHS OF THE HINDUS AND BUDDHISTS, Ananda K. Coomaraswamy and Sister Nivedita. Great stories of the epics; deeds of Krishna, Shiva, taken from puranas, Vedas, folk tales; etc. 32 illustrations. 400pp. 5⅜ x 8½. 21759-0 Pa. $12.95

THE TRAUMA OF BIRTH, Otto Rank. Rank's controversial thesis that anxiety neurosis is caused by profound psychological trauma which occurs at birth. 256pp. 5⅜ x 8½. 27974-X Pa. $7.95

A THEOLOGICO-POLITICAL TREATISE, Benedict Spinoza. Also contains unfinished Political Treatise. Great classic on religious liberty, theory of government on common consent. R. Elwes translation. Total of 421pp. 5⅜ x 8½. 20249-6 Pa. $10.95

MY BONDAGE AND MY FREEDOM, Frederick Douglass. Born a slave, Douglass became outspoken force in antislavery movement. The best of Douglass' autobiographies. Graphic description of slave life. 464pp. 5⅜ x 8½. 22457-0 Pa. $8.95

FOLLOWING THE EQUATOR: A Journey Around the World, Mark Twain. Fascinating humorous account of 1897 voyage to Hawaii, Australia, India, New Zealand, etc. Ironic, bemused reports on peoples, customs, climate, flora and fauna, politics, much more. 197 illustrations. 720pp. 5⅜ x 8½.   26113-1 Pa. $15.95

THE PEOPLE CALLED SHAKERS, Edward D. Andrews. Definitive study of Shakers: origins, beliefs, practices, dances, social organization, furniture and crafts, etc. 33 illustrations. 351pp. 5⅜ x 8½.   21081-2 Pa. $12.95

THE MYTHS OF GREECE AND ROME, H. A. Guerber. A classic of mythology, generously illustrated, long prized for its simple, graphic, accurate retelling of the principal myths of Greece and Rome, and for its commentary on their origins and significance. With 64 illustrations by Michelangelo, Raphael, Titian, Rubens, Canova, Bernini and others. 480pp. 5⅜ x 8½.   27584-1 Pa. $10.95

PSYCHOLOGY OF MUSIC, Carl E. Seashore. Classic work discusses music as a medium from psychological viewpoint. Clear treatment of physical acoustics, auditory apparatus, sound perception, development of musical skills, nature of musical feeling, host of other topics. 88 figures. 408pp. 5⅜ x 8½.   21851-1 Pa. $11.95

THE PHILOSOPHY OF HISTORY, Georg W. Hegel. Great classic of Western thought develops concept that history is not chance but rational process, the evolution of freedom. 457pp. 5⅜ x 8½.   20112-0 Pa. $9.95

THE BOOK OF TEA, Kakuzo Okakura. Minor classic of the Orient: entertaining, charming explanation, interpretation of traditional Japanese culture in terms of tea ceremony. 94pp. 5⅜ x 8½.   20070-1 Pa. $3.95

LIFE IN ANCIENT EGYPT, Adolf Erman. Fullest, most thorough, detailed older account with much not in more recent books, domestic life, religion, magic, medicine, commerce, much more. Many illustrations reproduce tomb paintings, carvings, hieroglyphs, etc. 597pp. 5⅜ x 8½.   22632-8 Pa. $12.95

SUNDIALS, Their Theory and Construction, Albert Waugh. Far and away the best, most thorough coverage of ideas, mathematics concerned, types, construction, adjusting anywhere. Simple, nontechnical treatment allows even children to build several of these dials. Over 100 illustrations. 230pp. 5⅜ x 8½.   22947-5 Pa. $8.95

THEORETICAL HYDRODYNAMICS, L. M. Milne-Thomson. Classic exposition of the mathematical theory of fluid motion, applicable to both hydrodynamics and aerodynamics. Over 600 exercises. 768pp. 6⅛ x 9¼.   68970-0 Pa. $20.95

SONGS OF EXPERIENCE: Facsimile Reproduction with 26 Plates in Full Color, William Blake. 26 full-color plates from a rare 1826 edition. Includes "TheTyger," "London," "Holy Thursday," and other poems. Printed text of poems. 48pp. 5¼ x 7.
24636-1 Pa. $4.95

OLD-TIME VIGNETTES IN FULL COLOR, Carol Belanger Grafton (ed.). Over 390 charming, often sentimental illustrations, selected from archives of Victorian graphics—pretty women posing, children playing, food, flowers, kittens and puppies, smiling cherubs, birds and butterflies, much more. All copyright-free. 48pp. 9¼ x 12¼.
27269-9 Pa. $9.95

CATALOG OF DOVER BOOKS

PERSPECTIVE FOR ARTISTS, Rex Vicat Cole. Depth, perspective of sky and sea, shadows, much more, not usually covered. 391 diagrams, 81 reproductions of drawings and paintings. 279pp. 5⅜ x 8½.
22487-2 Pa. $9.95

DRAWING THE LIVING FIGURE, Joseph Sheppard. Innovative approach to artistic anatomy focuses on specifics of surface anatomy, rather than muscles and bones. Over 170 drawings of live models in front, back and side views, and in widely varying poses. Accompanying diagrams. 177 illustrations. Introduction. Index. 144pp. 8⅜ x11¼.
26723-7 Pa. $9.95

GOTHIC AND OLD ENGLISH ALPHABETS: 100 Complete Fonts, Dan X. Solo. Add power, elegance to posters, signs, other graphics with 100 stunning copyright-free alphabets: Blackstone, Dolbey, Germania, 97 more–including many lower-case, numerals, punctuation marks. 104pp. 8¼ x 11.
24695-7 Pa. $9.95

HOW TO DO BEADWORK, Mary White. Fundamental book on craft from simple projects to five-bead chains and woven works. 106 illustrations. 142pp. 5⅜ x 8.
20697-1 Pa. $5.95

THE BOOK OF WOOD CARVING, Charles Marshall Sayers. Finest book for beginners discusses fundamentals and offers 34 designs. "Absolutely first rate . . . well thought out and well executed."–E. J. Tangerman. 118pp. 7¾ x 10⅝.
23654-4 Pa. $7.95

ILLUSTRATED CATALOG OF CIVIL WAR MILITARY GOODS: Union Army Weapons, Insignia, Uniform Accessories, and Other Equipment, Schuyler, Hartley, and Graham. Rare, profusely illustrated 1846 catalog includes Union Army uniform and dress regulations, arms and ammunition, coats, insignia, flags, swords, rifles, etc. 226 illustrations. 160pp. 9 x 12.
24939-5 Pa. $12.95

WOMEN'S FASHIONS OF THE EARLY 1900s: An Unabridged Republication of "New York Fashions, 1909," National Cloak & Suit Co. Rare catalog of mail-order fashions documents women's and children's clothing styles shortly after the turn of the century. Captions offer full descriptions, prices. Invaluable resource for fashion, costume historians. Approximately 725 illustrations. 128pp. 8⅜ x 11¼.
27276-1 Pa. $12.95

THE 1912 AND 1915 GUSTAV STICKLEY FURNITURE CATALOGS, Gustav Stickley. With over 200 detailed illustrations and descriptions, these two catalogs are essential reading and reference materials and identification guides for Stickley furniture. Captions cite materials, dimensions and prices. 112pp. 6½ x 9¼.
26676-1 Pa. $9.95

EARLY AMERICAN LOCOMOTIVES, John H. White, Jr. Finest locomotive engravings from early 19th century: historical (1804–74), main-line (after 1870), special, foreign, etc. 147 plates. 142pp. 11⅜ x 8¼.
22772-3 Pa. $12.95

THE TALL SHIPS OF TODAY IN PHOTOGRAPHS, Frank O. Braynard. Lavishly illustrated tribute to nearly 100 majestic contemporary sailing vessels: Amerigo Vespucci, Clearwater, Constitution, Eagle, Mayflower, Sea Cloud, Victory, many more. Authoritative captions provide statistics, background on each ship. 190 black-and-white photographs and illustrations. Introduction. 128pp. 8⅞ x 11¾.
27163-3 Pa. $14.95

CATALOG OF DOVER BOOKS

LITTLE BOOK OF EARLY AMERICAN CRAFTS AND TRADES, Peter Stockham (ed.). 1807 children's book explains crafts and trades: baker, hatter, cooper, potter, and many others. 23 copperplate illustrations. 140pp. 4⅝ x 6.
23336-7 Pa. $4.95

VICTORIAN FASHIONS AND COSTUMES FROM HARPER'S BAZAR, 1867–1898, Stella Blum (ed.). Day costumes, evening wear, sports clothes, shoes, hats, other accessories in over 1,000 detailed engravings. 320pp. 9⅜ x 12¼.
22990-4 Pa. $16.95

GUSTAV STICKLEY, THE CRAFTSMAN, Mary Ann Smith. Superb study surveys broad scope of Stickley's achievement, especially in architecture. Design philosophy, rise and fall of the Craftsman empire, descriptions and floor plans for many Craftsman houses, more. 86 black-and-white halftones. 31 line illustrations. Introduction 208pp. 6½ x 9¼.
27210-9 Pa. $9.95

THE LONG ISLAND RAIL ROAD IN EARLY PHOTOGRAPHS, Ron Ziel. Over 220 rare photos, informative text document origin (1844) and development of rail service on Long Island. Vintage views of early trains, locomotives, stations, passengers, crews, much more. Captions. 8⅞ x 11¾.
26301-0 Pa. $14.95

VOYAGE OF THE LIBERDADE, Joshua Slocum. Great 19th-century mariner's thrilling, first-hand account of the wreck of his ship off South America, the 35-foot boat he built from the wreckage, and its remarkable voyage home. 128pp. 5⅜ x 8½.
40022-0 Pa. $5.95

TEN BOOKS ON ARCHITECTURE, Vitruvius. The most important book ever written on architecture. Early Roman aesthetics, technology, classical orders, site selection, all other aspects. Morgan translation. 331pp. 5⅜ x 8½. 20645-9 Pa. $9.95

THE HUMAN FIGURE IN MOTION, Eadweard Muybridge. More than 4,500 stopped-action photos, in action series, showing undraped men, women, children jumping, lying down, throwing, sitting, wrestling, carrying, etc. 390pp. 7⅞ x 10⅝.
20204-6 Clothbd. $29.95

TREES OF THE EASTERN AND CENTRAL UNITED STATES AND CANADA, William M. Harlow. Best one-volume guide to 140 trees. Full descriptions, woodlore, range, etc. Over 600 illustrations. Handy size. 288pp. 4½ x 6⅜.
20395-6 Pa. $6.95

SONGS OF WESTERN BIRDS, Dr. Donald J. Borror. Complete song and call repertoire of 60 western species, including flycatchers, juncoes, cactus wrens, many more–includes fully illustrated booklet. Cassette and manual 99913-0 $8.95

GROWING AND USING HERBS AND SPICES, Milo Miloradovich. Versatile handbook provides all the information needed for cultivation and use of all the herbs and spices available in North America. 4 illustrations. Index. Glossary. 236pp. 5⅜ x 8½.
25058-X Pa. $7.95

BIG BOOK OF MAZES AND LABYRINTHS, Walter Shepherd. 50 mazes and labyrinths in all–classical, solid, ripple, and more–in one great volume. Perfect inexpensive puzzler for clever youngsters. Full solutions. 112pp. 8⅛ x 11.
22951-3 Pa. $5.95

PIANO TUNING, J. Cree Fischer. Clearest, best book for beginner, amateur. Simple repairs, raising dropped notes, tuning by easy method of flattened fifths. No previous skills needed. 4 illustrations. 201pp. 5⅜ x 8½. 23267-0 Pa. $6.95

HINTS TO SINGERS, Lillian Nordica. Selecting the right teacher, developing confidence, overcoming stage fright, and many other important skills receive thoughtful discussion in this indispensible guide, written by a world-famous diva of four decades' experience. 96pp. 5³/₈ x 8¹/₂. 40094-8 Pa. $4.95

THE COMPLETE NONSENSE OF EDWARD LEAR, Edward Lear. All nonsense limericks, zany alphabets, Owl and Pussycat, songs, nonsense botany, etc., illustrated by Lear. Total of 320pp. 5⅜ x 8½. (Available in U.S. only.) 20167-8 Pa. $7.95

VICTORIAN PARLOUR POETRY: An Annotated Anthology, Michael R. Turner. 117 gems by Longfellow, Tennyson, Browning, many lesser-known poets. "The Village Blacksmith," "Curfew Must Not Ring Tonight," "Only a Baby Small," dozens more, often difficult to find elsewhere. Index of poets, titles, first lines. xxiii + 325pp. 5⅝ x 8¼. 27044-0 Pa. $12.95

DUBLINERS, James Joyce. Fifteen stories offer vivid, tightly focused observations of the lives of Dublin's poorer classes. At least one, "The Dead," is considered a masterpiece. Reprinted complete and unabridged from standard edition. 160pp. 5³⁄₁₆ x 8¼. 26870-5 Pa. $1.50

GREAT WEIRD TALES: 14 Stories by Lovecraft, Blackwood, Machen and Others, S. T. Joshi (ed.). 14 spellbinding tales, including "The Sin Eater," by Fiona McLeod, "The Eye Above the Mantel," by Frank Belknap Long, as well as renowned works by R. H. Barlow, Lord Dunsany, Arthur Machen, W. C. Morrow and eight other masters of the genre. 256pp. 5⅜ x 8½. (Available in U.S. only.) 40436-6 Pa. $8.95

THE BOOK OF THE SACRED MAGIC OF ABRAMELIN THE MAGE, translated by S. MacGregor Mathers. Medieval manuscript of ceremonial magic. Basic document in Aleister Crowley, Golden Dawn groups. 268pp. 5⅜ x 8½. 23211-5 Pa. $9.95

NEW RUSSIAN-ENGLISH AND ENGLISH-RUSSIAN DICTIONARY, M. A. O'Brien. This is a remarkably handy Russian dictionary, containing a surprising amount of information, including over 70,000 entries. 366pp. 4½ x 6⅛. 20208-9 Pa. $10.95

HISTORIC HOMES OF THE AMERICAN PRESIDENTS, Second, Revised Edition, Irvin Haas. A traveler's guide to American Presidential homes, most open to the public, depicting and describing homes occupied by every American President from George Washington to George Bush. With visiting hours, admission charges, travel routes. 175 photographs. Index. 160pp. 8¼ x 11. 26751-2 Pa. $13.95

NEW YORK IN THE FORTIES, Andreas Feininger. 162 brilliant photographs by the well-known photographer, formerly with *Life* magazine. Commuters, shoppers, Times Square at night, much else from city at its peak. Captions by John von Hartz. 181pp. 9¼ x 10¾. 23585-8 Pa. $13.95

INDIAN SIGN LANGUAGE, William Tomkins. Over 525 signs developed by Sioux and other tribes. Written instructions and diagrams. Also 290 pictographs. 111pp. 6⅛ x 9¼. 22029-X Pa. $3.95

CATALOG OF DOVER BOOKS

ANATOMY: A Complete Guide for Artists, Joseph Sheppard. A master of figure drawing shows artists how to render human anatomy convincingly. Over 460 illustrations. 224pp. 8⅜ x 11¼. 27279-6 Pa. $11.95

MEDIEVAL CALLIGRAPHY: Its History and Technique, Marc Drogin. Spirited history, comprehensive instruction manual covers 13 styles (ca. 4th century through 15th). Excellent photographs; directions for duplicating medieval techniques with modern tools. 224pp. 8⅜ x 11¼. 26142-5 Pa. $12.95

DRIED FLOWERS: How to Prepare Them, Sarah Whitlock and Martha Rankin. Complete instructions on how to use silica gel, meal and borax, perlite aggregate, sand and borax, glycerine and water to create attractive permanent flower arrangements. 12 illustrations. 32pp. 5⅜ x 8½. 21802-3 Pa. $1.00

EASY-TO-MAKE BIRD FEEDERS FOR WOODWORKERS, Scott D. Campbell. Detailed, simple-to-use guide for designing, constructing, caring for and using feeders. Text, illustrations for 12 classic and contemporary designs. 96pp. 5⅜ x 8½. 25847-5 Pa. $3.95

SCOTTISH WONDER TALES FROM MYTH AND LEGEND, Donald A. Mackenzie. 16 lively tales tell of giants rumbling down mountainsides, of a magic wand that turns stone pillars into warriors, of gods and goddesses, evil hags, powerful forces and more. 240pp. 5⅜ x 8½. 29677-6 Pa. $6.95

THE HISTORY OF UNDERCLOTHES, C. Willett Cunnington and Phyllis Cunnington. Fascinating, well-documented survey covering six centuries of English undergarments, enhanced with over 100 illustrations: 12th-century laced-up bodice, footed long drawers (1795), 19th-century bustles, 19th-century corsets for men, Victorian "bust improvers," much more. 272pp. 5⅝ x 8¼. 27124-2 Pa. $9.95

ARTS AND CRAFTS FURNITURE: The Complete Brooks Catalog of 1912, Brooks Manufacturing Co. Photos and detailed descriptions of more than 150 now very collectible furniture designs from the Arts and Crafts movement depict davenports, settees, buffets, desks, tables, chairs, bedsteads, dressers and more, all built of solid, quarter-sawed oak. Invaluable for students and enthusiasts of antiques, Americana and the decorative arts. 80pp. 6½ x 9¼. 27471-3 Pa. $8.95

WILBUR AND ORVILLE: A Biography of the Wright Brothers, Fred Howard. Definitive, crisply written study tells the full story of the brothers' lives and work. A vividly written biography, unparalleled in scope and color, that also captures the spirit of an extraordinary era. 560pp. 6⅛ x 9¼. 40297-5 Pa. $17.95

THE ARTS OF THE SAILOR: Knotting, Splicing and Ropework, Hervey Garrett Smith. Indispensable shipboard reference covers tools, basic knots and useful hitches; handsewing and canvas work, more. Over 100 illustrations. Delightful reading for sea lovers. 256pp. 5⅜ x 8½. 26440-8 Pa. $8.95

FRANK LLOYD WRIGHT'S FALLINGWATER: The House and Its History, Second, Revised Edition, Donald Hoffmann. A total revision–both in text and illustrations–of the standard document on Fallingwater, the boldest, most personal architectural statement of Wright's mature years, updated with valuable new material from the recently opened Frank Lloyd Wright Archives. "Fascinating"–*The New York Times*. 116 illustrations. 128pp. 9¼ x 10¾. 27430-6 Pa. $12.95

PHOTOGRAPHIC SKETCHBOOK OF THE CIVIL WAR, Alexander Gardner. 100 photos taken on field during the Civil War. Famous shots of Manassas Harper's Ferry, Lincoln, Richmond, slave pens, etc. 244pp. 10⅝ x 8¼. 22731-6 Pa. $10.95

FIVE ACRES AND INDEPENDENCE, Maurice G. Kains. Great back-to-the-land classic explains basics of self-sufficient farming. The one book to get. 95 illustrations. 397pp. 5⅜ x 8½. 20974-1 Pa. $7.95

SONGS OF EASTERN BIRDS, Dr. Donald J. Borror. Songs and calls of 60 species most common to eastern U.S.: warblers, woodpeckers, flycatchers, thrushes, larks, many more in high-quality recording. Cassette and manual 99912-2 $9.95

A MODERN HERBAL, Margaret Grieve. Much the fullest, most exact, most useful compilation of herbal material. Gigantic alphabetical encyclopedia, from aconite to zedoary, gives botanical information, medical properties, folklore, economic uses, much else. Indispensable to serious reader. 161 illustrations. 888pp. 6½ x 9¼. 2-vol. set. (Available in U.S. only.) Vol. I: 22798-7 Pa. $10.95
Vol. II: 22799-5 Pa. $10.95

HIDDEN TREASURE MAZE BOOK, Dave Phillips. Solve 34 challenging mazes accompanied by heroic tales of adventure. Evil dragons, people-eating plants, blood-thirsty giants, many more dangerous adversaries lurk at every twist and turn. 34 mazes, stories, solutions. 48pp. 8¼ x 11. 24566-7 Pa. $2.95

LETTERS OF W. A. MOZART, Wolfgang A. Mozart. Remarkable letters show bawdy wit, humor, imagination, musical insights, contemporary musical world; includes some letters from Leopold Mozart. 276pp. 5⅜ x 8½. 22859-2 Pa. $9.95

BASIC PRINCIPLES OF CLASSICAL BALLET, Agrippina Vaganova. Great Russian theoretician, teacher explains methods for teaching classical ballet. 118 illustrations. 175pp. 5⅜ x 8½. 22036-2 Pa. $6.95

THE JUMPING FROG, Mark Twain. Revenge edition. The original story of The Celebrated Jumping Frog of Calaveras County, a hapless French translation, and Twain's hilarious "retranslation" from the French. 12 illustrations. 66pp. 5⅜ x 8½.
22686-7 Pa. $4.95

BEST REMEMBERED POEMS, Martin Gardner (ed.). The 126 poems in this superb collection of 19th- and 20th-century British and American verse range from Shelley's "To a Skylark" to the impassioned "Renascence" of Edna St. Vincent Millay and to Edward Lear's whimsical "The Owl and the Pussycat." 224pp. 5⅜ x 8½.
27165-X Pa. $5.95

COMPLETE SONNETS, William Shakespeare. Over 150 exquisite poems deal with love, friendship, the tyranny of time, beauty's evanescence, death and other themes in language of remarkable power, precision and beauty. Glossary of archaic terms. 80pp. 5$^{3}/_{16}$ x 8¼. 26686-9 Pa. $1.00

THE BATTLES THAT CHANGED HISTORY, Fletcher Pratt. Eminent historian profiles 16 crucial conflicts, ancient to modern, that changed the course of civilization. 352pp. 5⅜ x 8½. 41129-X Pa. $9.95

THE WIT AND HUMOR OF OSCAR WILDE, Alvin Redman (ed.). More than 1,000 ripostes, paradoxes, wisecracks: Work is the curse of the drinking classes; I can resist everything except temptation; etc. 258pp. 5⅜ x 8½. 20602-5 Pa. $6.95

SHAKESPEARE LEXICON AND QUOTATION DICTIONARY, Alexander Schmidt. Full definitions, locations, shades of meaning in every word in plays and poems. More than 50,000 exact quotations. 1,485pp. 6½ x 9¼. 2-vol. set.
Vol. 1: 22726-X Pa. $17.95
Vol. 2: 22727-8 Pa. $17.95

SELECTED POEMS, Emily Dickinson. Over 100 best-known, best-loved poems by one of America's foremost poets, reprinted from authoritative early editions. No comparable edition at this price. Index of first lines. 64pp. 5³⁄₁₆ x 8¼.
26466-1 Pa. $1.00

THE INSIDIOUS DR. FU-MANCHU, Sax Rohmer. The first of the popular mystery series introduces a pair of English detectives to their archnemesis, the diabolical Dr. Fu-Manchu. Flavorful atmosphere, fast-paced action, and colorful characters enliven this classic of the genre. 208pp. 5³⁄₁₆ x 8¼. 29898-1 Pa. $2.00

THE MALLEUS MALEFICARUM OF KRAMER AND SPRENGER, translated by Montague Summers. Full text of most important witchhunter's "bible," used by both Catholics and Protestants. 278pp. 6⅝ x 10. 22802-9 Pa. $12.95

SPANISH STORIES/CUENTOS ESPAÑOLES: A Dual-Language Book, Angel Flores (ed.). Unique format offers 13 great stories in Spanish by Cervantes, Borges, others. Faithful English translations on facing pages. 352pp. 5⅜ x 8½.
25399-6 Pa. $9.95

GARDEN CITY, LONG ISLAND, IN EARLY PHOTOGRAPHS, 1869–1919, Mildred H. Smith. Handsome treasury of 118 vintage pictures, accompanied by carefully researched captions, document the Garden City Hotel fire (1899), the Vanderbilt Cup Race (1908), the first airmail flight departing from the Nassau Boulevard Aerodrome (1911), and much more. 96pp. 8⅞ x 11¾. 40669-5 Pa. $12.95

OLD QUEENS, N.Y., IN EARLY PHOTOGRAPHS, Vincent F. Seyfried and William Asadorian. Over 160 rare photographs of Maspeth, Jamaica, Jackson Heights, and other areas. Vintage views of DeWitt Clinton mansion, 1939 World's Fair and more. Captions. 192pp. 8⅞ x 11. 26358-4 Pa. $14.95

CAPTURED BY THE INDIANS: 15 Firsthand Accounts, 1750-1870, Frederick Drimmer. Astounding true historical accounts of grisly torture, bloody conflicts, relentless pursuits, miraculous escapes and more, by people who lived to tell the tale. 384pp. 5⅜ x 8½. 24901-8 Pa. $9.95

THE WORLD'S GREAT SPEECHES (Fourth Enlarged Edition), Lewis Copeland, Lawrence W. Lamm, and Stephen J. McKenna. Nearly 300 speeches provide public speakers with a wealth of updated quotes and inspiration–from Pericles' funeral oration and William Jennings Bryan's "Cross of Gold Speech" to Malcolm X's powerful words on the Black Revolution and Earl of Spenser's tribute to his sister, Diana, Princess of Wales. 944pp. 5⅜ x 8⅜. 40903-1 Pa. $15.95

THE BOOK OF THE SWORD, Sir Richard F. Burton. Great Victorian scholar/adventurer's eloquent, erudite history of the "queen of weapons"–from prehistory to early Roman Empire. Evolution and development of early swords, variations (sabre, broadsword, cutlass, scimitar, etc.), much more. 336pp. 6⅛ x 9¼.
25434-8 Pa. $9.95

AUTOBIOGRAPHY: The Story of My Experiments with Truth, Mohandas K. Gandhi. Boyhood, legal studies, purification, the growth of the Satyagraha (nonviolent protest) movement. Critical, inspiring work of the man responsible for the freedom of India. 480pp. 5⅜ x 8½. (Available in U.S. only.) 24593-4 Pa. $9.95

CELTIC MYTHS AND LEGENDS, T. W. Rolleston. Masterful retelling of Irish and Welsh stories and tales. Cuchulain, King Arthur, Deirdre, the Grail, many more. First paperback edition. 58 full-page illustrations. 512pp. 5⅜ x 8½. 26507-2 Pa. $9.95

THE PRINCIPLES OF PSYCHOLOGY, William James. Famous long course complete, unabridged. Stream of thought, time perception, memory, experimental methods; great work decades ahead of its time. 94 figures. 1,391pp. 5⅜ x 8½. 2-vol. set.
Vol. I: 20381-6 Pa. $14.95
Vol. II: 20382-4 Pa. $16.95

THE WORLD AS WILL AND REPRESENTATION, Arthur Schopenhauer. Definitive English translation of Schopenhauer's life work, correcting more than 1,000 errors, omissions in earlier translations. Translated by E. F. J. Payne. Total of 1,269pp. 5⅜ x 8½. 2-vol. set.
Vol. 1: 21761-2 Pa. $12.95
Vol. 2: 21762-0 Pa. $12.95

MAGIC AND MYSTERY IN TIBET, Madame Alexandra David-Neel. Experiences among lamas, magicians, sages, sorcerers, Bonpa wizards. A true psychic discovery. 32 illustrations. 321pp. 5⅜ x 8½. (Available in U.S. only.) 22682-4 Pa. $9.95

THE EGYPTIAN BOOK OF THE DEAD, E. A. Wallis Budge. Complete reproduction of Ani's papyrus, finest ever found. Full hieroglyphic text, interlinear transliteration, word-for-word translation, smooth translation. 533pp. 6½ x 9¼.
21866-X Pa. $12.95

MATHEMATICS FOR THE NONMATHEMATICIAN, Morris Kline. Detailed, college-level treatment of mathematics in cultural and historical context, with numerous exercises. Recommended Reading Lists. Tables. Numerous figures. 641pp. 5⅜ x 8½.
24823-2 Pa. $11.95

PROBABILISTIC METHODS IN THE THEORY OF STRUCTURES, Isaac Elishakoff. Well-written introduction covers the elements of the theory of probability from two or more random variables, the reliability of such multivariable structures, the theory of random function, Monte Carlo methods of treating problems incapable of exact solution, and more. Examples. 502pp. $5^3/_8$ x $8^1/_2$. 40691-1 Pa. $16.95

THE RIME OF THE ANCIENT MARINER, Gustave Doré, S. T. Coleridge. Doré's finest work; 34 plates capture moods, subtleties of poem. Flawless full-size reproductions printed on facing pages with authoritative text of poem. "Beautiful. Simply beautiful."–*Publisher's Weekly.* 77pp. 9¼ x 12. 22305-1 Pa. $7.95

NORTH AMERICAN INDIAN DESIGNS FOR ARTISTS AND CRAFTSPEOPLE, Eva Wilson. Over 360 authentic copyright-free designs adapted from Navajo blankets, Hopi pottery, Sioux buffalo hides, more. Geometrics, symbolic figures, plant and animal motifs, etc. 128pp. 8⅜ x 11. (Not for sale in the United Kingdom.) 25341-4 Pa. $9.95

SCULPTURE: Principles and Practice, Louis Slobodkin. Step-by-step approach to clay, plaster, metals, stone; classical and modern. 253 drawings, photos. 255pp. 8⅛ x 11.
22960-2 Pa. $11.95

THE INFLUENCE OF SEA POWER UPON HISTORY, 1660–1783, A. T. Mahan. Influential classic of naval history and tactics still used as text in war colleges. First paperback edition. 4 maps. 24 battle plans. 640pp. 5⅜ x 8½.   25509-3 Pa. $14.95

THE STORY OF THE TITANIC AS TOLD BY ITS SURVIVORS, Jack Winocour (ed.). What it was really like. Panic, despair, shocking inefficiency, and a little heroism. More thrilling than any fictional account. 26 illustrations. 320pp. 5⅜ x 8½.
20610-6 Pa. $8.95

FAIRY AND FOLK TALES OF THE IRISH PEASANTRY, William Butler Yeats (ed.). Treasury of 64 tales from the twilight world of Celtic myth and legend: "The Soul Cages," "The Kildare Pooka," "King O'Toole and his Goose," many more. Introduction and Notes by W. B. Yeats. 352pp. 5⅜ x 8½.   26941-8 Pa. $8.95

BUDDHIST MAHAYANA TEXTS, E. B. Cowell and others (eds.). Superb, accurate translations of basic documents in Mahayana Buddhism, highly important in history of religions. The Buddha-karita of Asvaghosha, Larger Sukhavativyuha, more. 448pp. 5⅜ x 8½.   25552-2 Pa. $12.95

ONE TWO THREE . . . INFINITY: Facts and Speculations of Science, George Gamow. Great physicist's fascinating, readable overview of contemporary science: number theory, relativity, fourth dimension, entropy, genes, atomic structure, much more. 128 illustrations. Index. 352pp. 5⅜ x 8½.   25664-2 Pa. $9.95

EXPERIMENTATION AND MEASUREMENT, W. J. Youden. Introductory manual explains laws of measurement in simple terms and offers tips for achieving accuracy and minimizing errors. Mathematics of measurement, use of instruments, experimenting with machines. 1994 edition. Foreword. Preface. Introduction. Epilogue. Selected Readings. Glossary. Index. Tables and figures. 128pp. 5³/₈ x 8¹/₂.
40451-X Pa. $6.95

DALÍ ON MODERN ART: The Cuckolds of Antiquated Modern Art, Salvador Dalí. Influential painter skewers modern art and its practitioners. Outrageous evaluations of Picasso, Cézanne, Turner, more. 15 renderings of paintings discussed. 44 calligraphic decorations by Dalí. 96pp. 5⅜ x 8½. (Available in U.S. only.)   29220-7 Pa. $5.95

ANTIQUE PLAYING CARDS: A Pictorial History, Henry René D'Allemagne. Over 900 elaborate, decorative images from rare playing cards (14th–20th centuries): Bacchus, death, dancing dogs, hunting scenes, royal coats of arms, players cheating, much more. 96pp. 9¼ x 12¼.   29265-7 Pa. $12.95

MAKING FURNITURE MASTERPIECES: 30 Projects with Measured Drawings, Franklin H. Gottshall. Step-by-step instructions, illustrations for constructing handsome, useful pieces, among them a Sheraton desk, Chippendale chair, Spanish desk, Queen Anne table and a William and Mary dressing mirror. 224pp. 8⅛ x 11¼.
29338-6 Pa. $16.95

THE FOSSIL BOOK: A Record of Prehistoric Life, Patricia V. Rich et al. Profusely illustrated definitive guide covers everything from single-celled organisms and dinosaurs to birds and mammals and the interplay between climate and man. Over 1,500 illustrations. 760pp. 7½ x 10⅛.   29371-8 Pa. $29.95

Prices subject to change without notice.

Available at your book dealer or write for free catalog to Dept. GI, Dover Publications, Inc., 31 East 2nd St., Mineola, N.Y. 11501. Dover publishes more than 500 books each year on science, elementary and advanced mathematics, biology, music, art, literary history, social sciences and other areas.